Vladimir Voinovich was exiled from the Soviet Union in 1980. His *Life and Extraordinary Adventures of Private Ivan Chonkin, Pretender to the Throne* and *Ivankiad* are among the most probing satires in any language. *Moscow 2042* is his first novel written in exile. He now lives in Stockdorf, West Germany.

Vladimir Voinovich

Moscow 2042

Translated from the Russian by
Richard Lourie

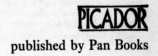

published by Pan Books

Originally published in Russian in the USA
under the title of *Moska 2042*
First published in Great Britain 1988 by
Jonathan Cape Ltd
This Picador edition published 1989 by
Pan Books Ltd, Cavaye Place, London SW10 9PG
9 8 7 6 5 4 3 2 1
© Vladimir Voinovich 1986
English translation © Harcourt Brace Jovanovich, Inc., 1987
ISBN 0 330 30732 0

Printed and bound in Great Britain by
Richard Clay Ltd, Bungay, Suffolk

CONTENTS

PART I

PART I

INTRODUCTION

Unfortunately, I don't have access to my notes. All my notebooks, pads, journals, and all the odd scraps of paper were left behind. There was only one slip of paper, crumpled, worn, and ragged along the edges, which had worked its way into the lining of my jacket and was returned to me by Frau Grunberg, the proprietor of our dry cleaner in Stockdorf. I could make out the following on one side of the slip: "4 sm. U nag. T.t.L.O.L." On the other: "Tomorrow or never !!!" The meaning of the tomorrow business is perfectly clear to me, and I will explain it in due course. But what does the writing on the first side mean? I can't remember for the life of me what the four "sm." could be or what the other letters could possibly signify.

For some reason, what intrigues me most is the second letter "L." Does it designate a thing, a person, an animal? It doesn't rouse the slightest association in me.

And it wasn't that long ago that my memory was perfectly excellent. Especially for figures. I always knew the number on my passport, work card, discharge papers, and my Writers' Union card. Believe it or not, I never make a note of people's phone numbers, I know them by heart as soon as I hear them.

But now? . . .

Now, sometimes it even takes a congratulatory telegram to remind me it's my birthday.

Still, I have no other choice but to rely on my memory.

I can easily foresee readers being mistrustful of this book and saying: This is too much already, he made it up, it couldn't have happened. I'm not going to argue whether it could have, but I will be most definite in saying that I never make anything up.

What I describe here is only what I saw with my own eyes. Or heard with my own ears. Or what was told to me by someone I trust greatly. Or not that greatly. In any case, what I write is always based on something. Sometimes it's even based on nothing. But anyone with even a nodding acquaintance with the theory of relativity knows that nothing is a variety of something and so you can always make a little something out of nothing.

I think this is sufficient reason for you to have complete confidence in this story.

It only remains to add that there are no prototypes for the people described in this book. The author has drawn all the main and minor characters of both sexes solely from himself, ascribing to them not only his imaginary virtues but the real shortcomings, faults, and vices that nature so lavished on him.

CONVERSATION OVER
A MUG OF BEER

This conversation took place in June 1982.

Scene of the action: English Gardens, Munich.

We were in an open-air beer garden. *We* means myself and an acquaintance of mine by the name of Rudolf, or Rudi for short. His last name was impossible for a Russian to remember. It wasn't quite Mittelbrechenmacher, nor was it was quite Machenmittelbrecher. Something of that ilk, not that it matters. Personally, I just call him Rudi.

We were sitting facing each other, with Rudi somewhat blocking my view. But, squinting my eyes a tad to the right, I could see a lake gleaming with sunlight; fat geese and naked Germans wandering along the shore. Actually, they probably weren't just Germans, but exhibitionists of all nations who had descended on Munich to take advantage of the local police's permissiveness, to see and be seen.

We were drinking our beer from quart mugs, which are called a "mass" here. To tell the truth, I'm not exactly sure whether it's the mug itself that's called a "mass" or the amount of beer it contains. Not that it matters. What matters is that we were sitting in a beer garden, drinking beer, and talking about whatever came up.

I think the first topic was horses. That's because Rudi owns a stud farm. He breeds horses and sells them to millionaires. Incidentally, he's a millionaire too, not that that matters either.

Though he deals in horses, his greatest interest is high-tech. He drives a luxurious Jaguar packed with all the latest electronics, and the set-up he's got at home is a whole other story. Computers, stereo televisions, automatic doors, just for starters. At nightfall the lights in his study go on automatically, but only if there is someone in the study at the time. If he leaves, the lights go off immediately. (Rudi claims that this device saves him at least four marks a month on electricity.) Needless to say, he has a musical computer that can synthesize the sounds of organs, violins, xylophones, balalaikas, and a host of other instruments, separately or all together. So, using one finger, one man can now perform a work that used to be the province of large orchestras.

Rudi is so fascinated by all this technology that I don't think he reads anything but technical journals and science fiction. He hasn't even read my books, although he does display them prominently and always brags to his other horse-world friends about having an unusual friend, a Russian writer.

He tells me (even without having read me) that I write too realistically, realism being a thing of the past. To be honest, such ridiculous opinions infuriate me, and I am always telling Rudi that his horses are also a thing of the past. But if some people still have need of horses, there still must be some use for a literature that depicts life as people really live it. People are much more interested in reading about themselves than about robots or Martians.

I had just said this to him in the beer garden where we were sitting. With a condescending grin, Rudi replied that we should compare the sales of my books with that of the average science-fiction writer. "Science fiction," he said self-confidently, "is the literature of the future."

That statement exasperated me. I ordered another mass and said that science fiction, like detective stories, is not literature but tomfoolery like the electronic games that induce mass idiocy.

But the warm sun, the cold beer, and the local way of life were not conducive to passionate argument. Not letting himself be caught up in my excitement, Rudi made a casual objection and mentioned

6

the name of Jules Verne who, he said, unlike the so-called realists, foretold many of the scientific achievements of our time, including man's flight to the moon.

I replied that foretelling scientific achievements was in no way the task of literature and that there was nothing original about Jules Verne's predictions. Every person has imagined space flight and underwater travel at one time in his life, and many ancient books described similar wonders long before Jules Verne.

"That may be," answered Rudi. "Still, science-fiction writers have not only foreseen technological discoveries but the evolution of modern society toward totalitarianism. Take Orwell, for example. Didn't he predict in detail the system that exists in Russia today?"

"Of course not," I said. "Orwell wrote a parody of what already existed at the time. He described a totalitarian machine that worked perfectly and could simply never exist in a real human society. Take the Soviet Union—its population only displays an outward obedience to the regime; in fact, people have nothing but contempt for the slogans and catch phrases. They respond by working poorly, drinking heavily, and stealing left and right. Big brother is the target of ridicule and the subject of endless jokes."

It should be pointed out that nothing could be more boring than to argue with Westerners. When a Western person sees that someone feels strongly about some point of view, that it is very important to him, he's ready to agree with it on the spot, which is not at all the case with Russians.

My quarrel with Rudi was fizzling fast and he was nodding agreeably, but I felt like heating it back up. And so I said that science-fiction authors have made up many things that have come true, but they have also made up things that will never come true, for example time travel.

"Is that so?" said Rudi, lighting a cigar. "You really think that time travel is absolutely impossible?"

"Yes," I said, "that's precisely what I think."

"In that case," he said, "you're very much mistaken. Time travel has already moved from the realm of science fiction into the realm of fact."

Needless to say, we were speaking in German, and, at that time, 1982, I did not have a very good command of the language (not that it's so much better now). And so I asked Rudi if I had heard him right, that technology now existed that made it possible to travel from one point in time to another.

"Yes, that's right," confirmed Rudi. "That's just what I'm trying to tell you. Today you can go to a travel agency, buy a ticket for a certain sum of money, and board a time machine for the future or for the past, whichever you prefer. By the way," he added, "at present the only such machine in Germany belongs to Lufthansa. The idea is a very simple one, technically. What's used is an ordinary space plane like the American shuttle, equipped, however, not just with simple rockets but with photon engines as well. When the craft achieves sufficient velocity to break free of Earth's gravity, the photon engines are switched on. In the second stage, the craft breaks free of the Sun's gravity. After that, it develops a speed almost equal to the speed of light, and time stands still for you, though it continues on Earth. When you land, you end up in the future. Or else the machine can generate a speed faster than the speed of light, and then you outpace time and end up in the past."

I was already a little tipsy from the beer, but I still had my wits about me and said, "Hey, cut the crap, will you? You know full well that Einstein proved it's impossible to achieve the speed of light, let alone exceed it."

Rudi finally lost his composure, spat out his cigar, and banged his mass on the table, something I never expected to see from such an even-tempered person.

"What Einstein said has been obsolete for years," he pronounced. "Euclid said that parallel lines never intersect and then along came your Lobachevsky and said that they do, and both of them were right. Einstein said that it's impossible and he was right, and I say that it is possible, and I'm right too."

"Listen, listen," I said, "don't go overboard. Naturally, I re-

8

spect you" — when I'm drinking I respect everyone — "but still you're no Einstein."

"That's true," agreed Rudi, "I really am no Einstein. I'm Mittelbrechenmacher, but I should also say that Lobachevsky was no Euclid."

Seeing that he had become extremely worked up, I said at once that in the end it didn't matter much to me who was the smartest one (Einstein, Lobachevsky, Euclid, or Rudi) and that I was ready to make practical use of modern technology, but was not interested at all in the laws on which it was based.

Which is in fact the case. I am writing these very notes on my word processor. I press the keys and the words appear on the monitor. A few other simple hand movements and the printer prints out those words. If I want to shift a few paragraphs around, the machine instantly does my will. If I want to change all references to Mittelbrechenmacher to Machenmittelbrecher or to Einstein, the machine can do that for me as well.

I use my electric razor, radio, and television every day of the week. Am I really obliged to know the theoretical foundation on which all those things operate?

I asked Rudi if he had flown on that time machine himself. He said that he had, and that once was enough for him. He had wanted to see the gladiators fight in ancient Rome and he had ended up in the arena himself and barely got out in one piece. Since then he had preferred to see such wonders on television or read about them in books.

Of course, I didn't particularly believe him, but then he said I could easily check the reality of time travel myself. All I had to do was pay a visit to his friend Fräulein Globke who worked in the travel agency at 5 Amalienstrasse.

"Still," said Rudi, "there's little chance you'll ever do any time travel."

"And why is that, may I ask? You said yourself that it's moved from the realm of science fiction to the realm of fact."

"Yes," he said with a grin, "yes, that's right. But the price of

9

the ticket has yet to move from the realm of science fiction. And why should you time-travel anyway and expose yourself to unnecessary risks? You're no lover of adventure."

That last phrase only indicates how little Rudi knew me. That's exactly what I am—a lover of adventure.

FRÄULEIN
GLOBKE

The decor in the travel agency on Amalienstrasse could not have been more ordinary. A spate of posters and brochures offered trips to see the pyramids of Egypt, the geisers of Iceland, the fjords of Norway, to sunbathe in the Bahamas, to ski the slopes of the Swiss Alps, or to take a sea voyage on the famous liner *Queen Elizabeth Two*.

I asked for Fräulein Globke and was directed toward a red-haired freckle-faced girl in one corner, half-hidden by the monitor on her computer.

To tell the truth, I had an attack of cold feet at the last minute. I thought that Rudi, the rat, was playing a practical joke on me, and the whole travel agency would come running over for a good laugh at the foolish foreigner. But when I told Fräulein Globke my name and my purpose in coming, she was not surprised in the least and did not burst out laughing, which both relieved and astonished me. Yes, she said, they truly could send any of their clients to any time and to any place on planet Earth, and she, Fräulein Globke, was ready to be of assistance.

My request struck her as quite modest. I wanted to travel to Moscow in 2032, that is, fifty years into the future.

"Fine," said the Fräulein, her manicured fingers tapping on her keyboard.

Letters and numbers began flickering on the screen. Fräulein

11

Globke looked at them, clacked her tongue, turned to me, and spread her hands in a gesture of helplessness.

"Aha, so you can't do it then, can you?" I said, gladdened by the chance to turn the tables on Rudi.

"Unfortunately," said the Fräulein with some embarrassment, "all the tickets for the flight have been sold. But if you're willing to fly *sixty* years into the future. . . ."

"What's the difference!" I said, interrupting her. "Ten years either way, what does it matter?"

"Wonderful!" she said, and, smiling radiantly, informed me that I had made the right choice in coming to them because they were the only travel agency in Europe organizing travel of this sort. And, if I was interested in the means of transportation. . . .

"Excuse me," I said, interrupting her impatiently, "I have some idea already of the means of transportation. It was explained to me in some detail by Herr Machenmittelbrecher."

"Mittelbrechenmacher," she corrected me politely.

I thanked her for the correction and said the practical, not the theoretical aspects of the flight interested me. What was the weightlessness situation and would the craft rock a great deal? "The thing is," I explained, "that when I drink, I sometimes get pretty rocky, even here on Earth."

"Oh," she said with a smile, "you can rest assured about weightlessness. Our electronic artificial gravity system is second to none. And there's no problem with rocking. But couldn't you re-frain from consuming alcoholic beverages during the flight?"

"What?" I said. "Refrain for sixty years? Fräulein, that's asking too much of me."

"What are you talking about?" she objected heatedly. "You're missing the point. It's here on Earth that sixty years will pass. For you the whole thing will take three hours. Like an ordinary flight from Munich to Moscow."

"Alright," I said. "That's clear. That I can understand. It'll only take me three hours to get there. But in fact sixty years will have passed. And I can't have a drop to drink in sixty years?"

"Stop it! Stop it!" She was so excited that her freckles swelled to twice their normal size. "What are you saying, not a drop? In the end, whether you drink is your own business. And by the way, there's no limit on the amount of drinks passengers can be served on this flight, plus they're all free of charge, of course."

"That's another story," I said. "Why didn't you tell me right away that drinks are free? If drinks are free, there's nothing left to discuss. I'll take a round-trip ticket, return in thirty days, in the drinking and smoking section, preferably with a window seat."

"Fine," she said with a nod. "However, I should warn you that our company does not guarantee your return flight. We, of course, will do everything in our power, but we don't know what political conditions will be at that point in the future. Naturally, our consul will always be at your service, but, just between us, who can guarantee that our country will still exist in sixty years and still have a consul there?"

Yes, of course, I thought, anything could happen in sixty years. But that was precisely the purpose of my trip—to find out just what *would* happen there.

"Alright," I said. "It doesn't matter. You can't guarantee my return. But if you can guarantee me free drinks, I'll take the ticket."

I gave her my passport. Fräulein Globke's slender fingers began dashing along her keyboard, as if performing a musical piece composed of letters and numbers. My first and last name appeared on the screen, my passport number, the flight number and departure date, followed by some other numbers which leaped across the screen, merrily multiplying. Finally, the numbers came to rest and formed a figure: 4,578,843.00.

"A round-trip ticket," said Fräulein Globke, "costs exactly four million, five hundred seventy-eight thousand, eight hundred forty-three marks."

"Oho!" I said.

"But if you pay cash, we can offer you a ten percent discount, which means that the trip will cost you. . . ." Her fingers stirred, and once again numbers leaped across the screen, forming a new figure. "Four million, one hundred twenty thousand, nine hundred fifty-eight marks, and seventy pfennigs."

"Now that's a different story," I said.

"Also, in the event that you do not return within three months, seventy-five percent of the cost of the return ticket will be refunded to your heirs."

"That sounds very good," I remarked. "I personally don't have that kind of money, but I think I can expect help from Herr. . . ."

"Mittelbrechenmacher," prompted Fräulein Globke.

Now that's people for you! Why do they always have to put in their two pfennigs worth? Did that Fräulein really think that I couldn't remember my best friend's name without her help?

THREE MILLION
FOR THE STORY

Needless to say, my hopes in Rudi were entirely misplaced. When I called him from a pay phone, he said he would have been glad to loan me the necessary funds, but, to his immense regret, he was having certain financial difficulties of his own at the moment. The thing was, he had spent his last six million on two stallions imported from Saudi Arabia, one of which had broken a leg just yesterday. Which meant bye-bye to three million.

As I later found out, this was a pure cock-and-bull story. Rudi was just nervous about lending me the money. I've noticed that, generally speaking, millionaires are tightwads.

I returned home, both out of sorts and at peace. It didn't happen, so it didn't happen. Wasn't fated. Maybe it's even better. I'm almost forty years old, an age at which it's time to start declining adventures when I can.

As for my wife, I noticed that she was particularly pleased by the turn events had taken. Because no matter what else I may be, I'm still her husband. And if I got bogged down somewhere there in the distant future, it's unlikely she could ever find another man like me.

My wife was so pleased that she even offered me a drink at dinner, something she usually does not do. And I, of course, did not play hard to get. I drank my first glass with her, my second and third when she was off talking on the phone, and the fourth with her when she came back.

"Yes," I said, "but still it's a pity it didn't come off. I really would have liked to have seen it."

"What's there to see? Do you think anything's going to change in that place?"

"In sixty years?" I asked. "You think nothing's going to happen in sixty years?"

Then she reminded me of the story of a neighbor of ours who had died recently. He had come to Germany from Russia long ago with his family and had not wanted to unpack his bags.

"They'll drive the Bolsheviks out soon," he used to say, "and we'll be going back. Why do double work, unpack and then pack all over again?"

The phone rang again. As soon as my wife left the room, I knocked off a quick shot, but she was back before I had time to pour myself another.

"It's some American for you," she said.

The American proved to be a correspondent for the *New Times*. He asked if I could see him tomorrow on some urgent business. To my question of what that urgent business was, he replied it wasn't something to be discussed on the phone. (And they say it's only in the Soviet Union that people are afraid to talk on the phone.)

"Alright," I said, "come see me, but not before ten. I work late and I get up late."

"OK," he said, signing off.

They say Americans are too free and easy. I don't see it that way. Most Americans I've met are well-mannered, tactful, modestly but neatly dressed, and very friendly. Of course, sometimes they do put their feet on the table, but, personally, that doesn't shock me at all. They're just relaxing. And they're right to. Relaxation is good for your health. But we Russians are always reflecting instead of relaxing, and that's bad for your health. I sometimes put my feet up on the table, but it doesn't help me relax. We're just not used to it.

My doorbell rang at ten o'clock on the dot the next morning. Opening the door, I saw a tall, well-built man in a light blue suit with dark hair parted on one side.

"Mr. Mac . . . ?" I said, having forgotten the rest of his Irish last name.

"Just call me John," he said with a smile.

I invited him into the living room and offered him coffee.

"Vitaly," he said, "I have a big favor to ask of you. Listen to my proposition and then, whether you accept it or not, don't breathe a word of it to anyone."

"Are you from the CIA?" I asked.

"No, what do you mean! I'm from the *New Times* as I told you. But I would prefer . . ."

"Would you like me to swear on the Bible?"

"It's not mandatory," he said with a smile. "Your word is good enough for me. I've heard that you're intending to travel to the Soviet Union, to the year two thousand and something . . ."

"Where did you hear that?" I said in surprise. "I didn't tell anyone about that."

"Don't worry, I won't tell anyone either."

"You can tell anyone you want, because I'm not going. A round trip ticket costs . . ."

"I know about everything," he interrupted. "But if the cost of the ticket is the only problem, our company is willing to assume all the expenses involved."

"All the expenses?" I said, incredulous. "Over four million marks? That's almost two million dollars!"

"And you'll receive another million as your fee for a detailed report on your trip."

"Three million dollars for a story?"

He grinned. "Vitaly, I can see that you still don't know your way around here in the West. This is not just any story. It'll be the sensation of the century. This century and the next one. It may even be worth more than I'm offering you, but our financial situation is not the best at the moment."

I promised John to think it over. He gave me his card and left, without finishing his coffee.

A CONVERSATION
WITH THE DEVIL

It would be a profound error to think that my decision was influenced in the slightest by this opportunity to earn fantastic and easy money. I don't claim to be indifferent to money, but I can definitely say that, for money alone, I would never risk a single hair on my head.

And I might not have accepted John's offer, but it had aroused the devil who dwells within me. Ever since that devil took up residence, his only thought has been to incite me to go on adventures. Sometimes he overdoes it, and I stifle him without the slightest pity. Then he quiets down for a while and gives no sign of life. In those periods my behavior is close to ideal: I refrain from drinking and smoking, I cross the street only when the light is green, I obey all traffic signs when I drive, and I give my wife every last cent of my earnings. At those times I'm a delight to everyone who knows me. My clothing is neat as a pin, I'm scrubbed, clean-shaven, well-groomed, and exceptionally pleasant to all.

But inevitably the devil wakes in me and starts with his pestering: "Why get up? It's still early, lunch isn't ready yet, you can sleep a little more. There's no rush, you're going to die anyway. You don't have to wash today, you washed yesterday. Stay in bed, have a smoke, fill your lungs with smoke. There are your cigarettes, over on the night table."

My devil is so persistent that I can't always resist him.

I shook a cigarette out of the pack, flicked my lighter, and took a drag.

"Bravo!" cheered the devil. "Cancer is the surest cure for smokers." His favorite saying.

"You idiot!" I said to him. "You shouldn't be inside me, but out working for the antismoking movement."

Puffing on my Marlboro, I began thinking about John's proposition.

It was an attractive proposition; still, it probably wasn't for me. Where would I actually be going? What would await me there in the distant future? I might get into awful trouble. And I'm no kid after all. I'm a solid citizen, a family man. I'm just about to turn forty. (Can that be true?) It's time to settle down, calm down. Avoid unnecessary excitement, stressful situations, and draughts. I should wear a bathrobe, fix myself some weak tea, and, at most, smoke a pipe, sit at my desk, and write a smooth-flowing novel.

"Of all human faults, prudence is most disgusting," snipped the devil.

"Get out of here!" I said. "Mind your own business. I'm sick of you."

"And I'm sick of you too," said the devil. "Especially in your virtuous moments. Listen, listen," he whispered, "you're well aware that prudence is imprudent. Today you're afraid of catching cold, and tomorrow a brick falls on your head, and so then what difference does a cold make? Why are you vacillating? Some good luck has come your way, take advantage of it. Let's go have a look-see at what those Communists of yours have dreamed up in the course of sixty years."

"Do you love the Communists?" I asked derisively.

"Do I!" cried the devil. "What's not to like? They're devils in their own way too, they're always coming up with some jolly new idea. Listen, let's go, do it for me, please."

"Alright," I said, "let's suppose I do go. But that'll be the last adventure you lure me into."

"Excellent!" cheered the devil. "Wonderful! And it's entirely possible that it will be the last."

"You imbecile!" I said. "Why does that make you happy? What will you do without me, if something happens to me?"

"Yes, right," said the devil sadly. "I admit it, I'd miss you terribly. But, to be honest, I'd rather see you dead than prudent."

"Shut up!" I said. "Don't bother me when I'm thinking."

"I'll shut up," said the devil meekly, and he fell still, knowing that his job was done.

And though I had told John that it was very unlikely that I would accept his offer and that I would call him in a week and a half at the earliest, I called him three days later and said yes.

SHADOWED

I think it goes without saying that, before undertaking a journey as risky as the one I had in mind, a person should see to the welfare of his family and make arrangements that may well be his last. Bank, post office, insurance agency, notary, I spent a few days in those and other such establishments.

While handling these affairs, I suddenly became aware, with a sense that had been honed in my Moscow years, that I was being followed.

I was very pressed for time, but, making use of my elementary powers of observation, I noticed that my telephone was behaving a bit oddly. Either I'd hear a rustling sound (a tape recorder?) or the phone would ding away by itself; either I'd dial and get a wrong number or someone would call my number by mistake.

For no apparent reason, my dog would start barking at night. I'd run outside but find no one there, though I once did discover a Stolichnaia cigarette butt right by my door.

Another time my eye caught a young Asiatic-looking man who bicycled past my gate and made too much of looking the other way.

Later on, my attention was drawn to an old green Volkswagen with a Frankfurt plate in one of the side streets near my house. Glancing outside, I noticed a copy of *Pravda* had been left on the back seat.

Just to be on the safe side, I reported what I'd observed to the police. They listened closely, but said that my suspicions were too vague and unspecific; still, if I came up with any definite proof that I was being shadowed, they would, of course, take the necessary measures.

All the same, the policeman with whom I spoke made a note of the Volkswagen license number, slipped the Stolichnaia cigarette butt into a cellophane packet, and placed it in the safe.

ABDUCTION

That same day something happened to me which might seem funny now, but did not seem so at the time. Having returned home from the police station, I decided to cast all suspicion from mind. I got out my bicycle and set off for a ride through the Stockdorf woods.

In my life as an exile, I have gotten into the habit of taking bike rides and have come to like them. I am very fond of the woods, mostly coniferous, that separate our village from the outskirts of Munich; they remind me of the woods around Moscow, with the difference that these are criss-crossed with asphalt and gravel paths, have signs at the intersections, and detailed maps along their edges. You get lost here only if you really want to.

I was going down my favorite path, which connects Buchendorf and Noirid; it's straight, paved, and always deserted on weekdays. I was pedaling quite fast, thinking about my upcoming trip, and apparently I was so caught up in my thoughts that I didn't notice what was up ahead on the road.

I still don't know what happened. Most likely a rope had been stretched across the path, I went flying over the rope, fell, and blacked out. Or perhaps some other means was used to stun me, I can't be sure. All I remember is that I was riding my bicycle and thinking. Then there's a gap in my memory, and I came to on a little couch bobbing under me.

Thinking I was in my own room, I assumed an earthquake was

23

taking place and I was about to jump up on my feet. But I noticed suddenly that, one, my body wasn't quick to obey me and, two, I was not home, but in some sort of mini-bus with curtained windows. The bus was in motion, and three men were sitting across from me, two in regular clothing, and one all in white, who had to be a doctor.

Good God! I thought. What's happened to me, what hit me, where are they taking me? I moved a little, pinching my various parts to check that my body was in one piece.

As soon as I showed some signs of life, the two people sitting across from me stirred, and the doctor said something in a language I couldn't understand. Taking a closer look at him, I saw that he was not a doctor at all, but most likely an Arab wearing the loose white gown of his people, a hood covering half his face. The others were probably Arabs too, but were dressed in European clothing. The two wearing suits were about thirty, but the face in the hood looked somewhat older.

After I came to, they first exchanged a few words and then the one in the hood began speaking rapidly, loudly, and with authority. Not only that, when he opened his mouth, a light-blue radiance emanated from his teeth which seemed to make the interior of the mini-bus even brighter.

When he had finished speaking, one of his companions nodded and began speaking in English to me. Calling me by my last name, Kartsev (preceded, of course, by the word *Mister*), he said that His Highness (meaning the one in the hood) offered me his profoundest apologies for having to deal so unceremoniously with me. Ordinarily, they would never have permitted themselves to act that way toward a person for whom they had such respect and esteem. It was only exceptional necessity that had impelled them to this act, for which His Highness deeply apologized again, and yet again.

Obviously, my memory had become clouded after what had just happened to me, and I didn't know exactly what His Highness was apologizing for, so I decided not to say anything.

"Still," continued the interpreter, "His Highness very much

24

hopes that you are now feeling fairly well and will not hold all this against us for too long. For his part, His Highness is ready to pay you compensation for the small loss which we have unintentionally caused you."

On hearing those words, His Highness nodded his head vigorously (not, however, revealing his face). Then he reached under the hem of his robe, his hand becoming entangled as it rummaged about, until he finally withdrew a leather pouch. It looked like a tobacco pouch, and he sat it down nicely on the narrow table between us.

"What's that?" I asked, with a sidelong glance at the pouch.

"A small personal gift from His Highness," said the interpreter with a smile (and His Highness smiled too with embarrassment). "A little gold."

I closed my eyes and asked myself who these people were and what was it they wanted from me. But, finding no answers, I opened my eyes and put those questions directly to them.

His Highness muttered something at great speed; then the interpreter said they were representatives of a certain small, but very rich Arab country. And, on learning of my upcoming trip . . .

"How did you find out about it?" I interrupted.

"In the East, they say that if you put your ear to the ground, you can hear the whole world," said the interpreter softly.

And so, having put their ears to the ground and found about my plans, they had decided to ask a small but delicate favor of me. Their hope was that at some point in the future, the great Soviet Union, great friend of the Arab nations, would stop keeping certain secrets secret. And they, my companions, would be very grateful to me if I could manage to obtain and bring back a detailed plan for an ordinary nuclear bomb, which they wanted solely for peaceful purposes. If I rendered them this service, His Highness would personally repay me, and the sack of gold I would receive in exchange for a few frames of film could be fifty times greater than the one there before my eyes.

My first impulse was to tell them to go straight to hell. But, to be honest, I wasn't sure that my frankness would be appreciated in a way that would be to my benefit. Then I decided to follow the good example set by Khadi Nasrudin who, as we know, at one point had promised the shah to teach a donkey to speak like a human being within twenty years. Nasrudin figured he had nothing to lose because in twenty years' time either the shah would die, or the donkey, or else he, Nasrudin, would stand before Allah.

Not wishing to appear too willing to carry out their request, I said that of course I would try (and not even so much for the money as out of my high regard for their country and for the person of His Highness) to do everything within my modest powers, but could not promise them anything hard and fast. I said that right now it was difficult for me to imagine what my country would be like after so much time, and I didn't know what information would be unclassified by then and what information would still be secret.

"You see," I said cautiously, "I would very much like to be of help to you, but, at the same time, any illegal action would run counter to my moral principles."

At this point all three of them began rattling nonstop in Arabic. Suddenly, His Highness said, speaking in pure Russian with almost no trace of an accent:

"We will not ask you to violate your principles and have no intention of coercing you into anything. But when you return from the glorious future to the difficult present, you may want to give some thought to yourself, your children, and your grandchildren."

"Your Highness," I said, stunned, "where did you learn such good Russian?"

"I studied at Lumumba University in Moscow," His Highness replied readily, and smiled, radiating that mysterious light again.

On that note our conversation ended, and five minutes later my abductors had deposited me, my bicycle, and the leather pouch on some side street.

On my way out of the van, I could not restrain myself and asked His Highness if he had platinum bridgework.

"What do you mean!" replied His Highness. "These are diamond crowns!"

26

A SURPRISE
ENCOUNTER

What kinds of gifts do you take with you on a trip sixty years into the future?

Pondering this question in the middle of Kaufhof, the well-known Munich department store, I was at a total loss.

The store had plenty of everything, but I couldn't imagine what to buy. Chewing gum? Jeans? Lighters? Calculators?

I had heard that Soviet-made chewing gum had already appeared in the Soviet Union. Of course, it had to take second place to Western chewing gum, but I didn't have the slightest doubt that in the span of sixty years, as a result of the technological revolution, historic party and government decrees, and the masses' enthusiasm for work, the production of chewing articles and their distribution to most segments of the population would probably have undergone radical change for the better.

As for jeans, I thought some progress was inevitable there, too, in sixty years; in any event, at least Polish, say, or Hungarian jeans would be available in Moscow.

All the same, I bought a pair of jeans. I also bought some ties, scarves, two collapsible umbrellas at five marks apiece, an electronic chess game, two cases of drafting tools, and cosmetics of every sort: lipstick, nail polish, powder, rouge, eyeliner, false eyelashes, things I knew would never be out of date.

I didn't forget myself either, of course. I bought film for my camera, tape for my Dictaphone, typewriter ribbons, notebooks, and a set of ballpoint pens. In addition, I stocked up on underwear, socks, gloves, soap, toothpaste, and bought a new Gillette razor and two packs of blades.

I bought all of those things knowing that, though they might be of incomparably higher quality in the future, I wouldn't be used to their new forms.

Spotting T-shirts with *Munich 1982* written on them, I immediately bought five. In the map and guidebook section, I found street plans of various cities, including the street plan of Moscow. I decided to provide myself with one of these, if only to compare the Moscow of today with the Moscow of the future. I picked up one street plan and began to study it, surprised by the amount of detail. Street plans like these were available when I lived in Moscow, but they gave only the most important streets, and not even all of them. On this map, I could find the little side streets and lanes where I once lived.

"Isn't there any street named after the writer Kartsev?" a voice said mockingly from behind me. Shuddering, I turned. Wearing a light green raincoat and a gray hat, with a grin on his face, was my former friend, classmate, and drinking buddy, Lyoshka Bukashev.

We had studied in the journalism department together, and later we both worked in radio, I in the literary section, and he in news. We used to spend evenings in the Journalists' Club. Sometimes there were two of us, sometimes three. Lyoshka would occasionally bring his friend Edik, a young man with curly hair who said he was a geneticist and an immortologist. The first time I met Edik, I asked him if he was doing research on prolonging life. He said that the problem of prolonging life held no interest for him. It was a trifling matter, a task for gerontologists. What interested Edik was not prolonged life, but eternal life.

"So, you're trying to find the elixir of life?" I had asked.

Edik said he was trying to find something else, but elixir was probably a good enough term for fools. I was about to take offense, but then he became embarrassed and said that in speaking of fools he had not meant me, but those bureaucrats who did not believe the problem was solvable, who would not give him a laboratory, and who did what they could to trip him up. Once he had even come close to going to prison for Mendelism-Morganism. Satirical pieces had appeared about him in *Krokodil*, and he was grateful to Lyoshka, who was the first radio commentator to speak well of his experiments.

Generally speaking, Lyoshka is one of those people who never does anyone an ill turn for no reason. As for good turns, he used to say, "I'm ready to do good within the limits of reason. Want me to lend you three rubles?"

His views were those of the complete cynic and careerist. But it took two tries to launch his career. The first try came during his first year at university. I remember that he was one of the oldest and the poorest of the students in our department. He had entered the university from the army and still wore his ragged uniform for the entire first year. He could not remember his father, who had been killed during the war. His mother, Polina Petrovna, worked as a street sweeper on Arbat Street, where she had a windowless room, seven and a half square meters.

Lyoshka used to say that not once in his life (not even in the army) had he eaten his fill. He did not enroll in the university to master journalism, but to join the ranks of those who eat well, dress well, and are not beaten up in police stations (as had once happened to him).

During that first year, though, Lyoshka Bukashev realized that people who are not beaten up in police stations can also be divided into various categories. He told me that real careers weren't made through professional channels but through "party and sexual" channels. I thought his observations were somewhat removed from real life, but later I saw that he was attempting to put them to practical ends.

He immediately took an active role on the Komsomol committee, quickly became our class's Komsomol organizer, *komsorg* for short, and a candidate member to the Communist Party of the Soviet Union. He did not let the sexual channels slip from his sight either, and began dating a student in our department, the grand-daughter of a famous Bolshevik hero. She, like Lyoshka, was enthusiastic about working for the Komsomol. In his second year, Lyoshka intended to marry and become a full-fledged Party member in the process. At the same time he was recommended for a leadership position in the department's Komsomol, a station from which Lyoshka's predecessors had risen to the uppermost heights of power.

So Lyoshka's nomination was up for a vote, and solely for *pro forma* reasons the audience was asked if there were any objections. His fiancée, her face streaked with tears, took the podium and said that, hard as it might be, she had to challenge Comrade Bukashev's candidacy. He was not what he appeared to be: He said one thing in public and another in private conversation. For example, when speaking in public he evinced only admiration for Comrade Lenin; with her, however, he always referred to him as Lenin-Shmenin.

Those were liberal times back then, and Bukashev was not expelled from the university. But he was not given a party card or elected to the leadership; he stayed in the Komsomol, but with a severe reprimand in his file. There was no longer any possibility of an important career, and Lyoshka worked in radio as a journalist of the lowest rank, writing articles about leading workers, high-speed smelting, and record milk production.

Promotion and salary increases came slowly until, almost by accident, he once again began working through party and sex channels. He met the daughter of the deputy minister of foreign affairs and was not about to let the chance slip him by this time. He married her, joined the party, and quickly made a career for himself.

He and I quarreled, and fate took us in different directions. I became a dissident, was expelled from the Writers' Union, and came close to being thrown in prison. In contrast, Lyoshka rose rapidly. He became a political commentator on television, traveled abroad where he carried out important assignments, and even, I heard, was in the circle that wrote Brezhnev's books for him. Needless to say, he and I did not see each other in those years, and now here we were, together in Munich.

"Hello there," he said in a friendly tone; he offered me his hand, which I perhaps should have ignored. But I must admit that my integrity always falters when such ceremonial gestures are involved.

After shaking hands, I asked what brought him to Munich.

"Nothing special," he said with his usual grin. "I came for a look at the stores."

To sting him, I asked if Moscow's huge department store GUM didn't have enough for him.

"GUM, my friend," he said in a tone both lofty and cynical, "exists for people who do not eat well, who dress poorly, and who are beaten up in police stations. And besides, there are lines there and I dislike lines. Do you know where they sell videocassettes here?"

I said I didn't, then asked him what he was doing here.

"Nothing interesting," he said dismissively. "Petty intrigues."

"And I thought you were involved with important political matters," I said.

"Important political matters," he retorted, "are mainly composed of petty intrigues."

For a moment neither of us said anything. Then I asked him if a big shot like him wasn't afraid to mingle in a crowd—you could never tell who was there.

"No, old friend, I'm not afraid. There are always several people among the customers who never take their eyes off me and guard my life better than they do their own."

31

"You mean you have your own people here?" I asked, stressing the word *your*.

"Of course, our people. . . ." He burst into laughter. "And yours as well. Listen, are you in any hurry?"

"No," I said, "why?"

"So then let's go for a beer?"

"Aside from the fact that your own people are following you, aren't you afraid to associate with me?"

"My friend," he said with a certain inward pride, "I can assure you that associating with you cannot harm me in any way. And it puts you in no danger either."

"But who knows with you," I said, wishing to offend him. "I have no idea what your mission is here."

"Whatever it is," he said, without taking offense, "you can be sure that I am not involved with any rough stuff. They have other people for that, and I don't even know who they are."

We got in my car, and I took him to the same beer garden in the English Garden where I had recently been drinking with Rudi. And this time too we each ordered a mass. Bukashev did the ordering. I noticed that, though he spoke German with an accent, he made no mistakes. The waiter was wearing lederhosen clasped beneath the knees. When Bukashev finished, the waiter cried "*Jawohl*" and ran to fill our order. Bukashev began asking me questions about my life here: Had I settled in? Whom did I see? Could I speak German? I said that my German was much worse than his, but seemed alright for everyday things.

Grinning as he had before, Bukashev remarked that no matter how difficult German might be for me, it couldn't be any harder than a Siberian eskimo dialect, which, had fate taken a different turn, I might have had to learn. He even hinted that he too had come to play a certain part in the resolution of my fate, and had immediately come out against the Siberian solution.

"And the others were for it?" I asked.

"Not all of them, but some were."

"And why were you against it?"

"I had three reasons, my friend," he replied unruffled. "First, as you recall, even as a boy I was ready to do good within the limits of reason. Second, I had some sentimental feelings for you. Third, to tell the truth, I like the way you write. Despite all the stupid things you've done, I think it would have been a shame to use a talent like yours for chopping down trees."

At once, he began trying to convince me (with complete sincerity, it seemed) not to waste time, but to get some writing done.

"Who's there to write for?" I asked. "You separated me from my readers."

"There's no need to exaggerate," he said. "In a way we did and in a way we didn't. Our country is big, the borders are long, people are traveling in every damn direction, you can't keep track of what they bring in. By the way, I myself brought in a good number of your books, no bull, fifty or sixty copies. And I'll grab a couple this time too."

"You Bolsheviks are strange people," I said. "You hound a writer, you exile him, then you smuggle his books back in. Doesn't that strike you as idiotic?"

"It is," Bukashev agreed readily, "it's perfectly idiotic. But there's nothing you can do about it. The system, you see, is idiotic."

I looked at him in disbelief. "You mean you know the system is idiotic?"

"So?" he said. "That surprises you? The system is idiotic and I serve it. But that doesn't oblige *me* to be an idiot. And the others aren't idiots either. Everybody understands everything, but there's nothing they can do."

"I don't understand," I said. "If you understand everything, why not try to change the situation? The power is in your hands."

"The power is in our hands, yes. The only question is how to use it. Think about it, let's suppose that power were in your hands. What would you do with it?"

"Ooooo!" I howled so loudly that a passing waiter carrying a dozen beers cast me a sidelong glance of fear. "If I had that power even for a week's time, the first thing I would do would be to smash your party to smithereens."

"I can see that," said Bukashev, not in the least disturbed by my blasphemy. "Alright, you would, and so then what?"

"I don't know," I said. "I don't even want to know. But whatever it was it would be better than your lackluster party."

"Listen to you!" He looked at me through his beer stein. "I can see you've become a total anticommunist."

"Nonsense!" I retorted. "I haven't become anything of the sort. I don't have anything against the so-called ideals of communism. Freedom, equality, fraternity, open borders, the withering away of the state, from each according to his ability, to each according to his need. What does that have to do with what you've been up to?"

"You're right," he said, wiping the foam off his lips. "it has nothing to do with it, to be blunt about it. But, after all, the USSR is not even seventy years old yet. That's just the blink of an eye in history. We committed follies and blunders because we were in too much of a hurry and tried to scale the stairs in one go. That doesn't work."

"And it won't in the future either," I said. "Utopias are utopian."

"How do you know if we're utopian or not." Bukashev finished his beer and set his mug on the table. "You can't force your way into Utopia. But if you think everything through and go step by step. . . ."

"Listen," I said, "why are you feeding me this crap? You can spout whatever nonsense you like on Moscow television and dupe the local yokels here, but not me. Do you really have any hope of convincing me that you believe in communism?"

"My dear man, I don't believe in anything at all," he said grinning. "I don't *believe*, I think. And it seems to me that there's still a chance."

"A chance?" I gasped with indignation. "After everything you've gone and done? What chance could there be?"

"I'm telling you there is a chance. A small one. It might be next to nothing. But it's still there. Listen, buddy," he said in Russian, grabbing the pants of a waiter running by, "bring us another round."

"*Jawohl!*" replied the waiter readily, dashing off to fill the order.

I watched him go in astonishment, then turned to Bukashev: "Lyoshka!" I said, calling him by his first name for the first time. "What's going on here? You spoke to him in Russian! How come he understood you?"

"I did?" he said with a puzzled tone. "I spoke to him in Russian? So, that means he's one of ours. Doesn't matter, pay no attention. It doesn't have anything to do with you."

The waiter came and set two mugs of beer on the table.

"Button that button!" said Bukashev derisively.

The waiter's hand went automatically to the button, but then he caught himself.

"*Ich verstehe Sie nicht,*" he said curtly, and walked away.

"Just try and work with people like that!" said Bukashev with a sigh. "Any little detail can trip them up. So, this is what I have to say. You know I was never an idiot. I never fell for any of that high-minded, raving nonsense. But there's no reason for me to lie to you. No point. And if I say there's a chance, it's because I've given the matter some thought. And I'm not the only one either. I know that you have a very low opinion of our leaders, but believe me there are people there who have their heads screwed on right."

I ran out for a quick leak, and when I came back, I said, "You know what—I don't know if you people have your heads screwed on right or not, all I know is that it doesn't matter either way. The system is rotten to the core, it's ossified, you know all that yourself, but you're still not capable of doing anything positive."

"And that's precisely where you're mistaken!" he retorted with unexpected heat. "We *are* capable of something. And we're going to do something."

"What are you going to do?" I said, staring right at him.

"There are some ideas," he said, not dropping his eyes. "But this is serious business, as you're well aware. It's almost impossible not to make mistakes in such a complex operation. Now, if you could only look into the future, say, fifty or sixty years, and find out what the results would be." He looked intently at me as he said this, then burst into laughter.

The last part of what he'd said had put me on my guard, of course. Had it just been chance, or was he hinting? And, if he was hinting, what did Bukashev want from me?

I expected that he would pursue the subject, but he seemed to put it out of his mind and once more began asking me questions about my life, speaking about his own in the process. Then he asked me about my plans for the summer, and again I couldn't tell whether he had an ulterior motive in asking this question or was just curious.

Trying not give anything away, I said I was planning to take a vacation and would soon be leaving for, well, . . . (I blurted this out without thinking) . . . Honolulu.

"Honolulu! The Hawaiian Islands!" said Bukashev dreamily. "You know, I've been a lot of places but I've never been to Hawaii. Must be nice there. Palm trees, sun, the ocean, and the Hawaiians with their ukeleles. Listen, you haven't seen my old love recently, have you?"

"Not recently," I said.

"I heard that she's become very religious."

"People change with time," I said evasively.

"Nonsense!" he retorted. "They just change what they worship. But they stay the same as ever. Yes, she did me in with that Lenin-Shmenin business. I thought I'd never get out of that one. Alright, it's been good to see you. But, seriously, no fooling around, do you want me to transmit a message to anyone in Moscow?"

Of course, I had plenty to transmit, but not through the likes of him.

"Listen," I said, "is it true what they say about you, that you're a major in the KGB?"

"Something like that," he said, taking pleasure in confirming it. "To be exact, a major general. But what does that matter? Do you think I met with you today to squeal on you? No, friend, I'm playing a different game, and the stakes are high."

He called the waiter over, and despite my protestations, paid for us both.

On the way back, I noticed in the rear-view mirror that we were being more or less openly followed by a green Volkswagen, but one which had a Cologne, not a Frankfurt, license plate. I mentioned this to Bukashev, but he dismissed it.

"They're ours," he said. "Don't worry, they're not following you, they're following me."

He asked me to drop him at the Vier Jahzes Feiten, the most luxurious hotel in Munich. One foot on the sidewalk, he suddenly asked if he might call me at some point.

"How can you call me, I'm leaving," I said.

"Oh, that's right!" he said. "For Honolulu. I forgot. But you're not leaving for good." He looked intently at me. "You'll be back some day and you might even feel like telling me about life in Hawaii. So I'll call you. I have your number."

It seemed that he knew more about me than I thought. But that didn't bother me particularly.

Driving away from the hotel, I caught sight of the green Volkswagen parked around the corner. I kept glancing into the rear-view mirror all the way home and made a few turns into side streets and blind alleys to make certain I was not being followed. The green Volkswagen did not reappear, and I caught no sign of any other tail.

On the way home, I switched on the car radio, which was always set to the station that plays Soviet Radio. It was broadcasting a concert at the request of the sea workers. First, the announcer's familiar voice read passages from Pushkin's *Bronze Horseman*, then the Bolshoi Theatre Orchestra played the dance of the young swans from Tchaikovsky's ballet.

"And now," said the announcer in a sugary voice, "a national artist of the Soviet Union will perform the Ukrainian folk song . . ."

"Hanka!" I said aloud, and predicted the future. As far as I recall, at all the concerts demonstrating the incredible flowering of our country's multinational art, they always play the same songs again and again. If it's a Russian song, it's either "Song of the Volga Boatmen" or "Dark Eyes." If it's Ukrainian, it's either a portion of "Natalka from Poltava" or this:

When Hanka gives me the eye,
My heart feels like it can fly.
Tell me, tell me if you can,
What's going to happen to this man . . .

I don't know why they perform this same song at all ceremonial concerts dedicated to the party congresses, Militia Day, or some other such thing, or why the woman who sings the song seems to be the same at every single performance — a tall, hefty woman in an ankle-length black-velvet dress cut low over a magnificent bosom. She lays her hands on that bosom, as if on a prop, entwines her fingers, and, with a cunning squint of the eyes, bursts forth in an infantile mezzo-soprano.

Hanka, you fox,
Hanka, you bluebird,
Hanka, you baby-girl . . .

Good God, I thought, won't anything ever really change in that country?

A PHONE CALL
FROM TORONTO

I was in the midst of my travel preparations when all of a sudden I got a call from Canada.

"Hello, old friend, this is Zilberovich speaking."

"Ah," I said, "hello, how's life?"

"There are problems," he answered simply. "Are you busy?"

"In what sense? Now, or in general?"

"Now and in general."

"Well, in general, I'm busy."

"Drop everything, buy a ticket to Toronto, and be there tomorrow."

I was taken aback by the proposition.

"What's with you," I said, "has your brain stopped working, or what? Why should I suddenly drop everything and dash off to Toronto from Munich? What do you think? You think I have nothing else to do?"

"Old man, this is not a subject for discussion. You'll rent a car in Toronto, something small and inconspicuous, get on the highway, take the sixth exit, drive exactly two miles, and you'll see a light-blue Chevrolet by the side of the road. It will have an antenna on the roof, blinds on the rear window, and its license plate will be smeared with mud. Follow that Chevrolet, keep some distance but don't let it out of your sight. That's it!"

"You idiot!" I shouted. "Before you start giving people orders, you should. . . ."

But these words were heard only by my wife, because the receiver had just been hung up on the other side of the planet.

"What is it?" asked my wife in alarm. "Who called?"

"You couldn't tell who it was? It was Zilberovich, of course."

"And what did he want?"

I told her.

My wife flared up. Not so much at Zilberovich as at me. "What's the meaning of this? What gives you the right? We may soon be saying goodbye forever, we have only a few days left together, and you're ready to spend them with anybody but your own family. It's your own fault, you've put yourself in a position where they can treat you like an errand boy. He thinks he's the center of the world and all he has to do is beckon and you'll come running."

Here, of course, she was not referring to Zilberovich.

I told her that I was very indignant, I had no intention of answering every summons, and, needless to say, was not going to Toronto. I said this with perfect sincerity, angry mostly with myself, and, at the same time, surprised by the strange mental force that was being exerted on me, despite the fantastic distance involved.

That force was somehow hypnotizing me, upsetting my equilibrium; there was no explicable reason for me to submit to it, and yet I could only keep from submitting to it by offering desperate inward resistance.

Does that make any sense?

I'll try to explain it more simply.

Zilberovich had not phoned me on his own behalf (he never had a behalf of his own), but on someone else's instructions. I was not that other person's subordinate in work, not dependent on him financially, and his attitude toward me could not affect my situation.

It would have been one thing if I respected that person and, for that reason, would have been ready to dash off to do his bidding, but that was not the case. Moreover, that person's pretensions to possessing the ultimate truth had made him a comic figure in my eyes.

All the same, whenever he summoned me, I simply became

rooted to the spot and felt it beyond my powers to refuse. And it was the same story this time too.

How should I have reacted to Zilberovich's call? I shouldn't have reacted at all. Someone had the idea that I should drop everything and dash off somewhere. I don't think I am obliged to anyone. I'm not even obliged to respond. I was up to my ears with things to do as it was.

But something was acting on my nerves and inclining me to think that it would be awkward not to respond.

Furious at Zilberovich's final words and those of his boss, and partially at myself, I mentally sketched out various refusals, beginning with the most arrogant, by telegraph: IF SOMEBODY WANTS TO SEE ME, LET HIM COME HERE.

Brief, clear, and to the point. But unrealistic. Because it was simply impossible to imagine a situation in which he would come to me, whereas it took no imagination to see me going to him.

But why, why, why? Why can't I stand up to this person who is of no use to me?

"What are you so worked up about?" my wife shouted at me. "Why are you smoking one cigarette after another, and what are you mumbling to yourself?"

"Was I really mumbling?" I asked in surprise.

"You're not only mumbling, you're making faces and giving someone the finger. If you can't just tell them to go to hell, send them a polite answer. Say you're sick, that you have a conference, that you have to finish writing your book."

"Sure," I said doubtfully, "but he'll say, Who needs your books?"

"So, if he does, you can say, Who needs yours? You have to fight rudeness with rudeness. If you put yourself last, other people do the same."

As always, she was right. But when she went to the bank, just to be on the safe side, I called the airport. Just as I had supposed, there were no direct flights from Munich to Toronto. To change planes in Frankfurt was too much. Where was the reason for me to try to overcome obstacles?

And yet, if you looked at it coolly, a change of planes without having to carry your luggage was no real problem. Not only that, I had a little bit of private business in Frankfurt, though of course I would never have traveled there for that alone. But, if you could kill two birds. . . .

A NEW
LEONARDO DA VINCI

I was first introduced to Leopold (Leo, for short) Zilberovich at the beginning of the sixties by his sister Janet, a classmate of mine at the university. Leo was one of the most prominent figures in literary circles of the time (or perhaps, to be more exact, on the literary fringes).

Tall, with long hair, wearing a dark soiled suit darned at the elbows and patched at the knees, he moved indefatigably about Moscow, a seemingly omnipresent figure in the editorial offices of the most liberal journals of the time, the Writers' Club, and all the poetry readings and theater premieres.

He was personally acquainted with all the known poets, prose writers, critics, and playwrights, whom he had won over individually with his knowledge and subtle understanding of their work. If need be, he could quote a four-line poem by one writer, or a line from another's novel or play, and would give the quoted passage an interpretation that was sometimes unexpected, but always original and flattering to the author.

I don't remember what he was involved in officially (I think he was a literary consultant somewhere), but his main calling was discovering and fostering young talent. His reddish, worn, grease-stained, and somehow scabby briefcase always bulged with poetry, prose, plays, and film scripts by young geniuses, whom he was constantly unearthing and trumpeting.

Many years later, when I'd ended up in the West, I encountered a great variety of literary agents who work in large offices and submit their clients' manuscripts to publishers. In other words, they do a business that is large and profitable. Zilberovich was doing the same thing, under Soviet conditions, but not out of self-interest. Not only that, poor as a church mouse himself, he bought food for the geniuses he had discovered without so much as even expecting a thank-you.

As soon as one of the talents began to publish and didn't need to borrow subway fare any more, he would cast Zilberovich directly out of mind. But Leo asked for nothing in return. His altruism was of such purity that he never even considered himself an altruist. Dropped by one genius, he would immediately find another and run around beating his drum.

By the way, he did this with me, too, at one point. He was simultaneously my admirer, sword bearer, and teacher. He knew everything I'd written, and nearly by heart. In those days, when I could only read my works to unselect audiences, Leo, of course, would always be there. He would find himself a place in the corner, and, his briefcase on his knees, he would listen intently. Whenever I was almost to a passage that worked well or contained a successful play on words, Leo would smile in anticipation, nod his head, exchanging glances with the audience, encouraging them to pay attention to what was about to happen. If the audience reacted favorably to the passage, Zilberovich's entire face would beam, and he would experience a surge of pride, as if he had fathered me.

When remembering that period of my life, I think that, of course, innate talent is the most important thing for a writer, but it's also important to encounter someone like Zilberovich early on.

Our romance ended when Zilberovich met Sim Simych Karnavalov. Hearing that name for the first time, I said that no half decent writer could ever have a name like that. A master of ceremonies or an accountant, but a writer? Never. At the time I could not imagine that. I would grow used to the name, however; it would not only seem normal to me, but would even assume great significance in my life.

I remember Zilberovich's first ecstatic account of Sim Simych Karnavalov, the former Zek who, after his release from labor camp, had begun working as a boiler operator in a kindergarten and writing "stunning" (Leo's word) prose. Earning sixty rubles a month, this man led a perfectly ascetic life. He didn't drink, didn't smoke, and ate the most frugal of meals. He wrote fourteen hours a day, allowing himself no indulgences, practically never associating with anyone because, in the first place, he feared stoolies, and, in the second, he valued every minute of his time. Still, with Zilberovich — Leo made a special point of this — Karnavalov would not only talk for an hour and a half straight, but would even read a few pages from his works.

"Well, and how were those pages?" I asked with concealed jealousy.

"My friend," said Zilberovich solemnly, "trust my taste. The man is a true genius." He managed to convey that though I too might be a genius in a certain sense, I still wasn't quite a true genius.

At that time Zilberovich lived on Stromynka Street, with his mother Kleopatra Kazimirovna and his sister Janet. They had a two-room apartment to themselves. This luxury, unheard of at the time, was theirs because Leo's grandfather, Pavel Ilich Zilberovich (Party underground-name — Serebrov) was a hero of the Civil War. Fortunately for future generations of Zilberoviches, he was also killed in that war. If he had died later in the camps, his grandson would hardly have had such a good apartment.

Leo's mother and sister lived in one room, and he had a room to himself. It was decorated entirely with pictures of people dear to his heart. The largest, a blowup of an old photograph, was of Grandfather Zilberovich at around age twenty-five, with a moustache like Chapaev's, wearing a leather jacket, and a Mauser on his hip. Grandfather Zilberovich was the only military man in the entire collection. The rest were Leo's favorite writers, starting with Chekhov and ending with me.

We often met in that room, and I read him my first short stories there. I wasn't the only one. Many poets and prose writers of my generation put in time there, and it was at Zilberovich's that I first saw and heard Okudzhava.

Even though I was somewhat jealous of Karnavalov, I never dreamed that he and Leo would become so close. But they did. Though not right away. By all accounts, Karnavalov was not very personable and in no hurry to let new people into his life. But when Zilberovich fell in love with someone, he wasn't so easy to get rid of either. He would call, drop by, offer his services, deliver things, pick up things, even retype manuscripts.

Once Janet telephoned me at two or three o'clock in the morning—Leo was missing. He'd gone out at seven o'clock, and he wasn't back yet. They'd already called the hospitals, and his mother was worried sick.

"And so what if he isn't back yet?" I said. "Is this the first time he ever came home late?"

She said, "No, it's not the first time, but we have an agreement, if he's detained, he'll call home by eleven-thirty."

The next morning Zilberovich called me and asked me to come to his place at once. It turned out that he had spent the whole night at Karnavalov's. Karnavalov had allowed him to read his novel, but the manuscript had to stay in the house. Zilberovich had read until daybreak, and now he was as happy as if he had just spent his first night with the woman he loved.

"Believe me when I say this," said Leo, pausing for effect. "This is a new Tolstoy."

I have to admit that I was quite stung by this assessment. I'd rather he had called Karnavalov a new Gogol, Dostoevsky, Chekhov, or even a new Shakespeare, whatever. The point was that he used to call *me* the new Tolstoy. To admit that two Tolstoys could exist simultaneously on Earth, and to take comfort in that fact, was, of course, well beyond my powers.

Naturally, I asked Leo what sort of novel this new Tolstoy had written. Leo was quick to reply that the novel was 860 pages long and was called *PDC*.

46

"PDC?" I said in surprise. "Is it about the police?"

"What do you mean, the police?" said Leo with a frown.

"But what's *PDC?* Doesn't it stand for preliminary detainment cell?"

"Well, yes it does, of course," said Leo, "but the novel is not about the police. And it's not just a novel either. It's only the first of a projected series of sixty."

I thought that I had heard Leo wrong and asked him to repeat the number. He repeated it. Then I asked him if this new Tolstoy had ever been in the nuthouse. Leo said that of course he had.

"Naturally," I said. "If a person is planning to write sixty thousand-page novels, there's a place in the nuthouse for him."

As a person of very progressive views, Leo grew enraged and began shouting at me that perhaps I should address such sentiments to the KGB and look for friends among the psychiatrists at Serbsky Institute. They'd know what I meant there. But he, Leo, didn't know what I meant.

We had a fierce quarrel. I slammed the door on my way out, thinking that I would never see him again. But that wasn't the first time I thought that, nor the last. The next day Leo brought me a bottle and said he had lost his head the previous evening.

But when we started drinking, he went on and on about his genius again and went so far as to say that he was not only a new Tolstoy, but a new Leonardo da Vinci. His was such an original talent that, considering the magnitude of his novels both in terms of size and content, he didn't call them novels or volumes but "slabs."

"The entire *Greater Zone*," said Zilberovich, "will be composed of sixty slabs."

"What is the greater zone?" I asked.

Zilberovich explained that *The Greater Zone* was the name of the entire epic.

"So, it's another book about the camps," I said.

"You fool, the camps are the little zone. But the little zone appears as part of the greater zone in the novels."

"I see," I said. "And so does PDC stand for—part of the little zone?"

"There you see," said Zilberovich, "a typical example of ordinary thinking. *PDC* is not a part of the little zone, but a novel about the embryonic development of society."

"Whaat?" I said.

"Listen closely to me now." Zilberovich threw his jacket over the back of his chair and began pacing the room. "Imagine that you're a sperm."

"Excuse me," I said, "but it's easier for me to imagine that you're a sperm."

"Fine," said Zilberovich, easily assuming his new role. "I'm a sperm. I am ejected into life, not alone, but in the company of two hundred million other tadpoles like myself. And we immediately enter what are not hothouse conditions but either an acidic or an alkaline medium in which only one of us can survive. And so all two hundred million begin battling for that one place. And all of them die but one. It becomes a human being. When he's born, he thinks he's one of a kind, but it turns out that he's one of two hundred million again."

"That's absurd!" I said. "There are four billion people on Earth, not two hundred million."

"Is that right?" Leo paused and looked disbelievingly at me. But he immediately found a retort. "On Earth, of course, that's right. But we're not talking about the whole Earth, just about our own country which is why the epic is called *The Greater Zone*."

"Listen," I said, "this is such poppycock that it's giving me a headache. *The Greater Zone*, *PDC*, sperm. . . . What do they have to do with each other?"

"You don't see?" asked Leo.

"No," I said, "I don't."

"Alright," said Zilberovich patiently, "I'll try to explain. The entire epic and each individual novel have many levels: the biological, the philosophical, the social, and the political. That's why there's a mixture of various ideas. That's why the intrauterine part of a person's life is viewed as preliminary detainment. He goes from preliminary detainment into life-long detainment. And only in death does freedom triumph."

48

"Who knows," I said. "Given the specific historical situation in Russia, life could be viewed as life imprisonment. But does he actually describe sperm as living people?"

"Of course," said Zilberovich, sighing for some reason. "As ordinary people who struggle to be imprisoned but obtain freedom when they fail. Is that clear?"

"It is," I said. "More or less. But a little abstruse. Now tell me straight out, is this novel, or all those novels, pro-Soviet or anti?"

"What a fool you are!" said Zilberovich, slapping his thigh. "Of course, they're anti. Do you think I would be telling you about them if they were pro!"

I don't want to be misunderstood here, but when Leo began to be fascinated by this Leonardo Tolstoy, running to see him and talking of nothing but him, I experienced this as an abrupt betrayal of me. The thing is that, without realizing it myself, I had grown used to having him always at hand, a devoted admirer, whom I could always send out for cigarettes or a bottle of vodka and put entirely out of mind when he wasn't needed. I had grown used to being able to go see him at any hour, read him some work, and hear him express his delight. But now he had started to change drastically. He was still happy to hear me read and even to praise me, but it wasn't the same anymore.

He no longer said, "marvelous, brilliant, stunning," now he said, "good, well put, not bad." Then he would plague me with some quotation from Karnavalov. Not only that, from the time he became Karnavalov's retainer, a sort of lordly condescension appeared in his attitude toward me.

I remembered all this in the airplane en route from Frankfurt to Toronto.

THE GENIUS FROM
BESKUDNIKOVO

No matter how jealous I was in those days in Moscow, and no matter how much I hid my envy behind jokes that sometimes succeeded and sometimes fell flat, my imagination was still fired by this new genius whom Zilberovich had discovered on the scrap heap. And when Zilberovich, making a point of being serious, informed me that, thanks to his—Zilberovich's—personal influence, Sim Simych had agreed to receive me, I, for my part, thanked Zilberovich with great irony for the honor and explained that only important officials agreed to receive someone; boiler operators and other such small fry did not agree to receive people, they invited them to drop by.

"Besides, I've seen enough geniuses in my time," I said. "They don't interest me all that much. But I may drop by there solely out of curiosity, nothing more."

Needless to say, I was taking a risk—Zilberovich might fly off the handle and not bring me there. But, to tell the truth, that wasn't much of a risk. Knowing Zilberovich inside and out, I knew that he wanted to boast about Sim Simych to me, and about me to Sim Simych. Because, mad as he was about his Leonardo, he sometimes remembered that I was of some value too.

To make a long story short, late one winter day he and I met and, taking a bottle of Kubanska along, we set off for the sticks, Beskudnikovo. We tumbled out of the suburban train onto an icy platform. Fine snow stung our faces, it was dark (all the street lights were broken), and there was the smell of frozen urine and something even more disgusting.

Then, to the barking of the local dogs, we dragged ourselves through back streets; we needed the agility of a tight-rope walker to avoid breaking a leg in the potholes. We finally found the kindergarten and that horrendous basement that stank of mice and sweaty clothing.

In one of those basement rooms lived the newly discovered genius, Zilberovich's idol. The room was about twenty to twenty-five feet square. The walls were covered with green wallpaper that had peeled in places and was wet and frost-marked in others. Just beneath ceiling level, there was a small window which was barred, like a cell window. The furniture: a rusty iron bed covered with a rough gray blanket; an unpainted kitchen table with a little cupboard for dishes; a sliding drawer containing a home-made knife, fashioned from a hacksaw blade; an aluminum fork that had long since lost one of its four prongs; and a mug, also cast aluminum, with its owner's initials, S.K., scratched into it.

The toilet proved to be a piece of board banded with roofing iron; someone had once painted it light blue, but the paint had now faded nearly entirely. On the shelf there was a piece of mirror the size of the palm of your hand, part of a safety razor (the blade holder and the blade, no handle), a shaving brush (also handleless, just the bristles), and a rectangular sprat can contained a soggy piece of soap of a sort, so black and foul-smelling that you'd have to look hard to find anything similar, even in a Soviet store.

There was nothing on the walls except for a small ikon in the far corner.

There were also two lights. One, a bare bulb, hung from the ceiling; the other was a table lamp, so to speak. Strictly speaking, it wasn't even a lamp, but a very ugly contraption made of wire and covered slipshod with newspaper that was burnt through in places. I should also mention the two bare stools, a bedside table, and a large leather chest with a padlock on it. In the corner by the door there was a country-style washstand with an aluminum basin beneath it and a coat peg, on which a sleeveless padded jacket, black with coal dust, was hanging.

Our host was wearing another padded jacket, this one a bit cleaner. He was also wearing quilted pants and felt boots with galoshes on top of them. He was a tall man, stoop-shouldered, with sunken cheeks and iron teeth.

"Simych, I'd like to introduce my friend. By the way, unlike yourself, he is a member of the Writers' Union," said Zilberovich loudly and with his usual free and easy manner.

Simych offered me his hand mistrustfully and, instead of saying how do you do, said, "Good."

He gave me the quick, guarded look typical of former Zeks. They say that modern airplanes have a special locator system that can identify planes in the air as either friend or foe. The Zeks have a different system, a sixth sense honed in the work camps over the years.

I have reason to believe that Simych did not view me as a foe, though he did act very strangely during our first meeting. Without any apparent irony, he still seemed to be trying to catch me out by asking questions:

"So, in other words, you're officially considered a writer? And you even have a document to that effect?"

"That's right," I said. "I am considered a writer. And I do have a document to that effect."

"And do you write your works directly onto a printing press, or just how do you do it?"

"No," I said, "what do you mean? I have an Underwood typewriter, that I tap out my books on."

Zilberovich could feel that we were off to a bad start and interrupted us:

"Simych, do you write with this pen?"

It was only when he asked that question that I noticed, next to the lamp on the table, an old-fashioned, nonspillable inkwell from which protruded a thick wooden pen with a gnawed end. The last time I had seen a pen like that was on a collective farm in the virgin steppe lands.

"Yes, I do," said Simych with a challenging look at me. "That's what I write with."

"But Simych," said Zilberovich, "I gave you a fountain pen. Where is it?"

"Oh, the fountain pen." He opened the drawer and pulled a plastic case with the union trademark from among the aluminum spoons and forks.

"And so why do you write with that piece of junk?" asked Zilberovich.

To be frank, Zilberovich's manner sometimes irritated me as well, but in this case I didn't think he had said anything so bad. Simych for some reason grew enraged and looked at poor Leo as if he wanted to burn a hole through him with his eyes.

"All world literature," he said with hatred in his voice, "was written with pieces of junk like this, and even worse junk, goose quills. Not with Underwoods or Overwoods, but with a piece of junk like this."

Then he became more kindly and even allowed Zilberovich to open the bottle. He didn't take a drop, but Zilberovich and I polished off his share. We took turns drinking from our host's mug, snacking on appetizers of processed cheese and onions.

I thought that we were already on firm footing, but when Zilberovich asked Simych to read something, he flew into a rage again and, looking daggers at Leo, said that he had nothing to read because he wasn't writing. And if ideas did come to mind from time to time, they were only in the sketchiest form.

It was plain that he still didn't trust me.

On the other hand, he trusted Zilberovich so much that he told him a great secret about his trunk. The secret was that all thirteen of the slabs already written, and the notes for the remaining forty-seven, were padlocked away inside that trunk. Needless to say, Zilberovich (a great keeper of secrets!) told me this that same snowy night as we made our way back to the train stop stumbling in the ice-covered potholes.

"Now do you understand?" said Zilberovich excitedly. "Now do you see that Simych is a genius?"

"Mister Zilberovich," I replied, "could you please explain to me, even if we are drunk, what your relationship to the opposite sex is?"

"What do you mean by that?" Leo stopped and turned his long-nosed face, blue in the darkness, toward me.

"What I mean is why do you, with the way you look and your prominent proboscis which legend has it matches another part of the body, why do you chase after geniuses when you could be chasing dames? Tell me the truth, are you gay, impotent, or what?"

"Listen," said Zilberovich, shivering from the cold and clutching the lapels of his coat. "Must you know everything?"

"I don't have to, but I'm curious," I said. "You don't have to answer the question."

"I can answer it or not answer it," he said. "But let me ask you a question. Can you tell me why you need all that, what's so good about dames?"

"Come on now!" I said, somewhat taken aback. "Of course there's nothing necessarily good about them, but the whole thing's interesting. The call of the wild. What are you, an idiot?" Now I was angry. "You don't know?"

"No," said Zilberovich, "I don't. Do you think I'm abnormal? I'm normal. All my parts work and I've tried it all. Alright, yes, it was pleasant. But all that fuss and bother before and after for only five minutes of pleasure!"

"So, you're saying you can't take the fuss and bother with women?"

"That's right."

"But with a genius you will?"

"With a genius I will."

"Then you're a fool," I said to Zilberovich.

"You're the fool," replied Zilberovich.

This was the only time I ever took an interest in Zilberovich's personal life.

THE LEADER
AND THE HERD

I have no intention whatsoever of telling Simych's whole story here, it's known well enough as it is. Thousands or even tens of thousands of articles, dissertations, and monographs have already been written on Karnavalov. There have been a few documentaries about him and even one feature film (though it was quite poor). Everyone in my generation clearly remembers Karnavalov becoming world-famous when he began publishing abroad. All the Soviet authorities — the Writers' Union and the journalists, the KGB and the police — entered a life-and-death struggle against him, but there was nothing they could do.

At the very beginning, when he published his first slab, the authorities simply lost their heads. That was a time when our government was flirting with the West, in the hopes of doing a little buying and stealing, and, after all the flap with Solzhenitsyn and all the others, they wanted to avoid any repetition of that with any writer.

For this reason, orders were given that Karnavalov be treated humanely. Have a chat with him, let him repent in the pages of *Literaturnaya Gazeta* and give his word not to publish any more in the West. The first time he was summoned to see an investigator, the conversation was mild. The investigator proved to have great admiration for the literary talent of the author of the slabs.

"I'm not a specialist, of course," said the investigator, "just a reader. But I liked your novel very much. I even cried in a few places." Saying this, he even sniffled and wiped his glasses to demonstrate how he had cried. "It's just a shame that the novel was published at such an unfortunate moment. At another time we would have welcomed it, but, right now, with the international situation so complicated, our enemies are of course trying to put your novel to very bad purposes."

The investigator proposed that Karnavalov prevent this from happening by rebuffing the international imperialists immediately in no uncertain terms in the pages of *Literaturnaya Gazeta*.

Simych promised to do this but, arriving home, immediately called a press conference for foreign correspondents, which he held in the boiler room. There, he delivered a very strong speech against communism and communists, whom he referred to either as predatory communists or, simply, predators.

The response was extraordinary. Simych not only became immediately famous as the greatest writer in the world, but as a hero. The whole world talked about that courageous Russian. And when the talk started to die down and the authorities only waited for the last of the uproar to pass so that they could devour him alive, he, being no fool, published another slab. The uproar was noisier this time, and his arrest threatened to cause an international scandal greater than the invasion of Czechoslovakia or Afghanistan.

The authorities were in a whirl, trying one thing after the other. They proposed that he leave the country on good terms. Not only did he refuse but, recalling the Solzhenitsyn affair, he appealed to all the countries in the entire world not to take him in if the predators ousted him from the USSR by force.

The authorities howled in confusion. No arrest came. Karnavalov's admirers (and they numbered in the thousands) followed everything he did and every action taken against him. The authorities were apprehensive that arresting Karnavalov openly might even spark a revolt. An automobile accident would have been too obvious. The only other choice was covert exile, but how and where could they exile him if all the Western governments would refuse him? Then the KGB carried out a brilliant and original plan.

Simych was arrested at eleven o'clock at night under conditions of the strictest secrecy. His relatives were kept isolated. Not only was his telephone disconnected, but his neighbors' were as well. Not a word of this would have leaked to the press if a UPI correspondent hadn't happened to be driving by. He saw them bringing Simych out of his building and shoving him into a Black Maria. But by the time he verified the information and sent it out over the teletype, Simych had already been parachuted from an airplane over Holland.

No, no matter what you say, and no matter what low opinion you may have of the KGB's mental powers, the idea was original.

But I'm getting ahead of the story. We met earlier, during the thaw, as people later called it. Everything was thawing and everyone was thawing. Even former Zeks. And even Sim Simych, most secretive of the secretive. I saw him again after that first night. With Zilberovich and without Zilberovich. Finally, observing that I had no ill intentions toward him, Simych began to trust me as well and even let me read not only *PDC* but chapters from the other slabs. He would go off to stoke his boiler with coal, and I would sit at his kitchen table and read frantically.

By the way, even back then I took special notice of one of the chapters of *PDC*. It was long, about a hundred pages, and stood out from the rest of the narrative. At the beginning of the chapter, there was a statement to the effect that this was not for those who enjoyed light reading but was for "dab" readers. Simych had of course found the word dab in *Dahl's Etymological Dictionary*, which he read regularly and used constantly in his work. And so I proved quite dab and patiently read that chapter through to the end, even though it was less like a chapter from a novel than one in a scholarly tome. It was called "The Leader and the Herd." There I found mention of the famous sperm, the one of two hundred million which struggles its way through. The chapter said that nature divides all living creatures — from the sperm to the higher creatures — into leaders and members of the herd. A great deal of space was devoted to the behavior of sheep, wolves, geese, seals, and all the laws noted by the author were, naturally, shifted onto human society, in which there is also a natural division between leaders and members of the herd.

Simych and I had our first serious quarrel then. He had just returned from the boiler room and was standing in the middle of his room, eating barley kasha from his bowl. He didn't offer me any, though, to tell the truth, I wouldn't have wanted any. I told him that I liked the chapter a lot, although there were essential differences between the animal world and human society. And though man is also a creature of the herd, he still has a more highly developed sense of himself as an individual, he aspires to freedom; generally speaking, people should not blindly submit to nature, and human society should be founded on pluralism. The word *pluralism* was in fashion then in our circles, and everyone used it, both aptly and inaptly. And I, too, had blurted it out unthinkingly. At the time I didn't know that this was the word he hated the most. What I had said so disturbed him that he began shaking all over and almost choked on his kasha.

"The pluralists!" he shouted. "They're even worse than the communist predators. You don't know what you're saying. Take a flock of geese. When they fly somewhere, they always have a leader. And, if there were no leader, just pluralists, they'd all fly off in different directions and die."

"I don't find the example very convincing," I objected. "That's not how geese do things. First one of them leads the flock, then another. They have a sort of goose democracy."

"Democracy!" bellowed Simych. "There's nothing good about democracy. If there's a fire, all the democrats and all the pluralists will be looking for one person to lead them out. Those vaunted democracies started falling apart a long time ago, they're dying, they're wallowing in luxury and pornography. And that doesn't impress our people. The only leader our people will follow is one who knows the way ahead."

This was the first time that I suspected he was referring to himself. Now some people say that he changed greatly after coming to the West. But I say he was always like that.

I remember one time (by the way, he was eating barley kasha

this time too), we were talking about Afghanistan, and I said that it was a terrible war. He replied that it was terrible but necessary. Because when we drive the predators out, we'll still need access to the Indian Ocean.

"Simych," I said, "before you start worrying about access to the Indian Ocean, you should give a little thought to straightening up the access to the boiler room. You could put down some boards, the mud's so deep out front you could drown in it."

But those quarrels were isolated, of course. All in all, I was so humbled both by his slabs and his actions that I set Simych above all the rest.

A LYRICAL DIGRESSION
ON BEARDS

What struck me most of all about Karnavalov was that he was without any vanity whatsoever, or the desire to be published, to become well-known, to receive royalties, to live in a good apartment, to eat and dress better. Later on I was very surprised when Simych, on the threshold of fame by then, began to attach significance to his appearance and even grew a beard. In my opinion, his beard didn't suit him and was out of keeping with his inner self. But here too I had to admit that he had known exactly what he was doing. He had known exactly when to have a beard, and when not to. If he had grown a beard as a boiler operator, even one down to his knees, it would hardly have done him any good. At most, he would have become known as the town madman by the residents of Beskudnikovo. And, of course, for that sort of reputation he would never have suffered the inconveniences that go with a beard, especially if you consider his job at the time—a beard was extremely dangerous with all that fire around. But when fame came, along with its throngs of admirers and journalists, when the time came to be photographed for book jackets and television interviews, a beard was just what the doctor ordered.

I have done massive research on beards which anyone who so desires can do in practically any library in the world. But, for those too lazy to go to the library, I will say briefly that I am deeply convinced that beards play a very important role in the dissemination of advanced ideas and doctrines, and in winning minds. I think that

Marxism would never have been able to win over the masses if Marx had shaved at some point, even if he'd been forced to do so. Lenin, Castro, and Khomeini could not have produced revolutions if they'd been clean shaven. Of course, power has sometimes been seized in one country or another, and territory has been subdued by people with just moustaches and sometimes even without. But no beardless man has ever yet been known as a prophet.

It also should be pointed out that there are beards and there are beards. To stand out from the general run, the wearer of a beard must avoid any hint of imitation. He should never grow a beard that could be called Marx-like, Lenin-like, Ho-Chi-Minh-like or Tolstoy-like. Otherwise, he will not be numbered among the prophets but among their followers. This was quite clear to Sim Simych, but he did not find a perfect solution immediately. At first, he went too far and grew a beard of such length that he would step on it himself, particularly when he was in a hurry. This was both inconvenient and pointless, because the beard was too long to fit into any photograph. He had to shorten it, and from then on the typical Karnavalov beard was one that barely covered his knees.

Some readers might wonder whether I'm devoting too much attention to beards. People tend to think that what matters most about a prophet is not his appearance, but his thoughts and ideas. This is a common delusion which I have been trying to dispel for many years, and, if the truth be told, with no success whatsoever. A prophet's thoughts and ideas are secondary. It is not our brains which a prophet primarily affects, but our hormones, and it is for this that a beard is needed, along with all the gestures, grimaces, and expressions that go with it. Sexually aroused, the crowd mistakenly assumes that it has mastered ideas for whose sake it is worthwhile to destroy churches, build canals, and kill their fellow men. It's curious that, while able to unleash the sexual energy of the masses, the prophets themselves are quite often impotent and have feminine voices. But this statement applies only in part to Simych. True, his voice was high, but I've heard that all the rest was in good working order, and, precisely because this ran counter to my concept, I was prevented from acknowledging him as a true prophet.

THE SUITOR

I am speaking so disjointedly here of events that I happened to witness because everything has gotten mixed up in my mind and, as a result of all my misadventures, I've lost my sense of past and future.

When Simych became famous, he was immediately accepted by one and all. He could only be spoken of in the most exalted tones; the slightest criticism was out of the question. And then he married Janet, in whose presence I could not say that I didn't like even some isolated phrase or sentence Simych had written. For her, everything that Simych did was so absolutely marvelous that even the term *genius* seemed insufficient.

But, by the way, she didn't think that highly of him right off. I remember the period when he not only surprised, but stunned me by falling in love with her at first sight. He had immediately decided to entice her with a copy of *PDC*, which he personally brought her to read in a legal file tied with brown string.

Now Janet doesn't remember this at all, but at the time she was very tough on *PDC*. "Tell me," she used to say to me, "why does he write so much and why are his heroes so uninspired, so spineless, so weak-willed? What are they supposed to be inspiring us to do, what's he driving at? Why does he paint Soviet life in only the blackest of colors? Can't he find anything positive about it? Of course, everyone knows there have been isolated errors and abuses, but the party has been straightforward in speaking of them. In the end, how long can you go on and on about the same thing? And you can't say only bad things happened here. After all, new cities were built, factories, power stations. . . ."

I had heard similar sentiments from Janet long before this conversation, although she had spoken before with greater confidence. Now some doubts had arisen in her, too, as to the justice of "our cause." Without noticing it herself, she had moved away from her old ideals but had not arrived at new ones.

One time I was on Stromynka Street without two kopecks to my name and decided to visit Zilberovich without calling first. Having climbed the four flights of stairs to his door, I nearly collided with a man dressed all in white sailcoth: sailcoth pants, sailcloth jacket, sailcloth shoes, and a peaked sailcloth cap of the sort popular in the early thirties (where had he ever come by that?).

"Hello, Sim Simych!" I said in greeting.

He gave me a strange look as if he didn't recognize me. Without responding, he began groping his way slowly down the stairs, like a blind man.

Kleopatra Kazimirovna let me in. She was terribly upset and whispered to me that a minute ago "that scarecrow" had proposed to her darling Janet.

"What gall!" she said with indignation. "With no position, and at his age. . . ." By the way, as to his age, Simych was all of forty-four at the time, but he looked much older.

Kleopatra Kazimirovna told me that Leo would be back soon, but that Netochka (her nickname for Janet) was at home. Then she went off to the kitchen.

In a cotton robe, Janet was sitting on the window sill and looking out (no doubt wanting to see him walk out the front door). On the round table in the middle of the room was a bottle of Algerian wine that had not been uncorked and a manicure set in a box lined in red velvet.

Janet was not usually particularly open with me, but this time she told me in detail about Simych's coming, how agitated he had been all the while they were drinking tea, and then how he had suddenly stood up and made her an old-fashioned offer of heart and hand. When she rejected his proposal, he grew incensed and promised her that she would bitterly regret her decision because the whole world would soon know of him.

"Can you imagine?" she said to me with excitement and indignation, but also with an uncertainty that wasn't like her. "The whole world will soon know of him! Can you imagine?"

"I can," I said in short.

"Why's that?" she said in surprise. "There are tens, hundreds of thousands of writers in the world, and every one of them is sure he'll be world-famous."

"That's right," I said, "every one is. And a few of them make it. You've read what he has to say about one sperm in two hundred million making its way into the big time."

"And you think Simych is the one?" she asked, concealing her own doubts behind mockery.

"He's very persistent," I said evasively.

"He's crazy," she said. "Do you know what line he was handing me? That he was just about of royal descent. He said that, that bookkeeper in a sailcloth cap!"

I think she forgot that she had said all of this long ago. Certainly I could never have brought myself to remind her of it.

DO YOU HAVE ANY
IDENTIFICATION?

I drove along local Route 4, following the instructions to the letter: the light-blue Chevrolet with the mud-spattered license plate was up ahead. I was trying to keep my distance in my rented Toyota, not coming too close to the Chevrolet, but not letting it out of sight either.

I wondered where the Canadian police were and why they were paying no attention to a mud-splattered license plate when, judging by the faded grass, there had been no rain in the Toronto area for a long time. Naturally, I was thinking about Simych, his eccentricities and odd ways, and about this idiotic cloak and dagger game with its covered windows and muddy plates. "He thinks he's another James Bond," I muttered to myself.

The driver of the lead car knew his business. He maintained a constant speed, made no sudden turns, and always used his turn signal in plenty of time.

Out past a town, which I think was called Laurenceville, there was a large pine forest bound in a neat chain-link fence. We had driven along about a mile and a half of fence when the driver of the Chevrolet made a right turn signal.

The only remarkable thing about the entrance to the forest was that it was nearly imperceptible. But at the very beginning of the forest there was a large white sign on the fence that read:

ATTENTION!!!
PRIVATE PROPERTY!!!
TRESPASSING STRICTLY PROHIBITED!
VIOLATORS WILL BE PROSECUTED!

Obviously, these warnings did not apply to the driver of the Chevrolet.

After another mile or so of gravel road, we finally came to a green iron gate in a green iron fence. Actually it was only I in my Toyota who came to this gate. The gate had opened for the Chevrolet and then had closed right in front of me.

I was surprised, naturally, but was in no rush to display any impatience, and I began examining the gate on which there was a broad arc-shaped iron sign with large Russian letters reading:

SOLACE

I already knew that this was what Simych had named his estate.

I hadn't even finished my cigarette when the gate opened and I drove through. But not very far. Just past the gate were an automatic barrier and a striped booth from which two cossacks emerged, one of them white, the other black, both with walrus moustaches and long swords at their sides. Upon closer examination, the white cossack proved to be Leo Zilberovich.

"Hello!" I said to him. "What's the costume for?"

"Do you have any identification?" he asked, not giving the slightest sign he'd recognized me.

"Here's some identification for you," I said and gave him the finger right in his face. The black cossack grasped the handle of his sword, but Zilberovich only frowned.

"You must show some identification," he repeated.

Now the black cossack opened the trunk of my car, which he closed right away, finding nothing there but a spare tire.

"Listen, Leo," I said angrily to Zilberovich. "I've been on the road sixteen hours because of you, so can the stupid games."

"We have to see some identification," persisted Leo, casting a quick glance to the black cossack, who then drew nearer and looked at me none too benevolently.

"Alright, alright," I said, giving in. "If you insist on playing this weird game, here's some identification." I handed him my driver's license.

He studied it closely, as if this were a checkpoint at a top-secret institution. He checked me against the picture and the picture against me several times. And it was only then that he greeted me with open arms. "How are you, my friend?"

"Go to hell!" I said, snatching my license back in a fury and pushing him away.

"Alright, alright, you've got reason to grumble," he said, giving me a whack on the back. "But you know that the KGB is after Simych and they can make up anyone to look like anyone else. Alright, let's get going. Let's get a bite to eat. Hey, Tom," said Zilberovich, addressing the black cossack in English. "Park his car up by the stable."

THE ESTATE

The estate on which I now found myself reminded me a little of the Writers' Club in Maleevka and a little of the government health spa in Barvikha, which I once happened on purely by chance. A long, three-story building with a semicircular porch and columns. In front of the porch was a large square paved in red brick, radiating asphalt paths whose edges were lined with white birches. To the left of the house were a pair of trim cottages with small windows, and, to the right, a small church with three modest cupolas. There were some other structures facing the main building at a distance. Further on, a lake gleamed with the setting sun.

On the square I noticed a striped pole with a plywood sign that read: CCCP.

"What does that mean, CCCP?" I asked Zilberovich.

"Where's that?"

"Over there, on the sign."

"Oh, that," said Zilberovich with a laugh. "That's not English, those are Russian letters."

"Was it stolen from the Soviet border?"

"Not at all. Tom made it. In time it'll all be clear to you."

A creature of the opposite sex wearing a red caftan, open widely above and below, was standing with her back to us and using a hose to water chrysanthemums. I had never seen anyone with a more misshapen figure in my entire life. It consisted mainly of an enormous behind, the rest seeming haphazard outgrowths.

Walking away from me, Zilberovich stole up to that behind and grabbed it with both hands.

"Heavens!" cried the owner of the behind, who turned around and showed herself to be a young woman with a common, freckled face. "Oh, it's you, my lord," she said with a rather foolish smile. "You're always sporting with me, and then Tom asks me how come I'm black and blue."

"Come see me, I'll powder the marks," cracked Zilberovich, giving her a friendly spank. Then, to me, he said, "This is Stepanida, Stesha for short. She's Tom's wife. He can't resist this work of art," he said giving the work of art another playful slap.

"You're all like dogs in heat, my lord," said Stesha, still smiling. "And you don't notice anything else about a woman."

We continued on our way and I remarked to Leo that his ideas on the issue of sex seemed to have undergone a change in the recent past.

"Not at all," said Leo with some embarrassment. "They haven't changed. But, you know, life here is so secluded and boring that sometimes you want to let in a little fresh air."

"And what does Tom say about it?"

"He doesn't say anything," replied Leo in a carefree tone. "He's a broad-minded person."

When we walked over to the porch, another creature appeared, and this one went bounding at my chest. It was a sheepdog of considerable proportions. I was about to kiss my life goodbye when I felt the dog licking my nose.

"Plushka!" shouted Zilberovich, dragging the dog off me. "You rotten rascal you! What kind of a dog are you! Simych was right to name you Pluralist."

"Pluralist?" I said in surprise.

"That's right," said Zilberovich. "It licks up to everyone indiscriminately. A real pluralist. But so as not to hurt his feelings, we call him Plushka."

The next to appear on the porch after Plushka was a Russian beauty wearing a red silk caftan, a cambric shawl, and boots of Moroccan leather. A large blond braid was wrapped neatly around her head.

"Heavens, look who God sent us!" she said, smiling radiantly at me.

It was Janet.

She ran lightly down from the porch and we kissed three times, the accepted greeting among foreigners who honor Russian customs.

"You haven't changed a bit," I said to Janet.

"I don't have the time to," she said. "We all work sixteen hours a day here. But you're grayer and you've put on weight."

"I know, I know," I admitted sadly. "It's true."

"Well, let's go take a little of the bounty God has provided."

We mounted the porch and found ourselves in a spacious, columned entry hall. A broad, carpeted staircase led to a landing with a potted palm, to the right of which was a double glass door with flowery curtains on the inside and a crucifix above it.

Janet crossed herself. Zilberovich removed his flat cossack fur cap and he too crossed himself. To my surprise, he was now completely bald.

"What, don't you cross yourself?" said Janet, looking askance at me. "Are you a militant atheist?"

"Not at all," I said. "I'm not a militant atheist, just a frivolous one."

In the refectory I threw my arms around Kleopatra Kazimirovna who, like me, had put on a lot of weight in the last few years. She was wearing a dark green dress, an apron of a slightly lighter shade, and a white headdress.

Leo hung his cap on a hook by the door.

We sat down at one corner of a large, uncovered oak table that could seat about twelve. The chairs were also oak.

Kleopatra Kazimirovna immediately brought in a cast-iron pot of cabbage soup from the kitchen, which adjoined the dining room, while Janet set out wooden plates and wooden spoons.

"What would you like to drink, kvass or juice?" asked Janet.

"There's no other choice?" I asked guardedly. Zilberovich stepped on my foot and winked to me.

"We don't keep liquor," said Janet dryly.

"Ah, of course you don't," I said. "But I do."

I bent to my Diplomat suitcase, which contained a bottle of German Gorbachev vodka that I'd purchased back at the Frankfurt airport.

"No liquor is consumed in this house," said Janet, stopping me.

O God! I thought in anguish, but said nothing. Zilberovich nudged me with his knee. I understood what this meant and asked for kvass, the taste of which I had already forgotten a little. The cabbage soup was absolutely tasteless, and my eyes began wandering about the table.

"Is there something you want?" asked Janet.

"Yes," I said, "some salt, if I may."

"We don't use salt because Sim Simych is a diabetic and on a salt-free diet."

"Oh, is that so!" I said in disappointment. "I didn't know. But I'm on a high-salt diet."

"Sure," said Janet, laughing good-naturedly. "You're on a high-salt, high-alcohol diet."

"That's right," I said. "And high-tobacco too."

"By the way," remarked Janet, "there's no smoking indoors here."

"No problem," I assured her. "It's warm, I can smoke outside."

The cabbage soup was followed by buckwheat kasha and milk, which, of course, don't require salt.

Kleopatra Kazimirovna asked me in detail about my life in Germany, my wife and children, how we were doing, what we were doing. I told her that my son was in a *Realschule*, my daughter in a *Gymnasium*, I was writing, and my wife was helping me and running the errands.

"Has she learned to drive?" asked Kleopatra Kazimirovna.

I said that she hadn't, that she went shopping on her bicycle.

"On a bicycle," said Janet. "But that's so inconvenient. Her dress could ride up or get caught in the wheel."

I explained that there was no danger of that because she wore jeans when she rode her bike.

"Jeans?" said Janet in astonishment. "You permit her to go around in jeans?"

"She doesn't ask my permission," I said. "But I don't see anything wrong with jeans."

"Netochka's become very strict here," remarked Kleopatra Kazimirovna with a mixture of pride and apology.

"Yes, I have," said Janet firmly. "A woman should wear what God has prescribed for her."

I replied that, to the best of my knowledge, God had created woman naked, and, as far as jeans were concerned, everyone wore them now, men, women, and hermaphrodites.

I was about to say more on the subject, but Zilberovich stepped on my foot so hard that I almost cried out, and, changing the subject, I delicately inquired why my host was not there.

"He's already eaten his dinner," said Leo.

"Will he be coming back or should I drop by and see him?"

Janet exchanged glances with her mother while Leo broke into laughter.

"Sim Simych does no business after dinner," said Janet.

"I see," I said with restrained displeasure, "but I'm not here on my own business."

"But he doesn't deal with business of any sort after dinner," repeated Janet. "His own, or other people's."

"It's true, old friend," seconded Zilberovich. "He simply cannot receive you now. He's studying *Dahl's Etymological Dictionary* right now and then he'll listen to Bach. He always listens to Bach before going to sleep. He can't fall asleep without his Bach."

I pushed away my kasha and rose. "You will forgive me, I hope . . . meaning you, Kleopatra Kazimirovna, and you, Janet, but I simply don't understand why I'm being treated this way. I didn't invite myself here. I don't have a minute to spare. I have a long and possibly dangerous journey ahead of me. The only reason I'm here is that Leo insisted. I lost a night's sleep, and with the changes of plane it took me sixteen hours to get here. . . ."

"Why are you getting so worked up, my friend?" Zilberovich took me by the arm and pulled me back onto my chair. "You've been traveling, you're tired. Get yourself some rest now. You and I can have a little talk while Netochka is making up your room . . ." He winked at me again with a glance at my suitcase. "You'll get in bed, have yourself a good night's sleep, and then tomorrow we'll get down to business."

A gentle melody streamed through the air. A great connoisseur of music, I immediately recognized it as Bach's "Well-Tempered Clavier."

ASTRIDE A
WHITE STEED

That goddamned Zilberovich!

The Gorbachev vodka I'd brought wasn't enough for him, and he pulled out his own quart of bourbon, saying that Americans considered bourbon the best drink in the world. Americans also cut the best drink in the world with a lot of soda, but we drank it straight, nibbling on pickles. Of course, it's foolish, even blasphemous to cut a drink like that, but to mix bourbon and vodka in one sitting is not the best idea either.

Ungluing my eyes with great effort, I looked around. I was lying on a wooden trundle bed with a rough mattress. I was in a strange sort of room, something between a prison cell and a monk's cell. There was an iron case in one corner and, in the other, a country-style washstand. (Could it be the same one I'd seen twenty-odd years ago in Simych's basement?) There was a tiny window at the top of the wall, through which the most cacophonous sounds were invading the room. Some son of a bitch was banging a drum and squeaking away on a fife. The nerve! At this hour of the morning. . . .

I lifted my hand for a look at my watch and was stunned. It was twenty to twelve, and I was still lolling in bed. And in a house where the master and all his assistants labored from dawn till dark.

God, why had I drunk so much? Why can't I be like everyone else — why can't I be like an American and just pour a little bourbon in a glass, cut it with soda, and carry on a calm, even discourse on Dante or taxes?

But our conversation had been interesting in its own way. At first Leo had been full of self-importance and secrets, but, as time passed and he came out of his shell, he blabbed a bit about the life they led there.

It was a very insular life. Simych wrote twenty-four pages a day. Sometimes he wrote in his study, and sometimes he strolled the grounds of the estate, making notes on the move. Finishing a page in his notebook, he would tear it off and toss it to the ground without looking where it fell, but Kleopatra Kazimirovna and Janet would rush to gather them up and keep them in order.

To skip ahead, I'll say that later on I saw this for myself—Simych out walking with his notebook, his wife and mother-in-law following silently behind him. As soon as he tossed off a sheet, they would pick it up, read it at once, then Janet would immediately evaluate it on her one-point scale. "A work of genius!" She would whisper it so as not to disturb Simych.

She once had had exactly the same opinion of Lenin. I remember when we were at university together, I borrowed a copy of one of Lenin's pamphlets from her (I think it was *The State and Revolution*). The word *genius* appeared in the margins like punctuation after every sentence.

Still, you shouldn't mix Gorbachev with Jack Daniels. I had a splitting headache, and I began thinking it was time to quit drinking altogether. I even vowed I would. Just take a hair of the dog and I'd be done with it for good. The drum was still booming and the fife was still squealing and frazzling my concentration.

I stood up on the bed and could just reach the window. But when I looked out, I could not believe my own eyes. On the square in front of the house, right by the striped pole with the CCCP sign, stood a Soviet soldier in full uniform with a submachine gun slung over his shoulder. I shook my head desperately. What was this? Was I seeing things, or had Soviet troops invaded Canada?

Squinting, I could make out Tom with a saxophone and Stepanida with a drum even bigger than her backside. Just as I had thought, they weren't playing, just tuning up.

Then two Russian beauties appeared wearing gaudy caftans and kerchiefs. One of them was holding a large loaf of bread in both hands, the other a tray with a salt cellar.

Then . . . I didn't exactly understand what happened next. First, I think, a bell pealed, then Tom started in on a rousing number and Stepanida beat the drum. At that very moment, a magnificent horseman, dressed in white and astride a white steed, began riding down the birch-lined paths from the far buildings.

The saxophone wailed, the drum boomed, and the dog by the porch tried to break free of its chain and began barking. The horse charged, chomping at the bit and tossing its head, but the horseman managed to restrain it and make it approach as slowly and implacably as fate.

He was all in white: white cape, white tunic, white pants, white boots. His beard was white and a long sword in a white scabbard hung at his side.

I opened the window all the way and stuck my head out to see and hear better. Peering intently, I recognized Sim Simych as the horseman, his face prophetic and severe.

Simych drew near the sentry. The saxophone and drum fell silent. Suddenly, Simych leaned to one side and in a single gesture drew a long and narrow sword, flashing in the sun. It appeared he was about to deprive the poor soldier of his head.

I closed my eyes. When I opened them again, I saw that the soldier had his hands up and his submachine gun was on the ground, but Simych was still holding the sword over the soldier's head.

"Answer me," said Simych resoundingly. "Why did you serve the predator authorities? Against whom did you take up arms?"

"Forgive me, Little Father," said the soldier in a voice that sounded a lot like Zilberovich's. "I didn't serve them of my own free will, I was forced by those satans."

"Will you swear to serve only me from now on and fight steadfastly against the predatory communists and pluralist spongers?"

"Yes, I will, Little Father, I promise to serve you against all your enemies, to defend the borders of Holy Russia from all who hate our people."

"Kiss the sword!" commanded the little father.

Falling to his knees, Zilberovich placed his lips to the sword. Simych crossed the imaginary boundary, and then the two beauties (by then I had no doubt their parts were being played by Janet and Kleopatra Kazimirovna) offered him the bread and salt.

Simych accepted the bread and salt, proffered his hand for the women to kiss, then, spurring his horse, bounded away down one of the side paths.

Evidently that was the end of the ceremony, for now they all went their separate ways.

While I was pulling on my pants, Zilberovich, still in uniform and carrying his submachine gun, looked in on me in the cell.

"You sure slept late!" he said in reproach. "You even missed our rehearsal."

"No, I didn't," I said. "I saw it all. But I don't understand what it meant."

"What's there *not* to understand?" said Zilberovich. "There's nothing *to* understand. Simych is in training."

"Does he really hope to return on a white steed?" I asked sarcastically.

"He does, old friend. Of course he does."

"The very idea is ridiculous."

"You see," said Zilberovich, choosing his words, "you met Simych in his cellar, poor and hungry, with a trunk full of slabs of no use to anyone. All his plans seemed ridiculous to you then. But now you see he was right and you were wrong. So then why can't you suppose that he can see farther into the future than you this time, too? Geniuses can always see things that are not given to us poor mortals to see. Our only choice is to trust in them or not."

I admit that what he said came close to offending me. His former high opinion of me, it was clear, was long a thing of the past. He exalted Simych and put me on the same level as himself, if not lower — *he* served a genius, whereas *I* was dangling on some limb of my own. But knowing how fickle Leo was, I decided not to take offense.

I glanced at my watch and asked Zilberovich if he thought I could get a ticket for the six o'clock flight at the airport or if I should reserve it in advance by phone. Zilberovich gave me a look between surprise and embarrassment (I couldn't tell which) and said that I would not be able to leave that day.

"Why not?" I asked.

"Because Sim Simych hasn't spoken with you yet."

"But we still have plenty of time for that."

"You have plenty of time," remarked Zilberovich. "But *he* doesn't. He wanted to receive you during breakfast, but you were sleeping. And every minute of his time is scheduled. He rises at seven. A half an hour's jog around the lake, ten minutes for a shower, fifteen minutes of prayer, then twenty minutes for breakfast. He's at his desk by eight-fifteen. At twenty of twelve he saddles Logos — "

"Who?"

"That's the name of his horse. Logos. And at twelve noon on the dot, rehearsal for his entry into Russia. After that he works again till two. Then lunch from two to two-thirty."

"That's very good," I cried. "Let him receive me during lunch."

"He can't," said Zilberovich with a sigh. "During lunch he looks through the readers."

"The what?"

"The newspaper," said Leo irritably. "You know he refuses to use words with foreign origins."

"But after lunch he has some free time, I hope."

"After lunch, he gives Stepanida a forty-minute class in Russian language, then naps for thirty minutes to restore his powers."

"How about after his nap?"

"After his nap he does a little exercise again, showers, has some tea, and works till seven. Then it's dinner."

"And he reads newspapers again?"

"No, the looker."

"The what?"

"The looker."

"I understand," I said, "you mean television. He relaxes. I'll see him then!"

"What do mean, he relaxes!" said Zilberovich, gesturing. "He watches only the news and only for half an hour. Then he works again until ten-thirty."

"Alright then, let him receive me after ten-thirty. Then at least I can leave tomorrow morning."

"From ten-thirty to eleven, he reads *Dahl's Dictionary*, followed by half an hour for Bach and then bedtime. But don't worry. He'll definitely receive you tomorrow. Just don't sleep through breakfast."

"The nerve of you people!" I said angrily.

"Which people?"

"I won't speak about the others, but you've got nerve, Zilberovich, and your Sim Simych has got three times what you do. It's not enough that you make me drag myself halfway around the world, you have to play games with me. He's on a schedule, he has no time. Well, for your information, my time has some value, too."

"Of course it does," said Zilberovich, livening up. "It's valuable to you. But his time is valuable to all mankind."

At that point I lost my head entirely. By the way, I simply cannot abide references to "the people" and "mankind." I told Zilberovich if Simych was of such value to mankind, he should address mankind directly, but I'd be leaving for the airport there and then. And I added my hope that they were going to reimburse me for my travel expenses.

"That's no problem, old friend. He knows everything and he pays for everything. But don't act like a fool. If you leave, he'll be so angry, you can't imagine."

In the end he talked me into it. I stayed.

After lunch, Zilberovich and I went gathering mushrooms. Then he took me to a real Russian bathhouse with a steam room and wooden tubs. When we entered the dressing room, I saw a dozen fresh birch branches on a bench in the corner. I chose one of the better ones and asked Zilberovich if he wanted me to pick one for him, or would one be enough for the both of us.

"I don't need one," said Zilberovich with an odd grin. "I've already been birched."

I didn't understand what he meant by that, but when Leo undressed, I noticed that his entire stoop-shouldered back was crisscrossed with purple welts.

"What's that?" I asked dumbfounded.

"Tom did it, the dog," said Leo without any malice. "Once he starts something, he goes all the way."

"I don't understand," I said. "Did you two get into a fight?"

"No," said Leo, smiling sadly, "we didn't get into a fight. He birched me."

"What?" I said in surprise. "What do you mean birched you? And you let him?"

"It wasn't his idea. Simych ordered that I be given fifty lashes."

I had just taken off my left shoe, and I froze, shoe in hand.

"Yes," said Zilberovich in a defiant tone. "Simych has instituted corporal punishment here. Of course, it was all my fault. He had sent me to the post office to mail a manuscript to the publishers. On the way, I stopped by a restaurant, spent a little time there, and left without the manuscript. I was almost to the post office before I remembered it. When I went back it was gone."

"What, there was only one copy?" I asked.

"Ha," said Zilberovich, "if there'd only been a single copy, he would have had me killed."

Flabbergasted, I fell silent. Then all of a sudden I slammed my shoe against the bench.

"Leo!" I said. "I can't believe this savagery. I can't imagine that in these times, in a free country, a grown, sophisticated, thinking person—an intellectual—was flogged in the stable like a serf. It's not only a question of physical pain, it's an insult to human dignity. Didn't you even protest?"

"Did I ever!" said Leo with excitement. "I went down on my knees before him. I implored him. Simych, I said, this is the first and last time that'll ever happen, I swear by my honor, it'll never happen again."

"And what did he say?" I asked. "Didn't he take pity on you? His heart wasn't moved?"

"Of course his heart was moved," said Leo, wiping a tear as it rolled from his left eye.

Now I was so riled up that I began running around the dressing room with my shoe in hand.

"Leo!" I said. "This can't continue. This has to stop at once. You shouldn't let anyone treat you like a dumb animal. Alright, my friend, get your clothes on and let's go." I sat down on the bench and began putting my shoe back on.

"Where are we going?" said Leo.

"To the airport," I said. "And from there to Munich. Don't worry about the money, I've got money up the nose. I'll bring you to Munich and help you get a job at Radio Liberty. You can be as anti-Soviet as you like there, and get paid for it, too."

Leo looked over at me with a sad smile.

"No, old friend, what do I need with Radio Liberty! My duty is here. Of course Simych is a willful man, but as you know, geniuses tend to be eccentric, and we should be patient with their eccentricities. I know, I know," he hastened to say, as if anticipating my objection. "You don't like it when I say 'we' and put you on the same footing with me. But I don't. I know that you have some talent. But you should also understand that there's an abyss between talent and genius. It's not for nothing that all Russia prays for him."

"Russia prays for him?" I said. "Ha-ha-ha. They forgot him there a long time ago."

Leo peered at me and shook his head.

"No, old friend, you're mistaken. Not only have they not forgotten him, on the contrary, his influence on people's minds grows with each passing day. People don't just read his books. They form secret groups and study his works in depth. He had supporters not only among the intelligentsia, but among the workers and in the Party, in the KGB, and on the military high command. And, if you want to know something," said Leo with a look back at the door, and then a whisper in my ear. "Last week he was visited by . . ." Now, his voice even lower than a whisper, Leo named a member of the Politburo who had recently arrived in America for a visit.

"You're full of it!" I said.

"I should drop dead if I'm lying," said Leo, picking a tooth with his fingernail like a hood.

I rose somewhat earlier the next morning. Leaving the house, I caught sight of two large vehicles with Washington plates. One was a car, the other a van marked American Television News. People were laying cable and carrying equipment into the house. Only one man was doing nothing, apart from smoking a cigar.

"John?" I said in surprise. "Is that you? What are you doing here? Do you work for television too?"

"Oh yes," said John, "I work for them all. But what are you doing here? I thought you were long gone. You'll have to pay a stiff penalty if you change your mind."

"Don't worry," I said. "I still have a week till my departure."

"I'm not worried," said John with a smile. "I know you've purchased the ticket. I didn't come here to see you but to do a short interview with Mr. Karnavalov."

With those words, he walked off into the house to take charge of rigging the equipment, and I decided to go for a walk by the lake. There I came upon Simych jogging, and he greeted me without breaking stride, as if we ran into each other every day on that path.

When I returned for breakfast, an entire team of cameramen, lighting men, and sound technicians were bustling about under John's direction. All the members of the household were assembled at the dining room table—Kleopatra Kazimirovna, Janet, Zilberovich, Tom, and Stepanida. They were all excited. My arrival caused a certain confusion, but it was cleared up on the spot.

The problem was, as Janet explained quite politely, that Sim Simych was going to be filmed at a typical breakfast at home, with his immediate family and closest associates, and since I fell into neither category, would I be so kind as to agree to take my breakfast in my own room?

That offended me, and I was on the verge of leaving. What was I waiting around there for anyway? For them to reimburse me? I was well-off enough now not to worry about such a trifling sum.

I was on my way out when the door was flung open and first John was wheeled in, his jean-clad butt in the air, his eye pressed to the camera, followed at once by Sim Simych in his sweatsuit. He was striding quickly, as if unaware of the cameras, uttering profundities on the go.

But he transformed himself instantly as he approached the table, and began acting like a well-mannered man of the world; he kissed his wife, then kissed Kleopatra Kazimirovna's hand, shook Stepanida's hand, whacked Tom on the back, nodded to Zilberovich, and then said to me, "You, I've seen."

He took his place at the head of the table, said that it was time for grace, and then cried out in Russian: "Our father who art in heaven . . ."

"That's OK," interrupted John, "that's enough, we'll have to translate it into English anyway. Now eat a little and talk. And if you can, give us a little smile."

"No smiles," said Sim Simych angrily. "The world is perishing. The West is surrendering one country after the other to the predators, communism's iron jaws are already at our very throats and will soon tear out our Adam's apples, and all you do is smile. Your life's too easy, you've gone soft, you don't understand that you have to fight for your freedom and sacrifice yourselves."

"How should we fight for it?" asked John politely.

"First, by renouncing everything you don't need. All anyone should have is what he absolutely needs. Take me, for example. I am a world-famous writer, but I live modestly. I only have one house, two cottages, a bathhouse, a stable, and a small church."

"Tell me, is the lake yours?"

"Yes, I also have one small modest lake."

"Mr. Karnavalov, whom do you consider the best writer in the world today?"

"You don't know?"

"I can guess, but I want your answer."

"You see," said Simych after a moment's thought, "if I say that I am the best writer in the world, that would be immodest. But if I say that it's not me, that would be untrue."

"Mr. Karnavalov, everyone knows that you have millions of readers. But there are people who don't read your books . . ."

"It's not that they don't read them," said Simych with a frown, "it's that they don't finish them. And others lie, saying they have when they haven't."

"But there are people who finish them, but don't share your ideas."

"Nonsense!" exclaimed Simych irritably, rapping his fork against the table. "Meaningless nonsense. What does that mean—they share my ideas, they don't share them? To share my ideas, a person needs more than a birdbrain. The predators' brains are besmirched with ideology, and the pluralists don't have any brains whatsoever. And neither of them understands that I speak the truth and only the truth, and that I can see many decades into the future. Take him, for example." Simych poked me with a finger. "He's also considered something of a writer. But he can't see past today. And instead of sitting down and working, he's off somewhere, to the so-called future. He wants to know what will happen in sixty years' time. But I don't have to go anywhere. I already know what's going to happen."

"That's very interesting!" cried John. "Very interesting. And just what is going to happen?"

Simych's face darkened; he moved his bowl aside and began shaking the crumbs out of his beard.

"If the world doesn't heed what I say," he said, looking directly into the camera, "there'll be nothing good about the future. Not in Russia or anywhere else. The communists will devour the whole world, themselves included. The Chinese will seize everything."

"And if the world heeds everything you say?"

"Oh then," said Simych, livening up and, in spite of himself, smiling a bit, "then everything will be fine. Then the whole world will be on the road to recovery, and the process will start in Russia first."

"How do you see the Russia of the future? Do you have any hope that a democratic form of governement will triumph there?"

"None whatsoever!" protested Simych heatedly. "Your much-vaunted democracy doesn't suit us Russians. A situation where every fool can express his opinion and tell the authorities what they should or shouldn't do is not for us. We need a single ruler who wields absolute authority and knows exactly where to go and why."

"And do you think such rulers exist?"

"They may not, but they could," said Simych significantly, exchanging glances with Janet.

"I'm terribly sorry," said John, after pausing to think, "but do you have someone specific in mind or is this just a theory?"

"Dammit!" said Simych, suddenly excited. He slapped his knee, stood up, and began nervously pacing the room. "You see, if I tell you what I think, it'll make for a terrible outcry, all the pluralists in the world will attack me like a pack of dogs. They'll say Karnavalov wants to be a tsar. And I don't want to be a tsar. I'm an artist. I think like an artist. I think in images. I take an image, reflect on it, and put it down in writing. Is that clear?"

"Yes," said John uncertainly. "For the most part."

"Alright then. I don't want to be a tsar. I still have not completed my tasks as an artist. But sometimes historical circumstances are such that a person must accept the mission for which the Lord has destined him. If there is no other person in the world who can do it, then he must take it upon himself."

"And if such a mission fell to you, you wouldn't refuse it?"

"I would refuse it if there were even one person who could carry it out. But there's no one. We're surrounded by mediocrity. And only if the Lord wishes to write a page of history with this hand . . ." Simych raised the hand that was holding the fork,

". . . will I. . . ." Simych did not finish his sentence, falling into melancholy, apparently doubting that the Lord would choose that hand.

"Alright then," he said resignedly. But he resumed a grand tone immediately. "Whatever will be, will be, but, for the moment, breakfast is over and it's time to go to work."

John asked Simych if he could film him working. Simych said of course they could. He was used to working under difficult conditions, and television cameras wouldn't disturb him.

"Simych!" I shouted. "While they're setting up, can you and I have our little talk?"

"No," said Simych, "I've already lost too much time as it is."

The next day I was not allowed at the breakfast table, because Congressman Peter Block was there to confer with Simych on nuclear disarmament.

I lost all restraint, flared up, and informed Zilberovich that that was the end of that—I was leaving.

"Hold on, hold on," entreated Zilberovich. "I'll straighten everything out."

Zilberovich returned five minutes later looking downcast. No, there was no way Simych could receive me today. The interview had taken so much time that he had written only four pages. He might even have to give up his afternoon nap and his lesson with Stepanida. The sole pleasure he would retain was his Bach, and that was only because he couldn't fall asleep without his Bach. And, if he couldn't fall asleep, the next day would be ruined.

I made no reply, but went back to my cell to pack my things. Bastards! Scum! I exclaimed mentally, tossing my dirty socks and wrinkled shirts into my suitcase. *His* time is valuable but mine isn't. They think I'm going to stay here waiting for them to reimburse me. Not on your life! I don't need their ticket. I'll pay for myself, I'm not poor. I won't stay here another second. I'm nobody's fool! I've had it!

I was about to slam my suitcase shut when I discovered that the slippers I always wore at home were missing. Where could they have disappeared? I had just begun glancing around the room when the door opened. Stepanida appeared in the doorway, holding a broom made of twigs and a dust pan.

"Oh, it's you, my lord!" she exclaimed.

"What do you want?" I asked.

"I just wanted to straighten up a little. I thought you were out, but now I see you're here. Maybe I should come back later?" Her usual idiotic smile flitted across her face.

"Wait a second," I said. "Have you seen my slippers by any chance?"

"Your slippers?" she said, and fell into thought as if I had asked her to prove a Pythagorean theorem. "Of course, the red ones, with no heels. Of course, of course, I've seen them. I put them under the bed so they wouldn't stink up the room. Just a moment."

She got down on her knees and crawled partway under the bed, aiming her indescribable backside at me. Her short skirt rode up, revealing near-transparent panties edged in fine lace.

O God! I have always looked with favor upon that part of a woman's anatomy, but I had never experienced a temptation like this one before. Those two hemispheres, brimming with mysterious energy, drew me like a magnet.

Struggling against myself, I tried to avert my eyes and asked irritably why she was taking so long.

"One second, my lord!" came her melodious voice from under the bed. "One minute, my eyes just have to get used to the dark."

"How dark can it be there!" I said and bent over, about to take a peek under the bed myself, when I lost my balance, my hands grabbing hold of those very spheres, which at once began wiggling.

"Oh, my lord!" she said in a frightened voice. "What are you doing?"

"Nothing, nothing," I muttered in a frenzy, feeling her panties slip off her like a snake shedding its skin. "Stay where you are. Get used to the dark. Everything's going to be fine. Now you'll see. Now I think you'll see something!" I whispered, panting, sensing her weakening, melting like butter.

I should say that I am a person of firm moral principles. All my friends know me to be an exemplary family man. But at that moment I simply went out of my mind. I lost all self-control. I moaned, I howled, I ground my teeth. And she too whispered sweet nothings, calling me dearest and darling, a rogue and a rascal, gratifying my pride by saying that she had never met a man like me before.

We only unglued ourselves from each other at lunchtime; I appeared rumpled and spent, barely able to put one foot in front of the other. At the table, Janet even asked if I were feeling ill; her shrewd brother did not say a word, but from the smirk on his face I could see that he had figured everything out.

I was put off that he knew and so intended to leave right after lunch, but no sooner had I picked up my suitcase than Stepanida appeared in the door and said with a lascivious smile, "My lord, do you need me to look for your slippers?"

And on it went. After Tom left to work in the stable, she came to my room; that night, when Tom fell asleep, soused on bourbon, she came to see me again.

I was so shook up by this sex-bomb that I lost all reason and was even ready to abandon my family, my plans, and stay on there, biting into her like a spider until I keeled over from exhaustion.

And so, when I learned that once again Simych would be unable to speak with me at breakfast because galleys had arrived from his publisher and he had no other time to read except at breakfast, I was even happy. But, a short while before lunch, just when I had sent Stepanida on her way, Zilberovich came running excitedly into my room and announced that Simych was demanding to see me at once.

GOOD

Simych was so lost in his work that he did not hear me enter. Bent over his desk, he was writing, and, by the way, not with his old-fashioned pen, but with a Parker ballpoint. The old-fashioned pen with the gnawed end which had once so impressed me was now stuck—with a bunch of other pens and pencils—into the aluminum mug with the initials S.K. scratched into it. Simych held his Parker in his fist like a chisel and put his shoulder into it as he wrote, tearing the paper. I couldn't see what he was writing, but, finishing a paragraph or line, he raised his pen and halted, moving his lips as he read it through. Reaching the end, he shook his head and exclaimed, "Good!" Then he put a period there, as if hammering in a nail.

Then he read another line, and again he said, "Good!" And another period. I looked at him with envy. Clearly, I was seeing a confident master at work.

I felt awkward about interrupting him but it was also foolish to keep standing there behind him. I coughed once, then once again. Finally hearing me, he shuddered, and turned around.

"Oh, it's you!" he said with impatience. "What do you want?"

I said that I didn't want anything, I had come simply to say goodbye and to hear his wishes.

"Good," he said with a glance at his watch. "I have seven and a half minutes for you."

"Simych!" I cried, beside myself with indignation. "You'll forgive me, but this is pure effrontery. I've been cooling my heels here for days because of you, and you only have seven and a half minutes for me."

"It *was* seven and a half, but now," he glanced at his watch again, "it's only seven. But that's enough. And there's no reason for you to get upset. This meeting will be of value for you too. You'll take *The Greater Zone* with you."

"*The Greater Zone*?" I said in surprise. "To Munich?"

"No, not to Munich, to Moscow, two thousand . . . what was it? Forty-two? That's where you'll be taking it."

"What do you mean? All sixty slabs?"

"I still haven't written all sixty," said Simych with a scowl. "There are too many distractions. I've only written thirty-six of them."

"And you want me to lug those thirty-six slabs with me to the future? For what? Don't you believe they'll be published there by then?"

"Of course they will," said Simych. "But I'm afraid they'll distort parts of it, make alterations. I want everything to be exactly right."

"I can understand that," I said. "But I'm just not going to lug thirty-six slabs with me. I have a hernia, and there's no way I can manage more than five."

"I see," said Simych, with a self-satisfied smile. "I shouldn't measure others by myself. But still I do hope you'll be able to manage."

He opened a small plastic box and withdrew a thin black disk the size of a hand. It looked like an ordinary personal-computer floppy disk, but apparently it had much greater storage capacity.

"Here you go," said Simych with a grin. "All thirty-six slabs. Don't strain yourself."

"And what I am supposed to do with it there?"

"That I don't know," said Simych with a sigh. "That depends on what it's like there. If everything's been published, proofread it all and check for mistakes."

Up yours! I thought to myself. It would take me a year to read all thirty-six slabs (I'm a slow reader), and I didn't plan to be there more than a month.

"If there are no mistakes, turn the disk in to the Karnavalov Museum."

"And what if there is no Karnavalov Museum?" I asked with guarded malice.

"If there isn't," he said, angry either at me or at ungrateful posterity, "that will mean that the predators are still in power. In that case, you. . . ." Here, his whole body began trembling and he began pacing the room. "Here's what you do. Find some computer and use this disk to print as many copies as possible. Then distribute them, the more widely the better. Just hand them out right and left. Let people read and discover what their voracious rulers are really like."

"Simych," I said softly, "how am I supposed to distribute the copies? You know that if the predators are still in power, they'll arrest me and maybe even execute me. . . ." I was quite careless in saying this and had not even finished the sentence before he flushed red and began shaking, his fist clenched.

"Young man!" he thundered, rattling the window panes. "Shame on you, young man! Russia is dying! The voracious predators are already crushing the bones of half the world. It's a time for sacrifices, and all you're worried about is yourself."

Still, seeing how embarrassed I was, he quickly overcame his wrath with mercy.

"Alright then," he said, "alright. Faint-heartedness is a fault common to many. It's because you don't believe in God. If you believed in God, then you'd know that suffering strengthens the spirit and cleanses it of impurities. If only you knew that our life on Earth is only a short spell, that God gives us repose from everything and eternal bliss. Think about it. And now go. Wait, I totally forgot something. Here's a note. Take it with you there too, and hand deliver it. Don't even think of opening and reading it." With those words he handed me a thick envelope sealed with wax. The envelope was marked in large letters:

"Leo!" shouted Simych. The door opened at once and Leo appeared, dressed simply in jeans and a T-shirt with a picture of Simych on it.

"Leo," said Simych with a nod in my direction, "he's leaving. Escort him out to the Montreal highway."

"Simych," said Leo in a rather free-and-easy tone of voice, "maybe he should have dinner with us and then go."

"That's not necessary," retorted Simych decisively. "He can eat on the plane. There's no point in wasting time."

I returned to Munich the following morning and tossed the letter to the future leaders in the waste basket. But I kept the floppy disk, without knowing why myself.

LONG
GOODBYES

I don't know about anyone else, but we Russians are in the habit of long and serious goodbyes. If a person is going off to war, or on a journey around the world, if he's traveling to the next town for a few days on business, or if he's going to visit relatives in the country, he'll receive a long and thorough send-off.

The poet said: ". . . And say farewell forever when leaving for a moment."

That's exactly what we do. We invite people over, we drink and make toasts to those who are leaving and those who are staying. It's a custom to sit for a minute in silence before a departure. And then later at the train station, the pier, or the airport, we kiss for a long time, we cry, say foolish words of farewell, and wave. In our house it was a tradition that my mother would not sweep the floor until the person who had left sent a telegram saying he had arrived safely. Some people may think this absurd, but all those rituals, a blend of age-old tradition and habit, are to my liking, and I find them full of higher meaning. We never know which farewell will prove the last.

". . . And say farewell forever when leaving for a moment."

To make a long story short, we threw a royal sendoff—with blintzes, caviar, champagne, and vodka. There were so many Russians and non-Russians that we were just about sitting two to a chair. Of course, we hadn't breathed a word to our guests about where I was going or for how long, but we acted so foolishly, mysteriously, and ambiguously about keeping this secret that our guests automatically began trying to guess whether my plan was to cross the Atlantic in a balloon or to spend time among the Afghan rebels.

I neither confirmed nor denied these conjectures, which caused even more absurd suppositions, including one that had me only pretending to leave so I could I lock myself up at home and write.

Among the guests was Rudi, who (I should make special mention of this) conducted himself with the utmost tact, betraying what he knew neither by word nor by allusion.

I must say that the send-off went quite well, though it was a bit on the long side. We threw out the last guest at quarter of three in the morning, and my wife had me out of bed by quarter of seven.

You can imagine my state as I, still not sober, suffering from a headache, heartburn, and the belches, dragged myself to the car with my suitcase, stuffed with presents for my future friends and descendants.

My wife ran out ahead of me, cursing me for walking too slowly. It seemed somewhat odd to me that she was in such a hurry to see me off. It was easy for her to walk quickly, all she was carrying was my Diplomat briefcase, in which I had hastily tossed everything I'd need right away: T-shirts, underwear, socks, and all the little implements you need to shave, comb your hair, clip your nails and brush your teeth.

As a matter of fact, we had plenty of time, but when we got to the car, we found that I had forgotten to turn off the headlights the day before and the battery was dead. We called a taxi, but then got caught in a traffic jam right before the airport; two buses had collided and the police had blocked the road. To make another long story short, we arrived at the airport after all the passengers had boarded.

I was so upset that I almost fell over when lifting my suitcase onto the scale. And when the clerk at the Lufthansa counter asked me whether I wanted *"rauchen oder nicht rauchen,"* I said *"rauchen"* and the breath I expelled when uttering that word seemed to make her momentarily comatose. The policeman who frisked me also appeared to feel unwell — he turned away from me the second his duty was done.

THE FACE AT
THE WINDOW

I did not have time to get a good look at our aircraft from the outside. Not only because there was no time, but also because entry was through the kind of mobile passenger walkway found in all modern airports. Inside, it looked like any other plane: seats, seat belts, windows, stewardesses. There were not many passengers. It was either something like twenty-five or something like fifty (I was seeing double).

I stepped across the knees of a pimply young man and took a window seat. Even though he was wearing large sunglasses, his face looked familiar, but I attached no significance to this. When I'm sloshed at least half the people I see look familiar.

Placing my Diplomat briefcase at my feet, I began looking out the window. The usual preflight preparations were going on. People in blue overalls were inspecting and adjusting things, and one of them, wearing headphones, was speaking into a walkie-talkie.

I think I dozed off for a while.

When I regained consciousness, the magical contraption was already moving down the runway, rocking slightly. It would stop, move, then stop again.

I looked out the window and could tell that we were in the middle of a long line of planes awaiting permission for takeoff. The first half of the line had turned to the right, which gave me a view of the planes ahead of us. The line was headed by two Lufthansa craft, then came one from Alitalia, then one from the Israeli airline El Al, followed by a Bulgarian Tu-154, an English Caravelle, and another German Boeing. When we finally made the turn, I could see that directly behind us was the pride of Aeroflot, an Il-62, ship number 38276, its dolphin-like nose to the ground as if it were on our scent.

Despite my memory having worsened due to my recent alcohol abuse, I memorized that number without any problem. The first half of the number multiplied by the middle number gave the last two numbers: $38 \times 2 = 76$. You'd have to be brain-damaged to be unable to memorize a number like that and, thank God, I'm not that far gone.

Of course, to see who was inside that Il-62 was out of the question, and I didn't even try. I was simply examining the plane and its general contours, when I saw, or seemed to see, a face pressed up against one of its windows. And who do you think it was? My former friend, Lyoshka Bukashev, of course.

I couldn't help but grin. I remembered the time in Moscow when I was constantly followed by cars packed with KGB agents like him. They had had powerful supercharged engines and I almost never was able to lose them. But now the situation was different. Now, even if he wanted to, Bukashev would have no chance of keeping up with me. By the time our craft crossed the bounds of the solar system, he'd still be looking down on the area around Munich.

My thoughts were interrupted by the plane's communication system. Herr Captain Otto Schmidt welcomed the passengers aboard, asked us to fasten our safety belts and temporarily refrain from smoking. He wished all a pleasant flight and expressed the hope that when we reached our destination this wonderful space plane and its passengers would not be devoured by dinosaurs or mutants spawned after a world nuclear disaster. Needless to say, all the passengers chuckled, and I joined in, though I must confess the joke did disturb me a little.

Meanwhile we were given permission for takeoff. Our craft

began with a stationary roar of its turbines, then it lurched forward and, with an awful howling and gnashing, began racing down the runway. It sailed past the line of planes; the airport buildings flashed past. The plane groaned, and suddenly the Autobahn, packed with cars of every color below us, was gone. I caught sight of a bend in the Isaar River, the BMW building's four column-shaped sections, the twin-spired Frauen Kirche, but all the other details blurred and blended. It was as if I were seeing the outlines of the woods and lakes through the wrong end of binoculars, creating an optical sense of even greater distance.

Farewell Munich! Farewell Germany! Farewell my old life! And farewell to the goddamn twentieth century!

PART II

THE FLIGHT

I suspect readers of this book will be interested in details of space travel: the effects of drag, the landscape of the stars, meteorite storms, encounters and confrontations with representatives of alien civilizations.

Alas, nothing of the sort happened during our flight. People with an interest in such things should read science fiction — a genre I personally have no taste for whatsoever. I limit myself to describing what actually happens, and do not add an iota. For that matter, I don't feel entirely comfortable about telling what actually did happen in this escapade. There are certain details I'd gladly omit — it is only my exceptional truthfulness that prevents me from deviating one inch from the facts.

And so, to tell the truth, I have only the haziest memories of the flight. I dozed off as soon as we were airborne. The first thing I remember is being awakened by a stewardess pushing the drink cart. Smiling precisely as she had been trained to, she asked me what I'd like to drink. Needless to say, I said vodka. She smiled again, handed me a plastic glass and a toy-sized bottle of Smirnoff. She was about to push her drink wagon on ahead when I touched her lightly on the elbow and asked her why she had given me a child's portion of vodka. She caught the humor and, with the same smile on her face, handed me a second bottle. I smiled too, and informed her that when I had purchased my ticket — paying a hefty sum for it in cash—I had been promised unlimited beverages. She expressed surprise and said that unlimited supplies of anything do not exist in nature. She then wanted to know exactly how many bottles would satisfy me.

"Alright," I said, "give me ten."

The figure I had mentioned was hardly beyond the limits of imagination. However, after rummaging through her cart and finding five more bottles of Smirnoff, the stewardess had to run to the front of the plane for the rest.

As I arranged the bottles before me, the person in the seat beside me (who had ordered a glass of tomato juice) removed his sunglasses and began following my actions with some interest. Then, apologizing for the intrusion, he asked if I really intended to ingest that horrendous amount of vodka. I explained that for a Russian, half a liter of vodka was the most rudimentary and, I would even go so far as to say, natural norm.

Without the sunglasses, his face seemed even more familiar than before. I definitely had seen that face somewhere. Two bottles later, I remembered exactly where. In Munich, at the central train station. By the ticket counter there had been pictures of left-wing terrorists for each of whom the police were offering a reward of fifty thousand deutsche marks.

And now those fifty thousand were sitting in the seat beside me.

The police, of course, always warn the public to be careful with terrorists and not try to apprehend them themselves, but I thought I could overpower this shrimp without any help from the police. Even if he were armed, there'd be little chance of his being able to use his weapon. Still, at the time I had no need of any additional deutsche marks and so, after polishing off another couple of bottles, I told him that I knew who he was. He denied it.

"Save your breath," I said. "I can see right through you terrorists, but I have no intention of turning you in. First, because I'm no stool pigeon, and, second, because there are no German police here."

He lowered his eyes and covertly shook my hand. Then, almost whispering, he said that his party valued nobility in people and would never forget the service I had done them. I asked him what party that was, and he readily replied that it was called "Thought-Idea-Action." Its goal was the replacement of the rotten capitalist system with a progressive communist one. Aware that propaganda for progressive ideas should be graphic and effective, members of the Party Executive Committee had carried out several extremely successful operations: they had attacked an American military base and had executed two well-known industrialists and a prosecutor after sentencing them in an underground revolutionary court.

"Unfortunately," said the terrorist, "our actions have not yet been understood by the broad masses. Corrupted by the capitalists' clever concessions and the greed of union leaders, the workers and peasants have still not realized their own class interests and are not willing to rise in a world-wide battle for the ultimate triumph of communist ideals."

"Yes, it's true," I seconded, "people don't want to fight because they're too well off. They've gone fat."

"Not only that," objected the terrorist, "to a significant degree, anticommunist propaganda generates a passive attitude toward revolution. It makes very deft use of the errors committed in the Soviet Union and Eastern Europe, and paints communism in the blackest of colors. I hope to put an end to those malicious fabrications."

"By what means?" I asked.

The young man was quick to inform me what his comrades in the struggle had decided. Learning of the possibility of time travel, they had packed him off to see communism with his own eyes and bring back irrefutable proof of its complete and absolute superiority over all other systems.

When I asked him where he had gotten the money for the ticket, he grinned and reminded me of the recent daring holdup of a Dusseldorf bank, in which one cashier and two policemen had been killed.

Without waiting for my next question, he explained that for

their party, killing people was an extreme measure, allowable only during the period of acute class struggle and for the noblest of goals. But, as soon as communism was triumphant, all prisons would be torn down immediately and the death penalty abolished forever.

Naturally I asked him what he roughly thought life would be like in that communist society of the future. His response was not at all rough, but quite definite. He replied at once that people would live in small-but-cozy cities, each of which would be covered by an immense glass dome. The sun would shine all year long in those cities; when the actual sun disappeared, quartz lights would come on automatically. Of course, there would be plenty of marvelous flora in such cities, the streets lined with palm trees.

"Under communism," he said, "everyone will be young, handsome, healthy, and in love with one another. People will stroll under the palm trees, carry on philosophical conversations, and listen to soft music."

"You mean there won't be any old age, sickness, or death?"

"None at all!" the young man assured me passionately. "I tell you everyone will be young, healthy, handsome, and, of course, immortal."

"Very interesting," I said. "And how do you intend to achieve this?"

"That's not our business," he was quick to retort. "We're men of action. We're engaged in a struggle. Let the scientists solve the problems of health and eternal youth."

Returning to the subject of the climate in the cities of the future, I remarked that of course it would be very pleasant to live in ideal conditions with constant sunlight and palm trees, but what about people who love snow, ice, and all the pleasures of winter?

Those people would also be given everything they wanted, he said. Special sections of the sunny city, where soft hills would be made of artificial snow, would be allotted to them. They could ski down those hills to their heart's content—even in rocking chairs on skis.

I also asked him if people would be free to read whatever they wanted under communism. He was slightly surprised by the ques-

106

tion and said that books with high intellectual and moral content would of course be available to everyone through public libraries.

In the meantime our lunch was brought (chicken, salad, cheese, a pastry, and orange juice). With appetizers like that, it would be a sin not to have a drink. I downed another three bottles and took a walk around the plane, striking up conversations with other passengers.

One woman around forty with a yellowish face was hoping to be cured of her cancer in the future. The representative of an important company was on his way to find out whether the Soviet gas pipe line to Western Europe would be operational in sixty years. Waiting in line for the toilet, I met a fellow Russian who was traveling to the future in the hopes of restoring the monarchy.

After various such conversations, I returned to my seat and had another couple of Smirnoffs. Possibly either from the drinking or the imperceptible but still real rocking of the craft, my mind became somewhat foggy, and so only bits and pieces of the remainder of the flight have stuck in my memory. At times I was so out of it that I even mistook Proxyimus Centaurus for the North Star. But all those heavenly bodies — the large, the medium, and the small — did not make the impression they should have.

In my time I've seen quite a few wonders, both those created by nature and by man. I've seen Elbrus and Mont Blanc, the Moscow Kremlin, the leaning tower of Pisa, the Cologne cathedral, Buckingham Palace, and the Brooklyn Bridge. And though I knew that when viewing such things you're supposed to experience something out of the ordinary and utter pronouncements that correspond to the sublimity of the sight, I never have experienced anything out of the ordinary. Though, of course, I've been known to utter the pronouncements.

I remember once in Paris when a building was pointed out to me. "Look, there's the Louvre!" I looked, and I thought, So, it's the Louvre, so what? I thought the same thing again watching the stars, planets, asteroids, and monoliths whiz past us. So what?

All the same, one object in space did stagger my imagination, and I might as well describe it right here.

The flight was nearly over. We were back in Earth's gravitational field and barely doing five miles a second when Captain Otto Schmidt's voice suddenly came over the intercom to inform us that to the right of our craft was an object that appeared artificial in origin. The passengers all pressed their faces to the windows. I did too (I was sitting on the right anyway). I caught sight of a spherical object resembling a gigantic aquarium, around two hundred feet in diameter, maybe larger (all measurements are extremely relative in space). It had the oddest antennae, swaying solar battery panels, and very large portholes that resembled lunar craters.

All the portholes were dark except for one. And it was through that porthole that I saw a truly fantastic vision. I could see a round and spacious room, brightly lit by an ornate crystal chandelier. The floor was covered with an Oriental rug, and the walls with walnut paneling. Near the porthole was a wide writing desk of excellent, old-fashioned workmanship, on top of which sat several telephones of various colors. There was a globe on one side of the desk and a television set on the other. I could make out a few other things along the walls: a leather couch, a cocktail table, and a bust of Lenin on a red pedestal. The overall impression was that of the office of some very important Soviet official, albeit unusual in shape.

At first I thought there was no one in the office, but then suddenly I caught sight of an enormous fish swimming out of the depths of the flying aquarium and drawing closer to the porthole. Actually,

I thought it was a fish, but upon closer inspection, the fish proved to be a humanoid creature, overgrown with a thick beard. Wearing an old pair of sneakers, frayed jeans, a crimson sweater, and, lazily moving the fins of his arms, the creature moved through space, nearing the porthole but not looking into it. The creature's gaze seemed to be fixed on something below it and its lips were moving, as if either talking to someone else or to itself.

Our speed relative to this strange structure was almost zero, and for that reason it was quite easy to see this creature—to be more precise, this person—moving his lips, frowning, and from time to time using a finger imperiously to point out something to someone.

Suddenly he raised his head (perhaps by chance), shuddered, and, floundering in weightlessness like an inexperienced swimmer, floated nearer the porthole.

"Hey! Hey!" shouted all the passengers on our flight in unison (as if he could hear them!), and began waving to him.

He overcame his problems with motion, grabbed hold of a handle of some sort, and flattened his face against the glass of the porthole. As he did that, he looked in our direction with an expression of despair seen only on the face of a man awaiting execution.

But what confused and stunned me the most was that this emaciated, balding, and shaggily bearded man was somehow reminiscent of the plump, prosperous, clean-shaven, and self-confident Lyoshka Bukashev. Of course, I realized that in no way could this be Bukashev, who had remained somewhere behind in the distant past. But, no sooner had I thought this than I noticed the man's gaze coming to rest on me. God! It gave me the willies. There was no way he could be Bukashev, but I couldn't imagine it being anyone else. And he had clearly recognized me. At the sight of me, his whole body shook and he began gesturing frantically as if trying to tell me something. My hand jerked instinctively to wave back, but apparently at that moment we shifted speed and the space station and its bearded prisoner suddenly lurched away from us, receding rapidly into the distance, diminishing as a balloon does when it escapes from your hand.

I wanted to discuss what I'd just seen with the young man beside me, but apparently he had paid the whole business no attention. In any case, when I turned toward him, he was reading some pamphlet, pencil in hand, underlining passages and making notes in the margins. I glanced over to see the name of the pamphlet. It was Lenin's well-known work *The State and Revolution* in German translation.

The sight of this person engaged in such a peaceable and ordinary pursuit soothed my mind, and I decided that I must have dozed off and the whole thing had been nothing but a drunken dream. In the hope of regaining my full faculties, I downed the last of the Smirnoff, but its effect was to finish me off completely—my mind dimmed again, and I fell right to sleep.

AIRPLANE NUMBER 38276

I was awakened by the stillness and did not understand right away what was happening. Our craft was no longer roaring, whistling, or shaking. Many of the passengers were already out of their seats, briefcases, bags, and suitcases in hand, silently crowding toward the exit.

Half drunk and half awake, I could not remember at first where I had flown from, or where I had flown to, or why. But after one look out the window it all came back.

Through the window I could see a field of scorched grass, cracked runways, and a large glass and concrete terminal in the mid-distance. On the top of the building, large letters spelled out:

MOSCOW

Under this word there was a series of portraits, and above the roof of the building a red star blazed in the rays of a warm July sun.

How could I remain unmoved? Excited, I sprang to my feet, but just then a voice on the intercom announced that the local airport personnel were unable to find landing stairs that fit our plane. The passengers were asked to stay calm and not crowd toward the exit. There would be a special announcement when we could deplane.

"We should have known," said the terrorist returning to his

seat. "Of course, to them this craft is antiquated. Their equipment doesn't fit it."

I didn't reply. I was looking out the window, unable to tear my eyes from what I was seeing. Beside us at the next bay was a banged up Il-62, listing hard to the left, and its number was . . . 38276.

But what could that mean?

I could make no sense of it. I could not understand how this antediluvian sloth, which couldn't even reach the speed of sound, had gotten here ahead of us.

Then it dawned on me: it was all a provocation!

Yes, of course! This whole flight-to-the-future business was nothing but a cunning setup, a ruse. They had certainly gone all-out this time!

It meant that Rudi, who had assured me that time travel was possible, and Fräulein Globke, and John, and my Arab abductors, and Lyoshka Bukashev, and the entire crew on this plane were all in on this meticulous KGB scenario to bring me back to Moscow—not in two thousand and something, but today. And fool that I am, I had swallowed that crude bait without blinking an eye.

Instantly sober, I began feverishly scouring my brain for a way out of the situation. But I couldn't come up with a single idea.

I suppressed my initial panicky impulse to flee, to hide in the bathroom, to seek cover under the seat. I always knew that foolish actions taken at critical moments only hasten disaster. But what to do?

"Hijack the plane!" prompted my devil, but without great conviction. "Hijack the plane, take hostages and the crew and demand that the plane return to Munich immediately."

I rejected the idea outright, as impossible to carry out. I had no bomb, no pistol, not even a pen knife, nothing I could use to threaten the crew. But as I looked out the window and thought the problem through, I suddenly noticed that the portraits on the front of the terminal were not the same ones that had been there when I'd flown out of that airport a few years before. The window was steamy and it was hard to see the faces, but I knew there was something different about them.

112

There were five.

The one on the far left depicted a person who looked a great deal like Jesus Christ. He was not wearing a robe, but a perfectly proper suit and tie and even, I think, a watch fob. The next portrait was of Karl Marx. The two portraits on the right were of Engels and Lenin. But I was not staggered by the portraits of the founders of the sole scientific worldview, and not even by the one of Jesus Christ (although he looked out of place in that company), but by the face of the portrait in the center. The bearded man, wearing an ample army tunic with a marshal's epaulettes, open slightly at the collar looked like . . . Whom do you think? . . . Yes, yes! Exactly like the Lyoshka Bukashev with whom I had drunk beer in Munich, whom I had seen at the Munich airport, and whom I thought I had spotted in that wondrous space device. This Lyoshka looked even more like the real Lyoshka, because his expression was as prosperous and self-confident as it was in real life, though his gaze was far more penetrating in the portrait.

I grabbed my head and groaned. O God! I thought. What does it all mean? Why do I keep thinking I'm seeing that goddamned Bukashev everywhere? Did I drink so much I've got a case of the DTs?

Alright, I said to myself, let's say I'm not in any spacecraft, just an ordinary Boeing. Let's say that the Proximus Centaurus and the space aquarium in which Bukashev was floating were no more than optical illusions perfected in KGB laboratories. Then what does that mishmash of portraits mean? Are they just tricks, too, to mislead me? No, that couldn't be.

Where to hang the portraits of the authorities, which portraits, and in what order, have always been questions of the utmost seriousness in my country, and in former times liberties taken in such matters could earn one a long sentence. I honestly could not believe that they would have hung those portraits only as a crude trick to ensnare a bungler like myself. So what did it all mean?

What was I supposed to think? That Lyoshka had flown faster in his Il-62 than I had in the Boeing? That during a three-hour flight he had risen to the rank of marshal, grown a beard, seized power, and ordered his own portrait placed on view? An absurd idea, but nothing any more likely came to mind.

As I strained my stupefied mind, two strange olive-drab vehicles rolled up to our plane. They looked like a cross between a brontosaurus and a locomotive. In any event, they appeared to be driven by steam, thick clouds of which jetted from the pipe at the front of each vehicle. These were armored troop carriers; as soon as they stopped between us and the listing Il-62, the hatches fell open and soldiers wearing short pants and carrying short submachine guns came tumbling out, one after the other, like mushrooms from a basket. They dispersed immediately and formed a cordon around the plane, training the barrels of their weapons at it.

Just then the intercom wheezed on and Captain Otto Schmidt informed the passengers that the Moscow authorities had been unable to locate landing stairs; we would have to use the emergency rope ladder and he, in the name of the crew and the entire Lufthansa airline, offered his profoundest apologies.

But people were already in such a hurry to be off the plane that they were not only prepared to use a rope ladder, they would have been willing to shimmy down a rope. All the more so since, as I had noticed, no one but me had been bothered in the slightest by the portraits.

The line began to move. I grabbed my Diplomat briefcase and found I was the last one in line. The young man who sat beside me was next to last. By the open door, two stewardesses smiled wearily as they wished the passengers a pleasant stay and reminded them that the return flight would depart in exactly one month.

To be frank, not knowing what awaited me below had me very much on edge. And so when I got to the stewardess, I asked if she could give me a few more little bottles of Smirnoff; opening my mouth wide, I pointed to the fire inside that needed extinguishing.

At first, she didn't understand. When she finally did, she quite coldly announced that their company provided passengers with beverages only during flights. For my information the flight had terminated.

114

Once again I opened my mouth, whacked my chest, and, using words and gestures, tried to explain how much I needed the vodka, since I had something of a *Kopfschmerz*, a headache, but she remained as indifferent as nature to my explanation.

In the meantime all the other passengers had disembarked. I walked over to the open door, looked down, and recoiled. It was a long way to the ground, and the rope ladder did not appear in the least reliable. And where was it written that, after paying the money I'd paid, I'd have to climb down ropes like a monkey? When I got a look at what was going on down there, I felt even more queasy. The passengers who had descended before me were standing ringed by soldiers, who had their submachine guns pointed at them. The soldiers herded the passengers to one of the armored personnel carriers, almost shoving them in one by one.

"Move it, move it, let's go!" shouted a thickset officer with four stars on his epaulettes, a captain apparently.

The vehicle screeched and puffed as it devoured the passengers who obeyed without a murmur. Only one attempted to offer any resistance, the young terrorist.

"*Genosse!*" he said, running over to the captain. "*Ich bin ein Kommunist!* You shouldn't be saying move it, move it! This is a time for peace and friendship. Not move it, move it!"

"I shouldn't be saying move it, eh?" said the captain in surprise. "Oh yeah?" He burst into laughter and kicked the poor man so hard he flew into the vehicle like a soccer ball into the goal.

The captain looked up questioningly at me.

Taken aback, I automatically stepped back into the plane, but immediately encountered something hard as steel. I looked behind me and shuddered. A bandy-legged soldier had the muzzle of his submachine pressed to my back. How had he gotten there? He stared at me unblinkingly with his Tatar eyes.

I needed no explanations and started for the exit when I heard a voice from below say something that startled me.

"Ramazaev!" shouted the captain. "Hands off the writer. He's not ours."

"Yes, sir!" cried Ramazaev, who leaped past me to the ladder. He took it in a trice, going from one crossrope to the next. There wasn't even time for me to wonder how they knew I was a writer when Ramazaev and his commanding officer hopped into one of the steam-belching vehicles, which lumbered away with a blast of its siren.

With no idea of what was going on, I looked back at the stewardess. Smiling, and with sudden quickness, she handed me a bottle of Smirnoff.

"*Danke schön*," I said. I was about to twist off the cap when I saw that a new group of officers had appeared below: three men and two women. The men also wore short pants, and the women short skirts, but of better-quality material than the first group's. All but one of them wore cloth caps. The men and one of the women had general's stars on their epaulettes, and the other woman, who was somewhat younger, was at most a captain.

One of the generals was evidently a priest. He was wearing a black cassock, but a very short one, only knee-length, the bottom half of which was striped. He wore the peaked headgear of an Orthodox monk, and a large star that may have been made of silver was on his chest. The star had a cross on each of its points, and he had the same sort of star and crosses on his headgear. The woman general had stripes on her skirt but, other than that, there was nothing eye-catching about her uniform. The generals wore many medals on their chests, but the woman captain had only two. It was clear that their heads were all close-cropped, because I could see no hair coming out from under the women's caps.

Having walked over to the bottom of the rope ladder, they stopped and looked me over from head to toe, squinting slightly from the dazzling sun, friendly smiles on their faces. I too smiled, but uncertainly, and continued to stand where I was, not knowing what to do. This game of peek-a-boo continued until one of the group of officers, apparently the ranking general, stepped forward. He was the tallest of them, and the plumpest, and his epaulettes had two stars, not one like the others.

"What's the matter, Vitaly Nikitich?" he said in a low, rumbling voice. "Climb down, we're waiting for you."

Plainly, the authorities were not only informed of my profession. My name was no secret to them either.

I hesitated, unsure of how to make my descent. Then, my mind made up, I lay down on my stomach and, in a highly humiliating fashion—feet first—I began crawling slowly toward the open door. I can imagine how ridiculous this looked from below. From above as well; one of the stewardesses standing over me lost her self-control and giggled.

When my legs were already suspended over the abyss, I panicked suddenly, feeling that I was on my way down but could find no point on which to brace my feet. I dug my fingernails into the synthetic carpeting, but it was too slippery. I could well have gone crashing to the ground, and that would have been the end of the adventure, but the stewardesses broke into a wild shriek, which brought Captain Otto Schmidt on the run from the cockpit. At the last minute, he grabbed me by the arms. With him holding me, I finally found a footrest on one of the crossropes.

"*Vorsicht, Vorsicht*," said Herr Schmidt in excitement.

First he let go of one hand, and, when I had grabbed on to the rope, he let go of the other. I began a cautious descent while those awaiting me below burst into applause. I thought they were mocking me, which made me angry. But anger lent me strength, and I covered the rest of the way with greater confidence, especially because the closer I was to the ground, the safer I was. My Diplomat briefcase came down the rope ladder after me.

On my way down, I did not rule out the possibility of my immediate arrest. But nothing of the sort took place. As soon as I felt terra firma beneath me, the officers drew near, and I noticed that all their decorations and medals were made of plastic. The head general walked over to me first, offered me a fleshy hand, and said with a smile, "Glorgen."

Thinking that Glorgen was his last name, I said mine as well, even though he must have known it. Then another general walked over, shook my hand, and said, "Glorgen." Assuming the two generals to be brothers, I introduced myself to him as well. To my surprise, both women and the clergyman also proved to be Glorgens.

There was an awkward pause after I had introduced myself to them all, but the head general made a sign to his companions who regrouped, and I found myself between the woman captain and the head general.

"Well now, Vitaly Nikitich Kartsev," said the general, still smiling. "On behalf of our small comlit delegation, I would like to extend our heartiest greetings on your return. As they used to say in the old days, welcome to your native land!" He spread his arms wide as if about to embrace me, but then immediately let them fall.

I hadn't managed a reply when the woman captain said: "Vitaly Nikitich, Comsor Smerchev heartily welcomes you on your arrival and says, 'Welcome to your native land!' "

118

"I heard," I said. "I'm not deaf."

"He says he's not deaf," said the captain to the general.

"Tell him," said the general, "that I am delighted that he looks so wonderful for his age and that he has not even lost his hearing."

While she repeated his words to me for no reason I could see, I looked at them with surprise: why did they think I should have gone deaf when I was only just pushing forty?

After expressing delight in my well-being, the general asked my permission to introduce the members of the delegation.

"My name," he said, "is Communi Ivanovich Smerchev." He also said that he was a lieutenant general in the literary service, the head comlit of the republic, and the chairman of the Jubilee Pentagon.

Thereupon Communi Ivanovich introduced the other members of the delegation, whose names and ranks I will list in the order they were introduced:

1. Dzerzhin Gavrilovich Siromakhin, a major general in SECO (State Security), first deputy head comlit of SECO, the second member of the Jubilee Pentagon.
2. Propaganda Paramonovna Bovinak, major general in the political service, first deputy head comlit in political education and propaganda, the third member of the Jubilee Pentagon.
3. Father Starsky, major general in the religious service, first deputy head comlit in religious nourishment, the fourth member of the Jubilee Pentagon.
4. Iskrina Romanovna Polyakov, a captain in the literary service, the fifth member and secretary of the Jubilee Pentagon.

Even though Iskrina Romanovna repeated word for word everything the members of the delegation said, I still missed a great deal. I had little idea what all those titles and posts meant, why they had such strange names, what a head comlit was, or what a Jubilee Pentagon could possibly be. And I also noticed that in my absence, the Russian language had acquired many new words, ideas, and expressions. After introducing himself and his companions, Communi Ivanovich asked (and the captain translated) if I had any questions.

I had so many questions I didn't know where to begin. For openers I asked what a Jubilee Pentagon was and whose jubilee it was meant to celebrate. Iskrina parroted my question.

Communi Ivanovich was glad to explain that a Jubilee Pentagon was a specially appointed creative pentagon committee charged with setting up and carrying out my jubilee on a high ideological level.

"*My* jubilee?" I asked, puzzled. "Oh, that's right, I'm going to turn forty in a couple of days. It slipped my mind entirely."

"Forty, you say?" said Smerchev, exchanging glances with his companions. Then, with a condescending smile, he continued, "No, no, Vitaly Nikitich, you're not going to be forty, you're turning one hundred."

"That's right, of course," I said, "one hundred." Forty plus sixty is a hundred. To be honest, that didn't occur to me either, even though I could have figured it out if I'd thought about it for a minute.

I even broke into laughter, and the entire Pentagon laughed benevolently along with me. Thinking of the vagaries of time, I muttered a few other meaningless words and interjections like: "Ah yes! How about that! Very nice."

"Tell me," I asked the general, "how is it you know me?"

None of them reacted to the question; they appeared not to have heard it. But when Iskrina Romanovna repeated it, they all broke into amicable smiles.

Communi Ivanovich spread his hands wide and said, "What do you mean, Vitaly Nikitich, how is it we wouldn't know you when we all made a thorough study of your works in instcominst."

"Comsor Smerchev says," repeated the interpreter, "how is it we wouldn't know you when we all made a thorough study of your works in instcominst."

"In what?"

"Instcominst," she repeated. "You mean you never studied in an instcominst?"

"What is that?"

"Instcominst is an institution of communist instruction."

"I see," I said. "And did you personally study my works in the instcominst?"

"What do you mean, Vitaly Nikitich! The study of preliminary literature is required for everyone in an instcominst."

I have to admit it, my wife is right when she says that constant alcohol abuse has a destructive effect on a person's mental powers. The more questions of mine they answered, the less I understood. And learning that there was such a thing as preliminary literature plunged me into depression.

"Fine," I said, "I'm very glad that you study preliminary literature in the instcominsts, but what I can't understand is how you learned I was coming."

The members of the delegation looked at one another again, but Communi Ivanovich smiled, spread his hands wide, and said, "So, you have such a low opinion of us then, Vitaly Nikitich? We don't claim that our intelligence gathering is perfect, but do you really think that after sixty years we wouldn't be able to handle, let's be frank, such a simple problem?"

"But it's time for us to go," interjected Dzerzhin Gavrilovich, who had been silent until then. "It's so hot here. Just like Honolulu," he added and then, grinning, glanced over at Communi Ivanovich.

"Well, Honolulu," said Communi Ivanovich, taking the ball, "might even be a little cooler. They have ocean weather there, it's damp and there's a constant sea breeze. While here we have a continental climate."

I caught their allusion and could appreciate the extent of their knowledge. And it was only then that I realized what had happened. In my conceit I had thought that I had left Bukashev far behind, but in fact he had flown to Moscow on his antedeluvian Il-62 sixty years ago, and of course had long since died. But his report on his meeting with me in Munich and on my planned trip had been included in my file.

No matter what you say, time's a strange and mysterious thing.

Then I remembered the vision I'd had in space and thought it at best a hallucination. I had been further confused by the portrait which closely resembled Bukashev on the front of the terminal. But, on the other hand, the members of the Jubilee Pentagon had a familiar look about them too.

To skip ahead for a moment, I'll say that in that Moscow of the future, I was to meet many people who looked very much like people I'd known in the past. Sometimes so much so that I went running to them with open arms and of course made a fool of myself each time. As I was to realize later, there's a limited selection of human features in nature, and only the inner essence of the personality is unique, irreplaceable. Still, in the past, the future, and in the present I have met many extremely replaceable people.

While engaged in these reflections, I was invited to proceed to the terminal where (as Communi Ivanovich put it) my readers and admirers were awaiting me impatiently. We set off toward the terminal. Iskrina Romanovna walked between me and Communi Ivanovich, to whose left was the short-legged and fat Propaganda Paramonovna, waddling like a duck. To my right strode Dzerzhin Gavrilovich, shoulders square, and behind him stomped Father Starsky, limping on the cement, his whole body twitching, his disheveled beard shaking, as he grimaced and winked all at once.

On the way I asked Communi Ivanovich why he didn't speak to me directly but always used the interpreter. "After all, we're speaking the same language, aren't we?" I asked.

After waiting politely for the translation, he explained that though we were indeed using more or less the same vocabulary, words in every language have both a dictionary and an ideological meaning (that I didn't know), and the interpreter was needed to translate our conversation from one ideological system into the other.

"Still," he added at once, "if this bothers you, let's try to man-

122

age without a translation. But in the event of any problems, Iskrina Romanovna is at your service. Do you have any questions?"

"Yes. Please tell me," I said with tremendous excitement, "what kind of political system is there now in your country?"

Smerchev looked at the others, stopped, and, placing his hand on my shoulder, solemnly informed me, "There is no political system whatsoever in our country, Vitaly Nikitich. Our country is the first in history, the first of all mankind, to have built a classless and systemless communist society."

"Are you serious!" I cried, clasping my hands. "Have you actually created real communism?"

"Well, of course, it's real communism," confirmed Smerchev.

"It's not *toy* communism," said Dzerzhin Gavrilovich, putting in a word of his own and, at the same time, giving me an odd look.

"Could it really, really, really have happened?" I muttered. "Me, I didn't believe in it. Me, I was a doubter. And to think of all the nonsense I spouted on the subject!"

"You did indeed," remarked Propaganda Paramonovna in a severe tone.

"So what if he did," said Dzerzhin Gavrilovich, coming vigorously to my defense. "That was a long time ago, and Vitaly Nikitich may well have been subjected to strong outside influences at the time."

That statement surprised me, and I raised an objection, saying that in my past life I had more or less successfully avoided outside influences.

"We know that," said Dzerzhin Gavrilovich. "Of course, you always stood out because of your independent judgment, but, you know, in life there are people who can have hypnotic effects on us. You might even take a highly ironic attitude toward such a person, but all he has to do is say a word and though you curse yourself, you're ready to run to the ends of the earth for him."

"Even to a hole like Toronto!" chimed in Smerchev merrily.

What the hell do they mean by all that? I thought. That they know everything about me? Of course, of course, they've had plenty

123

of time to compile a fat dossier on me. But then why are they bringing up the distant past and what use do they want to put it to now?

"In other words," I said, returning to the previous subject, "you're saying that you have built communism, is that right? I confess that I never expected it, never saw it coming. The thing is I was always on the weak side as far as having a progressive worldview goes. I never had much of a head for school, and I always got very poor grades in Marxist theory. But don't think I'm not very happy that things have turned out differently from what I'd imagined. Thank God I was wrong."

"Thank who?" asked Propaganda Paramonovna in a tone of surprise.

"He said, 'Thank God,'" Iskrina Romanovna repeated my words.

"God doesn't exist," said Father Starsky, darting over to me, his right foot stomping against the ground. "God absolutely does not exist, never did and never will. There is only the Genialissimo who is there on high." Starsky pointed a finger at the sky. "He never sleeps, all he does is work. He looks down upon us and thinks about us. Thank Genialissimo, thank Genialissimo," he mumbled like a madman, making strange motions with his right hand. It looked like he was crossing himself but in some new way. Using all five fingers he touched himself in the following places and the following order: forehead, left knee, right shoulder, left shoulder, right knee, forehead.

All the others stopped and began making that same motion, mumbling, "Thank Genialissimo, thank Genialissimo."

I looked at them with surprise, but warily as well. It appeared to me that they all might have been slightly touched by the heat.

"Vitaly Nikitich," said a concerned whisper. "You should star yourself too." It was the interpreter whispering. I looked over at her and grimaced, which was to say that I didn't know how to star myself. But, catching the look of astonishment in Propaganda Paramonovna's eyes, I made my hand do a little dance which clearly did not quite satisfy her.

124

Having completed this strange ritual, which made no sense to me, they all regained their calm at once. We continued on our way. As we walked, Communi Ivanovich explained that the building of real communism had become possible as a result of the Great August Communist Revolution, which had been prepared and carried out under the personal leadership and with the direct participation of the Genialissimo. "I hope you've understood," he said, "that the Genialissimo is our dear, beloved, and only leader."

"Yes, yes," I said. "I guessed that. Except I don't really see what the word Genialissimo means. What is it — a first name, a last name, a rank, or a post?"

"It's all those things," said Smerchev. "You see, we Communites all have names that we're given at birth which are later replaced by the names we're given when we're startized. Those are our startismal names. They reflect a person's basic activity. The name Genialissimo arose quite naturally. That's because the Genialissimo is simultaneously the general secretary of our party, holds the military rank of generalissimo, and, moreover, stands apart from everyone in the scope of his genius. In view of all his ranks and attributes, people used to call him 'our general secretary, genius, and generalissimo.' Well, as everyone knows, among his other virtues, our leader is also distinguished by his exceptional modesty. And he asked us all many times to call him by a name that was simpler, shorter, and more modest. And so, in the end, it was that simple and natural name that caught on — Genialissimo."

It must have been a long way from the plane to the terminal, because Smerchev also had time to explain how and why the Great August Communist Revolution took place.

From him I learned that the Genialissimo, then only a mere general in state security, had given considerable thought to the question of why communism, which was so well and scientifically conceived, was not succeeding in practice. He went over all the scientific sources and theoretical bases many times and in the most thorough manner, and he brought to light the mistakes which had been committed in the building of communism. At times vulgarizing the great teaching, previous party and state leaders had attempted to build communism without taking local and general conditions into account. At one point, even the great Lenin thought that he could build communism immediately throughout the planet by carrying out a world revolution. Later the position was taken that the first stage of communism, socialism, could be built only in one country. And that was done. However, the transition from socialism to communism proved much more complex than it had seemed at the start. All the attempts to build communism in one country proved failures. After analyzing these attempts thoroughly and developing his own revolutionary theory, the future Genialissimo, even back then, drew the sole correct conclusion that the root of the problem lay in the previous leaders having been guided by vulgarized ideas. Overly hasty, they failed to take into account the scale of the country, unfavorable weather conditions, and the backwardness of a considerable portion of the multiethnic populace. Ultimately, the future Genialissimo came to a decision—simple, but a decision of genius—that first there could be, indeed must be, communism in one city.

And so it was! Within a short period, communism was built within the limits of Moscow, which had become the world's first separate communist republic—Moscowrep.

"Excuse me," I said, "I didn't understand quite everything. Moscow is no longer a part of the Soviet Union?"

"It's not only a part of it, but it is still its geographic, historical, cultural, and spiritual capital," Smerchev informed me with pride. "But with his innate wisdom, our beloved Genialissimo worked out a theory that allows two social systems to coexist peacefully within the confines of a single country."

"Aha!" I exclaimed, glad that I was starting to understand. "It's like China. They also had a theory of two systems there at one time."

It was clear I had said the wrong thing. The members of the delegation exchanged odd glances.

"Why do you say that!" objected Father Starsky.

"Yes," said Propaganda Paramonovna with a smile, "your remark smacks of metaphysics, Hegelianism, and Kantianism."

"But why is that, why is that?" Dzerzhin Gavrilovich was quick to interject. "Vitaly Nikitich is only saying what he thinks. Isn't that so, Vitaly Nikitich?"

"Yes, of course, it is," I hastened to agree, with a look of gratitude for Dzerzhin.

"And as far as China is concerned," said Smerchev condescendingly, "there's no point in comparing that country with the great Soviet Union. China includes both socialist territories and pernicious centers of capitalist decadence like Hong Kong, Taiwan, and the island of Honshu. Meanwhile, the Soviet Union is an entirely socialist landmass with a communist core, which has become a powerful and inspiring example for other nations which have yet to reach this stage. An essential difference, you must agree."

As we drew nearer the terminal, I peered more and more intently at the portraits on the front of the building and then asked Smerchev who was that person who looked like Jesus Christ.

"What do you mean?" he said in surprise. "That *is* Jesus Christ."

"We worship him," said Father Starsky, flustered and stomping his foot, "not as any son of God but as the first communist, a great predecessor of our Genialissimo, of whom Christ once rightly observed, 'But those who will come after me will be stronger than I!' "

I was perfectly aware that those were not Christ's words, but John the Baptist's. Nevertheless, just to be on the safe side, I voiced no objection.

I noticed an old, half-effaced sign on the terminal's brick wall: "Attention! Doors open automatically!" But there proved to be no doors whatsoever; the doorway was no more than an opening in the wall. Smerchev came to a halt, allowing me to go ahead of him. No sooner had I set one foot inside the doorway than music began to blare and an enormous crowd of friendly people started waving small red flags, banners, and portraits of the Genialissimo and . . . I couldn't believe my eyes . . . of me.

Dzerzhin immediately dashed in front of me and began shouldering a path through the crowd, followed by Smerchev and myself. The slogans on the banners were more or less as follows:

LONG LIVE THE GENIALISSIMO!
WELCOME!
WE'RE THE BEST!
OUR STRENGTH IS IN PENTAUNITY!
GLORY TO THE KPGB!
WE STUDY AND RESTUDY PRELIMINARY LITERATURE!

Before I could even get my bearings, I found myself on something of a raised stage, behind a dais table covered with red paper. The members of the comlit delegation took seats on either side of me, in roughly the same order we had just been walking. Taking a seat behind me and a little to my left, Iskrina Romanovna whispered in my ear that she was there to help me if there was anything I didn't understand.

Communi Ivanovich stood and raised his hand. The music broke off and the crowd burst into cheers and applause. With another gesture Smerchev brought this to an end.

"My dear fellow Communites!" began Smerchev in an excited voice. "The Genialissimo has personally assigned me to introduce our dear, esteemed, and belated guest." Once again the audience burst into friendly applause. "For sixty years, courageously surmounting exceptional difficulties, he made his way here from the distant past to see with his own eyes both what we have accomplished and, on behalf of generations past, to pay profound homage to our beloved Genialissimo for his unflagging efforts for the good of our people and all mankind."

To be honest, I no longer recall much of what he said. All I remember is that he spoke very highly of my literary achievements in which I, as he put it, boldly castigated the faults of the socialist society of my time, for which I was unjustly punished by the Cultists, the Volunteerists, the Corruptionists, and the Reformists who had wormed their way into the Party. All the same, my courageous

128

and impartial criticism of my society's shortcomings played a modest but nonetheless positive role in the movement which ultimately culminated in the Great August Revolution.

Smerchev's speech was interrupted many times by the most enthusiastic applause, each time with the audience chanting the Genialissimo's name and mine. By and large, it was such a touching welcome that I can't find the words to describe it. One after the other, workers, engineers, students took the rostrum. To a drum roll, the banner of a Guards unit, which I was told bore my name, was carried into the hall. The Pioneers presented me with an enormous bouquet of flowers, tied a red Pioneer scarf around my neck, and recited poems of which I recall only this three-line verse:

> Here in the Moscowrep, every Pioneer
> Takes his lead from Kartsev's life,
> Kartsev's works, and Kartsev's glorious career.

As a matter of fact, all those who spoke and welcomed me promised to work, study, perform military service, and write as I had. It may be that some of them laid it on a bit too thick in their praise of me, but I must admit that all the same I did find what they said exceedingly pleasant, and tears even welled in my eyes.

They all quoted the Genialissimo frequently (the Genialissimo said, the Genialissimo observed, the Genialissimo has repeatedly indicated) but, strange as it may seem, the pronouncements, poetic turns of phrase, and sayings they ascribed to him were not (and of this I was certain) original.

Dzerzhin Gavrilovich and Father Starsky were among the speakers. The former, addressing the most flattering of compliments to me, called on the citizens of Moscowrep to make use of my arrival to display even greater communist vigilance.

"We do not have the slightest doubt," he said, "that Vitaly Nikitich has come here with the best intentions. But we should not forget that covert enemies can also penetrate our borders in the same way."

Father Starsky's speech was interspersed with quotations from Scripture which, to believe the priest, had been written by the Genialissimo.

"Primitive communists of the past," said Starsky, "having no knowledge of the Genialissimo's fundamental teachings, rejected without sufficient grounds the possibility of things that are now beyond dispute, like the immaculate conception, the resurrection, the ascension, and the second coming. That such things are possible has now been proven irrefutably by the achievements of modern science and religion. We have a perfect example here before us today. As we know, Vitaly Nikitich died a long time ago. But now he has been resurrected and has appeared to us. And if there are any Doubting Thomases, to use the Genialissimo's expression, among us here today, let him approach, touch Vitaly Nikitich, and see for himself that he has appeared to us in the flesh."

The next speaker was Progress Anisimovich Milovidov, a representative of a cosmonaut detachment. He reported on a unique space experiment that had been conducted in my absence. About nine months before, a cosmonaut couple, Raketa and Gely Solntsev, had conceived a child in weightlessness; they were under the care of a Doctor Pirozhkov, who had accompanied them. They now had reached their due date, and, in Doctor Pirozhkov's opinion, the child would be a boy. They were hoping the child would be born by the Sixty-seventh KPGB Party Congress and had already named it Congress. Milovidov read a radiogram from the cosmonauts to me: "We congratulate our beloved preliminary writer on his return. We are concluding an important biological-genetic experiment. Glory to the Genialissimo. The Solntsevs, Pirozhkov."

Everything I saw and heard at this meeting was terribly interesting, but it was all a bit tiring too. And so I was glad when Smerchev said that the main portion of the meeting was over and all that remained for him was to announce a ukase of the Supreme Pentagon.

Since this ukase applied directly to me, I memorized it verbatim:

Considering the outstanding services Vitaly Nikitich Kartsev has rendered to the cause of preliminary (precommunist) literature, and considering the lack of any criminal intent in his actions, the backwardness of his worldview, and his advanced age:

1. He is to be completely rehabilitated and henceforth is to be considered a full-fledged citizen of the Moscow Order of the Lenin Red Banner Communist Republic;
2. The rehabilitated Kartsev is to be given the rank of second lieutenant in the literary service and to be conferred with the startism name of Classic;
3. In connection with the forthcoming one hundredth birthday of Classic Nikitich Kartsev, his Jubilee is declared a national holiday;
4. The Jubilee Pentagon is to organize preparations for the Jubilee on a high ideological and political level and, in all labor collectives, to conduct rallies, meetings, and readers' conferences at which the basic works of Kartsev are to be restudied.

Naturally, the ukase had been signed personally by the Genialissimo.

To the strains of music, I was then handed a passport, draft card, and various other documents and papers, which I crammed into my Diplomat briefcase.

This amazing meeting concluded with a short concert conducted by a young woman who held the rank of lieutenant. A flock of girls in gauzy tutus performed the dance of the young swans. They were followed by acrobats, the Brothers Nezhdanov. While they were executing flips and somersaults, a full-figured woman with ruddy cheeks and bulging eyes approached the stage.

I swear, I recognized her at once! I had known her for my entire life, from birth to emigration. She never changed, she was always the same age, had the same complexion, and wore the same

131

black-velvet dress. Now that dress was much shorter than before, considerably above the knees, but the plunging neckline was the same as it had been in the past.

Seeing that woman so agitated me that I forgot all about the Brothers Nezhdanov and looked only at her. As soon as the acrobats had finished their act, the woman in black mounted the stage, strode to the center, and placed her bare arms across her ample and resplendent bosom.

"And now," said the mistress of ceremonies, "the Moscowrep national artist Zirka Nechiporenko will perform her rendition of the Ukrainian folk song, Ha . . ."

"Hanka!" I cried, clapping my hands.

The members of the presidium regarded me with amazement. I noticed that the audience seemed startled too. And the singer also looked back at me. But the mistress of ceremonies did not lose her composure and graced me with a smile.

"That's right! 'Hanka!' " she crowed.

Zirka Nechiporenko thrust one hip forward, winked at me, and, wringing her hands, trilled with great verve:

When Hanka gives me the eye,
My heart feels like it can fly.
Tell me, tell me if you can,
What's going to happen to this man.

Listening to her sing, I felt both weary and deeply touched. Finally, albeit belatedly, I had received the recognition I deserved. In fact, what had I earned, what had I accomplished in my past life? My only reward was to be called a hooligan, an alcoholic, a smuggler, a sexual criminal, an underling of foreign intelligence, a lackey of international imperialism, a speculator, a blackmarketeer, a parasite, a slanderer, a numskull, a wolf in sheep's clothing, a little dog barking from behind a fence, a Russian who had forgotten his ancestors, a Judas who had betrayed the motherland for thirty pieces of silver. But now it was growing difficult to remember all the insults that had been bestowed on me in the past by the Cultists, Volunteerists, Corruptionists, and Reformists. Now I had received recompense for all that in the love and recognition shown me by the Communites and by the members of the comlit delegation, who had already begun calling me by my new name, Classic (except for Dzerzhin Gavrilovich, who had started calling me "darling"). And so, when I was called on to say a few words in response, I was in a state of tremendous agitation.

I went to the rostrum, paused, and drank in all those handsome, inquisitive, inspired faces.

"Greetings, unknown generation of the future . . ." I began and then suddenly, unable to restrain myself, I began howling.

This was probably the effect of my excitement, weariness, and excessive drinking, all of which brought on a genuine fit of hysterics. I wept, laughed, and twitched all at the same time. I tried to get hold of myself, I strained every nerve, and then suddenly something quite strange happened. My body became weightless, I shot up to the ceiling, and sailed slowly over the audience's heads.

THE NATFUNCTBUR

A sharp smell returned me to consciousness. Someone was pouring cold water into my mouth and had thrust a piece of cotton batten saturated with ammonia to my nose.

Opening my eyes, I saw the face of Dzerzhin Gavrilovich bent over me. Seeing that I had come back around, he bent even closer to me and said in a rapid whisper, "Just one question: where's the key to the safe?"

I looked around and could make out that we were in a small infirmary-like room, and that all the other comlits were there too.

"I'm sorry," I said, my voice terribly weak. "I must have gotten a little too excited."

"It's alright, it's alright," said Smerchev. "Those things happen. We're going to take you to your hotel now, the very best hotel. You can relax and get some rest until you're yourself again."

They seemed to be in a hurry. I felt awkward about delaying them but, as a result of all the excitement (and it was time anyway), I was feeling the call of nature, actually two calls of nature, and, slightly embarrassed, I asked where the men's room was.

"The men's room?" Smerchev frowned and looked inquisitively at Iskrina Romanovna.

"What Classic Nikitich means is the natfunctbur," said Iskrina Romanovna with a smile.

"Oh, the natfunctbur," said Smerchev with a sigh. "Yes, of

course, the natfunctbur. I should have guessed. Well, that's understandable, that's natural. As the Genialissimo says, nothing human is alien to us," he said with a chuckle.

Iskrina Romanovna volunteered to show me the way, and I went with her, taking my Diplomat briefcase with me because of my old socialist habit of worrying it would be stolen. On the way, Iskrina Romanovna explained to me that a natfunctbur was a Bureau of Natural Functions. When we reached the door of the natfunctbur (which was so marked), Iskrina Romanovna solicitously inquired whether I required this facility for number one or number two. I blushed and asked what prompted her interest in such intimate details. She replied that she was not asking out of idle curiosity but because she wanted to help me register my function. Only later was I to find out what that meant.

Entering the natfunctbur along with me, Iskrina Romanovna turned to the intellectual-looking woman sitting in the corner; she wore a white smock, and her eyeglasses were attached to her ears with shoelaces. The woman handed me a sheet of gray paper on which I was to indicate my last name, startism name, year and place of birth, and my purpose in visiting the natfunctbur (on Iskrina Romanovna's instructions, I wrote in that space, "to surrender secondary matter"). I signed and dated the form, after which Iskrina Romanovna left and I was allowed to attend to my business, for which purpose there was a long row of holes directly across from where the woman sat.

Her presence embarrassed me, because I intended to do more than I had indicated in the form. The point is—if the reader has not forgotten (I at least hadn't)—that I still had the stewardess's parting gift of a bottle of Smirnoff, and now was the perfect time to make use of it. But when I went to the farthest hole and positioned myself so that the attendant could not see me remove the bottle, I thrust my hand into my pocket and discovered the bottle was missing. It wasn't in the other pocket either. I even turned both pockets inside out to see if they had any holes in them. They didn't.

All I could do now was to grin bitterly. They had built communism, but they still went through your pockets. And some low-life had taken advantage of the few minutes when I was uncon-scious. I had not been wrong to worry about my briefcase. By then I was so out of sorts that I ceased to be shy and, placing my briefcase in front of me, I set about doing what I had to do even with the attendant's eyes still on me.

Directly in front of me was a wall that had not been painted in ages and which was covered by every sort of drawing imaginable. Someone had also traced out in indelible ink, "Proletarians of all countries, wipe yourselves!"

I must say that personally I was very put off by this graffiti. It was beyond me how people who had reached the stage of commu-nism could still be capable of such vulgar humor. But the writing was very faint, and might have been made back in my time. I felt somewhat embarrassed for a generation that had been unable to think of anything wittier than this. I spotted something else under the graffiti—a three-letter word. It had either been written messily or else someone had tried to paint over it but with incomplete suc-cess, because it still showed stubbornly through. The word was "SIM." I laughed, which brought a look of surprise to the atten-dant's face.

"I'm laughing," I said to her, "because someone wrote 'SIM' here and I knew someone by that name."

These words seemed somehow to startle and perhaps even frighten her. She gave me a strange look, glanced over at the door, and placed a finger to her lips.

This made no sense to me, but I did think that the author of the first graffiti was essentially correct and that his advice should be taken. But do they have toilet paper? I thought with alarm. As far as I recalled, during the period of developed socialism, there never was any toilet paper in public toilets, and so the builders of a bright-er tomorrow would have had certain problems to overcome.

I looked around dubiously and at once saw for myself that dur-ing my absence radical changes for the better had in fact taken place. There was toilet paper! And not just some scraps of paper but an entire roll on a dispenser attached to the floor. Now there's communism for you! The toilet paper was, however, made of newsprint. All the better, I thought—if someone's taken the trouble to cut up newspaper and paste it together, that means that communist society has a high level of concern for human welfare. I grabbed the end of the roll and began pulling it toward me. And, to be frank, I was not well prepared for what I saw then. No, the roll had not been made from old newspapers. The newspaper itself had been printed in roll form.

I cannot begin to express how this staggered me. Naturally, when setting off on this long journey, I was ready for the most varied surprises. I expected to learn about unimaginable scientific achievements, manned flights to Mars or Jupiter, and I had supposed that Moscow would be a very different city by then. Marvelous shining buildings would soar to the skies and strange flying machines would dart between the buildings, and it was relatively easy for me to imagine other such wonders of future technology. But it had never occurred to me that the people of the future would find such a brilliantly simple solution to the toilet paper problem.

Needless to say, I began impatiently unwinding the newspaper in order to glean as much information as possible about the society in which I now found myself. The newspaper was still called *Pravda*. There were about two feet of pictures showing the decorations the newspaper had been awarded for its many years of tireless service in re-educating the workers. Under the name of the newspaper was a line to the effect that the paper was the organ of the Communist Party of State Security. Now I understood the abbreviation I had seen on one of the banners: KPGB. The Party had merged with the KGB.

Approximately another two feet were dedicated to the Genialissimo. First, there was a large half-length portrait of him in full dress with medals adorning his entire chest from chin to waist. The portrait was followed by a brief bulletin on the state of the Genialissimo's health. At first I was alarmed, thinking that something had happened to the Genialissimo, but then I noticed that the bulletin was entirely positive and was apparently published on a daily basis. It said that the Genialissimo was feeling fine after a productive night's work. His heart, stomach, kidneys, liver, lungs, and other vital organs were functioning perfectly. After performing a series of recommended physical exercises and ingesting a modest vegetarian meal, the Genialissimo had returned to his daily titanic labors for the good of all mankind.

The bulletin was followed by ukases signed by the Genialissimo. The Klyazma River was to be renamed the Karl Marx River. Decorations and medals were to be awarded to the institutions of corrective labor. The wording here was more or less as follows: "For great services rendered in the re-education of the workers and instilling them with an awareness of the communist ideals. . . ." Then came a long list of camps, of general, special, and strict regimes, institutions of prosecution and prisons of every sort, including one called the Dzerzhinsky Lefortovo Red Banner Academic Prison. They also printed various telegrams which the Genialissimo had sent in large quantities to various congresses, conferences, and meetings. Though I really had no time, I did read one telegram through. It was addressed to a congress of outstanding donors who, as the telegram put it, through their noble and self-sacrificing activities, were doing much to facilitate the fulfillment of the course charted by the party for comprehensive economizing and total recycling.

The entire newspaper was exceedingly interesting. There was an article on the value of thrift. A column about young people who wear long pants or long skirts and were crazy about bourgeois dancing. Cartoons, fables, an item by a phrenologist. Since I did not have the time to read everything, I tried to grasp the main elements. For example, from the article "Why We Love the Genialissimo," I learned that he was the national leader and held the five highest posts: general secretary of the CC KPGB, chairman of the Supreme Pentagon, commander in chief, chairman of state security, and patriarch of all the Russias.

I also learned that, because it was surrounded by a triple ring of hostility, the country was experiencing certain temporary difficulties and that a limited contingent of Soviet troops had been temporarily stationed in the Afghani-Pakistani Democratic People's Republic. Further, the entire country was successfully healing the wounds inflicted by the recently concluded Great Buryat-Mongolian War.

That was as far as I got because just then Iskrina Romanovna came running into the natfunctbur. "Why are you still sitting there, Classic Nikitich! People are waiting for you, and you're in here reading the newspaper."

I felt terribly embarrassed. "Iskrina Romanovna," I said, "how can you come running in here just like that. I feel awkward talking with you in this position."

"What does that mean, awkward?" she said. "Those ideas have no meaning to us. But people are out there waiting for you, and that is genuinely awkward."

All the same I asked her to leave and promised to hurry. I was sorry to part with the newspaper and would have been glad to take it along with me, but that crone of an attendant never took her eyes off me and, really, at the moment I had no place to put the newspaper. You couldn't hide a roll that size under your arm, and my briefcase was already bulging as it was.

Using the portrait of the Genialissimo and part of the bulletin on his health, I concluded my business, grabbed my briefcase, and rushed toward the exit.

Smerchev and his deputies, in fact, were waiting for me in the now-deserted auditorium, and they seemed to be nervous.

"Everything all right?" asked Smerchev. Before I was done replying, he said that it was time to leave for the city, that we'd been delayed too long as it was. I asked about my luggage and was told that my suitcase would be returned to me elsewhere.

We went outside.

The sun was at its zenith and scorching hot. On the cracked pavement, a column of vehicles was preparing to depart; it consisted of two armored personnel carriers (one at the head of the column, the other at the rear) and four old-time trucks with high, dilapidated sides on each of which was written in huge letters: DELE-GATION. The trucks were filled with the same people who had just welcomed me with such warmth in the airport terminal. They were packed in so tightly that they looked like a many-headed organism with blank, indifferent faces. I waved to them, but none attempted to wave back, possibly because none was able to work his hand free.

The personnel carrier at the head of the column blew its whistle and, emitting puffs of smoke and steam, the entire column pulled slowly away. In the rear truck, pressed up against one side, I saw the poor woman who had sung at the reception. Her long-suffering, submissive face was dripping with sweat. Our eyes met and I waved to her. She responded with a sour smile and turned away, clearly without any interest in me now.

When the column was out of sight and the smoke had cleared, there were still a few armored personnel carriers and a dozen or so cars, some steam-powered, some furnace-driven, waiting on the square.

Smerchev told me they had to switch to boilers and furnaces after the Cultists, Volunteerists, Corruptionists, and Reformists had destructively exploited the country's natural resources, finally exhausting the oil fields of Baku and Tyumen. Gasoline engines were now used only in military technology and special-purpose transport vehicles.

We walked over to an armored personnel carrier, by whose open doors stood a young man wearing a short, faded jumpsuit and a tank helmet. He was the driver of that ungainly vehicle, and his name, strange as it may seem, was just Vasya. The interior was half-sunk in darkness and as hot as a sauna. Taking a seat beside Vasya, I immediately became drenched with sweat and feared that I would not be up to this final leg of my journey. Smerchev and the others took seats on the long wooden benches that ran the length of either side.

Vasya battened down the armored door, gave a long blast of his siren, shifted some levers, and we were on our way. After making a series of complex turns around a traffic circle, Vasya finally brought his military vehicle out onto a wide road, which in my previous life had been called the Leningrad Highway.

Since that time the highway had fallen into a state of near total disrepair. The asphalt was cracked in some places, swollen in others, and, here and there, missing entirely. Vasya adroitly maneuvered past ruts and potholes, but sometimes either he was not paying attention or else the driving required more skill than he possessed, and we would go crashing down into some pit and then re-emerge on the other side.

Both sides of the highway were fenced by a continuous wall of reinforced concrete, about eighteen feet tall with three rows of barbed

141

wire along its top. The road was empty and looked peaceful. But from time to time good-sized hunks of brick or cobblestone would be hurled over the fence and onto the road. One brick hit the roof of our armored personnel carrier and shattered with a roar like that of an artillery shell.

"The Simites are up to their usual tricks," said Vasya without emotion.

"Semites?" I said. "You mean Jews?"

"Who?" said Vasya in surprise.

"They were a people in the olden days," Father Starsky explained to Vasya, leaning over the back of his seat. "Very bad people. They crucified Jesus Christ. But, thank Genialissimo, there are no Jews in our country. But there are still some out there in the First Ring."

I asked what the First Ring was. Smerchev joined in at this point and said that the communism which had been built within the greater Moscow area naturally elicited not only admiration, but also the envy of various elements of the population living outside its bounds. And so, of course, relations between the Communites and those living outside the boundaries of the Moscowrep were marked by a certain tension and even hostility, one which, as the Genialissimo had correctly observed, was ringlike in structure. The First Ring of Hostility was formed by the Soviet republics which the Communites called the filial republics, the Second Ring was composed of the fraternal socialist countries, and the Third by the capitalist enemy.

"In formal parlance," explained Smerchev, "we call them the Filial Ring of Hostility, the Fraternal Ring of Hostility, and, of course, the Enemy Ring of Hostility. But most of the time we just say the First Ring, the Second, and the Third."

"But how about those Semites?" I asked. "If they're not Jews, then who are they?"

"In the first place," said Smerchev with a smile, "they're not *Sem*ites, but *Sim*ites. And, in the second place, people like them aren't even worth talking about."

"Some think they are, some think they aren't," remarked Dzerzhin with a tone of doubt. But he did not take his idea any further.

Our carrier did not drive fast. Either because the road was blocked or for some other reason, we stopped quite frequently and then, gears grinding, we'd continue on our way. The vision-slit in front of me did not provide a wide view, but on the wall that separated the road from the First Ring, I did see innumerable portraits of the Genialissimo, though usually not in one piece. Just his beard, his boots, or his striped trousers.

I also saw a great variety of slogans, appeals, and greetings, some of which I knew from long ago though there were new ones as well. For instance:

> THE COMPONENTS OF OUR PENTAUNITY:
> NATIONALITY, PARTYALITY, RELIGIOSITY,
> VIGILANCE, AND STATE SECURITY!

I asked Smerchev since when had religion been considered compatibile with communist ideology. Father Starsky broke in to say that to win religion over to the side of communism was one of the tasks posed by the Genialissimo during the August Revolution. In the past, the vulgarizers had not taken into account the enormous educational powers of the church and had subjected believers to constant pressure. Now the church is considered the party's younger sister and has been granted enormous rights and powers, under only one condition—that the church not preach faith in a God who, as we know, does not exist, but faith in communist ideals and the person of the Genialissimo.

I also asked why they even had State Security (or SECO, as they called it) if the party itself, judging by its name, now dealt with state security. "Isn't there some contradiction in that?" I asked.

"None whatsoever," objected Smerchev firmly. "The party is the leading and guiding force in our society, whereas SECO is a branch of service. Is that clear?"

143

Now, recalling my first day in the Moscowrep, I think that though so much contradictory and absolutely unexpected information came raining down on me, I began to get my bearings rather quickly. For example, with no help from anyone, I figured out that the word *comcom* meant communist comrade, *comlit* meant communist literate, or writer, and the greeting *Glorgen* stood for Glory to the Genialissimo. And it seemed obvious why they said O Gen! instead of O God! But there was one key question for me: How did the Moscow Republic observe the basic principle of communism— from each according to his ability, to each according to his need? I asked Smerchev about this and he said that of course this principle was observed in the most direct possible way.

"So, does that mean that anyone can just walk into any store and take whatever he needs without paying?"

"Yes," corroborated Communi Ivanovich, "a person is given everything absolutely without charge. But we don't have stores here. What we have are comfoodests, that is, Communist Food Establishments, something like the cafeterias of your day. They are located in locpubasses meaning Locations of Public Assembly. We also have an extensive system of comdispoints, Communist Distribution Points, which serve Communites at the work place. There, every Communite receives everything to satisfy his established needs."

"I see," I said. "But who defines what he needs? Does he do that himself?"

"That's pure metaphysics, Hegelianism, and Kantianism!" exclaimed Propaganda Paramonovna gleefully.

But Smerchev pinned no labels on me, though he did say that my question struck him as odd. "Why should a person determine his own needs? He may not have sufficient preparation for this. He might have some, let's call them, impossible desires which he considers needs. He might want the moon and the stars. To determine what our needs are, there are the Pentagons, the Supreme Pentagon and the local ones. They're made up of party and religious activists, SECO workers, and others. Before determining what a person's needs are, you must first learn his physical and moral characteristics—his weight, height, ideological views, his attitude toward work, and the extent of his involvement with the community. Naturally, a person who is a good worker—who fulfills his production assignments, takes part in community affairs, and studies the Genialissimo's works diligently—has much greater needs than someone who is lazy or violates social discipline."

"But there are practically no people who violate social discipline in Moscowrep," said Dzerzhin Gavrilovich.

"There are very few such people," agreed Smerchev. "But still not everyone works as well as everyone else. Some people fulfill the plan by two hundred percent while others fulfill it by only a hundred and fifty percent, and to think that their needs are identical would be, I'd say, simply unjust."

CHECKPOINT
TWO

If my guess is right, it was about where the highway intersected with the old beltway, built back in my time, that traffic began slowing down. Pressing my face to the vision-slit and squinting through the sweat stinging my eyes, I could see we were on a broad stretch of road. A few long lines of steam-powered and furnace-driven vehicles were evidently organized in a hierarchy of sorts: large armored personnel carriers in one line, smaller ones in another, and quite small regular automobiles in another.

But there was no one ahead of us in our lane. At first, I thought this was just a matter of luck, but then I surmised that this lane was not for everyone—it probably had been designated just for important persons like myself.

But I was to learn at once that there were persons of even greater importance. A sudden, wild howl pierced the air and Vasya immediately pulled our lumbering bus to the side of the road, where we teetered at the edge of a ditch.

The howling crescendoed rapidly, and I caught sight of a vehicle that I knew from my past life. Racing past at enormous speed, and surrounded by a motorcycle escort, was a long file of old-model automobiles, their loudspeakers blaring, lights flashing. The first two cars looked like the Zils of my time, but the second one towed a black bus, attached by red and yellow hoses. Another Zil, bristling with machine-gun barrels, followed the bus.

146

As the cavalcade passed, all my companions starred themselves, then Smerchev sighed and whispered reverentially, "That was Him!"

"Who?" I asked. "The Genialissimo?"

Vasya broke into a loud guffaw, but Smerchev replied very seriously, "What do you mean! The Genialissimo doesn't drive around. That was the chairman of the Editorial Commission."

We set off on our way once more. A short while later, we came to a halt again, and Smerchev said that we'd have to step out to handle certain formalities.

I climbed out of that hell-hole dripping with sweat, more dead than alive. As I wiped my face with a handkerchief, I saw that we were in front of a long, low building; curtains covered its small windows entirely, and two men armed with submachine guns stood by an iron door marked:

CHECKPOINT TWO

A large steam vehicle stood in front of the building, puffing and panting. Raw pine planks hung from the rear of the vehicle's trailer. A wheel and a spring had been taken off the trailer, and two men in short, grease-stained jumpsuits were working on the spring; one of them held a large chisel and the other wielded a sledge hammer. As they worked, they carried on a conversation that did not make a great deal of sense to me. Twisting his neck unnaturally, the one with the chisel looked up at the sky from under the long peak of his cap and said, "Looks like there won't be any more movies today."

The other twisted his neck too and agreed, "Yes, the sky's too clear."

Having reached that conclusion, he missed with the sledge hammer and struck the finger of the man holding the chisel. The injured one jumped in the air, spun like a top, and then let loose a juicy tirade in the most "preliminary" language, every last word of which was familiar and warmed the cockles of my heart.

Meanwhile, Dzerzhin had walked over to the guards. At the

sight of him, one presented arms and the other opened the door of the building.

The spacious interior was reminiscent of the lobby of a large hotel on the first day of an important, perhaps even an international conference. In the middle of the hall was a series of small tables, each marked with a letter of the Russian alphabet. Smerchev and I walked over to the K table.

Without looking up at me, a lieutenant colonel took down my last name, startism name, and patronymic. Then she asked for my date of birth.

"Nineteen forty-two," I said.

"Nineteen forty . . ." she said as she wrote. Then, suddenly, she blew her top. "What's the matter with you? Do you think we have nothing better to do here? I've wasted a whole sheet of paper because of you. I'm going to inform your employer to dock you for the cost of the paper."

She was on the verge of tossing the paper into the waste basket, but Smerchev stopped her, whispering something in her ear. Her face was sullen as she listened, but all at once that expression was replaced by one of utter amazement. She looked up at me and clasped her hands.

"Oh, Gen! It really is you! Your face did look familiar, but I've only seen you on television. Well, I declare! You look wonderful! And a hundred years old! You don't look a day over sixty. You must eat nothing but vitamins out there in the Third Ring."

"In the Third Ring," remarked Propaganda Paramonovna, who had just walked over, "the workers live exclusively on secondary matter."

"Yes, yes, of course," the registrar hastened to agree. "Of course, secondary matter. But I've heard that it's vitamin-enriched."

After I had filled out the short form, I was asked to go to the far corner of the lobby, where there was a long zinc table of the sort I imagined pathologists used to dissect corpses. This time the role of the corpse was being played by my suitcase, which had already been opened, even partially gutted. The postmortem was

148

being performed by a large and beefy major, a customs official, I imagined.

The major recognized me at once. He spoke very ingratiatingly with me, apologizing frequently. "I beg your pardon, it's my fault, I'm very sorry for the inconvenience, in principle we would not inspect you under any circumstances but only because you might have brought something here out of ignorance, you understand, forgive me." After a few further apologies, he informed me that my luggage contained certain items which were not allowed into the Moscowrep.

"For example?" I asked, trying to remain unruffled.

"For example, this," said the customs official, picking up my Nikon camera, which he then opened.

"What are you doing!" I cried. "You've exposed the film! Do you mean to tell me taking pictures isn't allowed?"

"What do you mean!" said the major, alarmed. "Of course, pictures are allowed. Especially by you. You can do everything except what's forbidden. Here, please take your camera. Take all the pictures you want. I just took out the film but you can use the camera as much as you like."

"Are you out of your mind?" I asked. "What I am supposed to use it for without film? Hammering nails? Cracking nuts?"

"For Genialissimo's sake!" He placed his hand to his heart. "You can use it for whatever you like within the limits of your own needs. With all due respect and my apologies, photographic apparatuses are allowed here, but light-sensitive materials are not." With those words, he tossed onto the table the six other rolls of film which I had purchased in the Kaufhof before my departure.

"What you're saying, then, is that nothing can be photographed in this Moscowrep of yours?"

In a quandary, the customs official looked to Smerchev, then back to me. "Excuse me, I don't understand," he said. "In the Moscowrep you can photograph whatever you like, wherever you like, and whomever you like. You just can't use film."

"How can that be," I said in dismay. "I've seen your newspapers. There are photographs in them. They couldn't have been taken without film."

"Your observation is perfectly correct!" said the customs official with a little laugh. "But the photos in the newspapers are made for state needs, whereas your needs are personal. They know what can be shot on film but you, you'll forgive me, may not know. And because you don't, you might might start photographing some of the less savory aspects of our society, which would attract the attention of SECO. And what do you need that for?"

At the mention of SECO, I looked back around at Siromakhin who was standing right behind me. "Give in to him on this point, darling," said Dzerzhin Gavrilovich. "Better to give up a part than to lose everything."

Considering the discussion closed, the customs official pushed the film aside and continued his inspection. He told me then that I could use my tape recorder as much as I liked, but not the tapes and the batteries. He also removed the batteries from my Grundig portable radio. He conferred with someone by telephone concerning my notebooks and ballpoint pens, and they decided magnanimously that these items could remain in my possession. But then the major pulled out the floppy disk containing Sim Simych's slabs.

"What's this?"

"That?" I said in surprise. "You mean you don't know?"

The customs official shrugged his shoulders. "No, I've never seen anything like it."

"But don't you have computers?"

"Of course we do," said Smerchev. "But not that kind. Our computers are large."

"This isn't a computer," I tried to explain. "This is a disk which you *insert* into a computer."

"And what is it used for?" asked the customs official.

I said that you insert the disk into the computer and it records all kinds of programs and texts.

"And what's recorded on that one?" asked the customs official, holding the floppy disk up to the light obviously hoping to spot some writing on it.

150

"This disk contains novels by a preliminary writer. You must have heard of him, his name is Karnavalov."

"Karnavalov?" The customs official looked inquisitively at Smerchev who shrugged in reply.

"What?" I said in surprise. "You've never heard of Karnavalov?"

The customs official was embarrassed, and Communi Ivanovich blushed.

"Do you mean to say that you never studied Karnavalov even when you were in the instcominst?" I said.

It turned out that they had never heard of him. And never studied him. Now that's something! I thought. Who could have ever imagined that! I had thought that in the future just about everyone might be forgotten, but not Simych. Poor Simych! All the effort he'd put into those slabs only to have them completely forgotten in sixty years' time!

Since that was the case, why make a fuss over something that clearly had lost its value? When the customs official set the floppy disk aside, I voiced no objection. Ultimately, that wasn't my purpose in traveling there—to distribute slabs that no one had ever heard of. I'd be better off giving people one of my own books to read.

The official had just gotten to my books, which had been packed at the very bottom of the suitcase. He asked what these books were and, not without a certain pride, I said that they were my own.

"Your own?"

"That's right," I said. "My own. Does that surprise you?"

"You see," said Communi Ivanovich, coming to my aid. "Classic Nikitich . . ."

"Listen," I interrupted, "stop calling me that idiotic name. If you can't do that, at the very least just call me Classic and drop the Nikitich."

At another time I would not have said a word. But now I was very irritated by all the bizarre and meaningless rituals to which I had grown somewhat unaccustomed, after all the years I'd spent in the wilds of capitalist society.

"Alright, fine," Smerchev agreed at once. "If you don't want us to use your patronymic, we'll just call you Classic. All I wanted to say, my dear Classic, was that there is no private property in our society. Everything belongs to everyone here. And so those books cannot be considered your own."

The whole thing had me exhausted. I had a headache. From fatigue, from the heat, from a lack of sleep, from not having had a drop to drink for ages. And from all the impressions of the day.

"You see," I said to Smerchev, "no matter what you say, these books are my own. Not only as things that belong to me. But also because I wrote them myself with this very hand." As added persuasion, I even waved my hand in front of Smerchev's face. "I hope you'll agree that this hand is mine and belongs to me and not to everyone."

"So you're a believer in private property, are you then!" remarked Propaganda Paramonovna coquettishly, shaking her head.

"Listen," I beseeched the customs official and all the comlits together. "Why are you trying to drive me crazy? Why won't you let me keep my books? I have no intention of selling them or trying to grow rich off them. But I might want to give one to someone as a present."

"You intend to distribute them?" asked Propaganda Paramonovna in horror.

"What does that mean—*distribute* them?" I objected. "I'm not going to distribute them, I'm going to give them as presents. Would you like me to give you a copy?"

"What are you saying!" cried Propaganda Paramonovna in what seemed genuine fright to me. "I have no need of it. I don't read any preliminary literature."

I could see that they were all worked up, on edge. The conversation had taken a difficult turn. But I'm not made of steel either. Especially after the day I'd had. Unable to bear up under all the stupidity, I simply sat on the floor, clutched my head, and burst into tears. I have to say this doesn't happen often. I haven't cried since I was a child, and these Communites had brought me to tears twice in one day.

I noticed Smerchev nudge Iskrina Romanovna who ran over to me. "What's wrong! Why are you crying! Get hold of yourself! There's nothing to cry about. No reason to cry, my dear, sweet Clashenka . . ."

Clashenka? Then I realized this was a diminutive of Classic. Suddenly it all seemed so ridiculous that my tears turned to laughter. I could not restrain myself, I was choking on laughter, rolling on the floor. All the comlits clomped about in confusion around me, and I heard one of them say something about a doctor.

"I don't need any doctor," I said, rising and dusting off my knees. "It's over. It's all very clear and I won't make any more demands. You can throw out all my books, in the trash if you want—just explain one thing to me, will you? Why are you so afraid of them? After all, you told me that you had read them in the instcominsts."

"We didn't read them, we studied them," said Smerchev with a tender smile. "That is, some people studied them in detail, and the teacher gave the others a brief summary of the themes you dealt with and your books' ideological and artistic content."

"Aha!" I exclaimed in disappointment. "You *studied* my books. But reading them is still forbidden, just as it used to be, is that right?"

"What are you saying?" objected Smerchev forcefully. "Why do you have such a low opinion of us? Nothing is forbidden here. It's just that our need for preliminary literature has been entirely satisfied."

"Especially since preliminary literature is very often ideologically inconsistent," remarked Propaganda Paramonovna. "It contained a great deal of metaphysics, Hegelianism, and Kantianism."

"And a great deal of blasphemy against our communist religion," added Father Starsky, who had not said a word until then.

"And the method of socialist realism used by preliminary writers," said Propaganda Paramonovna, "has long since been condemned by the party as mistaken and harmful. There is only one correct method—communist realism."

"And generally speaking, my dear Classic," said Smerchev, "you

153

should realize that in the brief historical interval between our times and yours, our literature has grown by such leaps and bounds that, in comparison with it, everything you and your contemporaries wrote seems simply pitiful and feeble."

"Yes, yes, yes, yes," said Starsky, and they all nodded sadly.

"Still, not all of it," said Siromakhin, once again coming to my defense. "He wrote one remarkable book, which, I would even say, is on a level approaching that of the early examples of communist realism. Unfortunately," he continued, addressing me now, "you didn't bring it with you for some reason. But we'll find it . . ."

"And we'll correct it," prompted Smerchev.

"Yes, we'll correct it a little and, who knows, we might even reissue it."

I had no idea which book they were speaking of. But I no longer felt like asking. Or like arguing. And so when they confiscated my street maps of Moscow, my T-shirts marked Munich, and the chewing gum, I did not even ask why, sick to death of the whole damn thing. And when I was given a list of the confiscated items to sign, I scribbled my signature without so much as a glance at the paper.

THREE-WAY
SPLIT

But that was not to be my last ordeal. After customs we walked a short way until we came to a door marked:

SANITARY TREATMENT POINT

Smerchev apologized and said that it was absolutely necessary for me to go through sanitary treatment because the Moscowrep takes the most stringent measures against epidemic diseases being brought in from the Ring of Hostility.

Iskrina Romanovna offered to keep an eye on my valuables during the treatment, and I gave her my Diplomat briefcase, my watch, and my wallet.

The comlits remained outside as I entered what proved to be a dressing room with long wooden benches. On a bench in a corner, the two men from the steam-driven timber truck I'd seen earlier were undressing. Now their conversation was entirely friendly and they spoke in purest, unadulterated preliminary Russian, with constant references to the Genialissimo and his relatives on his mother's side. One driver's thumb had been bandaged with black insulating tape.

Watching them, I too began undressing. Strange as it may seem, and despite the unbearable heat outside, it was truly cold in there, and my body at once turned blue and became covered with goose flesh.

A woman in a white robe yawned with boredom behind a wooden partition. The drivers handed her their clothes, and each received a wooden bowl in exchange. After they walked away, I went over to her, handed her my clothing and received my wooden basin. It was wet, slippery, and without handles.

In the next room I encountered a woman with a large machine that had probably been built for shearing sheep, not people. She offered to cut my hair. I sat down, covering myself with the basin, and asked for a modified crew cut. Without answering or putting any covering over me, she immediately cut a broad swatch down the top of my head.

"Madame!" I cried, jumping to my feet. "What are you doing? Are you out of your mind? I asked for a modified crew cut."

At first she did not understand what I wanted from her, and then explained that all citizens of the Moscowrep had their hair cropped close as part of the struggle against undesirable insects. The hair was turned in at recycling centers. It hurt me to lose my beautiful head of hair but, as the saying goes, if they chop off your head, you don't cry for your hair.

I continued on my way and soon found myself in front of another door, this one with a sign that read:

HALL OF EXTERNAL WASHING

To one side of the sign was a piece of paper with the heading, "READ AND REMEMBER." These were the rules for bathers. They were written in elevated language and accompanied by an epigraph by the Genialissimo. "Everything should be beautiful about a person: his face, his clothing, and his body."

The rules began with a report of the enormous and unceasing work performed day in and day out by the Genialissimo and the party he leads for the benefit of the citizens of the communist republic. Because of the pains they had taken, nearly every Communite had the opportunity fully and regularly to satisfy his external washing needs.

156

However, as the Genialissimo constantly teaches, thrift should become a habit—it should become second nature, even first nature to every Communite. Wastefulness was to be avoided in washing, and water should be expended solely within the limits of a person's natural needs, which were not difficult to calculate. You simply multiply your weight in kilograms by your height in centimeters and divide that figure by the coefficient 2145. The result will indicate the individual's actual needs in basinsful of hot and cold water. I was somewhat worried about having to perform a mathematical operation that was beyond my powers before I could proceed to an external wash, but my worries were banished at once by the attached tables where all the possibilities had been precalculated. For a person of my height and weight—165 centimeters and 78 kilograms—exactly six basinsful would satisfy his needs.

The rules also indicated that those using the wash point were forbidden to:

1. Wash while wearing their outer clothing
2. Play musical instruments
3. Answer calls of nature
4. Damage communist property

And were categorically forbidden to:

5. Settle any disputes which may arise by using the wash basins or other washing implements

While reading the instructions, I noticed out of the corner of my eye two men walking past me, followed by a woman, and then by an entire family—husband, wife, and little boy. Then came another two women, and everyone, naturally, was naked. A certain hesitation set in, and I asked a fat man walking by where the men's section was. The question surprised him.

"What village are you from, buddy?"

"Stockdorf," I said.

"Staturtorf?"

"Not Staturtorf, *Stockdorf*," I corrected.

"I don't think I've heard of that one," said the fat man. "Where is it? Far away?"

"That's right," I said. "It's sixty years from here."

He looked at me as if I were an idiot and said that it was only in the Rings of Hostility that institutions were divided into men's and women's sections, but there was complete equality here and the difference between women and men had been almost entirely erased.

Squinting automatically and looking at the fat man's body I could see that, in his case at least, the difference had indeed been erased.

There was nothing of any special interest within the hall of external washing itself. A bathhouse like any other. Long stone benches, faucets along the wall, steam, a drone of voices. Men and women washed together and the only reason this surprised me was that it was taking place in Moscow. But I had already seen the sexes mixing freely like this sixty years ago in the Third Ring of Hostility.

It was a large area with many columns. On one column, I noticed an arrow and under it the words, "Satisfaction of sexual needs around the corner." So, there *had* been a great many remarkable changes in my absence! By the way, beneath this sign someone had scratched the word *SIM* with a nail. I was reminded again of Simych, and I thought what fun it would be to bring him there to that mixed bath house so he could see what ideas the predators had struck upon. I could imagine his outrage.

I took a few steps in the direction indicated by the arrow when the truck drivers I had seen twice before emerged from the steam in front of me. Holding plastic cups containing some dark liquid, and with obviously low intentions, they were accosting a frail-looking girl who, oddly enough, was not naked herself. Her private parts were covered by an oilcloth G-string, and her nipples by little stars. Though their purposes were playful, all three of them looked angry.

I was about to walk past them when the driver with the bandaged thumb stopped me with a question, "Hey, Pop, you want to go in on a three-way split?"

In another time, being addressed as "pop" might have caused me offense, and I might have smacked him in the face. But not this time. I was too happy that the sacred tradition of splitting a bottle three ways had survived under communism. The aroma of the liquid sloshing in their glasses reached my nostrils, and I must say it was none too appetizing. But the smell wasn't what mattered. A horse would have fainted from some of the stuff I've drunk in my time. And at the moment I would have gone for a glass of kerosene. But I was so exhausted that a glass of just about anything would have sent me straight to the floor, so I overcame my desire and, my hand on my heart, said in an edifying tone to the truck drivers, "Sorry, guys, count me out. I don't drink and I advise you not to either. Alcohol ruins the liver and has a negative effect on your mental abilities."

The truck drivers looked at one another in disbelief.

"We're not alkies," said the one with the bandage, though without great assurance. "And we're not asking you to split a *bottle*."

"Then what?" I asked in surprise.

They exchanged glances again, and the girl giggled.

"Come on!" said the bandaged one, perplexed. "What kind of question is that? You mean you don't know what you do with them?" he said, indicating the girl. "Let's go around the corner and satisfy ourselves."

"Three men with one woman?" I could not believe my own ears. "But that's a sin! How could you do something so disgraceful and shameless? After all, you're living under communism, for which millions have been killed by bullets, burned in fires, frozen in swamps!"

Despite my weariness, I read them a brief lecture on the October Revolution, the Second World War, the Siege of Leningrad, and the construction of various wonders of engineering. "And all that means nothing to you!" I said, and then spat on the floor and continued on my way.

"Hey, listen, Pop!" cried the bandaged one chasing after me. "Why are you blowing your top! Are you a nut or something? It's not us who's corrupt, it's the girls. They used to take half a glass

159

of soap," he said, indicating the glass in his hand. "That was no problem. You could satisfy your need and still get a good wash. But now they won't take less than three and that's why we need three people to chip in."

I felt ill at ease because there was something I had failed to understand here. I apologized, but said that unfortunately I could not take part in this particular deal because, number one, I did not cheat on my wife, and, number two, I had no soap, I'd left it in my suitcase. But then one of the drivers said that soap needs were satisfied right here, and he pointed to a booth in the corner where a fat woman was handing out glasses of soap. I walked over with my new friends and was given a glass of soap. I took one sniff and handed it to one of the drivers.

And was he grateful!

"Pop," he said, "I can see you're a newcomer and don't know your way around here yet. If you have any problem, come right to me. I work in comcolumn seven, everyone knows me there. My new name is Kosmy but everyone still calls me by my old name of Kuzya. And so if you need anything, a cylinder or a crankshaft, you come right to me. I'll get you whatever you want."

I thanked him and then went to find some water. All the walls and columns were plastered with waterproof signs that read more or less like this:

WATER IS THE SOURCE OF LIFE.
WATER IS THE PROPERTY OF THE PEOPLE.
WHOEVER WASTES WATER IS AN ENEMY OF THE PEOPLE.
ONE BASINFUL CAN WATER A HORSE.

As I approached the wall with the faucets, I noticed a poster on which a person looking like a Red Army soldier from the Civil War pointed a finger at me. By him were the words, "You used an extra basin!"

"Not me," I said. "I haven't even used one yet."

Of course, the Red Army soldier was only a drawing, but he looked so real that I automatically shrank from his gaze.

160

I satisfied only a third of my need, that is, of the six basins I received, I used only two. I fantasized that I might even be given a medal of some sort for such thrift, but, making no efforts to realize that dream, I headed for the exit.

My clothes were handed to me when I got there. They were still hot from the steam-cleaning. The plastic buttons on my jacket had melted, but my fly, which was made of metal, was still in one piece.

THE OATH

I was met in the well-lit and spacious room by Dzerzhin Gavrilovich Siromakhin, who asked if I'd had a good wash. He was alone. The others had already left, he told me.

"And now, my darling, the final formality, and then we can go get some rest."

We went through a door marked "Office of Ritual Needs Satisfaction." I was afraid that I might encounter something indecent again, but I was mistaken.

Three stout ladies, all holding the rank of general, were seated at high-backed chairs at a long table beneath a large portrait of the Genialissimo. It was clearly some kind of court. Their expression was quite severe, but the senior woman (the one in the middle) gave me a compliment that I'd already received once before, that I was very well-preserved for my age.

But then she too assumed a severe expression and declared that, when entering the basic sacred territory of the Moscowrep, I was obliged to take the oath of a citizen of the communist republic.

"Repeat after me," she ordered.

I don't remember the whole oath, of course. All I remember is that it began with gratitude to the Genialissimo for the honor he had bestowed upon me. As a communist citizen, I was obliged to observe the strictest discipline in the work place, in daily life and in social relations, to fulfill and overfulfill my production assignments, to struggle for comprehensive economizing and total recycling, to keep state, social, and professional secrets religiously, to cooperate closely with the organs of state security, and to communicate to them all anticommunist conspiracies, actions, utterances, and thoughts of which I was aware.

I had repeated everything to that point quite obediently, but here I stopped and looked over at the judges. "You know," I said, "there's something wrong about this. I must say, I am unable to inform on people."

"What do you mean you are *unable* to?" said the head judge in surprise. "I've heard that you are even able to write novels."

"That's right," I said. "Novels are one thing. Writing a novel is one thing, writing a denunciation is something else."

"Come on now!" she said soothingly. "It's much easier to write denunciations. You don't have to make up anything special. Just what you yourself have heard. Such as—who told a joke, where, and how people reacted. Nothing could be simpler."

"It might be simple for you," I said flaring up, "but for me it isn't. I wasn't a stool pigeon in my past life and I won't be in this one either."

All three of the judges' faces turned red simultaneously.

"Dzerzhin Gavrilovich," spurted the senior judge angrily, "why have you brought us such a green comcom? Why didn't you prepare him in advance? Go have a little talk with him and when he's seen reason, he can come before us again."

I could see that Dzerzhin was embarrassed. When we were back outside, he grabbed me by the arm and took me to a corner. "You've gone out of your mind, darling!" he whispered, looking timorously behind him. "Why are you doing this to me? How could you say things like that?"

"Things like what?" I asked.

"You mean you don't even understand what you said back there? You openly refused to cooperate with the organs and you even used the words *stool pigeon*. I can't imagine where you even heard that disgusting term. It's obsolete now. We, of course, have complete freedom within the reasonable limits of a person's needs, but people who use terms like that are not only punished in the rings of hostility but here as well. So, let's go back in there, but no monkey business this time."

"No," I said firmly. "Whether you like it or not, I didn't come here to inform on people."

"Oh Gen!" he muttered. "Are socialist prejudices deeply rooted in you! Is it so hard to repeat that oath? It's only a ritual, that's all. Swear that you'll inform, and then don't do it. Or else you can write false denunciations and give them to me personally. And I'll make sure nothing comes of them."

"That's it!" I said indignantly. "What do you take me for? If your brand of communism can't manage without denunciations, then I have no desire to spend another hour in your Moscowrep. I'm returning to Stockdorf at once."

"Alright, go then," he said, suddenly angry. "I'll order your suitcase returned to you at once and you can be on your way. If you have no interest in seeing how we live. . . . Yes, as a matter of fact, what do you need that for? You're accustomed to making up stories for your novels, so you can make up all the stories about us you want. That won't surprise us. We've had so much mud slung at us that a little more or a little less. . . ." He turned toward the window looking offended and dismayed.

It was unpleasant for me, too. I dislike offending people for no reason. And, besides, if I really thought about it — well, after all, I had dragged myself there, risking my neck, and so what was the sense of turning back right at the threshold without even taking one little look?

"Alright," I said. "To hell with you. I'll give in this time. But it's the last time."

"Good man!" Siromakhin jumped for joy. "I knew you were an intelligent person. As far as the denunciations go, let me tell you a secret: there's nothing to write them on anyway. The paper situation in the Moscowrep is a total" — here he drew the edge of his hand across his throat — "disaster."

PART III

THE ENJOYMENT
OF LIFE

"That was some trick you played on me yesterday," I said, giving Smerchev the once-over. "I thought that communism was like what I saw yesterday, and it's not that way at all."

"That's right. We of course knew that you're a humorist. And so we wanted to show you communism with a little humor too."

Smerchev and I were walking along a broad, palm-lined path. He was not in uniform, but wore a lightweight light-colored suit and sandals. The sun was at its zenith, bright but not blinding, warm but not scorching. Birds of incredible beauty sang from the branches of the palms, their voices truly those of paradise.

Strictly speaking, he and I were not walking but flying, lightly touching the earth then rebounding away. My entire body brimmed with an uncommon lightness, and I mentioned this to Smerchev.

"And have you figured out the reason why?" asked Smerchev with a smile.

"No, why?"

"Our scientists have invented a device that reduces Earth's gravity significantly."

"They've even come up with that?" I asked. "What was their purpose in doing that?"

"No special reason," said Smerchev. "Just to make life more pleasurable."

We were flying along tall, shining buildings. They reminded

me of some New York skyscrapers, but these were much more radiant and airy. They were all connected by transparent walkways in which palms and gloxinia grew.

The laughter of children and lovers was everywhere. Young rosy-cheeked men and young women with inspired faces flew toward us through air, moving as lightly as we were. All the young women wore short tennis skirts and had shapely, suntanned legs. They were all eating ice cream with chunks of candied fruit and casting loving gazes at me, all of them wishing to speak of grand matters with me, and I with them. People whirled in the carousels placed along the pink pathways, soared on swings, and flew through the air in orange boats.

A long, light blue banner billowed in the air, its message reading:

THE ENJOYMENT OF LIFE
IS THE FUNDAMENTAL AND SOLE DUTY
OF EVERY COMMUNITE.

We had already been out walking for a few hours, but the sun still stood at its zenith and was neither blinding nor scorching. I asked Smerchev how that could be, and he regarded me with the kindliest of smiles.

"You really don't know why? It's an artificial sun."

"Artificial?"

"Yes, of course it is. Our entire climate is artificial."

"How did you manage that?"

"Very simple," said Smerchev. "Simple as can be. The whole city is capped by a dome of rock crystal."

"Don't the seasons change?"

"There's no change of season, and no change in the time of day. It's always day, and it's always summer."

"But how can people sleep when it's always light?"

"That's simple too. They pull down the blinds. But people don't do much sleeping here."

I asked why, and Smerchev replied that people didn't sleep

because they didn't want to spare the time. Life was so good that they wanted to enjoy it every minute and every second.

"But when do they work?" I asked.

"They never work," was his answer.

Among the people who passed us were many that I had known in my former life and who had even died in my lifetime. They waved in friendship to me, and I waved back at them, not in the least surprised to encounter them. I knew that I was in paradise, even if it wasn't created by God but by man. I knew that if these people were able to construct an artificial sun and reduce Earth's gravity, there was nothing surprising about their having found a way to resurrect the dead.

By the way, the palm-lined path we were on was also something of a gigantic supermarket, lined with endless counters, stacked with gleaming arrangements of sausage of every sort, cheeses, sides of sturgeon, finely sliced salmon, red caviar, black caviar, pressed caviar, and eggplant caviar. There was every type of fruit and vegetable, the exotic and familiar, oranges, tangerines, artichokes, avocados, bananas, and pineapples.

And, needless to say, there were wines of every variety, cognacs, vodkas, mineral water, juices, sodas, and every beer imaginable in bottles, cans, and kegs, in a word, all the goods we could buy in our Stockdorf supermarket, or perhaps a little less.

But there are usually some people in our supermarket (sometimes on Saturday the line is six people long). Here no one picked up anything, they all just moved past without even a glance at the counters. Only the girls would pause for a moment to grab an ice cream cone or some dates and then with a laugh go flying on their way.

"But why isn't anyone buying anything?" I asked Smerchev, quite shaken by this sight. "Doesn't anyone have any money?"

"Of course no one has any money," answered Smerchev with a mysterious smile.

"Aha," I said, "that I can understand. I didn't have any money when I lived under socialism and it was pretty thin under capitalism too."

My remark amused Smerchev, who began laughing, though soundlessly for some reason. Still laughing, he explained that people didn't have any money because they didn't need any. Here everyone just took as much as he wanted, and everything was absolutely free of charge. But no one took anything because everyone's needs had long ago been entirely satisfied and they had no appetite for all that produce. All they ever wanted to eat was ice cream and dates.

"You mean I can take whatever I want and as much as I want?" I asked with suspicion.

Smerchev replied in the affirmative.

I went over to one of the counters. Uncertain at first, then getting into the swing of it, I began gathering groceries: two liter bottles of the Swedish vodka Absolut, a good length of Cracow kielbasa, a long roll, a few pieces of trout, a package of shrimp, a bunch of bananas, and jars of pâté, caviar, evaporated milk, green peas, asparagus, and a few other odds and ends. Some items I shoved into my pockets, others I held under my arms, and the rest, a pile higher than my head, I carried in my hands. Things started falling, and my pile was becoming smaller and smaller.

I raised my eyes to see if the can of condensed milk was still there and suddenly I caught sight of Rudi sailing through the air in his Jaguar. He waved to me with one hand; the other was around Fräulein Globke.

I wanted to wave back to Rudi, but the gesture I made caused the entire Tower of Babel in my hands to collapse, all the cans and bottles went flying, though without making any crash at all. Taking fright, I immediately began gathering everything up, worried that I'd be arrested immediately or that people would begin holding me up to shame. Citizen, they would say, aren't you ashamed to act like such a barbarian with the property of the people?

"Stop picking things up from the ground!" I heard a familiar and mocking voice say. "It's not hygienic."

I looked up and saw Lyoshka Bukashev, beardless in a white suit. On his arm, cuddling up to him, was Janet in a transparent dress. He was telling her a joke about Lenin-Shmenin, and her laughter was loud and wanton.

"But where's Leo?" I asked her.

"He's over there," she said. I looked and saw Leo on a bench kissing my wife. This I found unpleasant, not very unpleasant, just slightly unpleasant. I hopped up lightly into the air and streamed over to them.

"Aren't you ashamed of yourself," I said to my wife, "to be kissing another man while your husband's still alive! You know that kissing doesn't even give the man any pleasure."

"Poppycock!" said Zilberovich with Simych's voice. "Before, when I lived under socialism, nothing gave me any pleasure, except your novels. Now everything gives me pleasure, except your novels."

"You see!" I said to my wife. "He insults me and doesn't read my novels, but you give him kisses."

Then Smerchev bent close to me and whispered, "Classic Classicovich, there's no reason for you to act like a throwback believer in private property. We don't have any sort of private property here. Here all women belong to everyone, so your wife belongs to our entire society. Alright, pussycat, let's you and me go take a steam bath," he said to my wife and, taking her by the arm, went sailing away with her.

I raced off in pursuit of them but could feel that I was no longer flying but barely able to even run. I was on some sort of ploughed field, my feet splaying on the soil. And they had clearly turned Earth's gravity back on full force.

My wife in his arms, Smerchev was flying high above Earth, and I was no longer even running, but sliding along the mud. Then all of a sudden Father Starsky appeared before me in a long nightshirt, holding a candle.

"There is no God," he said softly. "There is only the Genialissimo, the Genialissimo alone, and no one but the Genialissimo."

"To hell with you and your Genialissimo!" I said, trying to shove him out of the way.

But he wouldn't budge. Bringing his face close to mine, he shook his scraggly beard, winked, and grinned. I could not get around him, and my wife was flying further and further away with Smerchev. In utter despair, I grabbed Starsky by the beard, bit his nose, and woke up with a pillow between my teeth.

AWAKENING

I continued gnawing the pillow for a long time after I'd woken, until I finally came to my senses. Feeling a little more like myself, I began looking around. Everything was dark and still, still and dark. Pitch black.

I rolled over onto my back and began thinking: Good Lord, what does it all really mean? Why is it that whenever I dream of my motherland, something bad always happens that makes me want to flee, and I wake up in a sweat?

I was so upset that I decided to wake up my wife and ask her what she thought the dream could possibly mean. My wife is a great interpreter of dreams and she believes that no dream is without its meaning, that they all bear some message for us which need only be deciphered correctly.

I reached out and groped in the bed beside me, but there was no one there. I began wondering where she could have gone in the middle of the night, but then it all came back to me, not that I believed one bit of it. Nonsense, I said to myself. It's all utter nonsense. Nothing of the sort could happen, and nothing of the sort did. I'm in my own bed in Stockdorf, and there's the window, and there's the light coming through the blinds. In a minute I'll go open the blinds and see my own yard, the three crooked birches by the fence and the rooster who parades around the yard.

I walked to the window, opened the blinds, and saw Revolution

Square and the Karl Marx monument. Actually, it was somewhat difficult to recognize Marx. In the sixty years of my absence, the pigeons had done such a job on his head that it had gone entirely gray.

Directly across the street from Marx, on the small square in front of the Bolshoi Theatre, was the statue of another bearded man, this one in military uniform and holding a pair of gloves, the Genialissimo, of course. Something struck me as odd about the Bolshoi Theatre. At first I couldn't put my finger on what it was exactly, but then it occurred to me: the horses were missing from the front of the building, as if they'd never been there at all.

The sun was already high in the sky. Vehicles of various sizes, enshrouded in smoke and steam, were tearing along Marx Avenue, and the sidewalks streamed with crowds of people dressed in short military clothing. Very few of them were empty-handed. Practically all of them were carrying something in their hands or on their backs or dragging it along behind them.

I felt that I'd gotten a good night's sleep and was well-rested. I was ready to go out for a walk and see how the city had changed in the last sixty years.

I dressed quickly and popped into the bathroom. There was a small sign on the hot-water faucet: "The need for hot water is temporarily not being satisfied." I rinsed my face and hands with cold water and peeped out into the corridor. The old hall attendant was sound asleep, her head on a night table. The book that had fallen from her hand was on the floor. I glanced at the title: *Problems of Love and Sex.* The work had been authored by the Genialissimo. I carefully placed the book on her night table and, trying to step as quietly as possible, walked to the elevator.

There was, however, a large padlock on the elevator. A small cardboard sign had been tied with a piece of string to the elevator shaft. It read: "The need to descend in elevators is temporarily not being satisfied." I found the stairs and used them to satisfy my need for descent. It was obviously not the main staircase, because I did not end up on the street but in a courtyard.

A LONGPANTSER

I was looking forward to a gulp of fresh air, but my nose was assaulted by a smell that sent me reeling. I will not describe it in detail except to say that it was like a latrine which is used as frequently as it is infrequently cleaned.

A long line snaked across the courtyard to a dark green kiosk; it was a line of soldiers of both sexes, mainly the lower ranks, breathing down each other's necks and holding plastic cans, old saucepans, and chamberpots.

There was a poster in a crudely constructed frame on the roof of the kiosk. It depicted a worker, a look of confident optimism on his face, and an enormous pot in his sinewy hand. The text at the bottom of the poster declared:

EVERYONE WHO HANDS IN SECONDARY MATTER
WILL FEAST ON PRIMARY, SERVED ON A PLATTER

"What are they handing out?" I asked a short-legged woman who had just walked away from the kiosk holding a can. Large plastic earrings dangled from her ears.

"They're not handing anything out. People are handing it in," she said, looking me over from head to toe, a bit too closely for my liking.

"And what are they handing in?" I asked.

"What do you mean?" she said, surprised by the question. "They're handing in shit, what else?"

I thought she was joking but, considering the smell to which I was gradually growing accustomed, the image of the worker on the poster, and the general look of the line, I became inclined to think she was serious.

"But why are people handing *that* in?" I asked incautiously.

"What do you mean why?" she cried in a nasty tone of voice. "What are you, soft in the head? He doesn't know why they're handing it in! And, if that's not enough, he's wearing long pants! And they say the young people are out of control. What else should we expect when their elders set this kind of example?"

"Exactly!" A somewhat stoop-shouldered man of around fifty walked over. "I also noticed he wasn't dressed like everyone else."

A crowd started gathering, some who had just finished at the kiosk, others from the end of the line. They all expressed displeasure at my curiosity and long pants, and even seemed on the verge of giving me a good drubbing. The woman voiced the opinion that even though I had a good drubbing coming, it would be a better idea to take me straight to SECO.

"What are you talking about, citizens!" I shouted loudly. "What does SECO have to do with this? If there are things I don't understand about life here, that's not my fault. I've just arrived, and I'm almost like a foreigner."

Someone in the crowd shouted that if I was a foreigner, all the more reason to take me to SECO, but no voice seconded his, and, at the word *foreigner*, the crowd around me began to dissolve. Only the woman with the earrings remained upset and tried to call the crowd back, assuring them I was not a foreigner at all.

"I can speak a little foreign!" she said, addressing the line which had now fallen silent. "Foreigners say 'bitte-dritte,' but this one speaks our language perfect."

While the line considered this point, I did not wait around for things to get worse; I sidled away, then streaked through a connecting courtyard to the street that at one time was called Nikolsky Street but was later renamed October 25th Street. Proud to have recognized this street at once, I raised my eyes to the corner of the nearest building to confirm that pride. What I saw utterly dumbfounded me. The blue and white sign fastened to the wall read: Kartsev Street!

Despite the warm and moving welcome the Communites had shown me the day before, I was still unable to believe that posterity held my merits in such high esteem. I even thought that this was somebody's misplaced idea of a joke and the sign with my name on it was hanging on only one building. But, crossing the street to Red Square, I saw identical signs on all the buildings. I felt simultaneously proud and belligerent. It even occurred to me to return to the secondary-matter kiosk, find that disgusting woman who spoke a little foreign, drag her there, and show her whom her idiotic suspicions had caused her to attack. But, being both lazy and forgiving, I abandoned the idea then and there. Especially since there were new impressions awaiting me.

If I were to describe, in detail, my feelings on what I saw that first day in Moscow, I would have to make too-frequent use of adjectives like surprised, astounded, struck, stunned, dumbfounded, and so forth. And indeed, just imagine coming out onto Red Square and seeing no Saint Basil's Cathedral, no Lenin's tomb, not even the monument to Minin and Pozharsky. All that was there was GUM, the Historical Museum, the Place of Execution, a statue of the Genialissimo, and the Gate of the Savior. The star on the gate was not ruby-red, but made of tin or plastic. And the clock on the tower read eleven-thirty, though in fact it was only quarter of eight. Peering more intently at the clock, I could see it wasn't working.

I stopped a comcom who was pushing a wheelbarrow containing a sack of sawdust and asked what had happened to everything that used to be there. Surprised by my question, he looked me over from head to toe and spent a long moment focusing on my pants. Then he asked which ring I was from. To avoid a direct answer, I said I was Latvian.

"I could tell," said the comcom. "The accent's a dead giveaway."

To my surprise, he proved well informed and willing to talk

(qualities I was rarely to observe among Communites). With a glance in both directions, he explained that all the things I was asking about had been sold to the Americans, either by the Corruptionists or the Reformists.

"What?" I cried. "Those enemies of the people even sold Lenin's tomb?"

"Keep it down!" he said, frightened. But before slipping away, he whispered to me that not only had they sold the tomb, but its contents as well, to some oil magnate who went around the world buying up mummies. Beside Vladimir Ilyich Lenin, his collection included Mao Tse-tung, Georgi Dimitrov, and four Pharoahs.

I was about to ask him the magnate's name when he suddenly took fright, grabbed the handles of his wheelbarrow, and began pushing it quickly toward the building that had formerly housed the Moscow Hotel. Shrugging my shoulders, I set off in the same direction. I intended to walk over to the Bolshoi Theatre, in front of which I had noticed an interesting statue of the Genialissimo when I'd been looking out of my hotel window.

Though it was quarter to nine and the crowds of blue- and white-collar workers had for the most part subsided there were still quite a few people on Marx Avenue (by the way, its name hadn't changed). As in my dream, a great many of them looked like people I had once known, some of them so much so that I almost went running to them with open arms. But then I'd get a grip on myself and remember that the only place I could find the people I'd known was (with luck) the cemetery.

As I'd noticed from the hotel window, everyone here was carrying something. Some had pots in their hands, others were holding net shopping bags or purses. One comcom was lugging a television set from which the screen was missing, another was bent beneath a sack of coal, and a woman walked along balancing on her head a striped and yellow-spotted mattress that was leaking straw. Overtaking the pedestrians, a bunch of school-aged children ran by. They had knapsacks on their backs and they were holding little brooms, which they whisked rapidly back and forth raising such clouds of dust you couldn't breathe.

Unable to restrain myself, I grabbed one of the school kids by the scruff of the neck.

"Hey, you little brat," I said, "why are you running around with a broom and kicking up all that dust?"

"And what am I supposed to do?" he cried plaintively, trying to struggle free of me. "I'm rushing to get to the instcominst. Classes start in ten minutes."

"Alright then, run along to school," I said. "But there's no need to kick up all that dust. Let the janitors take care of the dust."

"Who?" said the little boy in surprise. "What kind of janitors?"

I could see that I was making a fool of myself again.

"Regular janitors," I muttered, but let the boy go. I walked over to Sverdlov Square, which was now called Square of the Genialissimo's Four Exploits. The plastic sculpture of the man who had performed the four exploits towered over the square. The monument was at least ten feet tall, not counting the base. The Genialissimo was depicted in gleaming boots and an army greatcoat that the sculptor had left open, most likely so the viewer could behold the innumerable medals adorning the statue's broad chest. Seeming to slap his gloves against his right boot top, the Genialissimo looked out with a kindly smile onto the avenue, the traffic puffing clouds of steam, and at the image of Karl Marx frozen on the other side of the street. I walked around the statue, made an attempt at counting the medals on his chest, and had reached 140 when I lost track, gave up on the whole thing, and began walking down a street that in my time had been called Pushkin Street. Now it was known as Street of the Genialissimo's Preliminary Plans.

During this first stroll of mine, I had noticed that along with the avenues, streets, lanes, and alleys that had retained their names, there were also a great many whose names reflected the Communites' achievements and a great many devoted to one aspect or another of the Genialissimo's activities. For that reason, I was not very surprised to discover that Pushkin Square had been renamed the Square of the Genialissimo's Literary Gifts. And the monument on the square was not to Pushkin, of course, but to the Genialissimo. Still, Pushkin was there, too.

I would say that the plastic sculpture of the Genialissimo here was on a par with the one in front of the Bolshoi Theatre, but in this one he was wearing a summer uniform and not holding gloves. In his left hand he held a plastic book entitled *Selected Works*. The author's right hand rested upon the curly head of the young Pushkin, who was entirely lilliputian in stature; but the other figures composing a group portrait were even more diminutive. Of the other representatives of preliminary literature, I could make out Gogol, Lermontov, Griboedov, Tolstoy, Dostoyevski, and all the others from the later periods. I am pleased to report that I found myself in that group as well. I was standing behind the Genialissimo, holding onto the top of his left boot with one hand. Not finding Karnavalov among the lilliputians, I was once again presented with evidence that he was entirely unknown in the twenty-first century. I did discover one bearded man the size of a field mouse in that group of preliminary writers, but he was clearly not Karnavalov. It was probably Professor Sinyavsky.

Having circled the monument, I found myself once again at sock level with the Genialissimo. On the pedestal I read an inscription I knew from long ago: "I devoted my lyre to my nation."

Just then a large, red steam-bus pulled to a stop on the square and disgorged a horde of boys and girls, led by a woman with the epaulettes of a lieutenant. The children immediately began shouting and shoving, but the woman (who was clearly their teacher) took a few steps to one side, stretched out her right hand, and issued a command: "Form up by twos!"

Well-disciplined, the children formed up in even rows, stood straight at the command "Attention!" and relaxed at the command "At ease."

"And so, children," said the teacher in the tone of a tour guide, "what you see in front of you is a monument to our beloved leader, teacher, the father of all children, and the friend of all progressive humanity, the Genialissimo. The monument was executed out of high-quality plastic by the collective of the Red Banner Detachment of National Communist Sculptors, and was approved by the Editorial Commission and the Supreme Pentagon. Ivanov, what is the total number of monuments to the Genialissimo in Moscow?"

"One hundred eighty-four!" cried out Ivanov.

"Correct! One hundred eighty-four. And the one hundred eighty-fifth is now being erected on the Lenin Hills of the Genialissimo. All the existing monuments to our beloved leader reflect one aspect or another of his genius. One monument is to him as a revolutionary of genius, another as a genius of theoretical scientific communism, a third as a genius in its practice, and so forth. This monument was erected to his genius for literature. Semenov, how many volumes are there in the Genialissimo's collected works?"

"Six hundred sixteen," she was quick to reply.

"That's incorrect. Two new volumes came out yesterday. Komkov, stop fidgeting. And so, children, this monument is a sculptural group, the central figure being the Genialissimo. The secondary figures are his literary predecessors, the representatives of preliminary literature. You may be interested to know that each figure of each preliminary author has been sculpted in strict accordance with his literary stature relative to that of the Genialissimo."

Upon those words, I ran back behind the Genialissimo again, and again found the pitiful little figure that was me. My heart sank. The relationship between my stature and the Genialissimo's was, to be honest, not terribly flattering.

I continued to listen to the teacher and gleaned a good deal of useful information. I learned that the total size of all the preliminary writers was equal to the size of the Genialissimo alone. Moreover, the Genialissimo was like a mighty tree, growing up out of shoots that had had their day. As a tree drinks sap, so had the Genialissimo imbibed and transformed all that was best about preliminary literature, thereby obliterating any need for the latter.

"In fact," said the teacher, "just take the words that are inscribed on the base of the monument: 'I devoted my lyre to my nation.' Which of the preliminary writers would have been able to say anything so simple, so modest, and of such genius?"

"Pushkin could have," I blurted out to my own surprise.

One of the children started giggling, but fell silent at once. The teacher cast me an unfriendly glance, then returned to her pupils.

"Children, quick, back to the bus! Now we're going to see the monument to the Genialissimo's scientific discoveries."

The children darted back into the bus like bees into a hive.

Before plunging in after them, the teacher turned and regarded me once again.

"My advice to you, longpantser," she said, enunciating her words very clearly, "is to watch your tongue." And then, with a wiggle of her backside, which protruded from her short skirt, she disappeared into the steam bus.

I looked down at my pants, once again failing to understand what people here disliked about them. There was nothing special about them, they were quite a decent pair of pants. I didn't object if they wanted to go around in short pants, so why couldn't they leave me in peace?

VEGETARIAN
PORK

I started feeling hungry and began looking around for somewhere to get a bite to eat. On the other side of the street I noticed an establishment the door to which kept opening and shutting with all the people entering and leaving it. That building had once been a beer house and then later a dairy bar. There appeared to be something else of the sort there now.

High up on the roof of the building was a picture of the now familiar worker, a spoon in one sinewy hand, a fork in the other. There was even something at the end of the fork's prongs, but I couldn't make out exactly what it was. The worker had a friendly smile, and beneath the picture the following was written:

EVERYONE WHO HANDS IN SECONDARY MATTER,
WILL DINE ON PRIMARY, SERVED ON A PLATTER

The sign by the entrance read: COMFOODEST GOURMAND. I remembered Smerchev telling me that the word *comfoodest* meant communist food establishment.

As I ran across the street, an enormous steam truck pulling a trailer almost ran me over. Slamming on his brakes, the driver stopped his fire-breathing machine and heaped me with such choice abuse that it was easy for me to recognize Kuzya, my friend from the baths. Apparently, he had not intended to limit himself to swearing, for he was already racing at me and brandishing a crank handle.

183

"Kuzya!" I cried out in alarm. "Don't you recognize me?"

"Oh, so it's you, Pop." Kuzya lowered his hand, even seeming disappointed that his windup had been for naught. "What are you doing jaywalking like a fool? You better keep your eyes open, Dad, or you'll either get run over or get your head busted. You guys have it easier under capitalism. All you got on the streets there is donkeys and camels, but we've got technology here, as you can see for yourself."

He asked me how I was doing, if I needed any help, and reminded me yet again that if I needed a boiler, a cylinder, or anything like that, I shouldn't feel shy about going right to him for it. Then he pulled away, and this time I made it safely across the avenue to the front of the comfoodest.

The line wasn't long—sixty, tops. An elderly sergeant wearing a holey army shirt and a red armband stood by the entrance, punching holes in the gray slips of paper people held out to him.

While standing in line, I read an announcement on the wall which said that general nutritional needs would only be satisfied upon presentation of proof that secondary matter had been handed in.

Beside this notice were posted the "Rules of Behavior in Establishments of Communist Nutrition." They pointed out that thanks to the constant efforts of the KPGB and the Genialissimo's personal concern that Communites receive regular, high-quality nutrition, a great many remarkable successes had been achieved in this area. Food was becoming better all the time, its quality and nutritive value were constantly on the rise. As a result of rational nutrition, the Communites had scored great victories in the battle against obesity.

The following were listed as forbidden in a comfoodest:

1. Ingesting food while wearing outerwear
2. Playing musical instruments
3. Placing feet on the tables and chairs

4. Throwing uneaten food on the tables, chairs, or floor
5. Picking teeth with a fork
6. Pouring liquid nourishment on others
7. It is categorically forbidden to settle any differences which may arise using the remains of food, pans, dishes, spoons, forks, or other state property

To be fair, it must be said that the line moved quite rapidly. One after another, the people in line would hold out their slips of paper to be punched by the sergeant before they entered the establishment.

When my turn came, I rummaged in my pocket, but found nothing there except for a chance scrap of the newspaper *Zuddeutsche Zeitung* from sixty years back. I folded the scrap in two and held it out to the sergeant, who punched it without looking. Pleased to see that my old socialist and capitalist tricks were still working, I walked in.

I had the feeling that the primary matter here smelled more or less the same as secondary matter. On the wall facing the entrance, there was a large portrait of the Genialissimo and a saying of his: "We do not live to eat, we eat to live."

The comfoodest resembled a socialist self-service cafeteria— high tables with no chairs, the floor covered with sawdust. A long counter with dishes set out on it ran along the left side behind a partition made of light plastic tubing. The sight of the food alone was enough to make you want to run outside for fresh air. But in the first place, I was famished, and in the second, I had traveled there to study everything in detail and that included the food system.

I got in the line for the counter and, advancing along with everyone else, I soon reached the menu, which was posted on the wall and which I read with great curiosity. It consisted of four dishes listed in the following order:

1. Nutritional "Goose" cabbage soup with rice broth
2. Vitamin-enriched "Progress" vegetarian pork with a garnish of stewed cabbage

3. "Guards" boiled oat kissel
4. "Freshness" natural water

I beg the reader's pardon for quoting in such detail all the rules, lists, and menus I read, but I think they are necessary for one to form a more or less complete picture of the society I was in.

Young female comcoms in not-overly-clean uniforms were serving the customers quickly. Like everyone else, I received a plastic tray with a set of all the dishes the menu had listed. Metal chains attached two plates, two cups, and a spoon (all of which were also made of plastic) to the tray. There were two other chains (maybe for the fork and knife) but nothing was attached to them.

Taking a sniff of the food I'd been given, I instinctively frowned and decided that in some cases hunger can be satisfied through the nasal passages alone. However, I reiterate, I was moved not only by hunger but by an explorer's curiosity.

I found a table where there was only one woman taking slow swallows of her oat kissel. I asked her permission to stand beside her, and when she mumbled something I couldn't catch, I recognized her as the one who spoke a little foreign. And, judging by her hostile gaze, she had recognized me as well.

Tasting the cabbage soup, I guessed at once that its proud name referred not to the long-necked bird but to the little-known goosefoot plant, which I had had occasion to eat before when the collective farm was in full flower. Because I was starving, I was able to force down a couple of spoonfuls, but, to tell the truth, the "Progress" vegetarian pork, apparently made of pressed rutabagas, wouldn't go down. What I mean is that at first it did go down a little, but then it came rushing back up, so fast that I barely made it to the natfunctbur, where my fickle digestive system expelled it in one go.

THE PALACE
OF LOVE

On my way out of the natfunctbur, I came close to colliding with the woman who spoke a little foreign. Apparently, she had been waiting for me. As soon as she caught sight of me, she screeched maliciously and loud enough for all to hear: "So, you don't like our food, eh?"

I went outside without answering her. She dashed out after me. I started down what used to be Gorky Street but was now called Avenue of the First Volume of the Genialissimo's Collected Works. (Later I was to learn that communist Moscow had twenty-six avenues named after volumes penned by this author.)

The woman was dogging my heels.

"You're a fine one!" she muttered a few steps behind me. "You wear long pants, you don't want to turn in your shit, and you're squeamish about eating our food."

"Listen, you," I said, turning to face her. "For God's sake, will you leave me alone, I'm feeling sick enough as it is."

Apparently that was the last straw for her.

"Oho-ho-ho!" she cried, in an attempt to attract the attention of other people on the sidewalk. "He wears long pants, won't turn in his shit, he's squeamish about our food, and on top of that he's talking about some kind of god! And he's sick to his stomach! Our food makes him sick!"

"You can go stick it up your ass!" I said, unable to restrain myself. I crossed to the other side of the street.

Please forgive this extremely crude expression. In my previous life I never said anything like this to ladies. But this harpy had infuriated me.

I walked down First Volume Avenue not a little out of sorts. Somehow I didn't feel at ease in this communist kingdom. Of course, I would only be there for a month, but I was afraid that I wouldn't be able to survive even that length of time on vegetarian pork.

No, it was not that I wanted any advantages whatsoever. I wanted to live the same life everyone else did here. And not to interfere in anything. My job was to register the facts objectively and impartially, and to do this, I was prepared to undergo the most unexpected and risky of experiences. By and large, I have never been especially fastidious about food, but I simply could not stomach vegetarian pork and "Goose" cabbage soup.

Perhaps my worldview was to blame for it all. It was always backward, even when I lived under socialism. And later on when I ended up living under capitalism and was subjected to the daily pernicious and decadent influence of bourgeois propaganda and food, this may have not only affected my cast of mind but the working of my stomach. It had gone soft. This may not be a very scientific explanation but, to be blunt, I was not in the best of moods.

In that frame of mind I continued down the other side of the avenue where, under socialism, the Eliseevsky store had been located. Despite my gloom, I looked around, and did make a few observations and mental notes. For example, I was surprised that Nemirovich-Danchenko Street had not been renamed, even though that figure from antiquity was, as we know, one of the forefathers of socialist realism, which had been decisively condemned by the Party and replaced by communist realism.

But there was an even greater surprise in store for me on what had once been Soviet Square. The old familiar statue of Yuri Dolgoruki on horseback was no longer there. I mean, the horse was still there but Yuri Dolgoruki was no longer mounted on it. The Genialissimo had taken his place, a book of his in one hand, a sword in the other. And the square's name had been changed to the Square of the Genialissimo's Scientific Discoveries.

To tell the truth, the relationship of this monument to scientific discoveries was not at all clear to me. Alright, the book made sense, but what were the horse and the sword doing there?

I then switched my attention to the building that had formerly housed the Aragva restaurant. Needless to say, there was no Aragva there now, but high on the front of the building were three-foot-tall letters that read:

THE PALACE OF LOVE

I honestly did not understand the meaning of those words at once. But, approaching the building, I saw a sign by the massive doors which literally read as follows:

THE N.K. KRUPSKAYA STATE EXPERIMENTAL
ORDER-OF-LENIN BROTHEL

Oho! I said to myself. Now communism's starting to make sense! My mood took a definite upswing.

I thought that this establishment must only be open in the evening but, reading further, I learned that sexual services were provided to the populace from 830 to 1730, with a one-hour lunch break from 1300 to 1400. I glanced at my watch. It was exactly 9:42 A.M. Not the hour best suited for that sort of thing but, on the other hand, why not?

On the second floor there was a poster of a worker with a raised fist. The inscription was almost familiar by then:

HAND IN SECONDARY MATTER FIRST
THEN GO QUENCH THAT PRIMAL THIRST

Beneath the poster was a list of rules for the Krupstatexordlenbroth (this strange institution's name in abbreviated form). It said that sexual services were provided both for collectives—from factories, institutions, and social organizations—and for individuals as well.

I automatically recalled the truck driver Kuzya and his friend, who had tried to involve me in a disgraceful orgy at the wash station. The savages! How could they engage in such an intimate act in a group when there existed completely legal means for satisfying one's needs on an individual basis?

Those were my thoughts as my eyes continued to slide along the rules, from which I learned that sexual services were provided solely upon the presentation of proof that one had turned in secondary matter and that the following were forbidden in this establishment:

1. To bring anyone else along to be serviced on the side
2. To be serviced in one's outerwear
3. To be serviced in the hallways, on or under the staircases, in the natfunctbur, or any other place except those so designated
4. To use home-made contraceptive devices or any instruments of sadism or masochism
5. To play musical instruments
6. To damage communist property
7. It is categorically forbidden to settle any conflicts which may arise with sexual equipment

Here too, as in the comfoodest, there was an old man with an armband and a ticket puncher. I held out the same scrap of newspaper, but the other end out this time. Like the guard at the comfoodest, he punched it without so much as a glance.

The interior of this establishment resembled a polyclinic. There was a wide corridor with a linoleum floor and walls painted a dark green. Spaced evenly along both sides of the corridor were beige office doors and, to the left of the entrance, right past a dilapidated staircase, was a wooden partition with a small glass window and a sign: REGISTRATION. Coming my way carrying an armful of files was a young woman in a white robe that barely covered her means of production.

"Glorgen!" she said to me.

"Glorgen," I said and tried to grab hold of some part of her. But she dodged me nimbly, gave me a look of surprise and displeasure, and then began climbing the stairs, which afforded me a view of her better side.

"You don't want to, you don't have to," I said and walked over to the registration window. There I saw an elderly woman wearing eyeglasses with cardboard frames. She was knitting. I felt a bit awkward but, overcoming my embarrassment, I said I wanted to avail myself of the establishment's services.

Without saying a word, she pushed a scrap of paper my way. It was a form, of course, but a rather modest one. I filled in the blanks with my last name, startism name, and patronymic. To avoid unwarranted attention, I gave my age as sixty. Naturally, I wrote "none" in the space marked "venereal diseases."

I handed the form back to the old woman. She impaled it on a long rusty spindle, set her knitting aside, came out from behind the partition, and, still without a word, began walking down the corridor, her keys jingling. She opened a door marked "No. 6," let me in, and then left, saying nothing.

I closed the door and looked around. It was a small room with a single, uncurtained window. In one corner there was a narrow trundle bed covered with an oilcoth, with a plastic pail beside it. There were no pillows or bed coverings to be seen. A framed portrait of the Genialissimo hung at the head of the bed. His hairy chest was slightly exposed and this portrait too was accompanied by one of the Genialissimo's sayings:

LOVE IS A STORMY SEA!

In addition to the Genialissimo's portrait, the walls were covered with a variety of posters. There was a text of some sort in a wooden frame by the door. It proved to be the communist duties of the Krupstatexordlenbroth labor collective.

It stated that, in honor of the sixty-seventh KPGB Party Con-

191

gress, the labor collective was making unusual efforts and assuming the following obligations:

1. To raise labor discipline and the cultural level in satisfying the client's needs
2. Every twenty-fours to increase the usage of each cot space by no less than thirteen percent
3. To increase the collection of genetic material by six percent
4. To economize on materials
5. To study and take notes on the Genialissimo's book *The Sexual Revolution and Communism*; to pass an examination on it with no less than a B grade
6. To publish a wall newspaper regularly
7. To give all girls medals — "Ready to work and defend the Moscowrep"
8. To display great vigilance and inform the organs of SECO of any suspicious clients in a timely fashion

Since no one was rushing to serve me, I decided to have a look at the posters.

The posters depicted scenes from the daily life of the establishment's employees. A meeting of the director of the Krupstatexordlenbroth, Venera Mikhailovna Malofeev, twice awarded the Hero of Communist Labor, an Honored Worker in Sexual Culture, and a member of the Supreme Pentagon, with voters and workers from Ballbearing Plant No. 1. The Krupstatexordlenbroth collective taking part in the beet harvest, and another of them marching in the May Day Parade. Korennaya, a Class-Two sex instructor, reading a lecture entitled "The Genialissimo — our favorite man."

Having looked at all the posters, I sat down at the edge of the cot and began waiting. No one came. I was just about to go find out what the matter was when the door opened and the woman from registration peeped into the room.

"Are you finished?" she asked, regarding me over the top of her glasses.

"Finished with what?" I asked.

"What do you mean what?" she said in a severe tone. "Finished with what you came here for."

She slammed the door and walked away without waiting for me to answer.

I caught up to her in the hallway.

"Are you making fun of me?" I said, grabbing her by the elbow. "How could I be finished if nobody's come to the room yet?"

She gave me what I took to be a look of some surprise.

"And who were you expecting?"

Now it was my turn to be surprised.

"I was expecting one of your service people."

She seemed not to have understood me again. She peered intently at me for a long moment as if I were a madman, then said: "Comcom customer, are you from outer space or something? You mean to say you don't know this establishment satisfies customers' needs on a self-service basis?"

"That's him! That's him!" I heard a wild howl and saw the woman who spoke a little foreign come bursting through the front door.

Two policemen loomed behind her.

"That's him! That's him!" she shouted. "The spy! A real spy! He wears long pants, won't turn in his shit, he's squeamish about our food, and he speaks our language just like us."

"Alright, alright, my good woman," said the larger of the two policemen, whose narrow brow made him resemble a pithecanthropus. "We'll get this straightened out. Do you have a consumcard?" he said, addressing me.

"I do," I said and handed him the scrap of the *Zuddeutsche Zeitung* that had been punched at both ends. It was, of course, foolish and naive to hope that this trick would work again, but I often act on impulse, and it usually doesn't fail me.

This time it did.

The pithecanthropus turned the scrap of newspaper back and forth, held it to his eyes, then held it away. Extreme bewilderment on his face, he handed the piece of paper to the other policeman, who was also a big guy, but somehow frailer. He, too, examined the piece of paper and for some reason even blew on it.

"And what language is this written in?" he asked politely.

Assuming a look of surprise, I said that in my opinion any fool could see that it was entirely in Chinese.

"And you understand Chinese?" he asked, with what I took to be respect.

"Yes, of course, I do. Who doesn't?"

"We'll have to take you in," said the big one.

"In where?" I asked.

"You know, Intsec."

Guessing that Intsec stood for Internal Security, I offered no resistance.

The local Intsec station was in the other wing of that same building. The duty officer at the wooden counter wore three stars on his epaulettes. In the far corner of the room, four policemen of lower rank were playing dominoes.

"So, Comcom Duty Officer," said pithecanthropus, "we've caught us a Chinaman."

"What kind of a Chinaman?" said the duty officer with a look of surprise.

"An ordinary Chinaman," said pithecanthropus. "He wears long pants, won't hand in his shit, speaks our language, but understands Chinese. Here, look at this." He handed the duty officer the scrap of newspaper.

The duty officer spent a long time examining that strange scrap of paper and began turning it one way, then another; tensed, his lips moving, he even held the paper up to the light, apparently in an effort to discover watermarks.

"And why is 1982 written here?" he said. "Is this an old newspaper?"

"It is," I said. "It's an old one, from a museum."

"Alright then," said the duty officer, opening a thick notebook marked *Registry for Violators of the Compeace*. Then he picked up a wooden pen (the last time I'd seen one like that was seventy-five years ago in Beskudnikovo), which he dipped in a glass inkwell. "Last name?"

"Kartsev," I said.

"Odd," said the duty officer. "A Chinese last name, but it sounds Russian. And are you here for purposes of espionage or for no reason in particular?"

To tell the truth, I got a little cold feet at this point. Once they start with an espionage case, there's no getting out of it.

"Alright, guys," I said, "enough fooling around. I'm not Chinese. I was just kidding."

"Kidding?" repeated the duty officer, exchanging glances with the pithecanthropus. "What does that mean—kidding? Does that mean you're not Chinese?"

"Of course I'm not Chinese. Haven't you ever seen any Chinese? They have dark, narrow eyes and mine are round and blue."

"Oh, so then you're not Chinese!" cried the duty officer in a fury. "If you're not Chinese, then we'll have a different kind of little talk with you. Timchuk, give this guy a beating, communist style!"

Timchuk had a fist like a dumbbell. I seemed to have gone blind with rage and not only from the force of the blow. Spitting blood, seeing nothing, I raced at Timchuk and, had I gotten my hands on him, would certainly have made mincemeat of his entire face. But the domino players intervened at that point. Working together, they spun me around, twisted my arms behind my back, and threw me to the floor.

"You scum!" I cried. "What are you doing this for!"

They pressed my nose against the rough, stinking floor. I tried to kick myself free of them, cursing a blue streak as they twisted my joints.

"You bastards!" I shouted. "You bandits! And you're supposed to be communists!"

"Comcom Duty Officer," said a voice I recognized as Timchuk's, "you hear that, he's shouting insults about communists."

I was about to object that I wasn't against all communists, just bad communists; I was pro good communists. But they twisted my arms even harder, and through the sound of my own howl I could hear scissors clicking.

"Lift him up now," said the duty officer.

Beaten and bedraggled, I was in front of him again. Blood streamed from my broken nose and split lips onto my chin from where it splattered onto my shirt. The wonderful pair of pants I'd bought at the Kaufhof before my departure now looked like a pitiful pair of shorts raggedly torn off above the knees.

"Startism name and patronymic?" asked the duty officer.

196

"Up yours, you bastard!" I said, and spat blood in his face.

They say that at the moment of death, you see your whole life go past, like a movie. While Timchuk was winding up, I saw something of a movie too. But an unusual movie. I could see all the frames at the same time. I could see myself as a tomato-like misshapen infant being shown to its mother for the first time and at the same time I could see myself in kindergarten, on the presidium of the Soviet Writers' Union, in a Munich beer garden, and I could even see the coffin in which I was carried to my grave, except that I couldn't make out who the pallbearers were.

"Stop! Stop!" I heard a voice ring out and, coming back to my senses, I saw Iskrina Romanovna, who was literally hanging on Timchuk's raised fist.

"Stop!" she repeated. "Don't you dare hit him!"

The duty officer may have realized that he had committed an error of some sort but, still not wishing to admit it, asked Iskrina Romanovna what kind of bigshot I was that I couldn't be beaten.

"You mean you don't know who he is?" said Iskrina, maintaining her indignation. "This man is. . . ." She leaned close to the duty officer and whispered in his ear.

The situation turned right around. The duty officer dashed out from behind the counter and, almost falling at my feet, asked me to have mercy on him and his children, which he may or may not have had. Timchuk was beside him, trembling with fear, suddenly shabby and small.

Needless to say, my pant legs were returned to me with a bow, and a nurse, appearing out of nowhere, administered first aid, bandaging my nose and lips with insulating tape that smelled like tar.

"Let's go!" said Iskrina Romanovna, offering me her hand. The duty officer continued to bustle and cringe and beg for mercy.

"Alright, let's get going!" insisted Iskrina Romanovna.

"One second," I said, and, freeing my hand from hers, I smashed the duty officer right in the face with my elbow, causing blood to spurt in several directions from his nose.

"There," I said, "there's one socialist-style for you. And for you, you son of a bitch," I said, turning to Timchuk, "here's one Chinese-style."

I made a fist and punched him in the face, but it was I who howled like a banshee—Timchuk's face was made of brick.

THE SMELL OF
HER MOTHER

"Alright now, you tell me," said Iskrina Romanovna in a severe tone of voice when we were back in the hotel, "how did you end up in Intsec? Why were you in there?"

It was a terribly awkward moment. Touching my fractured nose with one finger, I said that I had just wanted to know about everything, to see with my own eyes how ordinary Communites lived.

"But why did the hallway attendant let you out?"

"She didn't let me out. She was asleep and I just tiptoed by her."

"You see that, she was asleep!" said Iskrina indignantly. "That's what relaxing vigilance leads to! No, there's no place for people like that in the Moscowrep."

"It's not her fault!" I cried, afraid of getting the hallway attendant into serious trouble. "She might have just gotten tired during the night and dozed off. And I was very quiet. I even took off my shoes so she wouldn't hear me." I had, of course, made up the part about taking off my shoes.

"Alright then, tell me the rest." Iskrina sat down in an armchair, regarding me with the severity of a judge.

I told her everything that had happened. About the line in the courtyard and the scene with the woman who spoke a little foreign. About the monument to the Genialissimo and the comfoodest.

"And what were you doing in the Palace of Love?"

I was utterly embarrassed.

"I see you have to know everything," I said. "But that's just it. I wasn't doing anything there. Because there was nobody in there with me. Even when I was a boy, I wasn't keen about that kind of self-service. And, at my age, the very idea is disgusting."

"No one was forcing you," she said curtly. "And if only because of the welcome you were given, you should have realized that you could have counted on something better. The places like the one you visited are designated for Communites with general needs. But, by decision of the Supreme Pentagon, your needs have been designated as high-level."

"Thank you," I said quite coldly. "But, if you care to know, I am against inequalities. And since I'm here, I want to be like everyone else, I don't want any privileges."

"Oh, how backward you are!" she exclaimed heatedly. "What does that mean—to be like everyone else? And to what inequalities are you referring? We are all equal here. Every Communite is born with general needs. But if he develops and improves himself, fulfills his production assignments, maintains discipline, broadens his horizon, then of course his needs also increase, and we take that into account. As far as I can see, you have no understanding at all of our life, and it's better that you don't go out alone. Especially since you have to get ready for your jubilee."

"Why do you keep pestering me about that jubilee!" I said angrily. "I don't want any jubilee. You're well aware that I'm not a hundred years old, but quite a lot less."

"It's true, you do look much younger," she agreed. "But all the same you're a hundred years old now. The Supreme Pentagon's ukase on the nationwide celebration of your jubilee will be made public tomorrow. It will be an event of immense political significance. And here you are acting recklessly. For that reason, the Creative Pentagon has assigned me to move in with you and give you an intensive course in personal preparation."

I gave her a look of suspicion.

"I don't understand," I said. "What do you mean you've been

assigned to move in with me? Are you intending to live in the same room with me?"

"That's right," she said. "In any case, until you get your bearings. There's plenty of room for two here."

"There's enough room, of course. Alright, order a folding bed brought up."

"What for?" she asked in surprise. "The bed's wide enough. You don't snore, do you?"

"I don't know," I said uncertainly. "I usually don't, but. . . . But listen," I said in excitement. "I still don't understand. You may consider me a hundred-year-old wreck, but I can't sleep in the same bed with a woman and just lie there like a log. There's a good chance I might experience a certain . . . how to say it . . . stimulation and . . . and then I simply could not vouch for myself."

Here, for the first time since I had known her, Iskrina laughed and said that I was not only backward but just plain foolish. Naturally, when going to bed with me, she had no intention of subjecting me to any tests that would exceed my powers. On the contrary, the Creative Pentagon had recommended that she satisfy any of my high-level needs as they might arise.

"And while we're on the subject," she said matter of factly, "you will probably require some instruction in this area as well. I suspect that your ideas of sex are just as barbaric as the rest of your ideas."

"Could be," I answered, confused and embarrassed. "I do have fairly wild ideas. And how about you, can you sleep with just anyone and get pleasure from it?"

My question seemed to have insulted and jarred her a bit.

"I don't sleep with just anyone," she said, "but only by the decision of our leadership. And this does give me pleasure, as does all socially useful labor."

To be honest, the whole thing had me very worked up. I began pacing the room and thinking what attitude to take. I never declined socially useful labor of this sort either, but after all there is still such a thing as marital fidelity. Not that I have never strayed, I had given in to weakness with Stepanida after all, but still I try not to cheat on my wife unless it's an absolute necessity. And I would attempt to make this clear to Iskrina.

"My dear Iskrina Romanovna . . ." I began.

"You can just call me Iskra," she interrupted with a smile. "Or even pussycat, if you like."

Needless to say, I immediately recalled that idiotic dream in which Smerchev had been calling my wife pussycat.

"And so," I asked, "does everyone call everyone pussycat here?"

"Not everyone. Just call me Iskra then."

Continuing to pace the room, I now began to look on her with new eyes. She was concave and convex in all the right places, and her knees were nice and round and suntanned. Of course, as a husband who tries to be unfailingly faithful, I should not have noticed such things, but, as a law-abiding person, I could not help but obey an organ of such importance as the Creative Pentagon.

"Alright then, my little Pusskrina," I said timidly, "if those are the duties placed on us, let's discharge them at once."

"Fine," she agreed, and moving from her chair to the edge of the bed, she unbuttoned her army shirt and revealed a plastic medallion in the shape of a star with rounded points.

To tell the truth, I suddenly felt a touch of fear. I was afraid that I would prove unable to justify the Pentagon's hopes. Socialist and capitalist prejudices were so deeply rooted in me that I needed to warm up to this sort of thing. Drink a little something. Recite a little Pushkin or Esenin, and, to get things going, a few sighs, hints, and touches were also required.

"Alright," I said, "we'll get right to it. But first I should take a shave, I'm all bristly."

I withdrew my Diplomat briefcase from under the bed, tossed it on the night table and, my back to Iskrina, I began rummaging through the bag. My razor was somewhere at the very bottom. Hurrying, nervous, I began tossing things right onto the floor — underpants, T-shirts, socks . . .

"What's that thing?" asked Iskra.

"What thing?"

"The thing you're holding in your hand."

"This?" I was holding a bar of Nivea soap. "It's just soap," I said. "Bathroom soap."

"It is?" she said, seeming confused. "Then why is it so hard? Is it frozen?"

"Why should it be frozen? Soap is usually hard."

"That's interesting," she said, even more confused. "May I take a little smell of it?"

"Of course."

I tossed her the soap across the bed. She caught it deftly and, bringing it close to her face, suddenly exclaimed, "Ah!"

"What's wrong?" I asked, worried.

Transfixed, she held the soap to her face, smelling it with her eyes closed.

"Iskra!" I cried in alarm. "Iskrina! Iskrina Romanovna, what's happened to you?"

Slowly she opened her eyes and peered at me intently for a moment as if not quite sure who I might be.

"That's how my mother used to smell!" she said softly and with a bashful smile.

PART IV

FAME

All of Moscowrep's mass media spoke only of me. Or rather, of me and the Genialissimo. They always began with him. First thing in the morning, all of Moscowrep's twelve television channels broadcast a bulletin on the state of his health, which always exceeded the bounds of praise. His pulse and blood pressure were always just a bit better than they needed to be. His lungs, liver, and kidneys functioned superbly, and the results of his urine and blood analysis were excellent. The newspapers and television never said a word about the Genialissimo's age, and the people I asked (Iskra, Smerchev, Siromakhin) only shrugged their shoulders and said that this age had never been of any interest to them, that the number of years the Genialissimo had already lived were of no importance because he was immortal.

I told Iskra that in my time it was only dead people, like Lenin, for example, who were considered immortal. She quite reasonably observed that my statement was devoid of any sense because only those who live forever can be considered immortal.

I said that past history had seen many rulers who were considered eternal or immortal, but who ended up dying anyway. My remark irked Iskra.

"What a comparison!" she said with great indignation. "Can't you see, don't you feel that there has never been anyone like the Genialissimo before. It's no accident that the press calls him a man for all seasons."

I was about to object that I had personally already outlived many people who were considered immortal but who subsequently died in the most ordinary fashion—from heart attacks, strokes, liver failure, or simple indigestion. But I refrained from this remark, remembering from past experience that such ideas are always considered seditious and had already landed me into serious trouble back in my own time.

I will continue to refrain from any such remarks and will refer only to the official reports on the Genialissimo. Not only do the people of the Moscowrep and the First Ring of Hostility consider him their leader, but the people of the other two rings also consider him their leader and teacher. They worship him and believe that by following his ideas they, too, will someday build a life as wonderful as the one the Communites have. They know that he is always thinking of them, pays close attention to all the details of their lives, and devotes all his time to the struggle for the common good.

This struggle, as far as I could tell, consisted entirely in composing replies to the greetings which the workers of the world sent regularly to their leader on the occasion of his birthday, the publication of his latest book, and of a new award being bestowed on him (which happened almost every day). In addition, every day he would send a great variety of messages, greetings, and appeals to every corner of the Earth, to people taking part in movements, congresses, and conferences.

But there was no question that, of ordinary mortals, I was the most famous. I was talked about on television from morning till night. Each day *Pravda* would devote up to nine feet of each roll to me. Writing extensive, detailed articles and reviews, the linguists, literary scholars, and critics discussed my life, my creative achievements, and my struggle with the Corruptionists. True, they never mentioned my books by name or quoted from them. At times they would even make strange statements to the effect that I was the first to reflect the Genialissimo's image in literature, though I had not done it very successfully; to be honest, I had no memory of that.

And even though I had never made any special pursuit of fame in my last life, what can you say—it's a nice feeling to turn on the television and the first thing you hear is your own name. Or to find your picture in a newspaper roll. It was nice to know that for my jubilee the working people were assuming increased quotas in the mining of coal, the smelting of steel, and were promising to use less primary matter and turn in more secondary matter. I had become so famous in a short time that, despite the severe paper shortage, I was literally deluged with letters and telegrams. I could no longer go outside; my hand was exhausted from signing autographs and shaking hands.

I should say that the way I dressed no longer caused me any problems. On the day after my ill-fated walk through Moscow, Iskrina brought me a pair of military shorts and an army shirt with a second lieutenant's epaulettes. This may not have been a very high rank, but still it was flattering—in my previous life I had not even made it to PFC. Now, when out strolling, I would from time to time glance over at my shoulders to make sure that my stars were on straight.

We know all of life's pleasures through contrast. If I hadn't wandered the streets on my first day in the Moscowrep, I would never have understood how much more of a pleasure it was to be a Communite with high-level needs than one with general needs.

In the Communist Hotel, where Iskrina and I were staying, we had a bright and comfortable room with rugs on the floor, two paintings of the Genialissimo, one in the peaceful bosom of nature, the other in the smoke of battle where he was dressed in field uniform, his hand stretched forward showing his soldiers the road to victory. And we had a luxurious bathroom. True, the hot water didn't work, but the weather was so hot that a cold shower was a pleasure.

I learned that the leaders of the Moscowrep divided needs into several categories. General needs were divided into the need to breathe, to eat, to take in fluids, to have clothing and shelter. Every Communite without exception had the right to satisfy these needs as stated in the first paragraph of the Moscowrep Constitution: "Every person has the right to breathe air, eat food, satisfy his thirst, cover his body with clothing proper to the season, and to live in a covered enclosure." These needs had been determined scientifically and were completely satisfied.

But there were needs whose satisfaction is not obligatory and so are determined in keeping with a person's merits. These are high-level needs, higher-level needs, and needs beyond classification. People in these categories complain that their needs are not always satisfied. Sometimes there are interruptions in the delivery of hot water (the case in our hotel) and electricity, problems with elevators and so forth.

Personally, I'm not complaining. The service in the hotel was perfectly fine, almost like capitalism. Every morning a red-faced waiter by the name of Proletarian Ilyich rolled a breakfast cart into our room. It contained fried eggs, ham, butter, red caviar, fresh rolls, and apple jam, but for some reason they didn't have any real coffee there, just as they had no real soap. Every morning the waiter would ask me, "What kind of coffee would you prefer, corn coffee or barley coffee?" And I would say that I would prefer coffee coffee. His mouth would drop open and he would emit a forced chuckle. Apparently, he had been informed that I was a humorist and was constantly joking, and he, as a true Communite, was obliged to have a sense of humor. I told him that I was not joking in the least and that in my time under socialism and capitalism coffee was made from coffee beans, but he thought I was joking again and he chuckled again.

They changed the linen in our room every day and, before going to sleep, I would put my shoes out in the hallway and would find them polished to a gleam the next morning. When seeing me retrieve them, the corridor attendant, Evolutsia Polikarpovna, would smile very tenderly to me, as a sign of her esteem, respect, and even love.

We took our lunch and dinner in the restaurant downstairs. It was a bright and comfortable place, with soft music. There was only one serious drawback in local life; the Moscowrep was a totally dry city. I heard that some Communites, to avoid breaking the dry law, ate dry tooth powder. Somehow that didn't appeal to me.

THE FIRST
DAYS

Just between us, I didn't have any regrets about my affair with Iskrina. She turned out to be a little on the quarrelsome side, but that's a failing found in women of all times and all nations. I liked her looks a lot. At first I was a little put off by her clean-shaven head and asked how that stupid fashion had started and didn't she think women looked more beautiful with normal hair. She said that Communites only grew their hair in the winter, but, in the summertime, as part of the struggle for total recycling, it was their duty to turn in their hair at a recycling center.

"And what do they do with the hair, stuff mattresses?" I asked.

"No, not at all," she answered artlessly, "I don't think they do anything with it. They just store it, that's all. It's a different story with secondary matter. We supply the Third Ring with that."

"Why?" I asked.

"We're under contract. At one point the Corruptionists signed a contract with them to deliver gas, but the gas ran out a long time ago. Our scientists refitted the gas pipeline and. . . ." Then, unable to restrain herself, she burst out laughing. I asked her what was so funny. Embarrassed, she would not say a word. But later on, I got it out of her—as a joke the Communites now called the former State Order of Lenin gas pipe the Lenin shit-line.

By the way, she insisted on using her favorite nickname for me—Clasha. I told her that Clasha was an idiotic nickname and asked her where she'd heard it. She replied that it was an ordinary diminutive and that she was not going to call me Classic, like everyone else. I readily agreed that Classic was a ridiculous name but said that I did not want to be called Clasha or Glasha either.

"If you have to stick me with some idiotic nickname, then just call me Talik, that's what my wife used to call me."

"I," she said, "am not interested in what your old lady used to call you. And whatever happened with you before we met is no concern of mine."

At first, she condemned my blue terry cloth robe as a sign of insane extravagance. Do people really walk around wearing robes like that over there in the Third Ring? she asked. I said that I didn't know about now, but that in my time many people did.

"That's the limit," she said.

Like all Communites, Iskrina thought that the level of prosperity was lower in the First Ring of Hostility than in the Moscow-rep, lower in the Second Ring than in the First, and that utter destitution reigned in the Third.

"Just look at this," she said, trying on my robe, closing it one way then the other. "There's plenty of extra material here, enough for two or maybe even three people."

Still, for all her communist good sense, she began wearing that robe more and more often and taking it off less and less often. She had also taken over my slippers, even though they were too big for her. The robe had a tasseled belt, but she was reluctant to use it. Whenever I would become irritated with her, her robe would slide open a bit, revealing a glimpse of what lay beneath. She had already understood that this simplest of tricks never failed to have its effect on me and that I would always race at her like a madman.

"Oh, Granpa!" she would cry, trying to fend me off. "What are you doing, Granpa! At your age, it might make you ill."

"I'll show you who's a granpa!" I'd bellow and then later, as through a fog, I would see her face, her eyes closed, as she bit her lower lip.

"There, you see!" she said to me one time. "I wasn't wrong when I said you were a savage."

212

"And I'll tell you what I think," I replied. "I think that you're discharging your duties with more zeal than regulations require."

"You should star yourself when you think those thoughts," she joked back in embarrassment.

THE AUGUST
REVOLUTION

From what I could gather from Iskra, television, and the newspapers, it was difficult to form any sort of complete picture of exactly when the August Revolution took place, and what was the main cause of it. Still, from various odds and ends of information, I came to the following understanding.

Before the revolution, when there was no such thing as the Moscowrep, the Soviet Union had been ruled by men of profound old age. That is, they were old in age but not always profound. They usually seized power when they were at the peak of their strength and health. And each time they set about bringing in younger men. But, in the time it took to bring in those younger men, they would usually have grown old themselves and, wise with age, would conclude that the most progressive form of government was senilocracy. And they would hold onto their posts until the day they died. The next generation of leaders would again set about bringing in younger men, but they, too, would not have time enough to accomplish this. Due to the high standard of living and medical progress, each new generation of leaders was older than the previous one. Things had reached a point at which, of the twelve members on the last Politburo, seven finished their years of service in a state of utter senility, two were permanently confined to wheelchairs, one was completely paralyzed, another deaf as a post, and the leader, who ruled over them all, spent the last six years of his life in a coma.

It was then that the Genialissimo launched the revolution, which was the result of the so-called "angry KGB generals' plot." I would very much have liked some details about this, but history was not one of Iskrina's strong points; she had spent too much time studying the preliminary language.

She had heard about those days only from her grandmother, who said that all the generals were young and vigorous, and all handsome to a man. When they took power, they decided immediately to do away with bad management, bureaucratism, bribe-taking, theft, favoritism, regionalism, cronyism, individualism, idle talk, glorificationism, verbosity, ostentation, drunkenness, phrase-mongering, hare-brainism, and bungling. They would step up discipline in production and fight for an overfulfillment of plans. They displayed great energy, meeting with the masses and delivering speeches, but no one toiled harder than the Genialissimo. He traveled throughout the country, demanding increases in oil extraction, steel smelting, and the cotton harvest; he studied the problems involved with the egg-laying abilities of a variety of hen types and kept a close watch on sheep litters. But, since the country was too large for him to keep an eye on everything, he decided to use advanced technology and instituted a regular series of inspection overflights in a spacecraft. From that vantage he could observe troop movements, quarry excavations, timber falling, the construction of various installations, and open-pit coal mining. He delved into everything. Sometimes he would even notice some workers taking too long a smoke break and would issue an order right there from space: those workers' boss was to be dismissed from his post, demoted, or brought to trial. Sometimes he would even notice an automobile breaking the speed limit or making an illegal turn, make a note of the plate number, and inform the registry of motor vehicles.

"He deals with trifles like that?" I asked Iskrina.

"Why are they trifles?" she objected with displeasure. "He deals with everything. And don't you forget that it was by following his ideas and his leadership that we built communism. And it only took one year after the August Revolution. And those inspections from space proved so effective that finally a decision was made to leave the Genialissimo in space forever and to divide power into the heavenly and the earthly. The Genialissimo rules things in general from up there, and earthly affairs are governed by the Supreme Pentagon and the Editorial Commission."

THE BUILDING OF
COMMUNISM

From Iskrina I learned that not only Muscovites but workers throughout the Soviet Union had labored to fulfill the plan to build communism in one city. With their help new buildings had been constructed and the capital was supplied with everything it needed all year long. Primary matter and consumer goods were brought in from all corners of the land. Foreign specialists had been invited there, including German sausage-makers, Swiss cheese-makers, and French designers.

Long before communism was declared, Moscow's warehouses had been well-stocked with Pepsi Cola, a variety of Italian pizzas, American hamburgers and chewing gum, jeans specially ordered from the West, T-shirts with the words "I love communism" written on them, and various types of West German two-ply, patterned, and textured toilet tissue.

At the same time, measures were taken to protect Moscow from people coming in from the First Ring of Hostility, especially people who lived in the provinces of Kalinin, Yaroslavl, Kostroma, Ryazan, Tula, and Kaluga who, on the pretext of visiting the capital's sights and museums, would at the end of every week carry out savage raids on Moscow's stores, emptying them of goods designated for Muscovites. To deprive them of this pretext, the Exhibition of Agricultural Achievements, the Tretyakovsky Gallery, the Kremlin Armory, the Pushkin Art Museum, and the Leo Tolstoy Museum (now the Museum of Preliminary Literature) had been moved outside the limits of Moscow. The same was done with the railroad stations at which those who lived in remote areas had to change trains in Moscow.

The workers of the Lyuberetsky Reinforced Concrete Works had built the eighteen-foot panels for the wall around Moscow. Toward that same end, the collective of the Leningrad Kirov factory had produced enough barbed wire to wind around the entire Earth four times. Workers in the German Democratic Republic (the Second Ring of Hostility) shared their experience in setting up mine fields and deploying devices that fired automatically and which had been perfected to the degree that even sparrows chancing by would be gunned down.

In addition, the populace had been subjected to a process of selection on the basis of certain qualities. Approximately a month before the advent of communism, antisocial elements were resettled out of Moscow, including alcoholics, hooligans, parasites, Jews, dissidents, invalids and pensioners. The students were dispatched to remote construction battalions, and the schoolchildren to Pioneer camps.

On the day communism was proclaimed all the stores were bursting with goods and food.

However, since it was all so new, mistakes were unavoidable. Iskrina told me what she had heard from her grandmother. On the first day of communism even the most politically conscious workers acted completely unconsciously and, despite it being a workday, did not go to work but ran to the stores and grabbed whatever they could get their hands on.

A terrific crush resulted, and, in the Smolensk grocery store alone, fourteen people were crushed to death; in the Eliseevsky store, all the windows were broken, all the counters overturned, and the store manager lost an eye in the process.

The worst disaster took place in GUM, where the pressure of the crowds broke the railing on a third-floor walkway and people fell to their deaths, killing those on whom they landed as well.

To restore order, the communist authorities were compelled

to call in the troops. Tanks of the Kantimir and Tamansky Guards regiments were brought in to Moscow, and a state of martial law was declared for three days.

After this, the Genialissimo appealed directly to the populace of Moscow. He said that isolated errors and excesses had been committed when the communist system had been introduced into the republic. He had nothing but criticism and scorn for those Volunteerists who had decided to introduce raw communism helter-skelter. He said that insofar as people were unable themselves to assess their own needs soberly, he would now appoint supreme and local pentagons, however, even limited needs should not be satisfied without the strictest economization of primary matter and the complete recycling of secondary matter.

I asked Iskrina why no one demanded that we turn in our secondary matter. She said that Communites with high-level needs were free of that obligation, especially since our hotel's sewage system was so constructed as to begin the recycling of all secondary matter automatically.

"And those people who had been guilty of disturbances on the first day, they were punished, I hope," I said.

"To say the least!" she said. "The chairman of the State Committee on the Need Satisfaction and the chief of Intsec were convicted and . . ."

". . . executed!"

"What are you saying! Absolutely out of the question. The Moscowrep has abolished the death penalty forever. We have only one punishment here: exile to the First Ring. And that's where those people were sent."

"Well, that was a mistake," I said. "Of course, I realize that people should be treated humanely under communism, but there's humane treatment and there's humane treatment and it shouldn't be misused."

"Don't get excited, you silly man," said Iskrina, stroking my head. "Those people were exiled to the First Ring. And they still haven't abolished the death penalty there."

The next day Iskrina told me another staggering piece of information. Not only was there no death penalty in the Moscowrep, but even the death rate itself had been practically eliminated among rank-and-file Communites.

"How could that be?" I said incredulously. "Do you mean to say that your communist scientists have invented the elixir of life?"

The question confused her somewhat. She hemmed and hawed, then said that yes, there had been certain definite achievements as far as the elixir was concerned, but that the elimination of the death rate had been achieved through more reliable and economic means. It was simply that critically ill people, as well as pensioners and invalids, if, of course, they were not members of the Editorial Commission or the Supreme Pentagon, were resettled to the First Ring and lived out their days there. All that remained here were rare instances of death in accidents and of course heart attacks and strokes. But those were also isolated instances, because people with cardiovascular diseases were also dispatched beyond the limits of the Moscowrep in good time, and if someone should happen to suffer a heart attack or appendicitis, the ambulance would rush him to the First Ring.

"So, for the most part there are no people with heart problems or high blood pressure, no invalids or old people?" I asked.

"Absolutely correct," she corroborated. "And we also have no dogs, cats, hamsters, turtles, or any other such unproductive animals. People used to keep them. But it was all perfectly stupid, because none of those animals was of any use and they all needed to be fed."

"And so they were destroyed?"

"How can you even say such a thing?" said Iskrina indignantly. "Why should they have been destroyed? They were exiled to the First Ring too."

"You exiled hamsters and turtles?" I said. "And what happened to them?"

"I don't know," she said reluctantly. "Maybe they were eaten there. You see, here the population's need for primary matter is satisfied entirely, but there they run out of things."

Usually Iskrina tried to speak with me in the preliminary language, which she had learned not from literature, but from precommunist *Pravda* editorials. I have to admit that my knowledge of that particular language was rather shaky too. And, for that reason, I proposed that we try to communicate in the communist language, in which I had already made a little progress.

Television is a great help in learning the language. By the way, their system there is entirely cable. I thought that this was for the sake of good reception, but the real reason proved much more serious. The thing was that even before the August Revolution, the Americans had started using their satellites to beam programs onto Soviet television.

"And the introduction of the cable system neutralized this ideological sabotage?" I asked.

"Not quite," said Iskrina with a grin. "They developed a new form of provocation. They installed laser projectors on the moon, and now they show their decadent films right on the sky, using the cloud cover for a screen."

"What?" I said in disbelief. "Is that possible?"

"Unfortunately, it is," said Iskrina. "Needless to say, we're taking countermeasures. For example, SECO especially recommended the long peaks on our caps to protect people from radiation. But some politically unconscious people peep out from under their caps. And so new countermeasures have to be found."

"I see," I said. "This is what they do to people who look out from under their caps." I pantomimed wringing a neck.

"You're so backward!" said Iskrina, clapping her hands. "Ours is a humane society, we don't treat people like that. We just simply disperse the clouds. True, this does have a negative effect on the climate and the harvests, but we put the ideological struggle first and the harvest second."

"I can see that. It was like that in my time, too."

Still, it was a good thing I had Iskrina! Thanks to her, I now knew not only that the outside world was divided into rings, but that the Moscowrep itself consisted of three rings of communism. Though there are no very distinct boundaries among the rings, it can be said that the Communites with high-level needs live in the Central Ring and those with common needs in the Second Ring. The Third Ring was inhabited mainly by Communites whose needs were amenable to self-service. Bold economic experiments were permitted at the periphery of the Moscowrep. The Communites of the Third Ring were allowed to raise vegetables and small domestic animals—pigs, goats, and sheep—on their balconies. If these experiments prove successful, the positive experience of the Third Ring Communites could someday be extended to the Central and Second Rings as well.

THE CHURCH

The Communist Reformed Church was founded in accordance with a resolution of the KPGB Central Committee and with an ukase from the Supreme Pentagon, entitled "On the Consolidation of Forces." Both documents indicated that the Cultists, Volunteerists, Corruptionists, and Reformists had conducted a vulgar struggle against religion. By oppressing believers and offending their feelings, they had underestimated the enormous benefit that could be derived from believers if they were accepted as full-fledged members of society. The documents proclaimed solemnly the incorporation of the church by the state under one absolute condition: that faith in God be renounced. (It was the Editorial Commission which had introduced this condition into the final text of the documents.)

The goal the Reformed Church set itself was to raise Communites in the spirit of communism and with fervent love for the Genialissimo. Toward that end, confession was regularly available in the workplace and in the churches, where services were held to honor the August Revolution, the Genialissimo's birthday, Communist Constitution Day, and so on.

Needless to say, this church had its own saints: Saint Karl, Saint Friedrich, Saint Vladimir, and many heroes of all the revolutions (but first and foremost the August Revolution) and wars; heroes of labor had also been canonized.

The church always instills its flock with the belief that the truly righteous man is the one who fulfills his production assignments, observes production discipline, obeys the authorities, and displays constant uncompromising vigilance to all signs of alien ideology.

The church also engages in a ceaseless struggle against the propagation of new communist religious rites among the Communites.

FAMILY AND
MARRIAGE

Men over the age of twenty-four, and women over twenty-one are allowed to enter into marriage. Marriages are concluded solely upon the recommendation of a local pentagon. Recommendations are given only to persons who fulfill their production assignments, take an active lead in community labor, and do not consume alcohol. Marriages are concluded on a temporary, four-year basis. Then, with the pentagon's consent, they can be extended for another four-year period but can be dissolved before that time in the event one of the partners engages in antisocial behavior. Marriages are dissolved automatically when a partner's productive years are over (at forty-five for a woman, at fifty for a man).

I asked Iskra if there were some Communites who loved each other and wanted to live with each other but were not given their recommendation, or if there were any who wanted to continue living together after the age at which their marriages expired.

She said that of course there were.

"So how do they get out of the predicament?" I asked.

"They don't have to. They just keep living with each other, that's all. If they have a place. And, if they don't, there are always bushes and doorways."

As for people who did not have enough merit points to get married, they were free to make use of the various forms of sexual service. Their needs were satisfied right at their workplace by traveling teams from the Palace of Love, usually after work or during the lunch break.

THE EDUCATION
OF THE COMMUNITES

My account of the Communites' customs and ways would not be complete if I did not touch on the subject of their education, which occurs in the following manner.

At birth, a Communite undergoes the ritual of startism. Then he passes through two stages: a preliminary stage in kindergarten, during which he is given his first lessons in love for country, party, church, state security, and the Genialissimo. He learns poems and songs about the Genialissimo and is also trained to do secret work for SECO. In the cheery, natural settings of Pioneer camps, children learn to inform on one another, to report their parents' transgressions to their teachers and those of their teachers to the kindergarten principals. About twice a year, a national commission on communist education inspects kindergartens, and the children can inform on their principals to the members of that commission. In the kindergartens, the pupils' denunciations are viewed only as a game; no weight or significance is attached to them, with the exception of those cases in which children uncover serious plots.

By the time they are in the instcominsts, children learn how to compose written denunciations. Their teachers keep a close eye on those compositions to make sure they are written in good communist Russian and are interesting in form and rich in content. Needless to say, children study the regular subjects as well, but principal attention is devoted to works by the Genialissimo and works about the Genialissimo.

The ten-year program at the instcominsts is obligatory for all children. They enter it at eight and graduate at eighteen.

Each student who graduates in good standing from an instcominst is presented simultaneously with a diploma, passport, party card, draft card, and identification as a secret agent of state security.

"And how about the ones that don't graduate in good standing?" I asked.

"They're exiled to the First Ring," said Iskrina.

PAPLESSLIT

I learned about the preparations for the celebration of my jubilee not only from television and *Pravda*, a fresh roll of which was always to be found in the natfunctbur in my hotel room, but from reports I received from Communi Ivanovich Smerchev and Dzerzhin Gavrilovich Siromakhin. Both generals called me every day or came in person to see me and keep me up-to-date on the successes achieved by the workers of the Moscowrep and the First Ring in connection with my jubilee.

Dzerzhin's reports were always accompanied by an odd smirk, whereas Communi was always solemn, even distinguished. He would reel off figures—how much had been produced and where, how many new brigades were engaged in special prejubilee drives, and how intensively the Communites were studying the Genialissimo's works.

At one point I said to him that if the Communites genuinely desired to celebrate my jubilee properly, they should not only acquaint themselves with the works of the Genialissimo, but with mine as well. Mine might not stand up in comparison with the Genialissimo's, but all the same the Communites might just find some interesting information in them too.

"Yes, yes, yes," agreed Smerchev. "That's been advised for some time now, and the leadership is reviewing this matter. But, in the meantime, perhaps you ought to be acquainting yourself with your communist successors, finding out about their lives and work, and how they are furthering the traditions you helped found."

"Of course," I said, "it's high time for that. I'm surprised that you didn't invite me to meet them before."

"We thought that you'd need this time to rest up. And besides, you've been on something of a honeymoon too. By the way, how do you like our Iskrina? Some comcoms have nothing but praise for the high cultural level of her services."

I looked at him with great surprise. What was that supposed to mean? But I really wasn't in a position to punch him in the nose. He was a general, after all.

"Listen," I said to Communi, "and get this straight once and for all. I will not allow anyone to make such scabrous remarks about Iskrina Romanovna in my presence."

"What do you mean! What do you mean!" said Smerchev in a frightened voice. "I didn't mean anything bad by that. I've never been serviced by her myself, but other people . . ."

"Alright," I interrupted, resigned to the fact that nothing got through to him, "let's drop the subject. So when can I go visit some comlits?"

"Right away if you like."

We went outside, where Vasya awaited us, not in an armored personnel carrier, but in an ordinary black steam car.

We pulled out onto Marx Avenue where it became the Street of the Genialissimo's Aphorisms and turned at the Lenin Library (which, to my surprise, still existed under its former name) onto Volume Four Avenue, once known as Kalinin Avenue.

On the way, Smerchev told me that, on the Genialissimo's personal instructions and in accordance with a resolution by the KPGB Central Committee "On the Reorganization of Artistic Organizations and the Intensification of Creative Discipline," all work done by the Communist Writers' Union had been thoroughly revamped. Formerly, writers had worked at home, which contradicted the basic principles of the communist system and was degrading to the writers themselves because it placed them in the position of cottage industry workers cut off from the people. This had evoked the rightful censure of the working masses who labored on kolkhozes, in plants, factories, and in institutions.

Writers were going to work whenever they saw fit. Some politically conscious ones would put in a full, honest day's work, whereas others set the length of their working day quite arbitrarily.

A commission looking into the union's activities uncovered flagrant abuses—some writers had not written a word in years. Those idlers were not even up to the motto of one of the representatives of preliminary literature: "Not a day without a line."

"Can you imagine such mockery of our working people?" said Smerchev indignantly. "To use a true, wise, and timely utterance of the Genialissimo, this is the same as if our heroic grain-producing peasants assumed the obligation of planting one ear of corn per day per person. Now that would be perfectly foolish, wouldn't it?"

I agreed readily, but asked what the communist writer's daily output quotas were.

"They vary," answered Smerchev. "It's entirely a question of quality. If someone produces good-quality work, his quota is lowered; on the other hand, if someone puts out low-quality stuff, he has to make up for it in quantity. Some of them operate on the principle 'Better less but better,' while others believe, 'Better worse but more.' But the main thing is that now writers are on an equal footing with all other comworkers. Now, like everyone else, they go to work at nine o'clock, punch in, and sit down at their desks. The lunch break is from one to two, the workday ends at six and then everyone can relax with the sense of having done his duty. Is this interesting to you?" he asked, just to be sure.

"Terrifically interesting," I said sincerely. "I've never heard anything like it."

"That's right, of course you haven't," said Smerchev happily. "I suspect there are a good many things here you've never heard of before." He then told me about the structure of the Communist Writers' Union. It consisted on two main departments, which were broken down into further departments of poets, prose writers, and playwrights.

"And what department are the critics in?" I asked.

231

"They're not in any," said Smerchev. "Criticism is the direct responsibility of SECO."

"I'm very glad to hear that from you," I said, deeply moved. "We had a perfectly stupid arrangement in my time. The organs of state security dealt with criticism then too, but in fact all they were doing was duplicating the efforts of the Writers' Union."

"That pernicious practice," said Smerchev with a frown, "is now a thing of the past."

I asked him a series of questions on more minor matters, for example, which were the genres most in fashion now? Prose? Poetry? Plays?

"All genres are equal here," said Smerchev. "We don't have genres that are in and genres that are out. You use whatever genre you know best to write about our glorious, beloved, and dearest Genialissimo."

"Stop! Stop! Stop!" I cried. "Excuse me, but I'd like to put a finer point on something here. What are you telling me? Do you mean to say that writers have to spend all their time writing about the Genialissimo?"

"What does that mean—*have to*?" objected Smerchev. "They don't have to do anything; they enjoy complete artistic freedom. This was their own decision. Now they are creating a collective work that is unprecedented in history and grand in scope—a multivolume collection of works under the overall title *Genialissimoiana*. This work will record every instant in the life of the Genialissimo and disclose the full extent of his thoughts, ideas, and actions."

"But how about your writers for children's and young people's books?"

"The children's writers write about the Genialissimo's childhood, the teen writers write about his teenage period, and the youth writers write about his youth. What could be simpler?"

He gave me something of a strange look. It seemed to me that he had started to suspect that I was either a fool or a spy. To dispel those suspicions, I explained that though we had had various literary organizations in the period of developed socialism, the rules had not been so thoroughly thought through at the time. Then, too, writers had described the lives of the leaders or the operations of various industrial and agricultural equipment, but some also figured out ways to write novels or poems about love, nature, and other such things.

Smerchev replied that nothing had changed in that respect—every communist writer was perfectly free to write about his ardent love for the Genialissimo, and perfectly free to write about nature and about the enormous changes wrought on the landscape as the result of the Genialissimo's leadership in the construction of snow barrier walls, new forestation, canals, and the reversal of the Yenisei River which now empties into the Sea of Aral.

I was about to ask him about the fate of other Siberian rivers, but just then our car pulled up in front of a building that looked to me like the old Writers' Building, except that it had had a lot of work done on it. A different sign hung on the building now:

ORDER OF LENIN GUARDS' UNION OF COMMUNIST WRITERS
MAIN DEPARTMENT OF PAPERLESS LITERATURE (PAPLESSLIT)

To my question of what paperless literature was, Smerchev smilingly replied that it was literature written without paper. So, it was with great interest that I entered the door Communi held open for me.

Yes, yes, I'd been right, it was the old familiar lobby of the Writers' Building. At one time its doors had been guarded by foul-tempered old women who would demand to see everyone's Writers' Union membership card. But there were no old women there now. They had been replaced by two guards with submachine guns who presented arms as soon as they caught sight of us approaching.

"He's with me," said Smerchev with a nod at me, and we encountered no obstacles.

The lobby walls were clean but bare, apart from a portrait of the Genialissimo in the act of composition and a wall newspaper called *Our Achievements*, at which I managed to get a peek. From the newspaper I learned that communist writers not only write but also constantly observe life and forge closer bonds with the masses by taking part in the potato harvest, sweeping the streets, and working at construction sites. There was a highly acerbic satirical piece criticizing one comlit who had managed to be late for work three times in one month.

That's all I had time to read because Smerchev dragged me off toward what had been the restaurant in my day. There was no restaurant there now but a long wide corridor with doors on either side, like in the Palace of Love.

"Let's drop in here," said Smerchev.

He pushed one door open and we were inside a steam room. I mean, at first I thought I was in a steam room. Because the people in there (about forty of them) were all naked to the waist. They were all sitting two at a desk and banging away at some sort of keyboards.

In front of them all sat a lieutenant colonel at a desk of his own. Our arrival seemed to throw the lieutenant colonel off momentarily, but he quickly barked out: "Stand up! Attention!"

The chairs scraped back, the naked people jumped to attention, except for one man in glasses at a desk in the rear who paid no attention to the command and continued banging away at his keyboard like a madman. His close-cropped head kept turning and he made strange faces, sticking out his tongue, sniveling and sobbing.

With frightened eyes, the lieutenant colonel looked back and forth from us to the man with the glasses, then shouted: "Stop, Okhlamanov! Do you hear me, Okhlamanov!"

But Okhlamanov clearly did not hear him. The man beside him first nudged him with his elbow, then tugged him by the arm, and then a second person came to his aid. Okhlamanov kept tearing loose like an epileptic and pecking away at the keyboard. Finally, one way or the other they managed to pull him away and it was only then that he saw that everyone was standing. He drew himself up, but continued to look at his desk out of the corner of one eye and his hands kept twitching out in the direction of the keyboard.

234

"Comcom Classic of Preliminary Literature," said the lieutenant colonel, reporting to me. "The writer workers in this subdivision of paperless literature are engaged in work on the theme of communist labor. Their work is keeping tightly to schedule. No one was tardy and no one is absent or out ill."

"At ease! At ease!" I commanded gesturing for them to be seated.

To the pleasant accompaniment of clacking keyboards, the lieutenant colonel told me that his detachment consisted of beginning writers or, as they were still called, subwriters or subcomlits. He was their leader, his position that of writer-instructor. In hot weather the subcomlits worked stripped to the waist in order to save wear on their clothing. All the subcomlits were sergeants. Lacking sufficient service time in literature, they were not yet permitted to express their thoughts directly on paper. But they were elaborating various aspects of various themes on their computers before their work went to the comlits who were the ones to create works on paper.

"You've never seen a computer before, have you?" inquired the lieutenant colonel.

"Of course he has," interjected Smerchev. "Classic Nikitich has not only seen a computer, he's even written several of his works on one."

"That's right," I said, no longer taken aback by Smerchev's information on me. "I indeed have done some writing on a computer, though mine was different than these. Mine had a screen on which I could see what I was writing and a printer that would let me print what I'd written at once."

"There you see!" exclaimed the lieutenant colonel with pleasure. "Your old equipment was too cumbersome. And, as you see, we have no screens, no printers, nothing superfluous."

"That's really interesting," I said, "but I don't understand how the sergeants get to see what they've written."

"They don't get to see anything," said the lieutenant colonel. "There's no need for them to."

"How can that be?" I said with surprise. "How can you write without seeing what you're writing?"

"What do you need to see it for?" said the lieutenant colonel, his turn to be surprised now. "We have a general computer for that. It collects everything, compares it, analyzes it, and then selects the most artistic, the most inspired, and the most ideologically impeccable words and reworks them into a single text of great artistry and ideological content."

I must admit that I had never heard of this sort of collective creativity before. And naturally I wanted to ask the lieutenant colonel a few more questions, but Smerchev, with a glance at his wristwatch, said that it was time for us to be going and he would be glad to explain anything I'd not understood.

It seemed to me that the lieutenant colonel was glad to see us go. Once again he issued the command: "Stand at attention" (and of course Okhlamanov failed to stand again). Smerchev and I said goodbye to the sergeants and left the room.

"Well, have you understood anything?" asked Smerchev with what struck me as a sarcastic tone.

"Not quite," I admitted. "I still don't understand where the sergeants' writing goes."

"It goes right here," said Smerchev, pointing to a door whose sign read:

ELECTRONIC PROCESSING OF PRELIMINARY TEXTS DEPARTMENT
ADMITTANCE WITH SERIES D PASS

The two stern-faced guards armed with submachine guns kept a careful eye on anyone approaching them.

I asked Smerchev why security was so strict and he replied readily that that area housed the top-secret computer that stored and analyzed the texts written by the beginning writers, selecting the artistically and ideologically best phrases and composing them into a unified whole.

"As you can well understand," said Smerchev, "our enemies

236

would very much like to infiltrate this area and insert their own ideological material into that electronic brain."

"And do you have many enemies?" I asked.

"Some," said Smerchev as if he were gladdened by the very existence of enemies. "Still," he corrected himself, "you have to remember that there are enemies and there are people who are simply immature, who, in their failure to master the basics of the leading worldview, express damaging opinions. And there are also those," he said, turning his face to me without breaking stride but smiling as he made a sort of clumsy little bow, "who do not understand the interdependence of phenomena and cannot tell the difference between primary and secondary matter."

"You mean there are people like that in the Moscowrep?" I asked.

"Yes," he said, assuming a look of sadness. "Unfortunately, there are. But," once again he hastened to correct himself, "we pay close attention to each and every person. We see a big difference between those who deliberately express views hostile to us and those who do so out of ignorance."

I did not say a word. I found Smerchev's words extremely unpleasant because they alluded to a remark I myself had made. And no one could have known about that remark, apart from Iskrina.

PRIMARY MATTER
IS SECONDARY MATTER

It was evening time, after dinner. We were sitting in our hotel room and I was watching television, to Iskrina's extreme displeasure. She thought that I wasted too much time in front of the set instead of spending it on something else. And by then I knew what that something else was. She was making me engage in that something else with such intensity that I was worn to a frazzle. I may even have been watching television just to get out of it. But perhaps that is overstating the case, because I found all television programs there terrifically interesting. Even a report on a donors' conference which apparently was taking place in the Hall of Columns of the House of Soviets. The hall was filled with men and women of all ages, bedecked with medals. As I understood it, they were donors of the fourth degree. That is, they contributed blood, secondary matter, hair, and semen — which they referred to as genetic material — regularly and in large amounts.

It was a lively congress. The donors shared experiences, telling how they fulfilled plans as individuals, families, and brigades. They told by what percentages they had fulfilled their previous obligations and promised to achieve even greater success in the future.

While I was watching, Iskrina was in an edgy state, and she flashed between me and the screen several times in her half open robe. At the same time, the silly plastic medallion she wore around her neck swayed back and forth like a pendulum on a grandfather clock.

"So why are you watching this nonsense?" she said, unable to hold back. "Haven't you had enough yet?"

"Leave me alone, don't bother me!" I said.

"Alright, alright, I won't," she agreed submissively, but a minute later she'd be back in the way again. "Does this *really* interest you?"

"Of course, it does," I said. "I never saw or heard anything like it."

"What's so new? Didn't they have donors in your time?"

"They had donors then," I said, "but in my time no one had come up with the idea of total secondary matter donation."

Then she began asking me questions, not so much, in my opinion, from curiosity, as to distract me from the television and drag me into bed. But, with the opposite aim, I began conscientiously answering her questions.

"You see," I said, "I lived in two different historical systems, as you know. Under capitalism, the situation as far as handing in secondary matter was concerned was fairly wretched, actually it was nonexistent. Well, let's say donating blood and genetic material was organized after a fashion, but the rest was, you could say, just tossed to the winds. Things were much better in this area under socialism, though. We collected crumbs and scraps, wrote in the newspapers about the need to do this, and we discussed it on television. Something did come out of it, I suppose."

I told Iskrina that even in our Writers' Building near the airport metro station there was a garbage can on every floor. The smell was unpleasant of course, but everyone knew that this was necessary and useful. But now, I said, you people have gone whole hog.

"That's right," she said, "of course. I think we're far ahead in many areas."

"You're far ahead," I agreed, "but in my opinion you've still a ways to go."

"What's that supposed to mean?"

"What I mean is that you people, Communites, are obliged to turn in a lot of secondary matter, but you've got problems supply-

239

ing the primary matter that the secondary matter gets made out of."

This remark did not seem to be to her liking. She began nervously fingering her medallion and said, "Are you really doing without anything?"

"I'm not doing without," I said, though, to tell the truth, I was doing without certain things. "I'm not thinking of myself, not only of myself, but about other people. You can't demand the impossible of them. You have to remember there is no secondary without a primary."

My words made a strange impression on her. Her face suddenly changed expression, and she said that I should never say anything of the sort again.

I found that surprising and asked her why not. Had I said something seditious? I just said what everybody knows; even Marx made the point that primary is primary but secondary is secondary.

"What idiocy!" she cried, terribly worked up. "What you're saying is nothing but metaphysics, Hegelianism, and Kantianism. I don't know what Marx said, but the Genialissimo says—and this is the keystone of his teachings—that primary matter is secondary matter and secondary is primary."

And then she gave me such a look that I couldn't say a word. From past experience I knew that some genialissimos so madly adore their own pronouncements that they'd have your head if you disagreed with them.

"Alright," I said. "Alright. I'm sorry if I said something wrong." And to change the subject I asked her why she wore that medallion.

She said that it wasn't a medallion but a Sign of Membership, which she was given as a child immediately after her startism ceremony.

"What's inside?" I asked.

"Inside?" she said, seeming upset again. "And why do you think there's something inside?"

"No special reason," I said. "It looks like an amulet. And there's always something inside amulets. A lock of hair or a picture of the person you love."

240

"What nonsense!" she objected nervously. "Why should I carry someone's picture around? There's nothing in there. It's just a regular Sign, the kind all Communites have. A Sign of Membership. That's all."

I was surprised by her reaction. What had I said to make her so excited? I might have written this off to female skittishness, but after Smerchev's allusions, I began to take a different view of matters. Could she really be informing on me? I asked myself.

Smerchev proposed that we drink a cup of corn coffee together, and we dropped by the writers' sathineed (satisfaction of high-level needs) where only colonels and generals sat around at relatively clean tables. Despite my low rank, they all rose immediately to their feet and greeted me with friendly applause.

Among those present, I recognized Dzerzhin Gavrilovich, who sat in a far corner and waved affably to us. Dzerzhin was sitting with a very young general who, if it weren't for his rank, I would have guessed to be around twenty-five. Taking his rank into account, I still wouldn't have thought him more than thirty. His face looked very familiar, but I realized that this impression was deceptive. I have already encountered a good many people here who reminded me of people from my past life. I said Glorgen to both generals, and they responded in kind.

Smerchev said he was hurrying off somewhere and so would entrust me to the care of Dzerzhin Gavrilovich. "Fine," said Dzerzhin, waiting until Smerchev had left to introduce me to the young general, whose name was Edison Xenofontovich Komarov.

"Glad to meet you, very glad!" he said, shaking my hand vigorously. "As you Germans say, *sehr angenehm*. By the way, I love the German language, even though I don't have anyone to speak German with."

"Are you a writer too?" I asked.

"O, *nein*!" he protested heatedly, but merrily. "I work in a completely different field. Though there are many similarities between our professions."

"For example?" I asked.

"You see, I'm a biologist, and I'm working on the creation of a new form of human being. The difference between us is that you create your heroes through the force of imagination, whereas I utilize the achievements of modern science."

"And what kind of heroes are you creating?"

"It would be my pleasure both to tell you about it and to show you. As soon as you've got your bearings here and have a little free time, come to see me at the Comscicom . . ."

"Where?" I asked.

"*Komisch!*" cried the young general; then he burst out laughing. "You're the first person I've ever met who doesn't know what the Comscicom is."

"That's forgivable in Classic's case," remarked Dzerzhin Gavrilovich. "He's only been here a little while and he still has plenty to learn."

"*Natürlich*," the young man readily agreed, and explained to me that Comscicom stood for the Communist Scientific Complex, of which he, Edison Xenofontovich, was the director in chief.

"Are biological experiments conducted there?" I asked.

"Experiments of every sort," he said. "All the sciences are headquartered in our complex, and I am in charge of them all, but personally I am solely engaged in biology. You must come, I'll show you everything. But right now, please forgive me, I must go." He shook hands with me and with Dzerzhin Gavrilovich and disappeared at once.

When we were alone, Dzerzhin Gavrilovich spent a long while asking me about my impressions of everything I'd seen in Paplesslit. I spoke in the most positive terms about the level of technological equipment available to communist writers, but at the same time I voiced certain guarded doubts as to the artistic freedom those writers enjoyed.

"I was surprised," I said, "that they are all obliged to write so-called Genialissimoiana. I have no doubt whatsoever in the Genialissimo's many virtues, but still it seems to me that writers could be dealing with other subjects as well."

What I had to say did not seem very much to Dzerzhin Gavrilovich's liking. "And who told you, my darling, that they all were obliged to write Genialissimoiana?" he asked with a frown. "Was it Smerchev?"

"Yes, it was," I admitted, immediately apprehensive that I might be getting Communi Ivanovich into trouble. "It was he who told me all that."

"What idiocy!" exclaimed Dzerzhin with heated indignation. "What slander! And could a person as intelligent and observant as yourself really believe that poppycock?"

"And why shouldn't I?" I said. "I'm brand new here."

"Alright then, believe me," said Dzerzhin firmly. "I have a reputation for being a very straightforward and truthful person. Believe me, everything that the honorable Communi Ivanovich said to you was pure poppycock and nonsense. Our comlits enjoy a freedom unlike any other known before. And they don't write what they're told to, they're absolutely free to write whatever they want. If they want to write in favor of the Genialissimo, fine, and if they want to write against him, fine. No limitations are put on them."

"Strange, strange," I said, somewhat confused by these contradictory statements. "But I hope that what Smerchev told me about the computer that processes all the written texts and chooses what's best ideologically and artistically is true."

"Of course, it's true," Dzerzhin was quick to agree. "We really do have a marvelous computer. The best in the world. And by the way," he said, looking me right in the eye, "it's my brainchild. I invented that computer myself."

"You did?" I said, almost choking on my coffee.

"Yes, I did," said Dzerzhin Gavrilovich. "Don't you believe me?"

"No, I'm not saying I don't," I said in confusion. "But, all the

244

same. . . . If you've invented such a technologically complex piece of equipment, you must be one of the major inventors here."

"Yes, that's right," said Dzerzhin with lazy assent. "False modesty aside, I have to admit that I'm one of the most important inventors here. By the way, would you like a look at how my computer works?"

"Is that possible?" I asked with a certain incredulity.

"What a question!" said Dzerzhin spreading his hands. "It might be impossible for some people, but for you it isn't. Especially since the Genialissimo has issued personal instructions that you be acquainted with all that is best in our republic."

I must admit that I found the Genialissimo's unwavering attention to me exceedingly flattering.

Leaving the sathineed, we headed straight for the door to the room that housed this unique electronic device. The guards saluted us respectfully, by presenting arms. We passed into a relatively small room in which two other guards were stationed and a young-looking major, the duty officer, sat at an office desk beneath a portrait of the Genialissimo.

Spotting Smerchev, the major jumped to his feet and, stammering from excitement, reported that all had been quiet during his guard duty at the installation.

"Very good," said Smerchev. "Good man. I'm here with Classic to have a look at how the machine's working. Give us the guest book."

The book, bound in red leatherette, was brand new, and I don't think it had ever been used before. I asked what I should write in it.

"Well, just write that you've been shown the machine and that you pledge not to divulge anything to anyone about its construction or principles."

I did not find this overly burdensome. As I've already said, I don't know the first thing about the construction of computers, and for that reason I could not betray any secrets concerning them even under torture.

After I'd done what had been asked of me, Dzerzhin ordered another door opened, one I had not noticed before. It was a narrow iron door, something like the kind found on submarines. First, the wax seal on the door was broken, then handles and numbered dials were spun.

"It's like a vault door in a Swiss bank," I remarked.

"Is that so?" I had the impression that Dzerzhin had given me an odd look. "It really looks like one?"

"I think it does," I said, "though, to tell you the truth, I've never set foot inside a Swiss bank in my life."

"You've never been inside a Swiss bank?" said Siromakhin.

"Never," I repeated. "Why does that surprise you?"

"Nothing ever surprises me," said Dzerzhin Gavrilovich. "I was just thinking. . . . I have information that you have been in Swiss banks."

"Too bad," I said. "Unfortunately that information's unreliable."

"That's strange. . . ." He was still having problems with the door. "Usually my information's highly reliable. Or could you have been there by some other means?" He stopped fiddling with the lock and peered intently at me.

"What do you mean by that?" I asked.

"What I mean is that some people in your profession possess highly developed imaginations and can use them to penetrate whatever place they like, even Swiss banks. Is that true or not?"

"In a certain sense it is true, of course," I agreed. "A bank can be penetrated by means of the imagination, but to walk off with what's inside, that's another story entirely."

"Well," said Dzerzhin with a smile, "to walk off with what's inside is something a lesser man can do, but to penetrate a bank with the mind from a great distance, and to see what's inside, is well beyond the powers of most people."

He finally succeeded in opening the door. It opened with a rusty squeak, and Dzerzhin Gavrilovich and I found ourselves in a dimly lit corridor at the end of which was another door very like the one we had just entered. It was only after the first door had closed behind us that Dzerzhin began to open the second.

"And now," he said somewhat grandly, "close your eyes and give me your hand. Try to imagine what the room is like. And then when you open your eyes, it'll be interesting to compare what you imagined with what you see."

Anticipating something out of the ordinary, I was glad to take part in that game. Conscientiously, I closed my eyes and with Dzerzhin leading me by the hand, I began walking forward, taking uncertain steps.

The door banged shut behind me.

Dzerzhin released my hand and I attempted to picture the place where I now was. I imagined a vast room lit by fluorescent lights, a host of monitors with green screens, flickering signal lights of various colors, and silent people in snow-white lab coats working the keyboards.

"Open your eyes!" commanded Dzerzhin Gavrilovich.

I'm sure you all know the feeling of walking down a dark staircase and thinking there's one step left and confidently putting your foot forward only to find there is no step there. Even if you don't break or strain your foot, it's still an awful feeling.

And so just imagine what I felt when I opened my eyes and saw a small room lit by a single bare bulb, forty watts at best, which did not contain a computer or anything of the sort; there wasn't even a stool in the place. There were only four rough walls made of poorly whitewashed brick and a bunch of wires with bare ends protruding from one wall.

"What's this?" I asked, absolutely flabbergasted.

"This is my invention of genius," said Dzerzhin with a self-satisfied grin.

"Are you trying to say there's no computer here?"

"I'm not trying to say anything," said Dzerzhin with a shrug. "I think that what you see, or, to be more precise, what you don't see, speaks for itself."

"No, listen, I still don't understand," I said with anxiety. "Does

247

this really mean that everything those sergeants write isn't recorded anywhere?"

"That's a good word for it—*recorded*," said Dzerzhin happily. "That's it exactly, none of it is recorded anywhere. A perfect, exact, and very apt definition—it is *un*recorded."

"And do the sergeants have any idea of that?"

"My darling, why do you have such a low opinion of them? What's interesting about our society is that everyone knows everything, but everyone pretends to know nothing. Is that clear?"

"Nothing's clear," I admitted.

"Alright, I'll try to explain. To the best of my knowledge, in your time, roughly speaking, there were two categories of writers. Writers people wanted to read and writers people didn't want to read. But no one published the ones people wanted to read, and the ones no one wanted to read were published. Is that right?"

"It is," I said uncertainly. "It wasn't exactly like that, of course, but generally speaking. . . ."

"I'm speaking generally," said Dzerzhin. "And so, at that time, the Corruptionists chose a strategy that was incorrect, not well thought through and, let's be blunt, very shortsighted. They banned some writers, thereby assuring them popularity and stimulating great interest in their works. And others, on the contrary, they published in enormous editions, which was completely pointless because no one read them. A tremendous waste of paper and money. And, just imagine, in your day to pay a regular writer a thousand rubles, at least a hundred thousand had to be spent on the publication of his book. And do you know how much paper was needed? A nightmare! Now, the situation has been simplified considerably. We allow nearly all writers to write whatever they want. For example, there's a writer named Okhlamanov."

"Yes, yes, I noticed him."

"Naturally, he's hard to miss. What do you think he writes?"

"I'd be hard pressed to say," I said falteringly, "but he did have a sort of inspired look on his face."

"To put it mildly," said Dzerzhin with a grin. "All madmen

are inspired. And so this inspired madman writes the same thing over and over again: 'Down with the Genialissimo! Down with the Genialissimo! Down with the Genialissimo!' Day after day, eight hours straight."

"You know this and you tolerate it?" I asked in amazement.

"Of course, if it had been written on paper, we would hardly have tolerated it, but my invention allows us to wink at such things."

"But listen," I said, staggered, "if all the writers know or at least suspect that everything they write won't end up anywhere, then why do they keep on doing it?"

"Oh, my dear man," said Dzerzhin with a weary smile, "as you well know, there are people who just want to write. And they couldn't care less what comes of it."

We were still in the room, and I was looking at the bunch of bare wires when I suddenly noticed a short word written in quite large letters beneath them. The word was *SIM*.

I asked Dzerzhin Gavrilovich Siromakhin what the word meant. He grinned and asked me what I thought it could mean. I said that I didn't know, but that I had come across the word before, sometimes even in the most unseemly places.

"But didn't you ever come across that word even before you came here?" he asked with a certain veiled cunning.

"I did. I knew a writer by that name — Sim. But as far as I can tell, the word over there on the wall," I said, pointing to it, "doesn't have anything to do with that writer."

"And why do you think that it doesn't?" asked Dzerzhin.

"Because no one knows that writer here."

"Is that what you think?" Once again Dzerzhin flashed me that odd grin. "What would you say if I told you that, on the contrary, everyone knows that Sim of yours here, and many people revere him, and that we call such people Simites? What would you say to that?"

"I'd say that was rubbish. Sim Simych Karnavalov lived in the last century."

"So he did," he answered pensively. "But Marx lived in the century before that, and even now Marxists aren't extinct."

When saying this, he pursed his lips and grimaced, as if to say that he was not displeased but rather surprised by the prolonged existence of Marxists. But I was not in the least surprised by the tenacity of the Marxists. Something else surprised me.

"Excuse me," I said to Dzerzhin. "There's something I don't quite understand. Do you mean to say that there are many followers of Sim Simych Karnavalov's teachings in the Moscowrep?"

"Not only in the Moscowrep, but in the First Ring as well," said Dzerzhin Gavrilovich. "I'll even tell you that there are more Simites than Marxists here. Not only more, but practically everyone you see is in fact a covert Simite."

"What are they like?" I asked.

"If you're interested," said Dzerzhin, "I can tell you a little bit about them."

I was interested, of course, and here is what I heard from Dzerzhin Gavrilovich. The Simite movement had come into being during Sim Simych's lifetime, meaning during mine too. At that time it was not yet a movement, but a numerous, if disjointed, throng of admirers. Then a small group of schoolchildren in the higher grades formed an underground organization that they called SIM. When questioned by the police, they would always deny any connection between the name of their organization and that of the writer Karnavalov, claiming that SIM was an abbreviation that stood for Society of Irremediable Monarchists. But when their homes were searched, copies of one slab or another from *The Greater Zone* were confiscated from nearly every member of the organization, one of whom had even done his own linguistic structural analysis of *PDC*. Needless to say, neither hide nor hair was left of that organization, but new groups sprang up at once, new associations and societies, and they all called themselves SIM, even though each invested the word with a different meaning.

By exiling Karnavalov from the country, the authorities of that time had hoped to put an end to the movement, but they had miscalculated seriously. The movement not only did not diminish, but, quite the opposite, it gained such sweep that it became a genuine threat to the security of the state. The Simites met in little groups for the express purpose of reading, studying, copying and distributing Karnavalov's works. To put a halt to this, SECO (then still known as the KGB) was compelled to make strenuous efforts. Finally, they succeeded in crushing all organized Simites. From that time until now, nearly all of Sim's works had been seized and destroyed. It could be that someone in the First Ring still might have a few of Sim's books in hiding, but in the Moscowrep that was entirely out of the question.

"So that means, one way or the other, you squashed the movement?" I said hopefully.

"What do you mean!" said Dzerzhin with a bitter grin. "On the contrary, crushing it was just the beginning. The movement took on forms that are impossible to combat. It has no organizational structure, no one joins it, and no one leaves it. There are no little groups, no lists. Anyone can consider himself a Simite but won't admit it to anyone."

"So how do you know they exist then?"

"That's no problem," said Dzerzhin, pointing to the wall. "Someone had to write that, after all. And, as you know, this is a top-secret installation. One of the most secret in the entire Moscowrep. Nevertheless, someone infiltrated this room and wrote that word on the wall. That's really something!" he said with a wave of his hand. And then he told me a story that was perfectly improbable.

Relatively recently, it had come to the attention of the Editorial Commission and SECO, that in books, newspaper articles, official statements, and personal letters, there had been a sudden rash of certain words being used quite frequently and not always properly — words like *sim*plification, *sim*ulate, *sim*ile, *sim*ian — and many semiliterate types had begun writing words like *sim*aphor and *sim*antics, and expressions like "it *sim*s to me." It cost the Editorial Commission no little effort to expose and curtail sabotage of this ilk.

"But is everything under control now?" I asked.

"Almost," said Dzerzhin. "Unfortunately, there is one word in the language which cannot be changed even by the Editorial Commission."

"There really is such a word?"

"There is," said Siromakhin sadly. "And that word is Genialissimo. Do you understand what that means? It means that every person who uses the word *genialissimo*, orally or in writing, at the same time is also using the word *sim*."

To my question of what the Simites' goal was, Dzerzhin replied that they were banking on a restoration of autocracy, or, as they called it, SIMonarchy, in Russia.

"That's the limit!" I said. "Can there really still be people in the twenty-first century who believe that a monarchy is the solution?"

"And how!" said Dzerzhin with a fervor I found odd. "The idea of a monarchy is very much alive and popular. And if you look deeply into the eyes of the Communites, you will detect their hope that the monarchy will one day be restored."

"What strange things you're saying," I said. "And who do the Simites want as their tsar?"

"You haven't guessed that yet?"

"No."

Dzerzhin walked over to the door, took a look through the keyhole, and, certain that no one was there, drew close to me and said, "They want Sim Karnavalov as tsar."

"Karnavalov?" I said in amazement. "Didn't he die in the last century?"

"Christ died two thousand years ago, but people are still waiting for him to come back."

A PERFECT
MOMENT

Sometimes I found Iskrina's ignorance shocking. For her, all precommunist history was just a tangle of bizarre events that happened at more or less the same time. I had gotten so used to this that I wasn't even surprised when she asked if I had known Pushkin personally. I explained that this was out of the question because I had been born almost a hundred years after he died, in a different epoch entirely. She was very surprised to learn that Pushkin had lived under the tsars.

"What rank did he have?"

I told her that Pushkin had held the rank of gentleman of the bedchamber which, in today's terms, would be something like a second lieutenant.

"That's all?" she said in surprise. "So why was he published then?"

"He was published because he was a great poet."

She began trying to persuade me this couldn't be so because only generals are great, not second lieutenants.

"Is that so?" I said, taking offense. "And how about me?"

"Your case still isn't clear. They might publish your book and at the same time promote you straight up to general. But *he* never rose to general."

"No, he didn't," I said. "But in those days writers were not judged by rank, but by the extent of their talent."

"And who determined the extent of their talent?" she asked.

I said that readers did. She didn't understand this and asked by what means they determined it.

"They determined it very simply. They'd read a poem and say, Great! What a writer! Pushkin! Son of a bitch! And if they didn't like something they'd say, What ridiculous crap, what raving lunacy. That's how they did it."

She didn't understand this either and asked me to tell her what Pushkin wrote about. I said that he wrote about all sorts of things, including love.

"Love for the tsar?"

"That too," I said. "But mostly he wrote about love for women. For example, there are the lines:

> *I remember a perfect moment:*
> *You appeared before my eyes,*
> *Like a fleeting vision,*
> *Like a genius of pure beauty.*

Her face covered by her hands, she listened, saying nothing for a long time after I'd finished. Then, with some excitement, she asked me to whom the poem had been dedicated.

"If you're interested in the woman's name," I said, "it was Anna Petrovna Kern."

"And what rank was she?"

"What nonsense!" I said angrily. "She didn't have any rank. She was just a woman."

"How could that be," said Iskrina, even more agitated now. "After all, he called her a genius."

"That's right, he calls her a genius of pure beauty."

"That's right, but you can't call just anyone a genius."

"Damn you!" I was beginning to lose my patience. "She wasn't just anyone. For him she was a woman unlike any other in the world."

"There, you see! She was unlike any other woman in the world. And, not only that, he called her a genius. So that means she was something like our Genialissimo."

"Good God!" I moaned in despair. "What does your Genialissimo have to do with anything? She was much more than that! She was a goddess. Your Genialissimo is . . ."

Meeting her gaze, one of horror, I faltered.

"I'm sorry," I hastened to make amends. "I didn't mean to say anything bad about the Genialissimo. I know that he is a great political figure, friend of all mankind, transformer of nature, and a multifaceted genius; but by today's standards Pushkin was backward, and to him Anna Kern was a genius."

"Alright, of course," she said, fiddling with the medallion on her chest. "Of course, he lived so long ago that there was a lot he couldn't understand. But it seems to me . . . forgive me for saying this . . . that you agree with him in some way."

"That's right," I said. "No question about it, I do agree with him in some way. Since in a certain sense I am also a person with obsolete ideas, I sometimes think that in fact a person is not born only to overfulfill production assignments, to consume primary matter and turn in secondary matter, but he also has an innate bent for things that are entirely useless — things like love, beauty, inspiration and. . . . Why I am telling you all this? Haven't you ever heard this before? In the entire Moscowrep isn't there at least one madman who writes about his feelings in rhymes?"

"Not in the Moscowrep there isn't. We exiled everyone we didn't need to the First Ring. And I've heard there are some people like that there. But not here."

"That's right," I said. "I forgot all about that. You don't have any pensioners, invalids, crooks, dogs, cats, poets, madmen . . ."

"And that's not to your liking?" she asked, still toying with her medallion.

I was about to answer the question, but her medallion made me lose my train of thought. I recalled that my last, passing question about the purpose of that seemingly innocent object had thrown her into something of a tizzy. Now I suddenly realized that she was not just wearing that doodad as a decoration, but that it served another purpose. Nothing could have been simpler to figure out, and only a dimwit like myself who never learned from experience could have failed to guess the truth immediately. But now it was perfectly clear to me that this doodad was in fact a microphone.

"How come you're not saying anything?" she said. "Keep talking, keep talking, you were speaking so well."

"I was? So well?" I repeated almost automatically. "And what was I talking about?"

"You were talking about poets, and about love."

"Oh, that's right," I said absentmindedly. "I was indeed. But you shouldn't forget that I'm a very backward person. I lived in the last century, under socialism; even under capitalism. I did not spend much time studying progressive doctrine and now I'm a hundred years old and sclerotic and senile and everything else, and, not only that, even back when I was a young man some people thought I was a fool."

"That's not true!" she objected strongly. "You're not a fool. You're very smart. You say things that I've never heard before from anyone."

I remembered being questioned once and having a man in a gray suit say to me, "If you were a fool, we would have forgiven you for everything. But you're not a fool, and you're well aware of what you're saying in your books." But he was wrong, because in fact I am a fool. If I'd been smart, I would have pretended to be a fool. But I was a fool and so I pretended to be smart. Still, in the sixty-odd years since that time, I had wised up a little. And so, in the most resolute fashion, I assured Iskrina that I was a fool and a backward fool at that. This seemed to cause her great dismay, and she slipped the medallion back into her blouse.

All the same, it turned out that literature on paper also existed in the Moscowrep. But it was created in a different building. As far as I could tell, this was the same thirty-story building that in my time had housed the Council on Economic Mutual Aid. Now it was the Directorate of Paper Literature (Paplit).

"So that means you have two literatures?" I asked Smerchev when we arrived for a visit.

"And how we do!" Smerchev said with a benevolent smile. "Of course we have two. And in your time there was only one, isn't that so?"

"Well, not quite," I said. "In my time there were two literatures too—Soviet and anti-Soviet. But, of course, both were paper literatures."

As I could see in the lobby, the comlits engaged in paper literature were much higher in rank than those in the paperless variety. In any case, everyone I encountered, apart from the guards, held a rank no lower than lieutenant, and they all walked with canvas files under their arms.

Generally speaking, the Paplit building was distinguished from Paplesslit by its superior technological equipment. Here, two of the sixteen elevators were working. We took one of those elevators to the sixth floor and, walking down a corridor with a red runner, we came to a massive door with a sign:

We entered a spacious waiting room, where a secretary with the rank of first lieutenant sat at a desk under a portrait of the Genialissimo. At the sight of us, the secretary jumped to her feet and informed Smerchev that the members of the planning commission had already arrived and were waiting for him.

"Fine," said Communi Ivanovich, kicking shut the door, which was upholstered in tattered black leather.

His office was even larger than the waiting room. The Genialissimo looked down at me from a life-size portrait, squinting in self-satisfaction, leaning on a column made of books. The spine of each book was neatly marked in gold letters: *Complete Collected Works.*

Directly beneath the portrait was an ample desk piled with stationery; on it there were several telephones of various colors. Another long desk, this one covered in green cloth, had been placed perpendicular to the first. Here, with notebooks open in front of them, several close-cropped officers wearing short-sleeved shirts sat and waited.

When we entered, they all leaped up and began applauding me. Even Smerchev joined in. I clapped a little in response to them, then went around to each, offering my hand democratically, introducing myself. Then I took a seat beside Smerchev.

When we were all seated, the secretary and another woman entered the room carrying trays with glasses of tea. Smerchev and I were served tea with lemon in brass glass-holders; the officers were given neither glass holders nor lemon.

I asked Smerchev in a whisper why there was a difference – did it mean that the comcom officers didn't like tea with lemon? Smerchev spread his hands and, whispering too, said that they might like it with lemon, but they had no need for it.

Before opening the meeting, Communi Ivanovich gave me a brief explanation of the work he and his subordinates were engaged in. As the head comlit of the republic, he was in charge of creating *Genialissimoiana* on paper and was coordinating the efforts of var-

259

ious comlit subdepartments. The subdepartment now meeting in that room had been assigned the important task of creating the volume entitled *The Years of Anxiety*, about the heroic part played by the Genialissimo in the Buryat-Mongolian war. Eight of the projected ninety-six chapters had already been written and today. . . .

"Today, boys," said Smerchev, as if they were sitting around the kitchen table, "we're going to tackle a new chapter: 'The Night Before the Battle.' This is the battle for Ulan-Udze. I'm not going to tell you what great, I would even say, *enormous* political significance this chapter is to have. As you remember, at the time of this truly historical battle, the Genialissimo was still an ordinary general. But, even back then, he had already displayed his talent for command, and in full. And so what we need here . . . which one of you deals with descriptions of nature? Is it you, Zhukov?"

"Yes, sir!" said Zhukov, jumping to his feet.

"Sit down, sit down. So, Zhukov, since we're faced with the task of describing the night before what could well be called the decisive battle, we will have to employ correspondingly intensive means in the artistic area. You know how to describe nature, of course, there's no question you're a past master at that. But, on the other hand, sometimes you get too carried away with nature and forget the political and military factors. And sometimes you even become too abstract, with the moon and the clouds and the river and the nightingales you describe. That's fine in and of itself, and sometimes it even comes off quite beautifully, but there are times it's not appropriate. Now you've got to really use your head and do some serious thinking. This isn't just any night, but the night before the main engagement. Your description of nature should have something threatening about it. If you want to depict the moon, you should have it just peeking through from time to time, but most of the time covered by black clouds, or, to use a stronger expression, covered with ominous clouds. It goes without saying that you'll need all those night sounds and rustlings. No need for any nightingales, save that for the part about the victory, then you can write about nightingales as much as you like. What we need here is birds that create a mood of anxiety, do you follow? Ravens, for example. What kind of cry do ravens make at night?"

"None whatsoever, Comcom General!" said Zhukov, jumping to his feet. "They make cries in the daytime and at dusk, but at night they're silent."

"Alright, if ravens don't make cries at night, find another sort of night bird that does, owls or something like that."

"I'll describe bitterns, Comcom General. They make the most alarming cries."

"Very good," remarked the general with satisfaction. "That's using your head. And as a matter of fact we can use crows for the morning panorama. They'll gather on the eve of the battle, knowing they'll have something to feed on soon. I think you've understood your task now. Let's move on to the next issue. Where's my note on that? Aha, here it is. His Thoughts Before the Battle. Let me explain the situation. It's the eve of a serious engagement with the Buryat-Mongolian invaders. And of course thoughts of all sorts arise in the Genialissimo's mind. Not gloomy thoughts of course, because as a great optimist he believes in ultimate victory. His thoughts at this moment should be wise, profound, and, I would even say, philosophical. This part is for you, Savchenko. You're our philosopher, this is where your talents come in. When describing the Genialissimo's thoughts, you should always keep in mind that these are great thoughts of genius. And his main ideas should be reflected in those thoughts. Needless to say, what those thoughts on the eve of battle should reflect is the Genialissimo's characteristic historical optimism. His thoughts might go more or less like this—Though I may die, my life will not have been in vain. It will have been given for the general good. Do you follow me here?"

"I do," replied Savchenko evenly.

"Now, as for the description of all the military preparations, troop positions, and weapons, I have no worries on that score because we have Malevich to take care of all that," said the general, indicating one of the colonels. "Malevich, as a great specialist in these matters and a former staff officer, you will do an excellent job here. And you, Shtukin, also have a pretty good sense of what's involved in military engineering."

The planning session was coming to an end. The two proof-readers were ordered not to let any grammatical errors get past them, and the poet Merzev was given the special task of supplying the chapter-to-be with colorful epithets and vivid metaphors. On that note, the planning session closed. Communi Ivanovich wished all those present artistic inspiration and great success in their work.

Taking their notebooks and pencils, the officers filed out, leaving Smerchev and me alone.

"So," said Communi Ivanovich, "now you've seen how we work. As you can imagine, it's a tough job running such a large collective. One person writes one thing and another person writes another thing, and sometimes the one just won't go with the other, and you have to make them do it all over. How many people wrote your books?"

"What do you mean how many?" I said in surprise. "I wrote them by myself."

"By yourself?" said Smerchev in astonishment. "All by yourself? And you described nature and love and your hero's experiences and kept an eye out for ideological errors too?"

"There were some things I didn't do," I said. "I mean, of course, I tried to make sure that my heroes were stable, ideologically speaking, but since I wasn't all that stable myself, they sometimes turned out to be very bad characters indeed."

"Just as I thought," said Smerchev, shaking his head. "Of course, it's simply impossible for one person to write a major piece of work so that it is both on a high artistic and a high ideological level. Stay here with us, and we'll give you an entire brigade of writers. All you'll do is give them instructions, they'll do the writing, and you'll put your name to it."

I did not have time to reply with a joke to Smerchev's proposition, because his office door flew open and in dashed Siromakhin in a lather. He whispered something to Smerchev and then informed us that we were to leave at once for the Kremlin.

PART V

INSIDE
THE KREMLIN

We arrived at the Kremlin at the end of the workday, around five-thirty.

I noticed that Dzerzhin was quite at home there as well.

We walked down long, wide corridors with red runners on the floor and through large halls that had enormous windows, ponderous, many-tiered chandeliers, and large busts in the corners, some marble and some bronze.

As we walked, I tried to figure out where the Georgiev Hall and Chamber of Facets were, but I could not figure it out, and found myself thoroughly unable to concentrate.

Many of the doors were under guard; as we passed each, two guards with submachine guns would present arms and click their heels.

Finally we ended up in a spacious room, in the center of which was a large green table. Many portraits decorated the room. To the left, a full-length portrait of the Genialissimo in uniform, his boots gleaming, holding a pair of white gloves in one hand. He seemed to be in the act of slapping them against his boot top and gazing at the opposite wall, where Christ, Marx, Engels, and Lenin looked back rapturously at him.

In one corner of the room, a middle-aged secretary in a colonel's uniform sat at a desk with many telephones. Greeting our arrival with the friendliest of smiles, she disappeared behind a leather-covered door and returned at once to invite us in.

The office I entered was large and old, something from my past life. It contained costly furniture, leather sofas and armchairs, and a long conference table. A writing desk with a dozen telephones of various colors was in the far corner, and there, before a half-length portrait of the Genialissimo, sat an imposing older man unrolling a *Pravda*. Completely bald, his skull gleamed, and he wore a marshal's epaulettes on his shoulders.

Coming out from behind his desk, he surprised me by not being in short pants, but wearing light blue jodhpurs, with red stripes down the sides, and high box-calf boots. A large variety of medals hung from his light blue military jacket, the very highest ones among them.

Dzerzhin introduced us, and I learned that this man was the Genialissimo's deputy at SECO, chief marshal of the Moscowrep, five-time recipient of the Hero of Moscowrep medal, Hero of Communist Labor, and Hero of Socialist Labor, Beria Ilich Maturin.

Beria Ilich embraced me like a brother, whacked me on the back, and said, "So, it's you!" Then, turning to Dzerzhin Gavrilovich, he asked how preparations for my jubilee were progressing. Dzerzhin reported that the preparations were going full steam ahead, the workers were vying with each other in taking on even greater responsibilities, the Editorial Commission was ready to issue a mass edition of my books, but . . .

"We'll deal with that 'but' right now," interrupted the marshal. He seated me in a leather armchair, taking the other for himself while Dzerzhin sat down on the couch. First, the marshal inquired as to how I was feeling and how I liked it here.

I looked around again and said that I liked his office, it was beautiful and spacious.

"No," said Beria Ilich, "I wasn't asking about my office, I mean how do you like it here in the Moscowrep?"

"By and large," I said, "it's alright, I like it. It's very interesting."

"And do you like the weather?"

"Yes, I do. Perfect communist weather. The sun is out and there's not a cloud in the sky."

266

"That's right," he agreed. "It's a pretty decent summer. But, unfortunately, there are also times when it's cloudy. We try to combat that, but we're not always successful. And sometimes those periods are even too protracted. Still, it's bad without *some* clouds. It gets too hot. What do you think?"

I said that, yes, it was quite hot.

"Yes, it is on the warmish side," he said. "Not the usual summer for our climate zone. Of course, it's much nicer when the sun shines but doesn't blind you, when it warms you without roasting you. And date palms grow and girls in short tennis skirts walk around eating ice cream and look at you with eyes full of love, isn't that so?" he asked, and looked at me as if he were peering into my very soul.

I felt I had broken out in sweat. I thought, My God, what's happening? How does he know my dream? I hadn't told anyone about it, not even Iskra. Even though their technology is backward, can they still spy on your dreams?

"There are a few things we can do," said the marshal with a grin, thereby indicating that he could not only spy on dreams but read minds as well.

"And we know how to read books," chimed in Dzerzhin, a remark that threw me for a loop.

To tell the truth, all this had started making me feel a little queasy.

"Of course," continued the marshal, "real life and dreams are two different things, success doesn't come so easily in real life. And communism turned out somewhat differently than we'd planned. Marx let us down a little. He was wrong."

"In two different phases," interjected Dzerzhin. It should be mentioned that he was entirely uninhibited in the marshal's presence.

"That's right," said the marshal, "in two different phases. Against the background of all world history, it's not so significant, but we feel it. Marx's mistake was in promising the complete impoverishment of the workers under capitalism, but this occurred . . ."

"Is occurring," corrected Dzerzhin.

"But this occurred," repeated the marshal angrily, "under communism. And, of course, a person with a humorous turn of mind might even find all this something to laugh at. There's plenty to laugh at here. Our short pants, our newspaper published in the form of toilet-paper, the shortages of primary matter. But is it a good thing to laugh at the poor? Well, is it?"

"It isn't," I admitted, feeling very embarrassed. "But I was only laughing to myself."

"Not only to yourself!" objected Dzerzhin, turning his head.

"Not only to yourself," seconded the marshal, peering intently at me. "And so, Classic Nikitich, I'd like to have a little talk with you about art. That's a very interesting subject, no end to it. What is art, why does it exist, where does it get its strange and mysterious power, those are questions no one can answer. To the best of my knowledge, you think that art is no more than a reflection of life, is that right?"

"That's right," I said. "That's more or less what I think."

"But that's absolutely wrong!" shouted the marshal, and, leaping up from his chair, he began dashing about the room like a young man. "Classic Nikitich, there's something I want to tell you. Listen carefully to what I say. Your point of view is absolutely wrong. Art does not reflect life, but transforms it." He even made very vigorous gestures, as if trying to mimic the transformational power of art. "You understand," he repeated excitedly, "it transforms life. And even more than that, art does not reflect life, life reflects art. And now you'll laugh at our beliefs . . ."

"What do you mean, for God's sake," I said hastily, "I'd never dare do that."

"Alright, alright," said the marshal, knitting his brows, "but you still aren't able to understand that we know far more about you than you could have ever imagined. But not only about you. Our knowledge of everything is much deeper and broader than the knowledge available to the people of your time. And we know with perfect exactitude that primary matter is secondary matter and secondary matter is primary matter."

"That's nothing but nonsense," I said to my own surprise.

"That's metaphysics, Hegelianism, and Kantianism. In reality, primary matter is primary matter and secondary matter is secondary matter."

For all that life had taught me, it hadn't taught me to button my lip. How many times had intelligent people tried to instill one elementary lesson in me: don't shoot off your mouth the second some idea comes into your head. Think a little, see if the idea's worth telling to anyone.

My untimely remark had a very definite and perhaps even negative effect on both the marshal and Dzerzhin.

Without another word, Beria Ilich returned to his chair, sat down, and began staring off somewhere past me. Dzerzhin looked over at the marshal. Both of them remained silent, and their silence lasted for quite some time. Then the marshal drew his hand across his face as if rubbing the weariness away and said softly, "Classic Nikitch, the question of matter is not subject to discussion. Primary matter is secondary matter and secondary matter is primary matter. You can refer to Marx and others who taught you in your day that matter precedes consciousness, but those teachers of yours contradicted themselves. They demanded consciousness from people but avoided giving them material remuneration. The theory and the practice were in contradiction. Here they are in perfect harmony. But let's talk about something more interesting: your novel, for example. I recently read it again from cover to cover. What can I say? An interesting book. It even represents a stage in your work that you would hardly have reached in Siberia."

Once again he peered into my soul, and once again I felt queasy. Suddenly he burst into laughter and began speaking in a much warmer tone of voice: "As I've already said, it's quite a wicked novel. It's as if you picked up an awl and jammed it in where it would hurt the most. But it's rich in fantasy, and not in the least boring to read. To tell the truth, I laughed a lot, and sometimes I even cried. Yes, it was a case of what I'd call laughter through tears."

"That's right," said Dzerzhin in support. "It isn't a book that just goes for the laughs."

"Yes, indeed," said the marshal in support of Dzerzhin, "it's

269

more serious than it seems at first glance. Though I must say that in your description of the darker sides of life here, you might be overdoing things. You also seem to be savoring and taking pleasure in the seamier side."

"And there's a lot of naturalism," remarked Dzerzhin.

"Yes," said the marshal, "you lay it on a little too thick with the naturalism. For example, when I read the passage about the vegetarian pork, I feel like vomiting, just like your hero."

"Excuse me," I interrupted. "That didn't happen with one of my heroes, that happened to me. I've never described that anywhere. Perhaps one of your agents was spying on me at the time."

"There's no need for that," said the marshal with a frown. "There's no need to tell us fairy tales. You're not stupid, and you can see that we know everything about you. But the dream you describe, that's another story. I was even surprised. It turns out that you're able to write about the good things too. When I read about the sun shining all the time and the palm trees growing and the birds singing and the girls in their little tennis skirts. . . . When I came to that description of the dream (though at first you don't know it's a dream), I thought, The son of a bitch can write! And I expected all the rest to be in the same vein. There I was all excited, and you hit me with that business about the vegetarian pork!"

The marshal spat and then, hands behind his back, began pacing his office.

"Couldn't you have left the pork out? We gave you everything. You're given fried eggs and ham and pâté and caviar of every sort. What else do you need? Coffee? We didn't know that you were such a diehard coffee drinker. Fine, you can have whatever kind of coffee you want. By the way, we can order some brought to us right now. What kind would you like?"

"Turkish," I said, entirely certain that they had never even heard of it.

The marshal clapped his hands and the secretary appeared at once in the doorway.

"Three coffees!" said the marshal. "Turkish for him, capuccino for me and. . . ."

"Corn coffee for me," said Dzerzhin modestly.

The secretary left and returned one second later carrying a tray. I was given a cup of real Turkish coffee. It may have been just because I was longing for it so badly, but I never drank a cup of coffee that tasted better in my life. Emboldened, I asked the marshal what need category he was in.

"I haven't thought about that for a long time," he said. "I suppose I'm beyond needs now. But let's go back to your dream. If you dreamed of such a beautiful life, why didn't you develop the idea any further? After all, the fact is that we all live on illusions. Dreams are primary matter, and life is secondary matter, and this is easy to prove. Sometimes we have bad dreams but we don't always want to wake up from them. But when something bad happens in life, we always want to go to sleep. And that's only right. Because dreams are much richer than life. In our dreams we eat what we like, we have the women we want, in dreams we die and come back to life, but in real life we can only do the former."

Just then the secretary, looking flustered, ran into the room and whispered something in the marshal's ear. Now in a flurry himself, Beria Ilich sprang to his feet and grabbed the receiver on the red telephone.

"Yes," he said, "Maturin here. Yes, sir! I will! We'll be right there." He hung up the receiver and looked over at me, his face betraying great excitement.

"We've been summoned by Horizon Timofeyevich."

"Who?" I said in surprise, surprising him all the more.

"You mean you still don't know who Horizon Timofeyevich is?" Beria Ilich looked over at Dzerzhin, who looked back over at me. I shrugged my shoulders.

"Horizon Timofeyevich Razin," explained the marshal, still in an excited state, "is the chairman of the Editorial Commission and could essentially be said to be the Genialissimo's deputy on Earth. And listen, please do not argue with him. Agree to everything he

271

suggests. In the extreme, we can make some changes later on. I'll be keeping an eye on you. Of course, you could look better, but it'll do. Straighten your collar and let's go. You wait for us here," he said to Dzerzhin.

THE GENIALISSIMO'S
DEPUTY

Once again we walked through halls and down passages, the guards snapping to attention, clicking their heels, and presenting arms.

The secretary to the chairman of the Editorial Commission was an older man with the rank of colonel general. All the same, he fussed about like a sergeant.

"Aha, so it's you!" he said, nervously thrusting his hand out at me. "Horizon Timofeyevich is just finished with his treatment and so he has a little time for you. Please come in."

Opening the door, the secretary entered first, but stopped to allow me and Beria Ilich to pass. Finally, and for the first time, I saw an old man in Moscowrep. And what an old man he was! He sat in a wheelchair, not at his desk but in the center of the room. Two hoses, one yellow, one red, ran from the wheelchair to the wall behind him. The old man himself was a total wreck: head drooping to one side, tongue hanging out, arms limp and lifeless. A thick wire attached to a horn-shaped microphone protruded from his left ear. The old man seemed to be sleeping. But, as soon as we entered, the nurse standing beside him gave him an injection directly through his pants. He shuddered, woke up, and tried to straighten his head, but it fell to the other side. His eyes, however, remained nearly entirely open.

"Who's there?" he asked, eyeing us with displeasure.

The marshal strode briskly over to him, picked up the speaker attachment and, placing it to his lips, reported respectfully, "On your orders, I have brought Classic to see you."

"Aha," said Horizon, barely able to make his tongue work. "Claffic. Fo, come over here, Claffic, come over here."

I drew nearer and took the speaker from the marshal's hand. "Hello!" I shouted into the horn.

"Fofo," muttered the chairman, "I'm feeling fo fo. You fee the two hofes? The yellow one fupplies me with primary matter, and the red one is a fuction tube for fecondary matter, to keep my organifm alive."

He tried to raise his head again and even achieved some success this time, but could not maintain it, and his head fell forward onto his chest. The nurse came up from behind him, set his head vertical, and stayed there to hold it in place. The old man seemed to perk up even more. And something akin to curiosity appeared in his eyes.

"Fo that's what you look like!" he said with evident approval. "Handfome, handfome. How old are you?"

"I'll be one hundred soon, Your Excellency!" I shouted into the speaker.

"Ftill young," observed the chairman. "I'm already a hundred and four. That's not fo much either. What pank is that?"

Taking a quick look down at my pants, I said, "If you're referring to my pants, Your Excellency, I had nothing to do with it, these are the pants they gave me. I came here wearing a nice normal pair."

"What are you talking about!" whispered the colonel general angrily. "Horizon Timofeyevich is not referring to your pants, but your rank."

"Yes," said Horizon Timofeyevich to Beria Ilich, "his pank fould be made higher, he's a claffic, after all."

"It'll be taken care of immediately!" Beria Ilich shouted into the speaker. "We'll promote him to major. Or even colonel."

"Why a colonel?" said Horizon. "Make him a general. And you, my beauty," he said, trying to raise his eyes to the nurse, "don't hold my head like that. When I give it a little fake, let go of it a little."

But the nurse did not let go of it and even shook it herself.

"Fplendid," said the Chairman in approval. "That will fuffice. Fo, you've agreed to take out all those fims and fo forth?"

Not understanding him, I glanced over at Beria Ilich and saw him winking vigorously at me. I nodded.

"Fplendid," said the chairman, the nurse nodding his head for him. "Everything fuperfluous muft always be removed, and what ifn't fuperfluous. . . ." Without completing his sentence, he fell back to sleep, his tongue dropped out again, and the nurse let his head rest to one side.

I looked over at the marshal, who then looked to the colonel general, who spread his hands wide and said, "That's it! Horizon has given his instructions and is resting now."

The nurse took hold of the wheelchair from behind and, gathering up the hoses, wheeled the chairman away, while the three of us tiptoed back into the reception room.

Beria Ilich sighed deeply and looked over questioningly at the colonel general.

"Everything's fine," said the colonel general with a smile. "Horizon Timofeyevich was in a very good mood, and he even made a few remarks."

"Yes, of course," agreed the marshal, "entirely apt remarks." He said the same thing to Dzerzhin, who greeted us with the question, "How did it go?"

"And so did you understand everything?" he asked me. "The demands weren't great at all: a few more dreams, a little less unnecessary realism, and take out all the Sims. Agreed?"

"No!" I said.

"What?!" The marshal jumped up, and Dzerzhin reached for his pocket. But he immediately took his hand away, walked over to me and said affectionately: "Agree, darling, people don't usually disagree here."

Close to my wit's end, I clutched my head. "Listen," I shouted. "Why are you plaguing me? What is it I'm supposed to correct? What novel are you talking about? And who is this Sim? If you mean Karnavalov, yes I knew him and I even used to go visit him in Toronto. But I never shared his views, and, what's more, I threw his letter addressed to the current leaders in the trash before I came."

"We know that," said the marshal with a smile. Then he exchanged glances with Dzerzhin. "And now throw Karnavalov himself out."

"Out of what?" I asked.

"Out of your novel, my darling," said Dzerzhin with a smile.

"Out of what novel?" I asked wearily. "Don't you understand, I've never written any novels about Karnavalov."

I sank into a chair and got out a cigarette. My hands were shaking, and I couldn't strike the match. Meanwhile, a strange, oppressive, and, I would even say, ominous silence had settled in the room.

"Alright," said Beria Ilich finally. "You're so upset and you spoke with so much conviction that I almost believed you. But there are still the facts. And facts, as they say, are stubborn things. Alright. Fine. It's time that I showed you something."

He rose heavily, walked over to a safe, and, his back to me, began working the combination.

"Beria Ilich," said Dzerzhin in a free and easy tone, "I see your safe is exactly like those in Swiss banks."

"It is a Swiss safe," replied the marshal. "It even says so on it: 'Made in Switzerland.' "

The safe opened. The marshal rummaged about inside for a good while and then finally withdrew a book with a reddish cover and set it in front of me.

"Recognize it?"

I picked up the book and began examining it. I read the title— *Moscow 2042*—then shifted my eyes to the author's name and saw that it was mine. There wouldn't have been anything so surprising about that. At one time or another every writer holds in his hands a book he himself has written. But the point was that, as far as I could recall, I had never written any such book.

"Well, what do you say now?" said the marshal.

"One minute," I said.

I looked over the dust jacket, turned to the title page, and read the publication information. It was dated 1987. But I had left Stockdorf in 1982. The fact of the matter was that I had yet to live in 1987.

"There's something haywire here," I muttered, then took a peek at the beginning of the book. There I found a description of my conversation with Rudi, my visit to Fräulein Globke, my abduction by the Arabs, and my meeting with Bukashev. Everything was detailed and accurate and, most important, written in my own style.

It made no sense. I could imagine that in sixty years' time someone could have researched all the details and, on the basis of reports by secret agents and other archival material, could have created a novel like this. But that someone could succeed in penetrating my mind and imitating my style, that I absolutely could not believe, because, just between us, my style is quite inimitable.

I glanced into the middle part of the book, my eye at once caught by a chapter entitled "New Word on Sim."

"Interesting?" said the marshal, looking over my shoulder.

"One minute," I said and, with mounting interest, read that rather short chapter.

I had thought I'd known everything about Sim, but there proved to be a good deal of substance I didn't know.

It turns out that, during my absence in the twentieth century, he had torn himself away from *The Greater Zone* long enough to dash off four slabs of memoirs entitled *SIM*.

The book the marshal had presented to me as mine said that I had read all four of those slabs (which I personally find very difficult to believe); not only that, the book said that, on the one hand, I had read the slabs long before arriving in the Moscowrep but, on the other hand, it said that I'd read them after I'd come back home.

They said that writers shouldn't explain everything, shouldn't spell everything out for the reader. The writer should allow the reader the opportunity to do a little work, expend a little effort of his own and find things that the writer himself had failed to see. If that's the case, then you figure out how it came to be that I read my own book before I had written it. Yes, go ahead if you want and think it all through. As for me, the whole business has my head reeling, and for that reason I'm simply going to recount what I managed to read in Beria Ilich's office.

I read that the first chapter of the first slab of Sim's memoirs began with a description of an ordinary morning in the life of an ordinary Soviet boy whose father is in prison and whose mother brings packages to the prison. The boy goes to school, comes home, and starts doing his homework. He's in the third grade and cannot fathom why they have imprisoned his father, a former Baltic Sea sailor, a commissar on the cruiser *Aurora*, and later the people's commissar for higher education. But even though the boy's soul is in pain, he still has to keep up with his schoolwork.

On that day, his mother gone, the young Sim ate dinner alone and then sat down to his lesson. His literature assignment was to memorize a new patriotic poem:

> *In the great outdoors, on a green oak tree,*
> *Two brave falcons were having a talk.*
> *And all people knew who those falcons were:*
> *The first one was — Lenin,*
> *And the second — Stalin . . .*

Sim says of himself that even back then he had a phenomenal memory. He even memorized that predator poem in no time at all, but then he grew thoughtful, wondering why he, who had taken a critical view of reality since childhood, was unable to picture Lenin and Stalin, sitting on an oak tree like two birds.

And just as he was subjecting that poem to critical analysis, there was a knock at the door. Sim opened the door to behold a filthy, tattered old wanderer with a bushy, tangled beard and a knapsack on his back. The old wanderer asked for a drink of water, and after he'd finished it and brushed the drops off his beard, he looked intently at Sim and asked: "What's your name, child?"

"Sim," answered Sim.

"That's right," said the wanderer, "Sim. Alright, now listen to me and remember everything I tell you, my lad. You shall be the tsar of the Russians. You shall be Sim the First." And with those words the wanderer vanished, as if into thin air.

By his own admission, Sim was an impressionable boy, and the old wanderer's words caused profound confusion in his soul.

Alone again, he tried to continue memorizing the poem, but now nothing would stick in his mind. Just the reverse, all of a sudden thoughts quite odd for a Pioneer leaped into mind.

280

> *And all people knew who these falcons were:*
> *The first one was—Lenin,*
> *And the second—Stalin . . .*

"And the third one is me!" said Sim suddenly to himself and, as he himself wrote, he was excited immediately by a keen foretaste of an uncommon destiny.

He told his mother about the old wanderer's visit. Dejected because her parcel for her husband had been rejected again, she let the story go in one ear and out the other. But later on it came back to mind, and she asked Sim to tell her the whole story again from the beginning and asked many questions about the old wanderer— what he looked like, what he was wearing. She scolded Sim for being too trusting and told him that from now on he was always to ask who was at the door and not to open it for strangers.

"But, Mama," said Sim, "why did he say I'd be tsar?"

"There's no shortage of crazy people," said Sim's mother. "They blab whatever comes to mind. They have a bad influence on children's minds. They should all be thrown in jail."

But that same night, having first made him swear a terrifying oath, she revealed the secret of his uncommon origins to him. Sim Glebych Karnavalov was not Sim Simych's father. His real father was Nikolai Alexandrovich Romanov, Emperor and Autocrat of All the Russias . . .

Sim Simych's mother, Ekaterina Petrovna, told him that, just before the Revolution, when her husband was serving on the cruiser *Aurora*, she was working as a laundress in the Winter Palace and became intimate with the tsar. The tsar was not engaging in debauchery, but did this solely to help save the Russian crown. He felt that, one way or the other, a revolution was in the offing, his heir was seriously ill, and the future was uncertain. That is why, with the consent of his wife Aliks, the emperor could bring himself to take such an unusual step. And on the night of their secret rendezvous, he implored Ekaterina Petrovna in the name of Christ that, if God sent her a boy, she should guard him like the apple of

281

her eye and only when the time came, when there was a sign from above, was she to reveal his true identity to him.

While I was reading, both SECO men, Beria and Dzerzhin, kept peeking over my shoulder, checking my reaction, and displaying considerable impatience. As soon as I would turn my head for a second to think through what I'd just read, Beria would ask me, before I had my wits about me, what I thought of it all.

"It's raving lunacy," I said.

"Is it?" said Beria Ilich in a clipped voice. "Is it lunacy? Is that what you think? Why?"

"It's all lunacy," I said. "Just take the time periods involved. I don't know, maybe some geniuses have a gestation period of nine months, but nine years . . . To be honest, I don't quite understand why you're so upset by what Karnavalov says. After all, it's perfectly absurd."

"That's exactly right, it's absurd," agreed the marshal. "But the point is, as history demonstrates, it is absurd ideas, to be more precise, idiotic ideas that have the best chance of winning the mass's minds. And that is why Sim. . . . By the way, do you happen to know why he has such a strange name?"

I did happen to know, because I had heard the story of his name's origin from the lips of Sim Simych himself. His father had also been called Sim by his comrades in arms, his full name being Simeon. Simeon Glebych. But he liked being called Sim, and so he decided to name his son Sim. When people asked him what the name meant, he would say, "Simple. SIM stands for Smash the Ixploiters of Money."

"That's not right," someone would say. "It's exploiters, not ixploiters, and so you should have named him Sem."

But Karnavalov would have none of it. Sem sounded too bourgeois, the boy's name was Sim.

"He told you all that himself?" asked the marshal.

"Yes, of course. And more than once."

"But could you speak of this publicly?" asked Dzerzhin, who had been silent for a long time until then.

"Why not? If you set up a reading for me . . ."

"We will set one up, of course," interrupted the marshal. "That's just what we're doing. That's the purpose of the Jubilee Pentagon—there's a mass campaign on, and your novel will even be published. The celebration will feature the best people of our republic, leading actors will read passages from your works, and they may also do some singing and dancing. And just maybe," he said with a cunning squint, "there'll be a performance of your favorite Ukrainian song. But we have a favor to ask of you, something on which the Editorial Commission insists—that you remove all references to Sim. He adds nothing of beauty to your novel, on the contrary, he even makes it clumsy and ponderous. Expunge those references, that's all. What do you think?"

To tell the truth, I couldn't think. Because, apart from the chapter "New Word on Sim," I still hadn't read it.

I figured that they of course would offer to let me read the whole book through then and there, but for some reason they were stalling and, from a few of the marshal's remarks, I deduced that they were afraid to give me my own book because if I read it I might fall under its influence. But Dzerzhin came up with an idea: if I read the book I would indeed fall under its influence, but, if I corrected it and reread it, the final result would be that I would come under the wholesome influence of the corrected version, and that would be a good thing.

The marshal thought for a moment then said that Dzerzhin was probably right, and it might be worthwhile to allow me to read a little more of my book, and that he would try to secure permission. He might be able to push it through the Supreme Pentagon, convince the Editorial Commission, and for that he was even prepared to meet with Horizon Timofeyevich.

"What are you saying!" I said. "Why bother an old man with such trifles? Why do you have to go through all those pentagons and commissions? Why can't you simply give me that book, if only for a night? I'll read it and give it right back."

The marshal looked at me as if I were mad.

"You're a strange person," he said after a moment's thought. "This is the printed word, after all. You don't even have a pass for it . . ." His face brightened with a thought and he turned to Dzerzhin Gavrilovich. "Listen, Siromakhin, drop by and see Morozov. He wanted to see you about something."

"Morozov wants to see me?" said Dzerzhin with a dubious glance at the marshal.

"Go see him, go see him," repeated the marshal impatiently.

As soon as Dzerzhin left the room, the marshal began acting oddly. First he crept over to the door Siromakhin had just closed and peeped through the keyhole. Then he ran over to his desk, pulled all his phone lines out of their sockets, cast a doubtful look at the ceiling, and beckoned me over.

"Listen," he whispered, shoving me into a corner, "I'll give you the book for one night. But no one must know. Even the woman you're living with."

"Fine," I whispered back. "I'll lock myself in the natfunctbur and read it there."

"And not a word to Dzerzhin either. No one at all. And if you happen to get picked up with that book, you're not to admit that you got it from me."

"What am I supposed to say?" I asked, extremely surprised.

"Whatever you want. You can say that you smuggled it in through customs. You can say that you found it in a steam bus or in a garbage dump. Whatever you want, just don't give me away. Do you swear?"

"I swear!" I said solemnly. "But I don't understand who might pick me up apart from your own people."

"Oh, are you naive!" he said with a dismissive wave of the hand. "In this republic you can't tell who are your own people and who aren't. Alright, keep it until tomorrow."

I had just managed to stuff the book into my shirt when Dzerzhin returned and said that Morozov was in a meeting and he couldn't get in to see him.

"Well, if that's the case, it's alright," said the marshal in a carefree tone, and he winked to me with Dzerzhin noticing. "You're both free to go now," he announced, extending his broad hand to me. "Very nice to meet you, Classic Nikitich."

A STROLL

A strange feeling overcame me when Dzerzhin and I reached Red Square: the feeling that I was a free man again, but that it could have turned out otherwise.

Night had already fallen and the sky overhead was strewn with stars that seemed especially bright against the background of the blacked-out city.

"So, how did you like our marshal?" asked Dzerzhin with a grin.

"I think he's an interesting person." No sooner had I said that than I saw an illuminated flying object sail slowly over the square from west to east.

"Look at that!" I said, nudging Dzerzhin.

"Where?" Dzerzhin craned his neck and, seeing what I'd seen, starred himself. I starred myself too. I did this quite automatically and realized that I was becoming a true Communite.

Dzerzhin offered to see me back, and we began cutting across Red Square. The evening was warm and still, and the streets entirely deserted. I don't think we saw a single person along the way. Dzerzhin remained silent and so did I, thinking about all the strange things I'd seen and heard that day. But I had the feeling that there would be another revelation before the day was done.

"Listen," I said to Dzerzhin, taking a more familiar tone now, "why are you all so worried about Sim Simych? I can see that you might be bothered by his followers, all those Simites, but Sim himself has been dead for a good while now. If he were alive now, he'd be. . . . How old would he be?"

"One hundred and sixteen," said Dzerzhin.

"There you go. One hundred and sixteen. . . . Of course there are those wild mountain people who live even longer than that, but I'm sure Sim died a long time ago."

We were already in front of the hotel by then and Dzerzhin had his hand on the door to open it for me.

"First read the book you've got inside your shirt, and then we'll have a little talk."

STEPANIDA
ZUEVA-JOHNSON

I have the most varied and conflicting memories, and they've become so mixed in my mind that even I can't tell which of them are primary and which are secondary.

I remember that I locked myself in the natfunctbur that night and read my book in secret from Iskrina, and that later I hid the book behind the television. But this memory is contradicted by another which tells me that I did not read any book whatsoever, but rather read about it in the Lenin Library. Dzerzhin Gavrilovich and I were driven to the library by good old Vasya, who on the way choked with laughter as he asked me if I knew the main feature of communism. I shrugged my shoulders and Vasya, with a glance at Dzerzhin, who was sitting in the back seat, whispered to me that the main feature of communism lay in erasing the difference between primary matter and secondary matter. Dzerzhin, however, overheard, and brandished a fist at Vasya, though good-naturedly, it seemed to me. Stepping out from the steam car, I decided to make a point of showing Dzerzhin my knowledge of the Lenin Library, and I at once headed straight for the main entrance.

"No, we don't go in that way," said Dzerzhin. "That's the entrance for the general public."

"You mean we can't use the general entrance?" I asked.

"Of course, we can," said Dzerzhin, "but that's not where we're going. In there you can get only works by the Genialissimo or on the Genialissimo, and what we need is something else."

287

We turned the corner, walked the length of the entire building, and finally ducked in through an inconspicuous door modestly marked Department of Preliminary Literature. Then came a system of hallways, in each of which we were stopped and had our papers thoroughly checked. Finally, we reached the main depository, which consisted of vast, interconnected rooms.

By the way, having been in that library countless times in my past life, I had never seen this entire collection, and had only the foggiest notion of it from the catalog. And now I was seeing it all. The collected works of all the world's greatest writers from Homer to Solzhenitsyn. From ancient parchments to the cheap editions of the present day.

There were readers seated at tables in each of these rooms, one, sometimes two, maybe even three readers, but never more than that. And they were all in SECO uniform, their ranks no less than major. Surrounded by stacks of books, they were all making notes, apparently intending to put this reading to use in the ideological struggle.

But one reader, a woman, a lieutenant colonel in SECO, was putting her privileged position to personal use. She was reading *Anna Karenina* (I noticed the title), and, all vigilance lost, was almost weeping out loud.

Naturally, I felt like spending a while in the depository, but Dzerzhin hurried me on, and, after passing through a few more rooms and corridors, found ourselves in front of a door marked: The Obscurantist Works of S.S. Karnavalov.

Here guards not only checked our documents, but even frisked our pockets. Discovering Dzerzhin's pistol, they asked that he surrender it to the head of the guard for safekeeping.

It was only then that we entered the room (actually, it was made of at least three rooms joined together) containing not only editions of all sixty slabs in Russian and a hundred foreign languages, but also extensive literature on Sim himself: memoirs, research, press collections and dissertations.

But there proved to be even more than that here. In the room next to this one, Dzerzhin Gavrilovich introduced me to a frail and sharp-nosed woman who introduced herself as SECO Lieutenant Sovetina Kulyabko.

On Dzerzhin's request, she readily explained that this room contained information gathered by secret agents on Sim's origins, life story, his way of life, habits, tastes, the strong and the weak points in his character, his sexual oddities, the files drawn up on him in school, the Komsomol, the orphanage, and the university, reports on his connections with various people, love relations, friendships, acquaintances as well as professional and chance relations. Kept in storage here were samples of his handwriting, his fingerprints, the records of the interrogation of his supporters, and innumerable photographs and slides, taken both openly and by hidden cameras, even at night with infrared light.

Having at once offered to show me some of the slides, she hung a small screen on the wall, pulled down the shade, switched on the projector, and began loading it with slides. It was all very interesting. There were pictures of Sim Simych at various times and in various situations. In one he was still quite young, seen with a group of orphanage pupils. There were pictures of him in the camps (full face and profile). There was a photograph for his passport after he left the camp—his face was weary and emaciated, yet stern.

Then there was a time gap, followed by photographs from nearly every day of his life. Dozens of wedding pictures of him and Janet. A day of triumph—holding his first book. At his desk. Out skiing. On his bicycle. Holding a cat. Then another arrest, prison, and even a picture of him being pushed out of the plane with a parachute on his back. Of course, there were photographs of him taking part in countless meetings, conferences, and press conferences, and meeting the president of the United States in the White House.

But some of the photographs taken by a hidden camera or with infrared light were too revelatory. I am sure that if I described in detail what I saw up there on the screen, this book would gain another hundred thousand readers. It's a pity that my innate moral good taste does not permit me to depict scenes of this sort.

I will say though that Simych did cause me some confusion. Knowing of his profound religiosity and famous asceticism, I naturally was shocked to see him in undignified positions not only with Janet but with other members of the opposite sex. There were no fewer than a dozen such women, some of whom I knew personally. One was a well-known woman novelist, a second was a famous American movie star, and a third was. . . . The face of the third woman wasn't visible but there was no problem recognizing her from behind. Seeing Stepanida and Sim in that posture, I felt a sudden flare of jealousy that even made me shudder and grit my teeth.

"What's the matter?" asked Lieutenant Kulyabko, sounding worried.

Embarrassed, I said that the last picture had been a little unpleasant to see because I had been quite close to that woman at one time.

"We know that," said Dzerzhin.

Lieutenant Kulyabko said that the slides depicting the details of my relationship with that woman were also available and she would be glad to show them as well.

"No! No!" I cried. "Anything but that! Can't you please destroy them somehow?"

"What are you saying now, my darling!" said Dzerzhin with a slight smile. "Those slides are part of history, and it would be criminal to destroy them. Alright," he said both to me and to Lieutenant Kulyabko, "we've seen the show. Now give us something to read, for example Stepanida's intelligence reports."

"Stepanida's intelligence reports?" I said in surprise. "Did she really write intelligence reports?"

"Did she ever!" said Dzerzhin. "Stepanida Zueva-Johnson was one of our best intelligence agents. Working with Tom Johnson, a former marine she had recruited, she supplied us with a great deal of priceless information."

STEPANIDA'S
REPORTS

I read Stepanida's reports in the library for three days in a row, nonstop. Every morning at eight-thirty, Vasya would come by the hotel for me, then take me back at eleven o'clock at night.

No, no one forced me to work there that long. I was so engrossed in my reading that sometimes I didn't even break for lunch. Especially since the nearest sathineed was located in the Kremlin, whereas on the library premises only general needs were satisfied; the mere memory of vegetarian pork was enough to kill my appetite.

The reports were written in the form of letters to a friend. Supposedly to someone by the name of Katya. In fact, I think, this Katya was a department head or perhaps even the head of the entire KGB.

A good move, I must say. Ordinary letters with a patina of common speech and writing mistakes. All of it in plain form, no code used. And if Sim Simych himself had intercepted those letters, he hardly would have guessed what they really were, for all his perspicacity.

In fact, they said everything there was to say about Sim Simych. Everything about his life, the way he worked, what he was working on, what ideas he was espousing, what he was talking about, his health, and even (women are low!) how he was in bed.

Outwardly, she referred to him with great respect, calling him the "Little Father." But, in fact, her assessments were cool-eyed, sober, sometimes sarcastic, and too subtle for a poorly educated village woman.

Here, for example, is her description of their ripening intimacy.

"Anyway, Katusha, there was a big stir in our little local socetie lately, a guy who's supposed to be a famous Russian came here. All the papers had write-ups on him and he was on the teevee every time you turned it on, a fine figure of a man tho, with an awful beard and a high voice.

"He speaks out against communism and for the Russian Orthodox religon, but he lets the Americans have it too for forgetting about God.

"He says that instead of sacrificing themselves they've gone soft and weak from good living. And greedy, predatory communism is already at your throat and they'll soon be sinking their iron teeth into it. . . .

". . . The writer decided to settle in our parts because as he says, nature here reminds him a lot of central Russia. He bought himself a farm and forty acres of land with a woods and a lake and he's planning to put up a fence around the whole thing.

". . . He lives a solitary life with his family, never goes out, and they say he works up to eighteen hours a day. But he does go to services at St. Georgy's. You can get real close to him there even tho he's always surrounded by his own people and his bodiguard Zilberovich (an Orthodox cossack and ex-Jew) always keeps a sharp lookout for anyone approaching and shoulders everybody away.

". . . I understand. Katusha, what you mean, I used that part to recruit Tom at one time. But Tom is a southerner and impressionable, but the writer lives in a world of his own images, and what's going on in front of him slips right by him, though I've tried more than one thing on him. Every time he goes to church, I try to get right in front of him and kneel down and bow my head to the ground, but though I put it right under his nose he doesn't notice a blessed thing. Tom says I'm a fool, and if I want to show off my best part, why cover it in blue jeans.

292

". . . Tom turned out to be a clever devil, black though he is. Now it's not me who takes a position in front of the writer but as soon as he sees me he moves over and gets behind me and starts praying and praying. I can feel the fish going for the bait, it won't be long now before he swallows it.

". . . He swallowed it!

"Yesterday after the service, that little Jew of his calls me aside and says that a certain famous person needs a secretary and translator who could live on the famous person's estate and provide him with certain small domestic services. And then he says—I've heard you meet all the requirements.

"I said that of course I had all the requirements for domestic service, but that I doubted my abilities as a translator since my knowledge of English was only so-so. But if the famous person needs a maid, then I was even very suited for that job. But, I said, there's one drawback with me, I've got a black husband.

"And then little Jew says we're not racists and we'll give your husband a job too, the famous person needs an extra bodiguard. . . ."

In later letters, Stepanida tells Katusha about settling with Tom on Simych's estate, describes what their duties were, details everything that happens on the estate, and even provides a colorful account of her intimate relations with her employer, which usually took place in the daytime when she was cleaning his office. Sometimes the purely feminine prevailed and she would praise her master and speak with enmity of his wife.

Day after day she observed life at the estate, describing in detail how the "Little Father" worked and prepared for his return to Russia.

He didn't share his plans with her, but sometimes he would give her a smack on the bottom and say, "Don't worry, Steshka, we'll drive out the predators, and I'll bring you and Tom to Moscow. Tom will be a count and you'll be a countess." When Stepanida would express her doubts about Tom becoming a count, since he was black, the Little Father would tell her, "What does that matter? It doesn't mean anything that he's black. As long as he's not a communist or a pluralist. And as for him being black, Peter the Great had his own black man whose blood ended up in Pushkin's veins. What matters is what a man's got inside."

While reading Stepanida's reports, her profiles on the residents of the estate and its visitors, I sometimes laughed so hard I cried. But, when I came to the place in which she described my own arrival, I became profoundly indignant. What a brazen, treacherous, immoral bitch!

No, I am not going to repeat here all her foolish and ridiculous fabrications about me, in which she refers to me as "Pot Belly" and portrays me as a sponger who tries to curry Sim Simych's favor. I never did anything of the sort in my entire life! But the main thing is that she purposely used her behind to seduce me too. And not because she felt a natural attraction to me, but for the basest of reasons: to detain me at the estate so that I would not leave before they wanted me to. And then at the end, having depicted our relations in the most idiotic manner, she drops her country speech and coldly and matter of factly observes, "Sexually speaking, he is of no interest."

Now does that take nerve or what? I, *I* am of no interest! Then who is? And so then why did you cry out that you'd never had a man like me in your life, you bitch?

But what could I have expected from someone like her? A KGB woman is a KGB woman. And it's no accident that I have always been very mistrustful of people in that profession.

DZERZHIN'S
REVELATION

I was so angry and upset that I decided to stop reading and walk back to the hotel without waiting for Vasya. I handed the folder to Lieutenant Kulyabko, watched to make sure she recorded its return in her register, and went outside. Dusk was starting to fall, but it was quite sultry. Clouds had gathered over the Lenin Hills, and thunder was rumbling off and on, but, judging by the wind direction, it seemed the storm would pass to one side.

I crossed Volume Four Avenue (formerly Kalinin Avenue) and walked down the Street of the Genialissimo's August Theses (formerly Granovsky Street) toward First Volume Avenue. To my left was the building that had once housed the Kremlin Polyclinic. It was still something of the sort, if the crowd of long limousines with internal combustion engines was any indication.

Just then, with a wild howl of sirens and flashing lights, a strange motorcade, like the one I'd seen before, consisting of four armored personnel carriers (two in front, two in back) and two long limousines connected by flexible hoses, pulled up near me. I realized that the chairman of the Editorial Commission had arrived, and I stopped to see how they would drag him out of the car (with the hoses or without them?). But suddenly an Intsec man armed with a submachine gun was beside me and telling me that stopping or even looking around was not permitted. He slid back the bolt on his weapon. A word to the wise is sufficient. I set off at a rapid pace, both bowing my head and averting my eyes at the same time.

At the beginning of Afterword to the First Volume Lane, a long line had formed in front of a water main. The line moved slowly because, to satisfy people's needs, only two plastic mugs were chained to the water fountain. The people in line were worked up and shouting to the old woman distributing the water not to give any more than a cup per person. I would have stood in line, but seeing that this would mean an investment of no less than two hours, I went on my way.

Someone called me, I turned around and saw Dzerzhin Gavrilovich running my way with a joyful smile. He told me that he had just been in Horizon Timofeyevich's escort and, catching sight of me, had decided to jump out and walk with me.

"But why does the chairman need an escort of armored personnel carriers?" I asked. "Do they think somebody's planning an attempt on his life?"

"That's right," said Dzerzhin. "To look the truth right in the eye you'd have to say there's somebody planning something against every member of the leadership. You know, there are many secret Simites among the people on the sidewalk here, those people in line, everywhere. The majority of them might be Simites."

"I don't understand," I said. "If that's the case, what's SECO been doing?"

"Oh, my darling," said Dzerzhin with a gesture of chagrin. "It's hard for you to make sense of it all. You're still new here. The thing is that SECO is entirely staffed by CIA agents."

"Now listen," I said with anger, "why are you handing me that crap, if you'll pardon the expression. I'm aware that hostile agents could infiltrate SECO, but, if you want my opinion, saying SECO is CIA through-and-through is utter nonsense."

"Alas, you're still so naive," said Dzerzhin, cunningly narrowing his eyes. "Unfortunately, what I just told you is not utter nonsense but the whole sad truth of it."

The sad truth, in Siromakhin's telling, was that over the course of many years, the CIA had infiltrated SECO step by step. "It's like a cancer, you see," said Dzerzhin, adopting a scientific and instructional tone. "First the cells accumulate slowly. But when their number reaches a critical mass, they seize control of everything. It's the same with the CIA agents. At first, they infiltrated one by one. But later on, when they were a majority in the leadership, they seized control of everything. Now their impudence has reached a point where a cleaning woman can't be hired by SECO without Washington's permission."

"I can't even begin to imagine that," I said.

"Yes," agreed Dzerzhin, "let's be frank, it's no easy thing to imagine."

"But if what you're saying is the truth and you know that all the SECO agents are really CIA agents, then why don't you arrest them?"

"That's all we need!" said Dzerzhin with a laugh. "Even though they are CIA, they call themselves SECO, and, as SECO agents, they're the ones who do the arresting—and of whoever they want."

"Yes, interesting," I said, thinking aloud. "But how come the army is looking the other way? Can't they deal with this situation?"

"They could have. Even though there are plenty of CIA in the army too. Still, the army *could have* dealt with it."

"And so why didn't they?" I asked impatiently.

"Don't you see? If our army smashed SECO, the Americans would respond by smashing their CIA, which is entirely staffed by SECO people, and that wouldn't serve any purpose of ours."

Needless to say, I couldn't make heads or tails of the picture Dzerzhin had drawn for me.

We parted at the corner of Volume One Avenue and Fourth Addendum Lane. On the way back to the hotel, I wondered why Dzerzhin had told me all that hogwash. Was he drunk, crazy, a provacateur, or just pulling my leg?

Suddenly a thought stopped me in my tracks and I went rushing back.

I caught up with Dzerzhin at Inspiration Square, grabbed him by the elbow, and, very agitated, asked him, "Listen, if SECO is staffed with nothing but CIA, then which one are you with?"

He peered at me for a moment, yanked his arm free of my hand, and said: "Alright, my darling, let's get things straight once and for all. To avoid any possible problems, you are never to ask me any more questions like that. OK?"

"OK," I said, and walked away.

THE SECRET OF
THE MEDALLION

I don't think it would be an exaggeration to say that I had come to
see and hear a great deal that was surprising in the Moscowrep. But
I found Dzerzhin's revelation simply staggering. I returned to the
hotel in high agitation and intended immediately to ask Iskrina what
her thoughts were on this subject. But she was busy watching a
soccer match on television.

I sat down beside her on the bed and began watching too. I
knew the two teams but now their names had grown somewhat
elongated. One team was called the State Academy Order of Lenin
Spartacus Team and the other the State Academy Order of Lenin
Dynamo Team. The players were well along in years, somewhere
between forty and sixty. I asked Iskrina why the soccer players were
so old. She said that naturally such important teams could only take
on the best players with high-level needs, and to reach the best-
player rank took some time.

The game was on the sluggish side. The players didn't run but
strode importantly about the field, rolling the ball slowly along.

I asked Iskrina what the score was. She said the score would
only be revealed during the twenty-fourth minute but that the final
score would be five to four in favor of Spartacus.

"How do you know?" I asked.

"It says so in the TV schedule."

"You mean to say someone fixed the score before the game?"

"Of course," said Iskrina. "The Athletic Pentagon plans everything out long before the match. Was it different in your day?"

"Completely different," I said. I told her that in my day the players had been younger and the score was determined spontaneously as the result of competition.

"I don't understand what you mean by spontaneously," she said. "Someone had to set the final score."

"No one had to set it. The players ran around the field kicking the ball and trying for a goal, and the team that got more goals had the higher score."

"But that's Volunteerism," she said indignantly. "And so whoever runs the fastest and kicks the hardest, scores the most?"

"That's right," I said, "that's exactly right. Though it is true that when corruption was in full bloom, sometimes one team would bribe the other and then the score would be determined in a different way."

"There you see," said Iskrina. "It was fertile soil for abuses. Nothing like that could happen now. Now the Athletic Pentagon determines the score based on the team's position, how disciplined the players are, how much they've studied the works of the Genialissimo, and what category of needs they fall into. It is out of the question that any team with general needs could score a goal on a team with high-level needs and not pay some price for it!"

"That's ridiculous," I said. "But if you know the score in advance, why watch the game?"

Iskrina shrugged her shoulders. "But when you're writing a novel, you know how it's going to end."

"That's just it, I *don't* know," I said. "I mean, when I set to work on a novel, I do have some plans but then the characters start doing what they want and which one of them strangles the other is up to them. It's the same story with this Sim business. Your people are putting a gun to my head to make me take him out of my book, but I can't, I can't bring myself to do it."

She hopped off the bed and turned off the television.

"Tell me," she said in a whisper, "what did that Sim look like?"

"What did he look like?" I said. "Well . . . about . . . average height. With a beard."

"Look in here," she said and pulled out her plastic medallion. "Is that him?"

It felt like something supernatural had happened. As if some invisible presence had flown in and out of the room. In the small photograph inset in the medallion, regarding me with a fixed and unfriendly gaze, was none other than Sim Simych Karnavalov.

THE NOVEL

"Well, did you read it?" asked the marshal when I pulled the fairly wrinkled book out from inside my shirt.

"Yes, yes, I read it," I said, although I had to admit to myself that already I couldn't recall how I had ended the thing. We were alone in his office. He had ordered his secretary not to let anyone in or any calls through.

"And what did you think?" he asked, looking me in the eye.

"In my opinion—not bad," I said. "Not bad at all. I would say it's good, even splendid."

"Yes," he agreed, "the novel works, it's interesting. But still, did you read it with a critical eye?"

"Of course I did. I always read with a critical eye."

"That's just what I wanted to hear you say!" said the marshal, coming to life and starting to move quickly about the room. "You see, you can come to terms with a person who thinks critically. But you can't come to terms with someone who doesn't. And what shortcomings did you find in your novel?"

"Shortcomings?" I repeated the word in surprise. "I don't understand what shortcomings you have in mind."

The marshal gave me a strange look. "How to put it," he said, a bit perplexed, "it seems to me that all books, even the very best, have shortcomings of one sort or another."

"Of course they do," I readily agreed. "All books but mine.

And that's because when I write I immediately cross out all the shortcomings and leave only the very best passages. Though when reading the novel this time, I did notice a comma that really didn't belong, but it's the proofreader who has to take the whole blame for that. I can't imagine how he let that slip past."

Beria Ilich Maturin stayed silent. I fell silent, too. He wiped the sweat off his forehead. I made the same motion, though there was no sweat on my forehead.

"That's what you say," said Beria Ilich with dismay. "But you're wrong. There are always shortcomings. For example, there's a whole collective of authors working on *Genialissimoiana*, but even they make mistakes from time to time. And in your book. . . . Let's have a look at it."

"Alright, let's," I readily agreed.

"Good." He opened the book and ran his eyes down the first page. "Alright, we can start here with the introduction. Right at the very beginning you say that everything you write about really happened or else was entirely invented by you. Which one is true?"

"Well, you see," I said, puzzled, "how should I know which one's the truth. As you people say: primary is secondary and secondary is primary. And, if that's so, then there's no difference between invention and reality."

"Alright, let's say there isn't," he agreed, and then began turning the pages. "But you portrayed that capitalist very well, very satirically, that . . . what was his name . . . Machenmittel-brecher?"

"Mittelbrechenmacher," I corrected politely.

"That's right, of course, Michelmaten . . . I understand. And so, that horse trader of yours, did he deal in white horses too?"

"White horses?" I said in surprise. "Aha, I see what you mean. To tell you the truth, I don't know. I don't think he usually chooses them by color. What matters to him is that they run well. And that's why he prefers Arabian horses."

"Aha, of course. Speaking of that, the Arabs who abducted you. . . . Don't you think it's curious that they would pin their hopes on you to get hold of some secret information for them here?"

"That's their problem," I said. "Maybe they were judging me according to themselves, and so they thought I was capable of betraying my motherland for a sack of gold. I must say, I wouldn't betray my motherland even for two sacks of gold."

"Yes, yes, yes," the marshal hastened to agree with me. "Believe me, no one has any doubts as to your patriotism. Alright, let's drop the subject. Whether any of that is true doesn't matter. But this," he said, opening to the page with the first mention of Sim, "this is no good at all. And this is how we deal with such things." From a plastic desk penholder, he withdrew a finely sharpened pencil, which tore the paper as he drew a line from the upper left corner of the page to the lower right. He was just about to make an X by drawing another line when I cried, "Stop! Stop! Stop!" I grabbed his hand. "You can't do that. You can't cross it out like it was nothing. I may have nurtured and cherished that page, I may have lost a night's sleep when composing. . . . I may have licked it like a newborn calf. . . ." I tried to show him how I might have done that. "And then you come along with your pencil and out it goes."

The marshal listened to everything I had to say with great bewilderment. "But why," he said. "But why? *Why* did you bring in Sim Simych? Don't you understand we have no use for him here?"

To be frank, this conversation had started to seem rather moronic, and I became a little angry. "What is this?" I said. "What kind of conversation is this? What kind of a stupid way is that to state the issue? Sim Simych is of no use to you. He's obviously of some use to me, and I categorically forbid you to cross him out."

"Is that so?" Beria Ilich's expression suddenly changed, and now he was regarding me with mockery. "You're forbidding me? Do you have even a rough idea of the difference between your military rank and mine?"

"I don't give a damn about your rank," I said, but then I bit my tongue in fear. Who the hell knows, I thought, maybe that's the wrong tack. Marshals are very touchy people.

"Beria Ilich," I said, almost tenderly. "Don't misunderstand me. If, in fact, I was the person who wrote this novel, that means that I wrote it, figuratively speaking, with my heart's blood, and put my soul into it, and you just want to take it and mangle it."

"Hold on, hold on, hold on," said the marshal. "What are you getting so keyed up about? You should realize that this is a serious communist state matter. If you don't do what we want, we can't reissue your novel and we can't celebrate your jubilee."

"To hell with it, to hell with your jubilee!" I said in a rage.

"It's not mine, it's yours."

"It's yours, it's yours," I repeated insistently. "You need it, not me. I can do without it. A lot of people have died without having a hundred-year jubilee, and I can live without one too."

"Alright then, if you're that selfish, then you can do without it, but there are other things worth worrying about a little, too. As you know," he said mildly and insinuatingly, "our Communites have made all the preparations for your jubilee. They have worked in the sweat of their brow, they have overfulfilled their production quotas, they have lived only for this, they've been counting the days. They have been looking forward to your jubilee as they would some great holiday. And on what is no more than a whim, you're willing to ruin their holiday."

Good God! Now I was the one sweating. I couldn't for the life of me remember how this conversation turned out in the novel and I was feeling tremendously resentful toward Maturin and toward all the other Communites. "I don't understand why this makes you so upset," I said. "I can understand that the Communites would like to read a little something besides *Genialissimoiana*, but if you agreed to publish my novel, why do you want to correct it?"

"Not correct it, *improve* it," Maturin quickly interjected. "Remove the excess. That's not only my own personal opinion. The comlits agree with me, and so does Horizon Timofeyevich who, despite his extremely full schedule, made time to look into this matter and urgently . . . do you understand, urgently," repeated the marshal in an openly threatening tone, "urgently requested that you give it all a good thinking through."

Dammit! As a rule I'm a reckless risk-taker, but when people like this marshal threaten me, I know it's serious business. "I don't even know what to say," I said in confusion. "Alright, give me the book for another night, I'll take another look at it and . . ."

"Correct it," he prompted.

"I won't correct it. I'll do some thinking," I said. "And if something can be done . . ."

"And of course it can," said the marshal.

"That's easy for you to say," I said with a sigh. "You have no pity on any novel. . . . Well alright, I'll give it some more thought."

"Very good," said the marshal happily. "So we have an agreement. You'll read it again, you'll have a look, you'll think about it, and then you'll come here tomorrow and we'll do everything that needs doing. Listen," he said, then walked over to the door, put his eye then his ear to the keyhole, and walked back to me, "I have something special for you." He spent a long time fiddling with the combination before he opened the safe door and withdrew. . . . And what do you think he withdrew? Of course it was the very same bottle of Smirnoff vodka that had disappeared just after I'd landed in the Moscowrep.

Naturally, I didn't say anything about that to him. We shared the bottle. And the interesting thing is that even this paltriest shot of vodka gave me no pleasure. I was surprised myself, and thought that perhaps I had not become a real Communite, but this was a sure sign that I had been cured of my alcoholism. This is going to make my wife so happy, I thought, as I clinked glasses with the marshal.

EDISON
XENOFONTOVICH

I was so fed up with all those idiotic negotiations about the reworking of my novel that I was very glad to be invited by Edison Xenofontovich, whom I had met briefly in the sathineed, to visit the Comscicom he headed.

I realized how important Edison Xenofontovich was when he did not send any old steam-puffer for me, but a real limousine that ran on gas. And the chauffeur was no ordinary driver, but a colonel. We pulled out onto First Volume Avenue and began racing directly away from the city center.

But we didn't race very far. Somewhere just past the Second Ring of Communism, we had a flat and, while the colonel changed the tire, I got out of the car for a breath of fresh air. But the air proved not at all fresh, smelling like a pigsty that had not been cleaned in ages. And the sounds I heard around me were pig-like. Grunts and squeals. I looked around expecting to see some ground-level livestock enclosures, but that was not at all what I saw. What I saw were pigs, squealing and grunting as they looked down upon us from all the balconies of the six-story building in front of which we had stopped. Not only that, there were pigs looking at me from all the other buildings' balconies, as far as my eyes could see.

I have to admit it made me somewhat uncomfortable. What is it? Some sort of communist pig city? Or a new breed of pig people? But then I realized, a realization confirmed by the chauffeur, that we were in one of the districts of the Third Ring where, as I've already mentioned, people are allowed to raise productive animals on their balconies, but not in excess of one head per family.

(I'll say here that later on I was to read various newspaper reports on this experiment, articles with titles like "Signs of the New" and even "A Pig on the Balcony." But the latter, I think, was actually a satirical piece about some bad person, and it might even have been about me.)

After changing the tire, the colonel drove even faster and we soon came to an inconspicuous forest road with a sign that read, "No Entry."

After a short while we came to gates, a guard booth, and two sentries, who checked our identification very thoroughly. I counted sixteen such guard booths and gates along the road. We were stopped at all of them, our identification carefully checked at each, and we were saluted and allowed to pass every time.

After the final gate, the road suddenly veered down into some underground structure. We traveled about a fifth of a mile underground and stopped again in front of a blank gate with an almost unnoticeable little wicker gate to the right of it.

We walked through that gate and soon found ourselves in a spacious room with a few tables with magazines on them, leather couches, armchairs, and two or three artificial palm trees in stout tubs. It was here that we were welcomed by Edison Xenofontovich wearing a white lab coat.

After greeting one another, I said that he must have had a brilliant career to have made general at his age.

"At my age?" he said with a sly tone. "And how old do you think I am?"

"Well, somewhere around twenty-five, twenty-six," I said, though without any great assurance.

Edison Xenofontovich burst into uproarious laughter and then winked at the colonel, who was also chuckling. I have to say I found their mirth somewhat offensive and, puffing myself up, I remarked that, in my opinion, I had not said anything so funny.

"Come on now, come on!" the young general hastened to re-assure me. "Of course, you didn't say anything funny. I wasn't laughing at what you said, I was just laughing. Sometimes I just have attacks of laughter, that's all."

Then, after exchanging a few words with the chauffeur, he said that he could go now. And he suggested that he and I take, as he put it, a short-but-educational stroll.

Leaving the hall, we came out onto a large underground street lined with four-story buildings that all shared a single roof. There was no steam traffic on that street; it may have been banned there. Some people went on foot and others by bicycle. As soon as they noticed the person accompanying me, they either smiled obse-quiously or tried to duck around the nearest corner. Many people recognized me, smiled at me, walked over, and asked to shake my hand or have my autograph.

It turned out that there was an entire underground city there. The streets were straight and divided the city into identical squares, more or less like Manhattan.

The Comscicom, as Edison Xenofontovich explained, was the scientific nerve center of the Moscowrep. The very best scientists, assembled from every corner of the land, worked there. The city housed 116 scientific research institutes, which were working in all areas of contemporary science.

"Of course, we can't go round to all the institutes," said Edison Xenofontovich, "but we might take a peek into this one. It was founded, thanks to you."

"Thanks to me?" I said in surprise as I looked over at a sign that read, "Institute of Information Extraction (Instinfext)." This was indeed an enormous institute with a great many laboratories. We visited a few, and in each of them entire brigades of professors and graduate students were subjecting little pieces of what looked like film to some sort of sorcery. They would examine them under microscopes, X-ray them, dip them into chemical solutions, and prick them with needles.

In each laboratory I asked the scientists what they were doing.

They would look over to Edison Xenofontovich who would laugh merrily and say, "You guess."

I would strain my imagination to the limit but always drew a blank.

"You still haven't guessed?" he asked when we were back on the underground street.

"I still haven't," I said.

"Do you remember that square black thing you brought with you?"

"You mean the floppy disk?" I said.

"That's right, you can call it that. We call them diskettes."

"But why are they cutting them into pieces?"

"What do you mean? They're trying to extract the information from them."

Clutching my head, I fell into a laughing fit. Edison Xenofontovich frowned and asked what I found so amusing. Still choking with laughter, I explained that a floppy disk is something you insert into a computer, not like the kind they had now, but the old-fashioned ones they had in my time. And the floppy disk had to be in one piece and not damaged in any way. And if you insert it into the computer, it starts working and puts out text either on the screen or directly on the printer. "Have you ever seen any computers like that?" I asked him.

"I personally have," he said. "But other people haven't. That obsolete equipment has been out of production for a long time now."

"In that case," I said, "your scientists are engaged in folly. With the methods they're using, they'll never extract anything from those little pieces."

"They don't have to extract anything from them," he said with a carefree gesture. "What they need is to have an institute, a director, a deputy director, a party organizer, a priest, a SECO chief, and laboratory heads. They extract plenty of profit from those positions. Extracting information from those pieces of the disk is of no consequence. As our Genialissimo correctly observed, 'Movement is everything, the goal is nothing.' Well put, wouldn't you say?"

310

"Not bad," I said. "And is your work like theirs?"

"Mine?" said Edison Xenofontovich with a laugh. "My work is much more serious. I run this entire complex. But I'm also a biologist, and I have my own institute, which is engaged in the creation of a new form of human being."

"A new form of human being?" I said.

"That's right," he corroborated, "a new form of human being. Does that surprise you? I've greater surprises than that in store for you. Come with me, I'll show you everything."

INSTCRENEWHUM

The Institute for the Creation of a New Human Being (Instcrenew-hum) was located close to the Instinfext, about four blocks away. There, too, we walked through various laboratories whose purposes were a mystery to me. Edison Xenofontovich introduced me to many of his colleagues. Without distinction as to sex, age, or rank (and some of them were quite elderly professors, docents, and doctors of medicine and science), he called them all by their first names and whacked them on their backs. In the cases of certain substantial ladies, he whacked even lower. But his manner, as far as I could tell, neither embarrassed nor shocked anyone. None of them was servile toward Edison Xenofontovich, but they all treated him with the respect due to a man senior in age, not only in rank. I, too, was gradually infected by their attitude toward their boss, and I ceased to be aware of the difference in our ages.

Edison Xenofontovich showed me thousands of baffling and complex devices, with boilers, vats, retorts, and test tubes, all artfully connected by a maze of metal, glass, plastic, and rubber tubing, in which things were bubbling, fusing, coagulating, and evaporating. In some of the laboratories there was a poisonous mist in the air that made my head spin and my gorge rise.

"*Interessant?*" he would ask in German, and would drag me to the next one without waiting for my reply.

At first, it really was interesting, but then later it all started to bore me. I told Edison Xenofontovich that it wasn't worth it to show me all their technology because I couldn't make heads or tails of it.

"Ah, that's right, of course," he was quick to agree. "We truly are involved in things here that are rather complicated if you don't have the background. Alright then, I'll show you something simpler."

We were walking down a corridor with many doors, exactly like the one in the Writers' Union, with the difference that these doors had little windows in them. Sticking my head through one of those windows at Edison Xenofontovich's suggestion, I saw something that startled and even somewhat shocked me. In a large airy room reminiscent of a hospital ward, naked men and women were copulating shamelessly on wide iron beds (of which there were about eight). But they did not seem to be doing so spontaneously; they were being observed by a group of specialists who were making measurements of some sort, taking notes, and issuing instructions as to who should do what and how. I unglued myself from the window and looked at Edison Xenofontovich in bewilderment.

"*Interessant*?" he asked.

"To each his own," I replied. "Personally, I was never big on peep shows."

"What? What does that mean—peep shows?"

He didn't even know what one was. Some professor! I explained to him that in my day certain of the absolutely corrupt capitalist countries had a form of entertainment designed to distract the workers from the struggle for their essential rights. For the price of a German mark or a quarter of an American dollar, a worker could peep through a little hole and see various forms of human copulation, and sometimes even humans copulating with special devices.

To my surprise, what I had said proved of very great interest to Edison Xenofontovich. He began questioning me in detail as to exactly how these shows were performed and what specifically went on there. Unfortunately, I couldn't tell him all that much. To tell the truth, I had taken a couple of quick peeks at such peek shows, but I usually didn't have the mark or the quarter it cost.

Hearing me say this, Edison Xenofontovich complained that the communist service industries had a woeful shortage of initiative and tended to yield such important spheres of influence to their ideological foes. He requested that I put what I had told him in written form, and at the next possible opportunity he would submit a proposal to the Supreme Pentagon for the establishment of such shows in those places where the Communites take public recreation.

"But you already have them," I said, pointing to the open window.

"What do you mean?" he said with a dismissive wave. "That's another matter entirely. This is not a peep show, this is a purely scientific institution. Can you guess what those people are doing?"

"Yes," I said, "I think I can."

"No, no, you can't," he said unequivocally. "You couldn't begin to understand what they're doing. What these people are doing is what I told you about before — creating a new human being."

"Why are you telling me something so obvious?" I said. "You think we had a different way of making new people in my day?"

"*Nein, nein.* You still haven't understood me here. I'm not just referring to a new human organism, I'm referring to a human being who differs fundamentally from his predecessors physically, intellectually, morally, and in terms of political awareness. In a word, I am speaking here of the creation of communist man. That was a task that had been posed in your time as well, but back then the stress was put on education and re-education. But, as time showed, that was a pernicious practice and a pernicious theory. In the process of education many people grew worse and not better. This was as stupid as trying to educate a donkey to become a horse."

"True, true," I said. "I'm in complete agreement with you there."

"I'm very glad to hear that," he said with emotion. "We're taking a completely different path now. We've decided not to waste time, not to educate and re-educate anyone, but simply to breed a new species of people. And that's just what we're doing. Take any animal, even take dogs. Yes, the simple dog. . . . So what is a dog then? A primitive animal. It does not possess reason. Nothing but reflexes. But there are dogs and there are dogs. There are hunting dogs, guard dogs, bloodhounds, house dogs, and decorative dogs. And many of those breeds did not arise all by themselves, but were created over a long period by purposeful crossbreeding. But, if we take the trouble to produce animals with certain definite instincts, then why should we look with indifference on humanity which, as the result of random combinations, is turning into a pack of mongrels? *Interessant?*"

"Very!" I said. "Terrifically interesting! And just what kind of human are you trying to breed: hunting humans, guard humans, or bloodhound humans? Or could it be decorative humans?"

"Ha-ha-ha-ha," Edison Xenofontovich broke into loud laughter. "That's very interesting. It might be worth it to try to breed a decorative human. But, my friend, you have misunderstood me here. What we're trying to do is breed humans for various purposes within the limits of a single species. You may recall what the Cultists, Volunteerists, Corruptionists, and Reformists did in your time. They sent scientists out to harvest potatoes, they forced cooks to run the state, and SECO people aspired to write novels. This was a foolish and unscientific redistribution of the cadres. Now all that will be completely different. Now we will breed various types of people for various purposes. For example, we'll want to breed conscientious workers and peasants for industry and agriculture. And, toward that end, we'll chose and combine the most productive workers. Those couples you just saw were exclusively recipients of the Hero of Communist Labor award, people who streamlined production or came up with new inventions. And in the same way we will breed people with propensities for military service, sports, science, or administration."

"Tell me," I said, "do you intend to breed writers the same way?"

"*Natürlich!*" he exclaimed. "But it's a little trickier with writers. We've observed that writers usually fall into one of two opposite categories: they have either a highly developed artistic imagination or a high level of ideological development. And what we want to create is a writer who would combine artistic talent with an evolved communist ideology. And for that reason we don't breed male writers with female writers but male writers with female professors of Marxism."

"Have you given any thought to creating a person who would combine all of the very best features?"

"Bah!" said Edison Xenofontovich with a flick of irritation. "Not only have we given that some thought, we've even achieved some great success in that pursuit, though it's been fantastically difficult. You see, such a person cannot be created by the old means. For many years I have been collecting genetic material—sperm—from various outstanding persons, geniuses, physicists, mathematicians, writers, directors, Heroes of Communist Labor, and Nobel laureates. I extracted the chromosomes, one by one. Then I put them together in every combination imaginable. I spent something like thirty years on that. . . ."

"Thirty years!" I said with a suspicious look at his youthful face.

"Maybe it wasn't thirty. Maybe it was less. It doesn't matter. Something else matters here. I did experiment after experiment. Sometimes they worked. But not always. Sometimes they were born blind, deaf, and dumb, and without arms or legs. Some of them had certain abilities, others had none. One time I created an intellectual. I gave him a head the size of a pressure cooker. And I stuffed that pressure cooker with all the knowledge that mankind had amassed. He spoke twelve languages fluently and could literally read every language there is."

"And so he must have become a great scientist?" I said.

"What are you talking about!" said Edison Xenofontovich with a gesture of dismay. "He turned out to be an ordinary intellectual. Big head, plenty of knowledge, but not a single idea. I had to annihilate him."

"What did you do to him?"

"I dissolved him in sulphuric acid," he replied impassively.

"And you didn't feel sorry about it?" I asked in horror.

"No, I didn't. Nature produces endless numbers of such creatures even without my help. But I won out in the end. I succeeded in creating an absolutely universal genius. He was a genius in every field."

"Why use the past tense? Did you annihilate him too?"

Edison Xenofontovich did not have time to reply because just then I heard from behind one of the doors a hideous, inhuman howl that will echo in my mind forever.

"What's that?" I asked bewildered, looking over at him.

"Don't pay it any attention," he said with a confused smile and was about to lead me further when there was a second howl, one so shrill that I could walk no further.

"What's going on in this place!" I said. "It sounds like some-body's being torn to pieces."

"How could you think anything of the sort!" he said with a gesture of astonishment. "But since you're dying of curiosity, let's go take a look."

And with those words he kicked open the door from which the howls had issued.

My worst suspicions seemed confirmed at once. In the center of a bright room was a wooden post to which a naked middle-aged man, his flesh pale and flabby, was bound by ropes. A gorilla-like human being in a lab coat was standing by the post, a plaited whip with a lead weight in his hand.

"What a nightmare!" I said, looking over at Edison Xenofon-tovich. "And you say that nothing out of the ordinary's happening here! What are you doing to that poor man?"

"That's just the point! We're doing absolutely nothing to him.

See for yourself." Edison Xenofontovich snatched the whip away from the gorilla and brandished it.

"Aaaaiii!" howled the bound man. "Don't beat me! I'm scared! I renounced all my beliefs! I admit that communism is the most progressive and most humane system."

"What are you yelling about, you worthless rag?" said Edison Xenofontovich. "Why are you renouncing everything you hold dear so easily? Look at him," he said turning to me. "There's not a whip mark on his back."

"I'm yelling because I'm afraid of pain," said the prisoner, sobbing. He turned his distorted face toward me and I recognized him as the representative of a West German firm who had flown to the future with me in the hope of learning how well the Soviet gas pipeline would operate. He recognized me too, and, his head twitching, he began pleading for help, interspersing his pleas with incoherent slogans about the superiority of communism to all other systems.

"Untie him and take him to a rest area!" ordered Edison. When the poor wretch had been taken away, Edison said to me: "So, there you see what lousy human material your capitalists produce."

He said this with such a tone of reproach that I automatically felt responsible for capitalism and all its faults, though I didn't remember ever having praised them.

"What's going on here and what does capitalism have to do with it?" I asked as if justifying myself.

"Capitalists are pathetic people," said Edison. "Just show one a whip and he'll renounce everything he believes in."

"I should say so! Who wouldn't at the sight of a whip like that. Capitalist or not, he's not made of iron. If he's beaten, he feels pain."

"Everyone does," remarked Edison edifyingly. "However, some people can stand up to it. And that's what I want to show you now."

He pushed open a door that led from that room to another just like it.

There was a post there, too, and a man tied to that post. His

319

entire back was welted with whip marks, much worse than Zilberovich's when I'd seen it in the bath house. The welts were swollen
and several had split open. In addition to the whip marks, two stars
had been neatly carved into the man's shoulder blades and blood
was streaming from them.

"Oh Gen!" I cried. "Who is this man? And why are you tor-
menting him so?"

Just then the man turned toward me and his puffy face and
bleeding nose made it no easy matter to recognize the young terrorist who had sat beside me on the flight. He looked at me without
saying a word and then his head—now covered with gray hair—fell
to his shoulder and he passed out.

"Why are you punishing him like that?" I asked softly.

"Us, punishing him?" said Edison in surprise. "How can you
even think that? We don't do that sort of thing. This is not a pu-
nitive agency but a scientific institution. We are testing the firmness
of various people's beliefs, and we've demonstrated by experiment
that communists, like this young man, display a steadfastness and
will unmatched by anyone else. He has not renounced his beliefs,
nor has he doubted them for a single second."

"Aha! I see. So you're doing this to him for scientific purposes.
Have you perhaps tried red-hot iron or, say, molten lead then?"

"Look at that!" said Edison happily. "I can see that the exper-
imentalist in you has been aroused. I find your ideas extremely valuable. You could be right. I'll order a steel bar brought to a white
heat and then jabbed into his . . ."

"Edison Xenofontovich!" I cried. "For Gen's sake, don't do
that! Don't do it! I was only joking, and it was a very stupid joke,
too."

"What's so stupid about it?" he objected. "Not stupid at all.
We've been wondering what to do to him next, but we've run out
of ideas. But then you come by, look at things with a fresh eye, and
immediately come up with something new."

"Listen," I said, very disturbed, "I beseech you, leave that man
alone. Of course, he's done a lot of harm in his short life, but surely

he's paid for his sins in full by now. Why put him to such a painful death?"

"What are you saying!" Edison Xenofontovich objected heatedly. "Do you actually think we have any intention of killing him? A valuable specimen like him! We're going to guard him like the apple of our eye. We're going to test him a little more, then we'll patch him up, fatten him back up, and take some genetic material from him. We could use more of that breed. Our people have shrunk in stature, especially our young people with their moral and ideological instabilities . . . When we've extracted sufficient genetic material from him, then we'll . . ."

"Annihilate him," I said.

"Why are you always harping about annihilation!" he replied irritably. "We will treat him humanely. We'll put him to sleep, embalm him, and display him in a museum as a man of unparalleled steadfastness. A man who stood up to everything to the very end, without a moan, without begging for mercy, without betraying his ideals. A man who lost his life, but remained true to his convictions."

I could see Edison's eyes dampen with tears.

"And what will you do with the capitalist?" I asked. "You'll annihilate him, of course, won't you?"

"We won't annihilate him either. We'll recycle him, we'll turn him into secondary matter and send him back to his homeland. If they want that merchandise, they can have it."

My long conversation with Edison Xenofontovich might appear to have been uninterrupted and to have taken place in one location. In fact, during the course of that conversation, at my urgent request, the young terrorist was taken down from the post, wrapped in a sheet, and carried off. Then Edison Xenofontovich and I left the laboratory and walked to his office, which was itself a small laboratory, guarded at the entry by an entire squad of SECO men armed with submachine guns.

There was no one inside, not counting a certain strange creature who was standing by a sink, washing and wiping test tubes of various sizes.

This creature, naked except for something like a loin cloth, was most likely of the female sex, as indicated by its droopy breasts, but at the same time it was somehow too formless and ageless to be a woman. It could have been thirty years old or it could have been sixty.

Moving slowly, sluggishly, the creature paid us no attention and went on with its work, dolefully singing an old song: "Young, yes, I'm young, but my clothes are plain, and no one will marry this girl."

"Well, Supey," said Edison Xenofontovich, "everything washed and dried?"

"Yes," said the creature, "it's all done."

"*Willst du schlafen?*" he asked it in German.

"*Ja,*" answered the creature, not in the least surprised.

"What else would you like to do?" asked Edison Xenofonto-vich, in English this time.

"Nothing," answered the creature in English.

"Don't you want to run around a little or do some reading?" asked Edison Xenofontovich, speaking Russian now.

"No, I don't," replied the creature in Russian. "I just want to sleep."

"Well then, go get some sleep," he said. Tossing the towel in the corner, the creature slowly left the room.

"That's a strange name for a woman, isn't it—Supey?" I asked.

Edison Xenofontovich explained that Supey was a diminutive of Super, and that this creature was not a woman, not a man, and not a hermaphrodite either.

"What is it then?"

"It's an edited superman," he said.

That of course made no sense to me. Then Edison Xenofon-tovich opened a desk drawer and rummaged about in it until he pulled out a photograph. It showed a powerfully built, naked man who no doubt spent a lot of time working out. His muscles bulged through his skin, and everything about him radiated great strength and vitality.

"Do you recognize him?" he asked.

"No," I said quite definitely, "I don't."

"It's Supey before editing."

With a sad smile he told me the whole melancholy story. Su-pey had been his first success en route to creating a universal hu-man. He had a perfect physique and his inward development was equally harmonious. He was capable of both physical and intellec-tual labor. He could perform the most complex mathematical cal-culations with his mind, wrote stunning poetry, composed music of genius, and his painting had been snapped up by the best museums in the Third Ring. He performed miracles of athletics, could press over eight hundred pounds, run the hundred meters in 8.8 seconds, and could easily beat any heavyweight in the world (though he would do it only on points since he was an exceedingly kind person). He would simply parry all the blows, barely touching his opponent out of fear of causing him pain.

"Well, so then what happened to Supey?" I asked, extremely intrigued.

Edison Xenofontovich clearly did not want to tell me but, since he'd begun, he decided to finish. In the Moscowrep, all achievements, scientific and otherwise, required the approval of the Editorial Commission, to which body Edison Xenofontovich had submitted his creature as well. Supey went before the commission, lifted record-breaking weights, repaired the broken watch of one commission member, shot a hundred bull's-eyes out of a hundred shots with a pistol, proved Gauss's theorem, played Beethoven's "Appassionata" on the piano, read a passage from the *Iliad* in ancient Greek and the entire *Communist Manifesto* in German. And all the members of the commission gave Supey's own poems a standing ovation except for the chairman.

"And what about the chairman?" I asked.

It turned out that the chairman had been sleeping all the while. He did not even hear the other members of the commission congratulating Edison Xenofontovich and his creation. They poked and prodded Supey, bombarded him with the most capricious questions, all of which he, needless to say, answered without hesitation or error.

Then there was a discussion. Someone said that Supey's appearance was almost ideal, but that his ears stuck out too much and should be tucked back a bit. There were also some remarks as to the shape of his nose and eyes. Learning that Supey would require a great deal of food, one of the commission members suggested an operation to remove his stomach. Just then the chairman woke up and pointed out that Supey's outer organs were too prominent.

"What purpofe do they ferve?" asked the chairman.

Edison Xenofontovich had grown embarrassed and said that well, of course, they were there for purposes of propagation.

324

"Why fould he propagate?" said the chairman. "No need for that. Let there be juft one. We put him in a mufeum. Juft make him look decent, fo children can fee him."

"And you didn't object?" I asked, stunned by all this.

"Did I ever! I wrote complaints, explanations, I collected signatures from scientists, I went from one office to another, leaving no stone unturned, and in the end I even dealt personally with the Genialissimo."

"And he wouldn't help you?"

"You see," said Edison Xenofontovich, "the Genialissimo commands enormous power, but when a matter reaches the Editorial Commission, then even he is powerless. He did everything he could, but then he phoned and said that I'd have to yield to them, if only a little. Yield on the small point so you can keep what really counts. I had no other choice. . . ."

"And so you castrated your poor Supey?" I asked in horror.

"That's right," he said with a sad nod. "I castrated him. What can I tell you? Of course, he didn't lose everything. He's still very conscientious. He washes the dishes and sweeps the floor and does the laundry. But all the rest is gone. On the other hand, he can sing like a woman now."

THE ELIXIR

Now look where I've landed! I thought, as I gave the laboratory a once-over. What a strange place this is—they treat people like flies. First they experiment on them, then they embalm them, recycle them, castrate them, and annihilate them.

I would say Edison Xenofontovich's laboratory looked pretty much like any other. In one corner there was a modest writing desk and, above it, a large portrait of the Genialissimo in full dress with all his decorations. Off to one side of the wall was a photograph which struck me as quite strange. It depicted two decrepit boozers clinking plastic glasses.

To be honest, the laboratory equipment did not particularly interest me at first. I remember a large vessel made of stainless steel, in which some liquid was bubbling away. A multitude of glass tubes of various colors, connected by coil pipes of various sorts, led out of that vessel. It also had many instruments indicating temperature, pressure, and so on. Finally, the entire system split into two parts, each of which ended in a single tube and plastic glass. The label on one had a picture of a rose, and the label on the other had a skull and crossbones. A colorless liquid dripped slowly, very slowly, into each glass.

While looking all this over, I could feel Edison Xenofontovich an inch behind me, carefully observing everything.

"*Interessant?*" I heard him say.

"It is," I said. "It's interesting. Looks like a still for making homebrew."

Apparently he found my remark extremely amusing. He laughed so hard he went red in the face, tears streaming from his eyes.

"That's right," he said, wiping away his tears. "It is a still for making homebrew. An ideal still. But not for homebrew. Can you guess what it's for?"

All I could do was shrug my shoulders.

"You can't guess?" said he with delight, clapping his hands. "Give up?"

"I give up," I said.

"Alright then," he said solemnly but excitedly. "You're seeing something only two other people have ever seen: I am one and the other is none other than the Genialissimo. He visited my laboratory before leaving on his last space flight, and he stood right where you're standing now."

"Was the Genialissimo really right here?" I said, taking a step to one side.

"Yes, he was. In person, in the flesh. And do you know why? Because I have made the greatest discovery in the history of mankind. I have invented. . . ."

"The elixir of life!" I cried, pierced by intuition.

"That's exactly right, the elixir of life!" he said, giving me a whack on the shoulder. "Or, as I call it, BGI, Beverage of the Genialissimo's Immortality."

I was so stunned by what I heard that I was simply unable to assimilate the explanation and did not even commit the essentials to memory. All I remember is that Edison Xenofontovich told me that the human organism contains two types of some sort of fluid or perhaps it wasn't a fluid, in any case he called one the plasma of life and the other the plasma of death. Apparently, the two plasmas are intermixed in us and are engaged in a constant struggle, in which the plasma of death gradually overcomes the plasma of life. Most importantly, he had not only discovered these plasmas but had ultimately devised a way of separating them.

While delivering this short lecture, he picked up the glass with the rose on it and asked if I'd like to sample it. I'd like to see someone who'd refuse. However, the taste of the liquid proved so utterly repulsive that I came close to vomiting.

"You don't like it?" he asked with concern. "Frankly, it isn't all that tasty. But, for the sake of eternal life, a person could drink worse."

I was of a different opinion on the subject but, out of politeness, did not voice it.

"And now," he said ceremoniously, "take a look at this photograph and see if you can figure out who the people are."

I looked at the photograph of the two old men for a second time. One of them seemed to look like the Genialissimo. The difference between the face in the photo and the portrait on the wall was enormous, but nothing surprised me any more. And that decrepit and absolutely bald old man with the sunken mouth. . . . I shifted my gaze to Edison Xenofontovich. "Yes, yes," I said. "There is a certain resemblance there. Though it's very remote."

"Well then, if you've figured that one out," he said with a grin, staring, "see if you can find a resemblance between me and someone else."

"Edik!" I said, now having recognized him as the young biologist to whom Lyoshka Bukashev had introduced me something like eighty years ago in the Journalists' Club. "Edik, is that you!"

"It is," said Edik.

"You're bullshitting me," I cried out in the preliminary language.

"I should drop dead," replied Edik with a smile, in that same language.

I still couldn't believe it. I walked all around him, looking at him full-faced and in profile. I even pinched him, but I still had my doubts.

"So then tell me," I said in an uncertain voice, "the Genialissimo must be. . . ."

"Of course," he said with a sad nod, as if admitting something that was supposed to have remained a secret. "Did you really figure that out all by yourself?"

"I didn't have to figure anything out," I said. "The truth was right there in front of me. But I didn't have the imagination to accept it."

"That's precisely the point!" he said as if I had confirmed some thesis of his. "That's precisely the point, we still do not trust our own imaginations. We don't understand how perfect we are, and we think that there exists some objective world that does not depend on the way we view it."

"Edik," I interrupted, "you don't have to tell me all that. I've already heard that primary is secondary and secondary is primary."

"You've heard that but you don't believe it because of your defective imagination. You know, among other things, I've also studied madmen suffering from hallucinations of every sort. And I've come to the conclusion that there is no such thing as a hallucination. It's just that the person having the hallucination sees something we cannot see, while we see things that he can't."

"In other words, let's say, if I drink to the point where I get the DTs and start seeing devils, does that mean they really exist?"

"Of course," said Edik with a nod. "They really exist in your world, whereas in mine, as long as I'm sober. . . ."

"By the way," I interrupted, "it's terribly boring to be sober all the time. Your laboratory must have something for sterilizing all those test tubes."

Edik looked over at me and paused for a moment's thought.

"As a rule I don't consume alcohol," he said pensively, "but in this case. . . . I should be able to find something at home."

Edik's needs were obviously even higher than Marshal Maturin's. He lived near his laboratory in a large apartment with windows looking out onto an underground street. Even though the apartment was spick-and-span, you still felt that it was a bachelor's place. One of the rooms contained a rather sizable library containing both scientific works and an excellent collection of preliminary literature from Pushkin to Karnavalov. He had a copy of this novel as well. And what we drank there was distinguished, too—genuine French cognac bottled in 2016. Not only that, after we'd polished off the first bottle, he brought out a second.

We sat with the lights off, but there was some sort of lamp outside the window. Its faint light entering the room allowed me to discern the corner of the table and the bottle, though my drinking partner's hook-nosed profile did seem dark and flat, as if cut out of cardboard.

We continued speaking of the scope, power, and flight of imagination, and Edik so confused me with his arguments that I could no longer tell the difference between real reality and imaginary reality.

As best I remember, his arguments boiled down to more or less the following. Our world itself is the fruit of a higher design. God designed this world, settled us on it, and expected us to live in accordance with his design. But he did not endow us with the ability to fathom his design, and we began acting not as he had conceived, but helter-skelter, and we even went out of control. The same thing happens with a writer. He creates an imaginary world, populates it with his characters, expects certain definite actions from them, but then they start with all sorts of monkey business and end up distorting the original idea.

I had already grown unused to drinking and became tipsy rather quickly. Maybe that's why everything we said seemed exceptionally wise to me.

"What you're saying is very true," I said happily. "That's just what happens to me. I conceive things one way but then they turn out completely different."

"Precisely," said Edik. "It was the same story with our unfortunate Genialissimo. He had his own design too. When he came to power with his 'angry generals,' he wanted to establish a new order here. He began a war on corruption, bureaucratism, and inequality. And the main thing was that, after placing those generals in all the key posts, he introduced a new principle—the cadres were to be constantly changed and kept constantly young. Until they seized power, the generals had been in agreement with this policy. But when they were in power, their own ideas began to change. They wanted to remain in their posts forever. The Genialissimo had not realized this yet, and demanded discipline, work, and that they be accountable to the people. Then he decided to introduce another principle of equality: from each according to his ability, to each an identical amount."

"Oh, so that was it!" I said, grasping everything all at once. "And that was too much for the people around him, was it?"

"There you go again!" said Edik with sudden anger, whacking his knee. "I don't understand how you can consider yourself a writer when you think so primitively. Any fool knows that people with privileges never want to surrender those privileges. You don't need much insight into human psychology to understand that. In fact, it wasn't only the people around the Genialissimo, but the entire society that was irritated by his innovations. The point is that the principle of inequality creates fertile soil for complacency on all levels of society. The people on top are smug because they have more than the people in the middle, and the people in the middle are smug because they have more than the people on the bottom."

"And what about them, what are they smug about?" I asked.

"You mean you've never met people who revel in the fact that they're on the very bottom? They can always rationalize their failure because of social inequality, and their own outstanding honesty, modesty, uniqueness. To be brief, the Genialissimo had encroached upon society's holy of holies. By taking an unassailable position, he made great advances, but at the same time he caused a dissatisfaction that grew greater by the day. And especially, of course, among the former 'angry generals.' And the angriest of them now was his closest friend, the deputy chairman of the Supreme Pentagon and the chairman of the Editorial Commission."

"Horizon Timofeyevich?" I said.

"Right. Of course he wasn't able to overthrow the Genialissimo, who had become a symbol, the subject of universal reverence, a sacred cow, but a trickier solution was found. One time when the Genialissimo was out in space on an ordinary inspection overflight, they decided not to let him return. Let him stay up there orbiting, we'll pray to him, we'll erect monuments to him, award him decorations, send him all sorts of greetings and reports, but meanwhile here on Earth we'll run things our way."

"Stop!" I said. "Don't tell me these fairy tales. In fact, the Genialissimo does not exist because he is just an invention of mine. Do you understand now, I fabricated it all."

"It's possible," said Edik with a shrug. "But that doesn't change anything, because all existing reality is the fruit of someone's idea. An idea is born out of nothing, then it is incarnated in life, where it displays a tendency to develop on its own. But if you have in fact made all this up, then it's high time to correct your work. That Sim of yours should go. Forever. Use any means to annihilate him. Later on you can also annihilate Horizon too. But the Genialissimo has to return to Earth. You and I have great need of him."

"We do? What sort of mutual interests do you and I have?"

"I'll explain. You see, the Supreme Pentagon and the Editorial Commission are made up of cretins and senile old men, and I cannot entrust my discovery to them. But, if you bring the Genialissimo back down to Earth, the three of us can put the elixir of life to the most effective use. We can use it to take control of the world and establish a new order on the Earth."

"I don't follow you," I said.

"I'll explain. The thing is that many people break the law and established rules of behavior because each of them thinks that he really doesn't have much to lose. That sort of person thinks: no matter what I do and what they do to me, I'm going to die anyway. The awareness that death is inevitable renders certain people fearless, even desperate. But the elixir will make everything different. In fact, we'll be able to rescind many punishments, including prison and the death penalty. Why? We'll simply distribute the elixir strictly on the basis of behavior. If you behave—you'll get your monthly portion. And if you behave well next month, you'll get it again. But anyone who displays any disobedience will be deprived of the elixir. Some temporarily, and some permanently. And so just imagine all those people, the majority of whom are well-behaved, all young, strong, and ruddy. Those who refuse to follow the example of the majority will grow old and sick, and lose their hair and teeth."

"But that's horrible!" I cried. "That's worse than the death penalty. That's even worse than what you've done to that poor terrorist. By the way, speaking of the terrorist . . . Couldn't you take some of your elixir and rub it on his wounds to help them heal?"

Edik gave me a bewildered look. "Why should they heal? I need him with those wounds. Everybody has to be able to see how he suffered, what he stood up to. I really don't understand how you can make such requests of me. Do you mean to say that they didn't break you of your abstract humanism back in the past?"

That threw me. Of course, they had tried to break me of it, and sometimes they made great efforts to. And, figuratively speaking, my heart had even hardened. But when I've had too much to drink, I start feeling sorry for everybody—even snakes, scorpions, and terrorists—and there's nothing I can do about it.

"You're a fool," said Edik. "Compassion is a foolish and useless emotion. It's the people who feel compassion that do the most damage of all. They hinder progress. And, while we're on the subject, they won't be getting any of the elixir either."

"Aha!" I said, catching him out. "That means the same thing is in store for me. I'll delete Simych for you, but you'll deprive me of the elixir and watch as I grow old and gray and lose my teeth . . ."

"What are you talking about!" objected Edik firmly. "Why do you think that of me? You'll live forever, but I can do you another favor—make you insensitive to suffering. One little operation and you'll be like a stone. Anyone at all can be cut into pieces before your eyes. He can writhe in pain, weep and moan, and your soul will be unmoved. You'll eat calmly, drink your wine, and enjoy the sunshine, the smell of flowers, and the love of women."

"Do you mean that I could really see someone being beaten and not suffer for him?" I asked.

"Let the person being beaten do the suffering," Edik replied evenly. "Why should anyone else suffer?"

I'd be lying if I said that I wasn't tempted by Edik's proposition. For a long time I'd been fed up with pity, compassion or whatever the hell else it's called. It had messed up my life, interfered with my career, ruined my appetite. What did I need it for?

I promised to consider his proposition. I mean, I think I promised to, though in fact now I am not even sure whether that conversation actually took place or was a dream or a delusion. But if I had imagined this conversation as I had everything else, then why can't I use the power of imagination to put an end to these adventures and return home to Stockdorf?

I tried to do that. I closed my eyes, strained my imagination to the limit, and, I think, even fell into some transcendental state, my entire body breaking out in a sweat. But I unglued my eyes and saw that I was not in Stockdorf. And I wasn't at Edison Xenofontovich's either. I was in my own hotel room. Iskrina wasn't there. Scattered on the floor by the bed were pages that had been torn from a book. I gathered them up and began reading them. The text seemed familiar, as if I had read it before, or perhaps even written it.

By the way, many notes had been made in the margins with pencils of different colors. The notes were mainly negative in nature and all pretty much the same. In some places there was the word "Bad!" In another, "This is too much!!!" (those three exclamation points were in fact used there). I looked through those pages and became engrossed in them, at the same time thinking that perhaps here and there it was indeed a little too much, but what was bad about it? On the contrary, it was not bad at all!

A GLOOMY
TIME

Stepanida spent more than twenty years on Sim Simych's estate, "Solace." And for all those years she faithfully recorded her observations on life there, referring to the estate owner either as "Little Father" or simply as "He," with a capital *H*. But, over time, those notes became shorter, more monotonous, and more despondent. Complaints that her best years were gone and wasted, and even hints that one day she'd like to return home, would sometimes break through.

One report was as laconic as could be: "Nothing new except we're all growing old."

Every day of all those years the Little Father kept to one and the same schedule: reveille, prayer, jog around the lake, breakfast, work, a ride on Logos, and then work, work, with short breaks for lunch and dinner, and, as usual, in the evening, research for new words in *Dahl's Etymological Dictionary* and the "Well-Tempered Clavier" before falling to sleep.

And no diversions. He didn't watch television himself and didn't like it when others did. Stepanida complains that she and Tom had to watch "Dallas" on the sly, turning down the sound all the way.

The estate knew only one period of life and hope (but a rather long one). This was the time when the leaders in Moscow were keeling over one after the other. In this period He Himself would sit down by the television in the evening and watch the funerals with pleasure, paying careful attention to all the reports and the commentary on changes and power struggles in the Kremlin; sometimes he would nudge Zilberovich in the ribs, asking, "What are they saying?" He was not strong in the local language himself.

He came to life in those days, spent less time grinding out His slabs and more riding Logos. He was often in a joking mood and even became more sexually active. But it all kept ending the same way. Having buried one old man, the predators would put one even older in his place, and on it went.

The Little Father's last flurry of hope had come when an infirm old man was finally replaced by a young, healthy one who held two higher degrees. The commentators vied with one another to praise the new leader's intelligence and wit, his clothes ordered exclusively from Dior, the fact that he read Voltaire in the original, and secretly attended church. To this new leader, the Little Father sent a secret message, instructing him to disband the Communist Party and restore to Russia its traditional form of monarchic rule.

He received no answer, and it soon became clear that the journalists had sung the new leader's praises too highly. He did wear Dior suits, but he hardly attended church, and the only writer he read in the original was Lenin.

When the Little Father was convinced of this, He ordered the television thrown out in the trash, ceased even asking what was happening in Moscow, and returned to his unending labors.

Stepanida notes this period as a turning point in the Little Father's morale. He continued to pile up the slabs, but now they cost Him more effort, He had lost His drive. And His memory was starting to go: memorizing proverbs became more of a problem from one day to the next. He'd learn six new proverbs, and forget eight. Sometimes when the occasion called for a certain proverb, He'd try to recall it, furrow his brow, snap his fingers, but, no, it wouldn't come. It would help if Zilberovich was around, because He was helpless without him.

The Little Father was going out riding less and less often, the dress rehearsals had petered out, and life had become quite boring on the estate.

It was sad and painful for me to read Stepanida's reports, which told of the Little Father losing faith in His own destiny and taking to drink (she was bringing more whiskey bottles and soda bottles out of His office every day).

And, then all of a sudden, there was this letter.

DISAPPEARANCES

Katusha my nearest and dearest,

I'm writing to you in terrible confusion. I don't know what the hell is going on here. This morning I woke up a little later than usual. I look over and Tom's not there. So I think—he went to the stables. Alright, I get up, tidy up, and go to clean for Him. Especially because He's out jogging then. I look in and the bed's all made like it was never slept in, and the office is all clean too. There's not a piece of paper on the tables except for some medical journal. There was still time before breakfast, so I went over to the stables to ask Tom if he knew what had happened. But Tom wasn't at the stables. That wouldn't have surprised me, but not only wasn't Tom there, Logos wasn't there either. I went looking for the little Jew, his door was locked, and he was nowhere to be seen outside either. Still, I wasn't thinking anything, I just thought maybe they went someplace together, I don't know, to the veterinarian. But it seemed kind of strange, because the veterinarian usually comes here and, if not, then it's something Tom and the Jew can deal with. The Little Father never deals with that sort of thing.

Still, I wasn't thinking anything. I started thinking when I went to breakfast and saw Janet and her mother there with tears all over their faces. I ask what happened? Nothing, they say. I ask where the Little Father is. They say He's gone and He won't be back. Is He dead, I ask them? I can see Kleopatra Kazimirovna tremble and look away, but she doesn't say anything. Then Janet says, yes, He's dead. So I ask about Tom and the Jew, where are they gone to. Did they bring Him to the morgue? By horse? Kleopatra Kazimirovna is still saying nothing, but Janet says, "Tom and Leopold Grigerovich are gone too." And so I ask, what, did they die too? They died too, she says.

Can you imagine how I reacted to that and what I said? I asked where their bodies were. And she says, it doesn't matter, it's none of my business. I say what do you mean it's none of my business. It's none of my business where your husband's body is, but where my husband's body is is very much my business. She doesn't give me any answer and I don't know what to do, should I call the police or not. Katusha, if this is your doing, then you should put me in the know because I have no idea what to do now. I await further instructions. . . .

That last sentence could have given Stepanida clean away and must have been written in a state of great haste and excitement.

Evidently, Stepanida received the instructions she was awaiting, because in her next letter, barely able to fake a folksy style, she reports that the Little Father had been very deep in thought during the days before he disappeared. He summoned the Jew and Tom many times and, locking His office door, spent a long time in conversation with them. Tom had not been himself either and gave unintelligible replies to Stepanida's questions (though she does mention parenthetically that he should have told her everything). Zilberovich, too, acted mysteriously, though he was in a good mood.

At one point, a few days before the disappearances, Stepanida noticed that the Little Father's lights were still on late, and she stole up to his open window and heard Him speaking Russian on the telephone with a person he called Mr. Rivkin. She only heard part of their conversation, which struck her as extremely odd, though it was only later that she figured out what it all meant.

"I don't understand what the hitch is," Sim was supposed to have said with unusual excitement. "Most horses are superior to people, but we have to realize that horses are on a more primitive level of development and their organisms are much simpler than ours. . . ."

Stepanida only began to get a hint of what the conversation was about when, after the Little Father's disappearance, she found a Xerox copy of an article from *The Medical Review* on His desk. Many passages in the article had been underlined, and in the margins there were notes made in the Little Father's own hand. The article reported on the experiments performed by Harvard professor Doctor Donald Rivkin on freezing the bodies of higher mammals. It said that there now existed sufficiently reliable means for freezing bodies that could remain in a state of suspended animation for nearly any length of time (almost forever). It also discussed the first experiments, not only on monkeys, but on live human beings who, incurably ill (usually with cancer), had agreed to submit themselves to freezing in the hope of remaining frozen until cures for their illnesses were found.

There was another Xerox copy on the desk, not an article, but the phone bill for the intercity call on which Stepanida had eavesdropped. This call had lasted four and a half hours, had cost a fortune, and, considering the fact that the Little Father hated to waste money, must have been of great importance to Him.

Here, as they say in books, Stepanida's reports broke off. A document attached to them dryly notes that, having fulfilled her combat assignment, Hero of the Soviet Union, KGB Major Stepanida Makarovna Zueva-Johnson returned to her Motherland, but was killed in an automobile accident en route into Moscow from the airport.

But that was not the end of it. I also read reports by at least a dozen agents who had been assigned to learn what had actually happened to Karnavalov and where he had disappeared. Some of the agents honestly reported that they had failed to turn up a single clue. Others repeated ridiculous rumors. In the end, only one produced any useful information—that recently a complex and cumbersome experiment had been conducted in Professor Rivkin's clinic, involving the simultaneous freezing of the organisms of three humans and one horse.

This was followed by something that made no sense whatsoever: "S.S. Karnavalov, his two bodyguards, and his horse Logos were shipped to Geneva in a frozen state and there deposited for unlimited storage in a vault in a Swiss bank."

"And there in that vault," said Dzerzhin Gavrilovich to me when we next met, "he remains to this day, waiting for his hour to strike. He's waiting for the communist system to collapse, and then he'll be thawed out and ride in here on a white horse."

"Yes," I said pessimistically, "a person like him is capable of anything. But I'm sure that our renowned communist intelligence people working in tandem with the renowned CIA have already learned in precisely which Swiss vault the pretender is being kept."

"Come on!" said Dzerzhin Gavrilovich with a bitter laugh, failing to pick up on my allusion. "If we knew where he was, we wouldn't need your help."

THE CREATIVE
PENTAGON

"I hereby declare this extraordinary session of the Creative Pentagon open," said Smerchev matter of factly. He cast a questioning glance at Beria Ilich, who was sitting beside him. His chin supported by his fist, Beria Ilich was looking off somewhere past my left ear, his expression that of someone who was there as an outsider with no intention of interfering in the functioning of the Pentagon.

"This session is a particularly secret one," continued Smerchev. "No one, apart from the stenographer, is to take any notes whatsoever." He paused and gave me a significant look; I showed that my hands were empty and patted my chest to indicate that I had nothing to write with, in my hands, on the table, or inside my shirt. "As the members of the Pentagon know, and as I am now warning anyone who may not know," he continued with another look in my direction, "nothing that happens within these walls is to be disclosed to anyone."

"If you count me and the marshal," I remarked, "this isn't a pentagon but a heptagon."

Finding my own remark witty, I laughed out loud. The members of the Pentagon exchanged tense glances. The marshal remained unruffled, but Communi Ivanovich, after a quick look at the marshal, mimicked something like a smile to let me know that my playful mood was out of place and not in keeping with the seriousness of the occasion.

343

Embarrassed, I shriveled and shrank, then began scrutinizing the members of the Pentagon one by one. They were seated as follows: Smerchev was at a table to the right of the marshal. Iskrina was at the end of that table with her pencil and pad (she was taking the minutes). From time to time I tried to catch her eye, but she was being cool and distant and would not look in my direction. The other members of the Pentagon—Propaganda Paramonovna, Dzerzhin Gavrilovich, and Father Starsky—were at a conference table. I was sitting a few chairs from Starsky near the far end of the table.

"I think," continued Smerchev, "that we should conduct this session without any unnecessary formality, and get right to the heart of the matter. I should point out at once that relations with Classic did not progress smoothly from the start and that certain difficulties had to be overcome. Personally, I explain the lack of understanding on both sides as the result of our having been raised and reared in different social systems. We have taken that factor into account and have been displaying a great deal of patience and humanity. We gave our guest a very warm welcome, we have put him up in the best hotel, and even placed him in the high-level-need category, though he had done nothing to deserve this. We intended to mark the one hundredth anniversary of his birth with a grand, nationwide celebration. The leadership of the KPGB, the Supreme Pentagon, and the Editorial Commission, with the Genialissimo's personal participation, have made an exceedingly bold decision: despite the temporary paper shortage, and despite our custom not to publish books that do not have a direct bearing on *Genialissimoiana*, we had intended to publish a book by our guest. But we requested that he make certain essential corrections and excise certain sections, which the book could easily do without. To perform this small task, he was supplied with all the necessary materials and familiarized himself with them, isn't that so?" said Smerchev, looking at me.

"If you're referring to the chapters from the novel I'm supposed to have written," I said, "then, yes, I've familiarized myself with them."

"You must stand when a general is speaking to you," whispered Starsky out of the blue.

I looked over at Starsky, then at Smerchev, who averted his eyes but said nothing. I realized he agreed with Starsky but was not going to press the point. As for me, I had no intention of standing: I wasn't going to play the little boy for them.

"Now you know everything," said Smerchev. "Sim Karnavalov is not dead, as you supposed at first; he is alive, stored in a Swiss bank, waiting for his day to come."

"But he won't live to see the day," remarked Starsky and all the members of the Pentagon laughed, a laughter that was both jolly and forced.

"Yes," seconded Communi Ivanovich confidently, "he won't live to see the day, if, of course, you give the matter some thought and are willing to meet us halfway."

"I have a question," I said.

"Go right ahead and ask it," said Smerchev, politely.

"Tell me. . . ." I looked over at Starsky and then for some reason automatically rose to my feet. "Have the things I read about in that novel been confirmed by independent documentation?"

"Of course they have," said Dzerzhin Gavrilovich who, opening a green file in front of him, began leafing through some papers. "They've been confirmed by the reports from Major Stepanida Zueva-Johnson, by information from intelligence agent Tom Johnson, and by the telephone bill for the conversation between Karnavalov and Professor Donald Rivkin."

"What perfect rubbish!" I said, starting to grow edgy. "All the nonsense you're referring to, all those reports, information, telephone bills, you took all that from my novel. And it's just a novel, a work of art—in other words, pure fiction."

"And quite malicious fiction at that," observed Propaganda Paramonovna, who had not said a word until then. She looked over at the marshal.

"You call it fiction," said Smerchev, "but, because of that fiction, the Simites in our republic are becoming more defiant with each passing day. For example, as recently as yesterday, at the base of the monument to the Genialissimo's scientific discoveries, unknown criminals placed an enormous heap of secondary matter with a note attached that read, "Our present to the Genialissimo."

"Oh Gen, what blasphemy!" exclaimed Father Starsky and, lifting his eyes to the portrait of the Genialissimo, he starred himself devoutly. The other members of the Pentagon starred themselves, and I followed suit before I slid into my chair.

"Judging by the size of the pile," continued Smerchev, "this was clearly not the work of one person, but of an entire organization. And of course the note was signed with a certain well-known three-letter word. The day before yesterday, a group of punks was neutralized. They had been meeting in private apartments where they wore long pants and long skirts and danced hostile dances. Once they were arrested they of course began to play games and claim that the length of pants is not political in nature. But it was also discovered that each of them had inserted into their Sign of Membership a small picture of the person they revere."

Upon hearing this, I glanced over at Iskrina without meaning to, but she continued dutifully to record the minutes and displayed no emotion at all.

"Alright then," said Smerchev, "let's not drag out the discussion. I only wish to tell our guest [I noticed that he was avoiding referring to me as Classic] that it is perfectly clear to us that he has no desire to correct the book he wrote or to do any more work on it. But this must be done, and so all of us—not only me personally but all the other members of the Creative Pentagon—urge you to delete the section where you have him come riding in on his white horse. You'll be better off and so will we. Why can't you let go of that part? Why are you so fond of it?"

Oh, Gen, these people were impossible! I stood up once again and began pacing nervously.

"My dear comcoms, ladies and gentlemen," I began, trying to sound as convincing as I could, "believe me, I harbor no ill against you. I would like to do everything you ask. Yesterday when reading certain sections of the novel, I even picked up a pen and I wanted to, I sincerely wanted to delete Sim Simych from it. . . ."

"And what prevented you?" asked Propaganda Paramonovna in a sarcastic tone.

"My own nature," I said. "The thing is, I would see the word *Sim*, I'd take aim at it, but I couldn't get my hand to move. Not only that, it's not so easy to delete him either. If I delete him, then I have to delete Zilberovich, too. . . ."

"Very good," interjected Starsky, "one Simite fewer."

"Not just one," I objected. "If I delete Zilberovich, then there's no point in having Janet. And if Janet's out, then Kleopatra Kazimirovna is out too. And so are Stepanida and Tom and the horse and Doctor Rivkin."

"So delete them all then!" cried Smerchev.

"But don't you understand, there'll be nothing left of the novel. All that will be left is meaningless nonsense. And you simply fail to understand me. If I had been able to correct my novels that way, I would not have had any reason to come here. What a career I could have had back then in the days of socialism, under the Cultists, Volunteerists, Corruptionists, and Reformists! I would already have been the secretary of the Writers' Union, a Hero of Labor, a Deputy to the Supreme Soviet and a Lenin-Prize laureate. I would have had royalties by the sackload. But I was incapable of that then and I am incapable of it now."

A heavy silence descended upon the room. The members of the Pentagon exchanged glances. Communi Ivanovich unbuttoned the top button of his field shirt, then buttoned it again. Suddenly, Propaganda Paramonovna jumped to her feet, waltzed up to me from behind, put her arms around me, and pressed her large breasts against my shoulder blades.

"Please, please, my darling," she whispered in the sweetest of voices. "Why are you resisting, why are you acting like a stubborn old mule. Please, help us, I implore you. I beg you as a woman." Suddenly she fell to her knees and threw her arms around my legs. "My darling, my sweetest. . . ."

Suddenly beside myself, I jumped to my feet, braced my hands on the top of her bristly head and began shoving her away from me. "Look at you!" I said. "Look at the scene you're making here! Aren't you ashamed of yourself!"

"You shameless lowlife!" I heard Starsky say. "Look who's talking about shame! Look who's on her knees before you! A woman! A mother! A general! And you . . . I'll tear your face to pieces!"

With those words, he came running at me, limping and stomping and attacking me with his fists. It was a good thing that I had just broken free of Propaganda's embrace and could grab Starsky's beard. Pulling it downward, I slammed his face against my knee. His face red with blood, he bounded away from me with a wild howl to the wall, pressing his back against it. He covered his face with his hands, but the blood seeped through his fingers, dripping onto his cassock and the floor.

The members of the Pentagon looked in amazement back and forth from me to Starsky. Then, for the first time, I caught Iskrina's eye and realized that she, too, was horrified.

"But this is out-and-out terrorism!" said Propaganda Paramonovna suddenly and ominously. And the room filled with a silence that gave me gooseflesh. Beria Ilich rose and left the room. I noticed that now everyone grew more relaxed, almost sighing with relief. Dzerzhin jumped up and ran over to Starsky.

"Let me see," he said quite crudely. "It's nothing so terrible. Tilt your head back and the bleeding will stop. Everything's all right," said Dzerzhin to Smerchev.

"What do you mean everything's alright?" said Propaganda Paramonovna indignantly. "How can everything be all right when people are being criminally assaulted?"

"Be quiet!" said Dzerzhin, cutting her off. He began pacing the room in circles. "Here's the thing. Our discussion with Classic has gone too far. We're requiring something of him but he doesn't understand us. And why?"

"Because he's our enemy, that's why," said Propaganda.

"Yes, that probably is why," said Smerchev with a sad smile.

348

"But why should that be?" said Dzerzhin, slapping himself on the thigh. "Why must he be an enemy? Why toss around words like that so soon? Speaking personally, as someone who works for SECO, I'm used to trying to find what's good, what's best about a person. We should try to understand Classic. The point here is that I've examined all the old cases against preliminary writers, and what I found was that many of them were abnormal and had to be treated delicately. Otherwise, they offered resistance. Just like he's doing. The whole point is that he's a creative person and he can't just be ordered to do one thing or another; we ought to offer him a wide range of choices to allow his art the scope it needs. Let's suppose he doesn't want to inform us where the vault is located. Alright, he doesn't have to. He doesn't want to delete his hero, that's understandable too. But, listen, my darling," he said, addressing me directly now, "you can come up with something yourself. Say you don't want to delete your hero, then have him die, that's all. And that will be the end of that. Or, say he wasn't frozen, but pickled, how about that?"

Dzerzhin looked over at me and all the others did the same. Even Starsky, fearing to lower his head, turned it slightly to one side and regarded me in bird-like fashion.

"What do you say?" said Smerchev. "It's a good idea, in my opinion. A productive one."

"It's ridiculous," I objected wearily. "Who's going to pickle a person? A person is not a cucumber or a piece of pork."

"It was just an idea," said Dzerzhin. "I wasn't really thinking. But maybe we can come up with a better idea. Let's say he was frozen and placed in a vault, but there was a hole in the vault and he defrosted and rotted. There's any number of possibilities here. You know better than I, you're the artist."

At that moment Iskrina glanced over at me, and I could see that she was categorically against any such changes. Had it not been for that glance, I might even have yielded. But now. . . .

"No," I said, sensing that my moment of weakness had passed. "No, it's not going to happen. And since you're treating me this way, I don't want anything more to do with you. I don't need any of your jubilees or other honors. I'm just going to wait for my spacecraft and then I'm going back home to Stockdorf."

"Without a visa?" asked Starsky nasally, squeezing his nose.

"What kind of visa?" I asked, on my guard now.

"What a question," said Smerchev with a smile. "We have definite rules when it comes to border crossings. You can't do anything here without a visa. If a person wants to go to the First Ring, or anywhere else, say Kaluga Province, he must have his visa."

"That," I said with a dismissive gesture, "only concerns Communites. And not only am I not a Communite, I was even stripped of my Soviet citizenship more than sixty years ago. And so I am not your subject in any way."

All the members of the Pentagon exchanged odd glances when I said this, but Communi Ivanovich smiled, spread his hands far apart, and, calling me by my real name, said with a tone of satisfaction, "No, Vitaly Nikitich, you *are* our subject. We've rehabilitated you, you see."

PART VI

THE SOCIALIST
HOTEL

"Where have you brought me?" I asked Vasya.

"Where they ordered me to," he answered. "You'll be staying there now." He pointed to a long, squat building, and while I was giving the building a look-over, he stepped on the accelerator, and drove away, enveloping me in a cloud of steam.

When the steam cleared, I could see by the light of the moon that the building was something like a barracks and that all of its windows were totally black. Above the door in the center of the barracks there was a dimly-lit peeling sign that read:

THE SOCIALIST HOTEL

There was a vacant lot across from the hotel, to the right of which stretched a high, reinforced-concrete wall topped with barbed wire, from which I concluded that I was at the very outskirts of the Moscowrep.

Not knowing what to do, I did nothing for a while, but then I decided to go in the hotel and had to push the door open with my shoulder. It opened with a terrific screech.

My nose was immediately assaulted by the smell of urine.

"How do you stand the stink?" I asked a middle-aged woman, a second lieutenant. She was sitting beside a night table on which an oil lamp made of tin cans was burning faintly. I wondered where she got those cans. I had never seen any canned food in the Moscowrep.

"What do you want?" asked the second lieutenant.

I told her that I had been transferred there from the Communist Hotel.

"Last name?"

I thought that as soon as she learned who I was, she would immediately swoon and ask for my autograph, but nothing of the sort took place. She spent a good while looking through some filth-stained book, running a crooked finger from one line to the next. Finding what she needed, she took a bunch of keys from the table along with the oil lamp, led me down a long corridor and, opening room number fourteen, she said, "This is your room." And then she was gone.

I fumbled along the wall, searching for the light switch, but there was none, just as there were no lights. But the moon was bright enough for me to see the narrow iron bed in the corner by a barred window and a wobbly night table. The bed had a rough blanket and a pillow that seemed stuffed with rotten straw. I don't think there was anything else in the room, apart from the plastic pot I found in the corner by the door.

To tell the truth, I didn't like any of this in the least, but I also knew that my stubbornness would cost me some day, and so I said to myself, To hell with it, I can spend a while here, too. There was one good thing—I'd at least gotten a room to myself, and not a cot in some dormitory where those who consume vegetarian pork do more than snore.

Needless to say I found no sheet under the blanket. What could I do? I set my shoes outside my door, but I didn't undress any further and lay down on top of the blanket.

I was so tired that I fell asleep right away, but woke up soon because I was being bitten by insects. I got up several times during the night; I'd shake the insects off and go back to bed. By morning I'd gotten a little sleep, but this time when I got up, I was horrified. The walls were crawling with bugs, the blanket rustling with lice.

Fleas were hopping on top of fleas. I tore off my shirt and saw that my whole body was covered with little red bite marks.

I've got to get out of here, but quick! I said to myself and darted out to the hallway. Of course, I hardly suspected that my shoes would have been shined, but my shoes weren't there at all.

There was a different woman on duty, this one a sergeant. When I asked her about my shoes, she looked a little surprised, but then informed me that the hotel wasn't responsible for items left out in the corridor. That I should have expected. When I asked her where the natfunctbur was, she told me that hotels of that class have no natfunctburs of any sort, but there was a container for secondary matter in my room. Meaning, of course, the plastic pot.

Naturally, I had no great desire to use that vessel, but, what can you do, I went back to the room. Interestingly enough, there was a strip of newspaper there too, one about eight feet long. Unrolling it, I immediately spotted a headline: "A Man from the Past." As I guessed at once, the article was about me, even though my name was never mentioned once.

It goes without saying that I'd had occasion to read that sort of criticism before, but I might have been more thick-skinned back then and did not take everything so much to heart; this time, I was deeply wounded by what I read. The article said that some disgusting character from the distant past had set about criticizing and spitting upon everything that we hold dear. When living in the period of developed socialism, he had seen nothing good in pre-communist society's forward progress, and, on assignment from Third-Ring intelligence, he had slandered and spat upon everything he saw. His activities, if they may be called that, deserve the strictest punishment, but, owing to the permissiveness of the Corruptionists then in power, he managed to escape retribution by hiding in the Third Ring where, to please his foreign benefactors, he set about defaming his country with a will, the country which raised him, fed him, clothed and shod him. And now here he is back with us again. Our society forgave the renegade for his past crimes. We hoped that after spending sixty years in the Third Ring he would have seen and thought enough to understand the principled difference between communism and a world where the workers have been reduced to such poverty that they even have to import secondary matter from abroad. In that hope, the Supreme Pentagon made a decision to grant full rehabilitation to the renegade. We welcomed him with open arms, but, as the saying goes, no matter how much you feed a wolf, he still belongs to the forest. Having lost all conscience, this lackey of international reaction even sees our period of mature communism in the darkest of colors, disliking everything so much he does not even differentiate between a comfoodest and a natfunctbur.

As we all know, the article went on, ours is the most humane society on earth. But it is severe with those who would break its laws and its rules of behavior. The article ended by calling on the Communites to defend themselves against my provocations by displaying the utmost self-discipline and vigilance, to close ranks with the party, the Supreme Pentagon, the Editorial Commission, and the person of the Genialissimo, and show stiff resistance to all hostile incursions.

Yes, that made for very unpleasant reading. I was even disgusted by the very idea of using this newspaper for the purpose for which it had been published. But, having nothing more suitable at hand, I went ahead and used it anyway. Then, I went back out into the hallway, not in the best of moods.

BOYCOTT

The woman on duty by the night table was darning a cotton sock that was stretched over a chunk of something. I asked her where I could wash up.

"Washing needs aren't satisfied here," she snapped quite rudely.

"Is there anywhere I can get my breakfast needs satisfied?" I asked poisonously.

"There's a comfoodest around the corner," she replied without lifting her head.

I went outside. The pavement had turned cold overnight, and my pampered, shoeless feet felt the cold. Not only that, the streets were covered with pebbles and scraps of plastic, which made walking quite painful. Curling my toes, I somehow hobbled my way to the comfoodest.

The line was short, around forty people. I was surprised to see so few people, but it was then that I realized I was in the Moscowrep's Third Ring, where most of the population were Communites with self-serviceable needs. And so that meant that people in the line had come there from the city center. Or maybe these people weren't Communites at all, but visitors from the First Ring, because none of them recognized me and no one asked me for my autograph.

The menu was posted on the wall by the door, and I read it. Thank God, they didn't have vegetarian pork. Only two dishes were listed: rice kasha made from wheat and tea made from oak leaves. This seemed like food I could consume without running any great risk to my stomach. But next to the menu was the now familiar announcement that Communite needs are satisfied only upon presentation of written proof that secondary matter has been handed in.

I ran back to the hotel. But the pot in my room was quite empty and had even been washed clean. Though I found this extremely awkward and began stammering with shame, I asked the woman on duty if she happened to know what had happened to the secondary matter in my room.

"The hotel takes no responsibility for the loss of items left in rooms," she said without looking at me, and I was certain that it was she who had done the filching.

What a predicament. Not having any secondary matter, I couldn't get any primary matter, but without the primary I couldn't produce the secondary. So did that mean I was going to die of hunger?

I must admit that at that moment it flashed through my mind that maybe the ideologists here were right, and secondary was primary and primary was secondary.

But what was I supposed to do now? The first thing to do was find Iskra, I said to myself. Of course, I knew that she worked for them, but still she and I had grown very close. Maybe she'll want to help me. I asked the woman on duty for permission to make a phone call.

"The telephone is only for business needs," she said, cutting me off without even a look.

I went outside again, figuring on calling from a booth, especially since public phones in the Moscowrep were free. One of the public phones by the hotel entrance was out of order, and another was minus a door and the receiver had been torn off. Another one around the corner had a receiver, but the glass had been smashed and I was afraid of cutting my feet. The next phone booth was about a block away. It had both a door and a receiver; the only thing lacking was a dial tone.

358

All the streets around there had stupid names—Outskirt Street, Residual Street, and Information Street. There was practically no traffic, though there was noise. Sheep bleated and pigs grunted on all the balconies. Somewhere a pig was being slaughtered, and its squeals were horrible.

I walked along Information Street to the Communist Terminal Metro station. There were eight phone booths there. Of them, seven were out of order. A middle-aged woman talked in the eighth one. I stood behind her, listening to her in spite of myself.

"What are you saying, Dusya," she said, "this isn't life. There's no life here. What? No, I'm telling you this isn't life, there's no life here. Not a bit. What do you mean! You mean this is life? This isn't life, it's a total mess. Who's complaining? No one's complaining. You asked me how's life, and so I just told you this isn't life. What kind of life is this without any life to it?"

I realized that this conversation had just begun and knocked on the glass. I was expecting her to be nasty about it, but she broke off the conversation as soon as she saw me and promised Dusya to call later, vacated the booth, and went into the station.

I grabbed the still warm and moist receiver and placed it to my ear. I expected to hear a dial tone, but there was none. Then I spotted a man with a canvas briefcase two booths from mine, and I ran over to him. He was just saying goodbye to someone and sent his regards to Planeta Semenovna. When I picked up the receiver he had only just hung up, it, too, was dead. Then in a fury I whacked the receiver against the phone so hard that it broke in two.

Turning around, I shuddered. There in front of me was an Intsec man with an enormous face. I thought I was going to have to explain why I had smashed the receiver but, paying me no attention at all, the Intsec man went into the booth, fitted the two pieces together as best he could, dialed a number and started talking.

But when he came out and I grabbed the phone it was dead again.

There was no room left for doubt. They were playing an idiotic game with me, one whose rules I had come to know quite well in my past life. Still, I had to pay Intsec its due, they had learned a thing or two over the last sixty years. In my day they hadn't been able to disconnect every phone in time. Now they could.

There's no substitute for experience. Rotating on my axis, I immediately spotted a couple embracing on a bench in front of the Monument to the Friend of Children (the Genialissimo with his arms around a young girl). I also noticed a middle-aged comcom in a straw hat reading a wall newspaper, a motorist tinkering under an open hood, and a young mother pushing a baby carriage past me. By the way, the carriage was empty (I snuck a peek).

What now?

BOYCOTT
(CONTINUED)

My life had turned into a total nightmare. The hotel was impossible: no air to breathe, plus all those insects, and, on top of it, no light, because, as the duty woman told me, I had no lighting needs. And, in fact, I had none, because although I usually use light to read, there was nothing to read here except for that miserable newspaper, pieces of which were still slipped under my door even though my need for them had entirely vanished. In every piece I would find something which bore a direct relation to me. Some of the headlines had become laughably familiar: "A Man from the Past," "Not in Tune with the Times," "Beware of Provocations!" "Forsaking His Kin," "The Judas of Stockdorf."

I was spending days on end aimlessly roaming about the city because I simply could not stay in the hotel. Just between us, I was dying to eat so badly that sometimes I even dreamed of vegetarian pork. But you couldn't get in a comfoodest without the proper paper. I tried my old trick and showed the comfoodest watchdog a scrap of *Pravda* but apparently the *Zuddeutsche Zeitung* looked more like the required document; this none-too-clever ruse was detected immediately and I almost caught it in the neck for that. I tried to fool another guard with an even simpler trick. Having stood in line until I was quite close to the door, I said to him, "Hey, look at that bird up there" and immediately pushed my way through the door. But, saying "I'll show you a bird!" the guard grabbed me by the scruff of my neck. I escaped from him, but it cost me the collar of my shirt.

They say that matter never disappears. But I could see that the matter of which I was composed was disappearing, and at a good clip too. I took a passing glance at my own reflection in a window and what I saw scared me. I looked like a visual aid for an anatomy class.

Curiously, none of the Communites seemed to know who I was. It hadn't been all that long ago that they all would say hello to me and besiege me for autographs. But now they simply did not see me, did not notice me, as if I were invisible. And when I would speak to one of them and ask for directions or the time, they would continue on their way as if they hadn't heard me.

Once in a while I would succeed in making contact with the person guarding some entrance. And so at the beginning, when I still had hopes of finding Iskra and was trying to work my way into the Communist Hotel, the guard not only did not allow me in but shoved me roughly away. I might have thought that he didn't know who I was, but quite recently that same person had been smiling ingratiatingly at me, bowing and opening the oak door wide for me. My attempts to find Smerchev and Dzerzhin also came to naught. I went both to Paplesslit and Paplit. But in both places the guards blocked my way by crossing their submachine guns, and one of them even brandished the butt end of his weapon at me. I asked him how I could get into Paplit. He said I'd need a pass. Where could I get a pass? At the pass bureau which is located inside the building. But you needed a pass to enter the building. In other words, the same sort of runaround I knew all too well from socialist times.

Of all the officials I knew, the only one I ever ran into was Father Starsky, near Paplesslit. "Father!" I cried, rushing to him. His face dropped when he caught sight of me, and muttering "Saints preserve us!" he starred himself against me as if warding off the devil and disappeared into the door of Paplesslit.

The rest of the Communites ignored me entirely. Sometimes this so enraged me that I was ready to be arrested and face a firing squad if only someone would acknowledge that I still existed. One time, I became so desperate that I heaved a chunk of brick at a Intsec station window. And what do you think happened? The Intsec men came pouring outside, took one look at me, turned around, and began picking up the pieces of glass, without paying me any attention at all.

Another time I walked up to a comcom at a steam bus stop and asked him for the time. He looked right through me, not reacting in the slightest, as if the sounds I made did not cause his ear drums to vibrate.

"My dear sir," I persisted, "I'm speaking to you. I'm asking you if you would be so kind as to tell me what time it is," and I followed this with a few remarks about his mother.

And, can you imagine, he didn't respond this time either.

That drove me wild and I went for him, knocked him onto his back (a big bull of a man, he toppled right over). Pinning him with my knee, I grabbed him by the throat. "Tell me what time it is, you son of a bitch, or I'll strangle you!"

And I would have strangled him too (he was already wheezing), but suddenly a crowd formed, tore me immediately off him, and then casually dispersed as if nothing had happened.

My suffering grew even greater when the weather took a turn for the worse. The nights were cold, and in the morning the pavement would be damp with dew. And though by then I was used to walking around barefoot, my feet still froze. On the other hand, the days were nicer now. Not too hot and not too cold. The sky was cloudy more often, and I noticed that the Communites looked up at the clouds with a hopeful look I could not fathom.

It's always uncomfortable to own up to one's weakness, but as an exceptionally honest person, I must report that my integrity was unable to withstand everything that had come crashing down on me. I always envied people who remained true to their beliefs no matter what. Among communists, there had been some who had kept their faith even after years in prison, even when their backsides were branded with red-hot steel and molten lead was poured down their throats. The young terrorist had overcome terrible tortures before my eyes. But I proved to be such a weakling that, after going hungry for a few days, I was prepared to sell all my foggy ideals, my immature beliefs, and secrets (if only I knew any!) for a mess of potage. But no one offered me any such deal. The agents from the Third Ring operated at such a level of secrecy as to be invisible, and the Simites, of whom I had heard so much, also made no efforts to contact me.

There were, however, some signs of them. Roaming the city and thinking only of my stomach, I nevertheless noticed that something was afoot. People were gathering in little groups, whispering about something, exchanging odd glances. And I kept encountering the word *SIM* more and more often. I saw it on fences, on the pavement, and even on the walls of official institutions. Sometimes the word was written in chalk, sometimes in charcoal, and once I even saw it written on a phone booth in secondary matter.

Waking up one morning, I discovered the word *SIM* in my own hotel room. It had been scratched into the wall with some sharp instrument. Naturally, I ran right to the duty woman, brought her to my room, showed her the word, and said that I had not written it.

"We'll look into this," she said, and ran off to report the incident. I was never to learn to whom she had reported and what consequences this produced, because an event took place the next night that eclipsed everything that had happened to me until then.

DALLAS

Night was already falling when, exhausted by my futile wanderings about the Moscowrep, ostracized, starving, unhappy, my feet scraped and bloody, I slowly shuffled like a sick man back to my hateful hotel room. What could I do now? I thought. To whom could I appeal for permission to leave if no one would speak to me? Maybe I could appeal to the Genialissimo himself. Though we did not share the same beliefs, still we had gone to school together, we had drunk together in the Journalists' Club, we had met in Munich, and finally, if, when he had been a plain general he had saved me from the "Siberian scenario," then why wouldn't he show mercy this time as well? Could it really be important to him, too, that I mangle that idiotic novel?

I already knew that his power over earthly affairs was not as great as it might seem at first glance here. Nevertheless if he personally said, "Leave the man alone! He's my friend!" or something along those lines, they might just obey, not daring to pretend they hadn't heard.

But how could I get my appeal to him? Was a direct appeal the only way? If he can see everything from up there and if he's keeping an eye on everything, then he might be observing me too. The next time he appears in the sky, I'll fall to my knees and reach out with my hands. . . .

I raised my eyes and only then did I notice that the entire sky was covered in dense layers of cloud. Probably not even the Genialissimo could spot me through a cloud cover like that. And I wouldn't be able to see him either.

"Do you think something's going to happen today?" I heard a young man beside me say. Surprised that someone would say so much as a word to me, I looked over and saw a frail-looking comcom who had tilted the peak of his cap slightly upward and was also staring at the sky.

"Like what?" I asked.

"What do you mean like what?" Tearing himself away from his bead on the cloud cover, the comcom shifted his gaze onto me, and I recognized him immediately as the subcomlit Okhlamanov from Paplesslit.

"Oh, so it's you!" he said in confusion, then he suddenly turned and quickly began putting distance between us. I didn't try to stop him. By now I was used to everything in that city.

Night had already fallen by the time I limped back to the hotel. I walked past the duty woman sitting by the oil lamp and just to be on the safe side said Glorgen to her. But she, as I should have expected, made no reply. Then I sat down on my bed, lapsing into the gloomiest of thoughts.

In all respects, it was probably the blackest night of my entire stay in the Moscowrep. Not a single star pierced the clouds, and the entire communist city was sunk in inky darkness. No matter how often I looked out the window, I saw no other windows, for none of them was lit. There were no streetlights on and neither was the flash of a single headlight to be seen. Somewhere in the distance, the front of a government building shone with a large, backlit portrait of the Genialissimo, one of his wise sayings gleaming in gold: "Mankind's age-old dream has come true!"

The pitiful remnants of that light, dispersing en route, entered my humble room, making a few of the things just about visible: the curves of the iron bedstead, the night table, two empty plastic clothes hooks on the wall.

Recently those clothes hooks had started putting ideas into my head that had never occurred to me before in my past life but which now seemed almost natural.

I judged my situation to be hopeless. I was living among alien and incomprehensible people, I couldn't fight my way in anywhere, I couldn't get anything I needed, and I couldn't picture any way of breaking out of this trap. And if I couldn't break out or was never able to tell anyone what I'd seen here, then what was the sense of living?

Those hooks were rather rickety, but I thought they could probably support my body, which had lost a lot of weight by then. The intention had yet to take shape in me, but I could already see myself, blue, emaciated, pitiful, my tongue hanging out and my legs bent up. I even pictured a muscular medic or a SECO man squeamishly removing my remains from the hook and throwing them onto a stretcher. I wondered how *Pravda* would react. Would it print something on the order of "A Dog's Death for a Dog" or say nothing at all and pretend that I had never existed?

While I was thinking these thoughts, my room was suddenly illuminated by a strange, all-pervasive light and then was plunged just as suddenly back into darkness. I had no idea what had happened. Had that lighting effect been caused by something outside my room, or had I just been visited by a revelation? One way or the other, my thoughts now took a sudden turn in a completely different direction.

What's the real truth here? I asked myself. Why should I stay here, what is the purpose of my dooming myself to utter ruin and never returning to my beloved Stockdorf, never seeing my wife and children again? It's only because my miserable nature requires that I perform meaningless exploits and will not allow me to delete something I wrote myself. I took a hard, clear-eyed look at my entire past and I thought, Why should I cling to my fictions, my images, and my words forever, if that's going to doom myself and my family to horrible trouble? Do those fantasies really matter more to me than my own well-being, not to mention my life?

No, they don't! I interrupted myself. Of course they don't. I

367

am not an idiot and not a madman, and I still have the common sense to realize that my own life is the primary matter, and the fictions are the secondary. You can make up a story one way or you can make it up another. And in the end you can always delete what you made up. No matter how sorry I felt about Sim Simych, I felt sorrier for myself. I had the clear and joyful realization that I could very easily delete everything that I had written—Simych, Janet, Kleopatra Kazimirovna, Zilberovich, Stepanida, Tom, and myself included. Not just delete it, but cut it out, crumple it up, and consign it all to hell. Give me that goddamned book, and I'll burn it this minute or annihilate it in some other way. I could imagine my pleasure in tearing the pages to shreds and hurling them in the fire.

"Manuscripts don't burn!" my devil maliciously reminded me, referring to one well-known preliminary writer.

"Get thee behind me!" I said with a wave of my hand. "Of course they burn poorly if you throw a whole manuscript in all at once, but if you ball up each page and throw them in one at a time, they'll burn perfectly well and there'll be nothing left."

Of all the ideas I had ever tried to put into practice, this was probably the simplest, the most brilliant, and the one most requiring immediate implementation. I couldn't waste another single second there.

I darted out to the corridor and started heading for the light of the oil lamp flickering in the distance. I had to tell the duty woman to connect me immediately with Smerchev, Dzerzhin Gavrilovich, Propaganda Paramonovna, or even Beria Ilich. I would tell them everything and then everything would go right back into place. They'd take me right to a sathineed and I'd satisfy my nourishment needs and then. . . . Then I'd do whatever they wanted.

I braced myself before speaking to the duty woman, expecting my request to meet with utter hostility. But she surprised me by speaking first.

"Listen," she said, sounding excited, "you're an educated person. Do you know where the Nevada desert is?"

That caught me off guard. I thought for a second then said that Nevada was in America.

"That means it's in the Third Ring?" she asked with evident satisfaction. "Just as I thought."

"Did something happen over there in the Third Ring?"

"You mean you don't know?" she said in surprise. She looked around and, certain there was no one in the hallway apart from the two of us, she whispered, "Our cosmonauts gave birth to twins in space, and then along with the doctor and the children, they landed in that desert and asked for political asylum. A fine thing, those traitors! Their Motherland raised them and fed them primary matter of the best quality, and then look what they go and do. And they're all poor over there, all they have to eat is secondary matter over there, isn't that so? Haven't you been there? You know what it's like there, don't you?" she asked, getting worked up for some reason and clearly not believing what she had been told about the Third Ring.

Out of my old pernicious fidelity to the truth, I started out to tell her what I had seen in America sixty years ago, but then I suddenly realized that this might be a step toward my own destruction.

"That's right," I corroborated, "for a long time now America's been nothing but a bunch of beggars, and secondary matter there is even. . . ." I wanted to think of something truly awful to say here, but never had the time. Light had come streaming into the hallway through the side windows and the open door.

"Movies! Movies!" shouted the duty woman; she ran outside, tilting the peak of her cap upward as she went. With no idea what was happening, I dashed after her and was frozen in my tracks.

The entire sky overhead was a many-colored blaze. A film was being projected onto hundreds or even thousands of acres of cloud. The images were quite clear. Two luxuriously dressed ladies were drinking champagne in a restaurant. A long Cadillac swam past. In an office furnished with antiques, an athletically built man was talking on the telephone, one hand in the air, holding a smoking cigar.

Looking closely, I realized it was "Dallas," the famous American television series, which in my time had appeared every week on television in America and all through Europe. "A Tuesday without Dallas is like coffee without cream," I remembered an ad from the Stockdorf commuter train.

The film was silent, but Russian subtitles ran over the clouds.

The two women were back on again. They had changed costume and were no longer in the restaurant, but at a roulette table in a casino.

"What luxury!" sighed the duty woman enviously, looking at me with a strange smile.

A crowd of people streamed past on the street, men, women, children, and old people. Many of them were lugging bedding, pillows, and blankets. It looked like a sudden mass evacuation. I nodded goodbye to the duty woman and merged with the flow of the crowd. Soon we were all on a vast vacant lot.

There was already an immense crowd there. Thousands, maybe even tens of thousands. They all sat quietly, some by themselves, some in little groups. They all stared up at the sky and no one said a word.

A conspiracy of silence.

While making my way through people sitting and lying on the ground, I accidentally stepped on someone's foot. The owner of that foot cried out in pain and started swearing at me but people immediately began shushing him and he fell silent.

I found a free spot, sat down in the dust and faded grass, and I, too, began gazing upward. Though I had seen some parts of the series sixty years ago, I had not remembered any of them, nor ever understood them. I didn't understand them in English and I didn't understand them in Russian. To me, "Dallas" was about people who were constantly changing their clothes, drinking champagne, driving around in Cadillacs, and talking about millions of dollars. There were the customary commercial breaks, ads for toothpaste, soap powder, and Japanese electric cars. But what held me was neither the story nor the ads, but the grandiosity of the spectacle in the sky and the reactions of the spectators down below. What I mean is, there was practically no reaction. As if in mass collusion, the spectators maintained utter silence, but when two former boxing champions began munching McDonald's hamburgers on that celestial screen, everyone around me began automatically smacking their lips. And suddenly I, too, so wanted a hamburger on a roll with a sparkling glass of Coca-Cola that I groaned with desire. This drew extreme displeasure from the audience. People shushed from every side and someone even punched me in the ribs.

But neither I nor anyone else got to watch the entire episode. Just when one character had casually handed another a check for fourteen million dollars, the roar of engines began to mount overhead, and when the heroine was tanning on the beach with her aging but fabulously wealthy lover, an entire armada of heavy bombers appeared and began to break pattern, strafing the clouds with tracers.

A second later the roar of motors on earth was heard and confusion swept the crowd. "It's a roundup!" someone shouted, and the word spread like wildfire: "Roundup! Roundup! Roundup!"

People jumped up, grabbed their bedding and pillows, and scattered at a run. As they ran, they raised so much dust that you couldn't see the film or even the person next to you.

I, too, jumped up, not knowing what to do. If this really was a roundup, then it would probably be better if I got caught in it (so I thought). For a long time my only dream had been for someone to pay me the slightest attention.

The roar of the motors grew louder and louder, both up above and on the ground. The dust was so thick my nose, ears and eyes were packed with it and I couldn't see a thing. All of a sudden a blinding light came from every side at once. I could hear feet pounding the ground, followed by shouts and shots.

Just then someone grabbed me by the arm and began dragging me away. Though the stranger was dragging me very rudely and very firmly, for some reason I felt he was a friend trying to save me. I did what he wanted, and when he started running, I started running too. A short while later we were in a narrow lane.

It was bright and noisy. I craned my neck and saw that the

371

planes were still circling and firing at the clouds. Using special shells to disperse the clouds, they had already succeeded in part. The sky had been torn to shreds, but on one cloud torn from the main body the aging millionaire was still handing a glass of champagne to his young, bomber-riddled lover.

My unannounced guide dragged me around the corner of a shed where, releasing my arm, he began to shake the dust off himself, coughing and sneezing. Looking at the back of his nobby head, I was sure that I'd seen him somewhere before. Just then he turned his face toward me and asked in a whisper, "Do you recognize me?"

It was Okhlamanov again.

THE LAST
SUPPER

We took a circuitous route through side streets, courtyards, and back ways, twice we darted across wide avenues, then walked through a mysterious, silent park, and again stole sinuously along, flattening ourselves against walls to avoid patrols and chance passersby. But, as I already knew, there were no chance passersby in that city.

When we stopped to catch our breath in another park, I asked Okhlamanov where we were going.

"To friends," was all he said, and we continued on our way.

The cloud cover had already been mangled, but the planes were still roaring, maliciously ramming the last remnants of illuminated vapor. The bare sickle of a young moon hung bashfully in the midst of the carnage.

After walking another five or six minutes, we passed a squat-looking building and came up against dense shrubbery.

"Now listen carefully," whispered Okhlamanov. "We're going to crawl under these shrubs until we come to a hole in the fence. There's a big street on the other side. I'll crawl through the hole first and run across the street. You wait a minute. If something goes wrong, I'll shout 'Help! I'm being robbed!' You wait there under the bushes until one of our people comes for you. It might even be someone you know. If you don't hear me shout, then after a couple of minutes you crawl through after me and run straight for the house directly across. Use the entrance on the far left, close the door behind you, and go down to the cellar. Be careful, it's dark there. Hold on to the railing on your way down."

This part of the operation went smoothly, and, a few minutes later, Okhlamanov was dragging me by the arm through a labyrinthine basement. Then he knocked on something, some sort of door opened and closed, a second door opened, and I could see a group of young men and women feasting by the light of an oil lamp beneath a large portrait of . . . Sim Simych.

"Ladies and gentlemen!" cried Okhlamanov, his voice deafening after the hush of the streets. "Look whom I've brought here! It's Classic. A full glass for Classic!"

The young people sprang to their feet at once, plastic glasses in their hands. A young woman wearing an ankle-length black dress made of dyed sacking ran over to me with a glass filled to the rim. "Drink with us!"

"But who are you?" I asked, gingerly accepting the glass.

"Haven't you figured it out, Vitaly Nikitich?" asked Okhlamanov with a smile. "We're your fellow Simites."

Everyone there looked curiously at me. In a far corner past the last table I noticed Dzerzhin, with a bad cut on his forehead.

"My dear comcoms," I said, looking for somewhere to set the glass down. "You've done a very clever job in staging this nasty provocation, but the trick won't work. I'm no Simite. I knew many people in my past life, and Sim Simych Karnavalov was one of them. But I was never in agreement with him, I never shared his ideas, and you won't take me in with this cheap trick."

Having said that, I automatically, and to my surprise, drank the glass in one gulp, and almost hit the floor. In my day, I've had occasion to consume denatured alcohol, varnish, even airplane brake fluid, but none of them even came close to what I'd just downed.

"Hurray for Classic!" cried Okhlamanov.

"Hurray!" shouted the others.

"By the way," I said. "The name Classic wasn't my idea. You're the ones who gave me that nickname. I make no claim to it."

"Three cheers for Classic's modesty!" shouted Okhlamanov.

"Glory to Sim!" cried another voice.

"Long live autocracy!"

Fools, I thought, what fools. Do they really think they're going to catch me with that cheap bait?

"Dzerzhin Gavrilovich!" I yelled. "Why are you hiding in the corner?"

"I'm not hiding," said Dzerzhin, coming out from behind the table and heading toward me. "I'm glad you're here with us. I knew from the start you were one of us and would help us. Give Classic another glass!"

The young woman in black brought me another glass. I took it from her. I had nothing to lose.

"Here's the thing," said Dzerzhin when he was near me. "This is no provocation. You can either trust us or not, but you have nothing to fear. No matter what, the Supreme Pentagon has consigned you to oblivion. Even if it turns out that we are provocateurs, we can't do anything worse to you than that. So, trust us, let's drink, and then we can have a little talk."

A LITTLE TALK
WITH DZERZHIN

Our conversation took place in the natfunctbur in the cellar. As a matter of fact, I remember next to nothing of the conversation, but I do remember what Dzerzhin told me. Great events were afoot. The people's dissatisfaction with the communist and socialist systems was reaching a head throughout the Moscowrep and in the vast territory of the First Ring. The Simites were increasing and threatening to become a spontaneous movement. At the same time, SECO ("Or, in other words, the CIA," said Dzerzhin. "Make of that what you will.") had received completely reliable information that Swiss doctors had begun defrosting Sim. And there was no question that Sim would be headed to Moscow as soon as he was defrosted. His arrival was inevitable, but the authorities were preparing to resist, and that resistance had to be thwarted. Their attention had to be distracted.

"How?" I asked.

"You have to make certain compromises so that they'll concentrate on your jubilee. It's so important to them, they'll use all of their energy on it, and we'll turn that to advantage."

"And just who are you people?" I asked. "And just who are you personally? A SECO general, a CIA agent, or a Simite?"

"Bah," he said with a wave of the hand, "that doesn't matter. In this country nobody knows who he really is any more. In any case, you must make concessions so the authorities will take the

376

bait, but also in such a way that Sim will remain intact, though under a different name."

"What name?" I asked. "In any case, you know that I don't share Sim's ideas and don't want to help him arrive here. I may even delete him from the book."

"Too late now," said Dzerzhin sadly.

THE JUBILEE

The crowds were vast. The checking of passes began at Vigilance Square. Details of mounted Intsec men had massed by the Bolshoi Theatre, and the only way in to the House of the Soviets was through a corridor formed of two ranks of submachine gunners. I was escorted by two SECO colonels, one of whom was a two-time recipient of the Hero of the Moscowrep medal. He told me that he had been awarded his combat decorations for forming mine-laying detachments during the Buryat-Mongolian war.

Clearly taking the information concerning my age too seriously, both of the colonels supported me by the elbow, and the two-time recipient was careful to warn me each time we were approaching a pothole or a step.

The Hall of Columns was already full. The stalls and balconies were packed. Television and radio journalists were fiddling with their cameras, microphones, and wires.

I was taken through a side door and found myself backstage in an atmosphere of nervous excitement. Under SECO supervision, stagehands were dragging pieces of scenery back and forth. Apparently the ceremony was going to conclude with a show. I saw performers I knew. A flock of young swans was limbering up backstage left. The acrobats, the Nezhdanovs, were sitting facing each other on little stools, their expression impassive. And the Ukrainian singer Zirka Nechiporenko was standing in front of a cracked mirror, sprucing herself up and practicing making eyes.

"Hello there," I said to her in Ukrainian.

She shuddered, turned around, and, recognizing me, said in a serious voice, "Glorgen."

Just then Smerchev appeared, looking concerned.

"The Jubilee Pentagon has just received a telegram," he said, handing me a yellow piece of paper whose contents I quote here verbatim:

I AM MARCHING TO MOSCOW.
TO AVOID UNNECESSARY BLOODSHED,
I PROPOSE YOU LAY DOWN YOUR ARMS
AND OFFER NO RESISTANCE. SIM.

"You see now," said Smerchev with a sorry smile. "And you say it's all fiction."

I read the telegram again.

"What the hell is all this!" I muttered. "Metaphysics, Hegelianism, and Kantianism." Then I spoke to Smerchev, trying to calm him down. "It's alright, Communi Ivanovich. The main thing is for you not to get excited, save your nerves. We'll be abolishing Sim in a minute."

The audience broke into stormy applause as soon as we came out on stage. Naturally, I was seated at the presidium between Smerchev and Dzerzhin. The atmosphere in the hall was tense, but protocol was strictly maintained. Dzerzhin declared the meeting of the Moscowrep's workers open, then gave the floor to Smerchev.

Smerchev went to the speaker's stand. In brief but colorful terms, he described my life and enumerated my literary merits, mentioning my outstanding contribution to *Genialissimoiana* and, in that context, making special note of my novel *Moscow 2042*.

"But the propaganda agencies of the Third Ring of Hostility," he said, "and all their other agencies have been spreading slanderous fabrications about that novel. They claim that the hero of the novel is supposedly a certain Sim, though we all know that no such person exists in reality. But no one is better equipped to speak on that subject than the author himself."

I strode over to the speaker's stand. Nervous and excited, I didn't feel that I was at a celebration, but at the sort of press conference which in my time was held for repentant spies and dissidents.

"Comrades!" I said, my voice trembling. "My dear comcoms, ladies and gentlemen! To begin with, allow me to express my deepest gratitude to everyone who helped make this wonderful occasion possible. My gratitude goes first to our party, its Supreme Pentagon, and the organs of SECO," I bowed to Dzerzhin, "the organs of religious enlightenment," I bowed to Father Starsky while at the same time giving him the finger from behind the speaker's stand, "and, of course, to our dear, beloved, glorious, and inimitable Genialissimo." I raised my eyes to the chandelier and starred myself in grand style. "I have lived a very long life, the majority of which I spent in a state of political unconsciousness. I must admit that, over the course of my life, I committed many unforgivable and almost irreparable mistakes. For example, I usually wrote my books while under the influence of alcohol, with no idea of what I was doing, and sometimes even without a thought as to what the Party, the people, and security expected of me. Because of my backward worldview, I often failed to notice any of the good that was occurring in the revolutionary development of our reality, which I distorted to please my foreign masters. So, for example, in my novel *Moscow 2042*, I devoted too much attention to a certain Sim, who is allegedly the heir to the throne of the tsars. In reality, no such person as Sim has ever existed. He was a fiction. In other words, I just made him up, pulled him out of my hat. I know that there are some so-called Simites here who are hoping for something like a second coming, but . . ." Here I raised my voice and tipped an imaginary hat, ". . . your hopes are in vain, ladies and gentlemen. Because Sim no longer exists."

I heard applause and turned to see the presidium applauding— Smerchev, Siromakhin, Propaganda Paramonovna, and Father Starsky. But the audience maintained a tense and unfriendly silence. Then a vague murmur ran through the crowd. SECO agents, positioned along the walls, began peering into the audience.

380

"Yes, my dear Communites," I said, prolonging the pause, "after reviewing my novel, I have decided to do a radical rewrite on it and, first and foremost, I will *delete* Sim."

The presidium gave me a standing ovation. The public grew even stiller. I took a sip of water, paused for a moment, then said softly, "Unfortunately, even now I don't have the principles and firmness to delete that character entirely. But I have renamed him. And he will now be known as Serafim, not Sim."

When uttering those words, I had no idea they would have such an impact on the audience. I don't think the members of the presidium foresaw this either.

A stir ran from the first row to the last. I could hear people asking each other, "What? What did he say? Bim? Cherubim?"

Suddenly, someone in the middle of the hall shouted out, "Long live Serafim!"

A tremendous uproar followed at once. The SECO agents leaped from the wall and waded into the audience to drag out the person who had shouted. But now it was not one person shouting, but nearly the entire audience. Suddenly, from the back rows two balloons bearing a sign SERAFIM flew up to the ceiling.

Now the agents went wild. They stopped looking for the person who had started the shouting and went after the sign. They stood on the backs of chairs, crawled over people's backs, and some of them jumped high enough to set a new indoor high jump record. The colonel who had twice received the Hero of the Moscowrep medal displayed exceptional composure, worthy of particular mention. Not losing his head in all the pandemonium, he immediately drew his pistol and, with two well-aimed shots, pierced the two balloons. The sign began slowly and hesitantly falling, showing first one syllable then another — SE, RA, FIM. But while that sign was on its way down, two others had risen to the ceiling.

Just then the other colonel (not the Hero) walked over with a piece of paper and said loudly to Communi Ivanovich, "A telegram from Geneva." I snuck up in back of Smerchev and read over his shoulder:

I AM MARCHING ON MOSCOW.
TO AVOID UNNECESSARY BLOODSHED,
I PROPOSE YOU LAY DOWN YOUR ARMS
AND OFFER NO RESISTANCE. SERAFIM.

That's the limit! I thought. It doesn't matter what name he goes by, he always gets what he's after.

Now, I can no longer remember the order of events. I later learned that word of Serafim's imminent arrival spread at once throughout the Moscowrep. The city was in turmoil. And, as usually happens in such cases, the citizens began displaying their dissatisfaction even without any serious cause. For example, at one factory in honor of my jubilee, each worker had been given a kilogram of sausage marked "Communist Delicatessen in Cellophane." One woman Communite took a bite of hers right away and said, "Citizens, this is shit!" and the other Communites also noted that this delicatessen primary matter looked much too much like secondary matter. As if they hadn't noticed this before and hadn't made jokes on that subject. They seemed to have worked themselves into a state in which they would have taken even genuine Hungarian salami for secondary matter.

The revolt spread to other factories. It could have been suppressed, of course, but somewhere in the New Kaluga District, the First-Ring Simites had forced their way through the gates of Moscowrep. First they ran to the comfoodests and other need-satisfaction centers, where they met with a great disappointment. They had thought the citizens of the Moscowrep lived solely on dates and ice cream. The force of that disappointment was so great that the Simites of the Moscowrep and the First Ring joined forces and began smashing everything in sight.

382

THE END OF
EDISON

It was a night of turmoil.

Heavy aircraft droned overhead from early evening until dawn. They made their descent right over my hotel and landed on Khodinsky Field. Later on I found out that six divisions of paratroopers and two motorized divisions had landed that night.

When the tank columns appeared, their din dominated the air. The glow of fires flared first in one place, then in another throughout the city, and shots could be heard. Back in my room at the Communist Hotel, the walls shook, the glass shattered, and the chandelier swung like a pendulum.

I wrapped my head in the blanket and fell asleep just before daybreak, but I didn't sleep long. Around seven o'clock there was an explosion that shattered windows. Later I heard that some idiot pilot had flown over the roof tops at supersonic speed.

It was a good thing the blanket was over my head. I shook the glass off the blanket, got up and went to the window. Tanks were standing on Revolution Square. A long line of soldiers holding mess kits stretched from the field kitchen on the Bolshoi Theatre's square. But basically things were calm.

I turned on the television at seven o'clock. The announcers Semenov and Malyavin appeared on screen. "Moscow speaking," said Semenov in a perfectly ordinary tone of voice. "Here's the latest news. Today our beloved Genialissimo has sent his congratulations for the labor victory won by the collective of the Order of Lenin, Order of the Genialissimo, and Order of Labor Glory Grade One Sock Factory, known as the 'Red Sock,' which, by mid-September, had already filled its quota for two years. . . ."

Then came reports of the achievements made by subway-construction workers and steel-mill operators, a growth in the donor movement, and an exhibition of children's drawings in the Tretyakov Gallery of the Genialissimo's Artistic Gifts Museum. They showed some of the drawings in which, as the commentator Malyavin said, the children with their innate spontaneity express their fervent love for the Genialissimo and their passionate loyalty to the cause of communism and state security. Not a single word about all those rebellions, fires, tanks, and planes.

I thought that they might at least mention it at the end of the program, but I never got the chance to see it. The telephone began ringing shrilly. It was Edison Xenofontovich, or rather, Edik, sounding very excited.

"Vitaly, don't be surprised. I need you to do something. It's very important, very urgent. Can you come here immediately?"

"Are you serious?" I said almost sarcastically. "Do you have any idea what's going on in the city?"

"Yes, yes," he said impatiently, "I know about everything. Still, I have something that's very, very important for you to do. There's an armored personnel carrier waiting for you outside the hotel, and it has a pass personally signed by the minister of defense. You won't have any problems with that pass. I'll be waiting."

Someone knocked at my door even before I had hung up the receiver. Opening the door, I saw a SECO colonel I knew from before who said he had been ordered to bring me to the underground city.

On the way there, I never took my eyes from the vision slit and was stunned to see how Moscow had turned into a front-line city in a matter of hours. Literally every street and side street was packed with troops. Officers wearing red arm bands directed traffic.

We did not in fact experience any problems, except for the

many ID checks that made it take some two and a half hours, if not more, for us to reach the underground city. I found Edik in his office, very wrought up.

"Well?" he said, "any problems on the way? I can see that there weren't any. If there had been problems, you wouldn't be here. It's horrible what's happening. It's all because of that Sim of yours. . . ."

"I have no characters named Sim," I interrupted to say.

"I know, I know, you changed his name. But I think he even prefers that. And now under the name of Serafim he's on his way here. The troops sent out to stop him all defected to his side without firing a single shot. I honestly don't understand how that could happen. Just yesterday people were praising communism, pledging their loyalty to the Genialissimo and delighting at his every word. And today they're destroying the monuments to him, burning his portrait, and switching en masse to Serafim's side. Could all their praises and vows of eternal loyalty have only been mass hypocrisy?"

"That's right," I said, "they could. The masses are usually hypocritical. Even back when ancient Russia accepted Christianity, the people were quick to throw the idols they'd worshipped the day before into the Dnieper River."

The phone rang. Edik grabbed the receiver.

"Yes, hello. What are you saying! Of course, of course, it should have been done. Where is he now? Aha. And what about Serafim? Already? So fast? If you get any more news, call me."

He hung up the phone and looked at me in confusion.

"It's all over!"

"What's all over?" I asked.

"It's the end of an era. Two hours ago the Genialissimo was arrested by a special SECO space detachment, brought back to Earth, and taken to Lubyanka."

"*Interessant!*" I said.

"*Interessant?*" he cried. "You think this is interesting? Then you might be interested to know that Serafim, accompanied by wild and furious mobs, has crossed the beltway and is now moving toward

385

the center of the city on the Genialissimo's Strategic Plans Highway."

"The what?" I asked.

"The Minsk Highway," said Edik. Deep in thought, he walked over to his experiment, picked up the glass with the rose on it and took a sip, which seemed to calm him down. "By the way," he said as if just regaining consciousness, "would you like a taste?" He held out the glass to me.

"No thanks," I declined, "I've already tried it."

"Listen," said Edik. "I have an idea. What kind of a person do you think Serafim is? He'd want a long life, wouldn't he?"

"Praise God, he's already had one."

"But of course he'll want to live even longer."

"Who wouldn't," I said.

"Exactly," he said laughing happily. "Who wouldn't. Everyone wants to but not everyone gets to. So, listen to me. . . ." He looked around, checked to make sure the door was closed, and then began speaking in a rapid whisper. "When you see him, tell him about me and my discovery. Tell him to issue an order that no harm be done to me or my work. And then I'll share it with him. I'll furnish him with a regular supply of the elixir, and he can live as long as he wants."

"God forbid!" I cried. "I beg you, don't do it. If he lives as long as he wants, he'll pile up so many slabs they'll crush us all."

"What do you mean!" he said. "He won't be interested in slabs now. Pay attention, what I'm saying is very important. If he gives orders that I'm not to be touched and my work can go on, then he'll practically live forever." He lapsed into silence and peered at me. Then, after a moment's thought, he said, "And you will, too. Until the elixir goes into mass production, only the three of us will have it. Me, him, and you!"

"You're forgetting one other person," I said.

"Who's that? Oh, of course! I don't think any elixir can help him now."

He picked up the glass, took another sip, then held it out to me. "Take a swallow, don't be afraid. It only seems disgusting in the beginning. After you've tried it a few times and you realize that it's making you young and immortal, the elixir will taste like the sweetest nectar."

The phone rang again, and Edik ran over to answer it. I took the two glasses and switched their places.

The street outside was in turmoil. Military steam vehicles kept pulling up and driving away. An ambulance with its siren wailing raced past, and a roaring fire engine followed.

"Yes, yes," Edik was saying meanwhile. "I understand. Absolutely, I will do everything in my power."

"What a nightmare!" he said after he hung up. "The mobs are grabbing high-level-need Communites and SECO men on the streets and tearing them limb from limb. Oh, Gen, I can't take any more!"

He grabbed the glass and in a fit of passion drained it in a single gulp. Then, with sudden second thoughts, he took the glass from his lips, and saw the skull and crossbones. His eyes were filled with horror when he shifted them to me.

"Listen," he said. "I think I grabbed the wrong glass. I drank the wrong one. I drank death!" he cried and threw the glass to the floor, where it went rolling under his desk. "Gen! Gen! Gen!" he wailed hysterically, clutching his head.

Suddenly he stopped, looked intently at me, and asked quietly, "Did you do it?"

"I did," I said with a crooked grin when I saw him go pale.

Of all the many amazing things I've seen in my time, none was more unforgettable than what I now saw. Edison collapsed onto the couch, seized his temples, and right before my very eyes began turning into an old, old man. In disbelief, I saw his hair rapidly grow long, turn gray, and fall out. His face lost color, wrinkling like a baked potato.

In a flareup of last strength, and with his whole body shaking, this pitiful old man jumped up, brandished his fists, flashed me a look of hatred, and then spat out all his teeth, which went clattering across the floor.

He looked from his strewn teeth to me, but without any hatred now, only meek humility. "You!" he said, his sunken mouth smiling. "*Ich sterbe*," he added softly. He lay down on the couch, curled up, and died.

I felt a little sorry for him, of course. We had, after all, met back in my past life and even had a drink together. But I knew that I had to destroy that useless elixir, and its creator too. If people aren't equal in life, they should at least be equal in death. But I had no time for philosophizing or grieving, because gunfire could now also be heard in the underground city.

I grabbed a metal rod that was standing in one corner and first smashed the test tube seething with the fluid of life then the one quietly gurgling with the fluid of death. The glass shattered, the liquids went running and formed two puddles on the floor. They began spreading, trying to flow together into one. Both puddles were transparent, you couldn't tell them apart.

The instant before they merged, I made a dash for the door realizing something bad was about to happen. The puddles formed a combustible combination as they ran together, and immediately blazed up, in a column of unbearably white flame which struck the ceiling and set it on fire like a sheet of paper. A chain reaction was taking place within the flames. The column turned into a whirlwind that began moving about the room, immediately igniting everything it touched. I saw the parquet floor char and rise, one end of the desk burst into flame, then the curtains caught and the windows started melting. My eyelashes and eyebrows singed, I bolted from the room.

The underground street had been seized by panic. People were running up and down the street, some armed, some not. A heavy armored personnel carrier raced past at enormous speed, its machine guns firing at random. The transport vehicle that had brought me there was still waiting by the sidewalk, calmly puffing clouds of steam. I jumped into the cab and, in a tone of command, shouted to the driver, "Let's go!"

He did not respond. I looked closer at him, and only then did I see the stream of blood flowing from his temple.

With great difficulty, I tore his hands off the wheel and shoved him out of the cab. Then, after getting a little feel for the pedals and gears, I swung the vehicle around and began heading for the exit from the underground city.

PART VII

THE SECOND
COMING

An immense crowd, running into the tens of thousands, buzzed
with excitement by the Triumphant Arch, and I was in the very
thick of it, buzzing along with everyone else. People were tearing
the Genialissimo's portraits and the banners with his sayings from
all the adjoining buildings. Not far from me, a group of young people had joined hands and were dancing around a burning effigy of
the Genialissimo, fashioned from secondary matter, of course. The
effigy smoked and melted and shed secondary tears.

"It's like burning him alive!" cried someone in joy.

I looked around and saw Dzerzhin Gavrilovich beside me. He
was wearing long pants and a cross on top of his undershirt, as if it
had slipped out by itself.

"You see," he said, stretching his arms apart to indicate the
crowd, "they're all Simites."

That stunned me. I asked myself where all those Simites had
come from and how had they managed to keep themselves hidden
until now. To tell the truth, I was even a little afraid of them, but
hoped they would treat me like an outsider and leave me alone. But
I was somewhat afraid for Dzerzhin Gavrilovich. Even though I
knew he was a Simite, people who didn't might just take him for a
former SECO general. I knew from history that in times of national
disturbances security people sometimes end up in very ticklish situations. But Dzerzhin Gavrilovich seemed not to display any signs
of anxiety.

"They're coming! They're coming!" suddenly shouted the old woman beside me. I had no problem recognizing her as the same troublemaker who had once helped land me at an Intsec station. Now she was in uniform, but her insignia were gone and she wore a cross, apparently cut from cardboard, around her neck.

"They're coming! They're coming!" others picked up the cry.

A wave of excitement passed through the crowd, and everyone surged toward the middle of the street. In the thunderous rejoicing, the moans and howls of people being crushed were almost inaudible and did nothing to dampen the mood of elation. All eyes were on the Minsk Highway, where something seemed to be happening, but I couldn't see a thing because my view was blocked by a tall, broad-shouldered worker wearing a pair of greasy overalls.

"Kuzya, is that you?" I poked his back.

"Hey, old-timer!" he said with a broad smile, recognizing me. "Look what's going on here. Yesterday we had communism, but nobody knows what we've got today." And then from an excess of feeling he added a tirade which I cannot bring myself to reproduce here.

Meanwhile the crowd had grown even denser. People were pressing on me from the left, the right, and in back. Suddenly I saw someone wearing a torn T-shirt and a plastic cross.

"Is that you, Communi Ivanovich!" I said in surprise.

"Keep it down," whispered Smerchev. "You know, the name my mother gave me was Coluni."

"You mean you had a mother?" I said, but could not hear the answer because the crowd had just risen, to an even higher pitch of excitement. Up on my tiptoes, at first all I could make out were the points of lances and then, elbowing my way forward a little, I glimpsed three epic figures slowly approaching the Triumphant Arch. In the middle, on a white horse, in white flowing robes and boots of white Moroccan leather, rode Sim Simych. And, swaying in their saddles on bays, were Zilberovich to his right and Tom to his left, both of whom had long moustaches and, despite the weather, wore tall astrakhan caps. They were both armed with long lances.

394

Sim Simych held a large sack in his left hand and greeted the exultant crowd by reaching into the sack and tossing American pennies left and right.

Simych and his retinue passed under the Triumphant Arch, then came to a stop. Simych raised one hand and the crowd grew silent at once. Someone ran over to Simych with a microphone, and I was surprised to see that person was Dzerzhin, who had just been beside me a minute ago. Simych graciously accepted the microphone from Dzerzhin's hands then suddenly cried out in a piercing voice, "We, Serafim the First, Tsar and Autocrat of all the Russias, do hereby most graciously declare that predatory communism has been totally destroyed and no longer exists. Are there any secret predators among you here?"

I was about to shout out that they were all predators here because every last one of them was a member of the predators' party. But I was far away, and Dzerzhin was close.

"There is!" he cried, and diving into the crowd, he dragged out Communi Ivanovich, who tried to resist. Communi Ivanovich tore free, sobbed, dug his feet into the ground, then finally fell to his knees almost right under the hooves of the new autocrat's horse.

"Admit the truth, did you serve predatory, devouring, diabolical communism like a dog?"

"I admit it, Your Majesty, I served them," babbled Smerchev, lowering his head. "But I didn't serve the idea, I only did it for my own gain and to satisfy my greedy passions. I'll never do it again, and I curse the hour when I became a predator."

"It's too late now," said the Tsar, with a wave of his hand.

A steam fire engine was parked by the arch with its long ladder fully extended upward, and a Simite perched on top of it was now lowering a rope that ended in a noose.

"Forgive me, Your Highness, have mercy!" Smerchev reached out to Sim Simych. Dzerzhin began pulling his former colleague by the legs, and Smerchev fell onto his belly and grabbed Logos's rear leg. Logos kicked out with his hoof, cracking Communi Ivanovich's poor head like a walnut.

I started feeling very on-edge. An utter humanist by nature, I have always been firmly against such forms of punishment. Personally, I'm in favor taking people like Communi out to the stables for a good thrashing, but I have never been an advocate of excessive cruelty.

But they were still at it. Since the issue of Communi had been resolved so rapidly and so radically, Dzerzhin at once left the former head comlit to writhe alone. Plunging into the crowd again, he dragged out Father Starsky. Eyes blazing and beard disheveled, he was brought before the newly-arrived Emperor.

"Do you admit that you served a diabolical, predatory, impious teaching like a dog?" asked the Emperor.

"I admit it, Little Father," said Starsky in a sweet, sing-song voice, not the least confused. "I admit that I served it, am now serving it, and will continue to my last breath to serve the radiant ideals of communism and the great leader of all mankind, the genius, the Genialissimo. . . ."

"Crucify him!" order the Tsar.

An enormous, crudely built cross appeared at once, and four Simites began nailing the unfortunate Father Starsky to that cross with large rusty nails. The product of the Moscowrep's progressive industry, the nails, of course, bent at once and the crucifiers had to pull them out, straighten them out, and pound them back in. Suffering incredible torment, Father Starsky would still not yield and, his eyes narrow slits, he howled, "Oh Gen, can you see me? Can you see the torments your humble slave Starsky is suffering for your sake?"

I don't think anyone can suspect me of any excess affection for Father Starsky, but now, seeing the courage and dignity with which he accepted a martyr's death for his own undeveloped beliefs, I was suffused with the deepest respect for him and a wave of compassion rose in my chest.

Starsky was still suffering on the cross and crying aloud as the Tsar and his retinue continued on its way. At the horsemen's approach, people fell prostrate, and I went down on my knees myself.

American pennies poured, ringing on the ground in front of me, and I managed to scrape up a few and slip them inside my shirt. Noticing another coin, this one a quarter, I was about to reach out for it, too, but just then a horse's hoof came down on top of it. I thought I'd be able to pick the quarter up as soon as the horse started up again. But the horse did not start up and an ominous silence hung over me now.

"Who's that?" I heard the Tsar's voice say. "Lift him up!"

Someone (it turned out to be Dzerzhin) grabbed me by the scruff of the neck, tore me from the ground, and set me on my feet. I lifted my head and encountered Simych's gaze. Narrowing his eyes, he looked at me so sternly that I even felt a tremble pass through my entire body. Zilberovich and Tom regarded me impassively, showing no sign of having recognized me. I think only Logos, who was shifting from foot to foot, looked at me with a benevolent eye.

"Is that you?" asked Simych softly.

Nervous and confused, I poked my chest with a finger and said, "Me?" But I came to my senses at once and admitted it. "Yes, it's me, Simych."

"Not Simych, but Your Majesty," Zilberovich corrected.

"Hello, Leo!" I said to him, surprising myself by giggling obsequiously. "You look very imposing on horseback."

"Did you carry out the task I gave you?" asked Sim Simych sternly.

"The thing is, Sim . . . or should I say Your Majesty?" I asked, bobbing like a fool and nodding my head, while thinking to myself, That son of a bitch is the limit! Even after sixty years in deep freeze, he remembers everything. "If you . . . if you're referring to the floppy disk, then, no, I didn't because. . . ."

"Seize him!" Simych flicked the reins and continued on his way, scattering pennies as he went.

THE GENIALISSIMO

I was taken down long, reeking, poorly-lit corridors. An iron door was opened and I was shoved forward into a cell which had almost no light. Only at the very top of the ceiling was there the faintest glimmer, coming from a small window the size of a school notebook. The blue light barely trickled through, outlining only the window itself across the background of the darkness.

I stood there in the midst of that impenetrable space, hoping that once my eyes grew used to the dark they'd be able to make out something, but they couldn't make out a thing. I tried moving to the right and immediately banged up against something hard. Judging by the smell, it was the pot. I could not hear any sounds, but I felt that I was not in there alone.

"Anybody here?" I asked, not speaking loudly.

"Yes," answered a soft voice that sounded familiar. "I'm here."

"Who are you?"

"The Genialissimo," was the voice's simple reply.

Inwardly, I uttered a few indecent words, which I will not include here. Evidently those dogs had not thrown me in prison, but into a mental institution. And, to top it off, I was in with a madman who had delusions of grandeur.

"Listen, you're not violent, are you?" I asked.

"What do you mean?"

"I mean that if you have a drop of sense left, you won't even think of attacking me. I'm a karate expert, and any attempt to use force on me could cost you dearly."

Needless to say, this was bull. I didn't know the first thing about karate. But I was well aware that madmen were a lot more reasonable and cautious when they thought they might catch it in the teeth.

The other person in the darkness remained silent, thinking over what I'd said. Then, calling me by name, he asked, "Vitaly, is that you?"

Now it was my turn to remain silent. Then I asked, "You mean that you're saying you really are the Genialissimo?"

"That's right," he said. "I am the Genialissimo. Or the former Genialissimo."

I thought for a moment then said: "How are you, Lyoshka? In my opinion, they were perfectly right to throw the two of us into a mad house."

"Why's that?"

"Because what we imagine to be happening right now could never have happened in reality."

"Why's that?" he asked again.

"Your question itself is proof of your illness. Judge for yourself. You and I were born at the same time, we grew up and were on our way to becoming old men in the last century. It's impossible that we've both ended up here together and that this also coincided with the arrival of that raving lunatic who now calls himself Serafim."

After a pause for thought, Genialissimo Bukashev said: "You've proved yourself that the concept of reality is very relative. In any case, it only exists in one form for us, as it is refracted through our imaginations. In other words, reality is only what we think we see in front of us."

"In that case, no reality exists for me now because at the present moment I can't see a thing."

"You don't have to see anything. Put your hands out in front of you and come toward my voice."

I did as he said, and a few moments later Bukashev and I were poking and prodding each other like blind men, to prove to ourselves that we were really there.

A NIGHT'S
CONVERSATION

We spent most of the night sitting on the narrow plank beds, quietly conversing, unable even to see each other's silhouette.

Genialissimo Bukashev had been arrested and brought to Earth by a special SECO space detachment two days before the final fall of the regime. If I'm not mistaken, this was the first time in history someone had been arrested while in orbit. (Although space prisons where people arrested on Earth were sent had existed even before this.)

"Do you remember our conversation in the English Garden?" asked my cell-mate.

"Do I ever!" I said. "I remember it very well. I even remember you saying you intended to build communism but, like your predecessors, you turned out to be a real utopian, a dreamer."

"You're mistaken, you little fool!" he said, quite merry all of a sudden. "I didn't turn out to be a utopian. I *did* build communism."

"You call this communism?" I asked indignantly. "This society of pitiful paupers who can't even tell the difference between primary and secondary matter? A society whose entire spiritual life has been reduced to composing and studying *Genialissimoiana*? Do you mean to say that that is what communism is?"

"Yes, I do, my dear man," he said with a grin that I didn't see, but felt. "This is what communism is."

"That's funny," I said, "I had a different picture of that dream which has been with mankind for so long."

"I did, too," he said. "But when people start realizing their dreams in real life, when they start moving en masse toward a single goal, something like what you've seen here is always the result."

"'You're speaking like a total anticommunist," I remarked.

"That's right," he agreed. "But with one big improvement. You know, the Americans say if it looks like a dog, barks like a dog, and bites like a dog, then it's a dog."

"Do you mean that you are in fact a total anticommunist?"

"At last, you've guessed," he said with ironic praise.

"An interesting confession," I replied with great sarcasm. "Bit too late to be of any help. Why are you telling me all this? I'm not your interrogator or an informer. And even if I were. . . . You're not really counting on anyone trusting you now, are you? Now, anyone you stop on the street will tell you he was always an anticommunist. Him you can believe, but you you can't. No, brother, it's not one of your better ideas, and it won't save your skin."

I could hear him sigh.

"Do you actually consider me stupid enough to think anything could save me now? No, my friend, I'm not counting on anything at all. I lived for many years on that elixir Edik was sending me. I drank it for the last time just before my arrest, it's worn off now, and the accelerated reverse effect has started. It will all be over quite soon. So, I have nothing to lose, and you should take what I say on faith and not ask for proof. You can call me whatever you want to. But what matters is not what I'm called, but what I've done. I built communism and I also buried it. Just think how people have fought that doctrine in the past. They formed little groups, parties, distributed leaflets, and then rotted in prisons and camps. And what did they accomplish? Your Simych tried to hurl those slabs of his at communism and he ended up in a freezer. No one understood one simple thing—that you have to build communism if you want to destroy it."

He lapsed into silence, and I did not encourage him to continue, because I needed to do some thinking too. A mystery that I had never been able to fathom before had now been revealed to me from an unexpected quarter. "Listen," I said finally, "according to your logic, we have to admit that all the people who brought us to communism were in fact its enemies."

"Isn't that obvious?" he said joyfully. "All those people from Marx to me who infected mankind with communism, also gave mankind the chance to come down with the disease and develop an immunity which will last for many generations into the future. But of the destroyers of communism, *I* was the greatest success, because it was I who brought that teaching to its ultimate absurdity in practice."

This he said with unconcealed pride then lapsed into silence again.

"*Interessant*," I said, imitating our late mutual friend. "Even very *interessant*. And were those always the ideas you held? Even back when we were together in Munich?"

"Well, no," he sighed in the darkness. "My ideas were somewhat different back then. At that time I still thought that . . . Yes, yes," he interrupted himself irritably. "I can feel you grinning at me. You think you knew it all long before I did. But I knew everything you knew. But you stood off to one side and mocked, whereas I tried to do something. In any event I did bring the historical experiment to an end."

"And are you pleased with the results?"

"Whether I am or not is of no significance," said Bukashev. "If you perform your experiment honestly, you have to accept the results, whatever they are."

Now I grew angry. "And do you think that you performed your experiment honestly? And was your personality cult part of that experiment? And were the endless portraits, the clunky, tasteless statues, and all that insipid Genialissimoiana also a necessary part of the experiment?"

Bukashev groaned and gnashed his teeth. "You can't imagine how much I hated all that. I asked them, I beseeched them, I ordered them to stop all that glorification. And what do you think happened? They replied with stormy applause, articles, novels, poems, and films about my exceptional modesty. Whenever I wanted to make some concrete reforms, and convoked congresses and meetings and told them we couldn't go on living this way, let's finally do something, let's try a new approach, once again the reply would be stormy applause and cheers. The newspapers and television would extol me for my exceptional boldness and breadth of vision. The propagandaists would go all out in quoting me: 'As our glorious Genialissimo has correctly indicated and wisely observed, we can't go on living this way, let's do something, let's try a new approach.' And that would be the end of that."

As a matter of fact, I didn't find anything novel about his confessions. Even back in my day, the Soviet system had operated in exactly the same way.

"Still," I said to Bukashev, "maybe your mistake was surrounding yourself with bureaucrats and yes-men who didn't know how to do anything but applaud. Maybe you should have sent them all packing to hell and gone directly to the people. I'm sure the people would have supported you."

"My friend," said the former Genialissimo sadly, "what people are you talking about? And who are the people anyway? Is there any difference between the people, the populace, society, the mob, the nation, or the masses? What do you call those millions of people who run enthusiastically after their leaders, carrying their portraits and chanting their senseless slogans? If you mean that the people are the best of those millions, then you have to admit that the people consist of very few people. But if the people are the majority, then I should tell you that the people are stupider than any one person. It's much more difficult to convince one individual of an idiotic idea than an entire people."

"You might be right," I said. "You might. But tell me, if you're so smart, how come you allowed your comrades to leave you up there in space?"

"I wasn't opposed to it," he said. "There was nothing left for me to do on Earth. When I saw that I couldn't change anything, I decided to let things take their own course. I knew the situation was out of control and sliding toward disaster. But I no longer had the power to slow things down or speed them up. I was tired, and I wanted to be far away from everything and everybody, but I could never find that on Earth. So, when they decided to leave me up there in space, I said to myself, Maybe it's better that way. They pretended I was their leader, and so did I. In reality, I was living a life all my own—I ate, I slept, I read books, I thought, and I waited."

"Waited for what?"

"For all this to collapse."

"And so," I said, taking him at his word, "that means you were doing the exact same thing Simych was? He was waiting in a deep freeze and you were waiting in outer space. What's the difference?"

I think the comparison offended him.

"The difference is," he said angrily, "that, before waiting for the ship to sink, I gave it a good shaking, while he was busy pointlessly piling up all those slabs of his. And then of course I wanted to see how the whole thing would end, which was the only reason I kept on drinking Edik's elixir."

"Do you know what happened to Edik?"

"Yes, I know, you poisoned him. And that was the right thing to do, he was an abominable and dangerous man. And his invention can't help me any more. And I don't need it anyway now. I lived long enough to do everything I wanted, I can die now."

I don't remember when and how I fell asleep. All I remember is that the cell was filled with light when I woke up. When I looked down from the upper plank bed, I saw nothing but a neatly made bed.

THE IMPERIAL
PROCLAMATION

"By the grace of God, We, Serafim the First, Emperor and Autocrat of All the Russias, in this Proclamation do most royally and most graciously declare that the diabolical, predatory, and blood-stained communist government has been deposed. The fetid KPGB party has been disbanded and declared outside the law. The propagation of communist ideology is tantamount to the gravest of crimes against the state.

"Russia is hereby declared a United and Indivisible Empire with a monarchist form of government. The division of the Empire into republics is rescinded. The basic administrative unit outside the capital will be the province, the provincial governors to be appointed by Us.

"The Empire consists of the territories formerly controlled by the KPGB, that gang of devils, and includes Poland, Bulgaria, and Rumania, each of which is to be a province.

"Power in all its fullness belongs to the Emperor, who will exercise it through Our appointed Governing Senate, Cabinet of Ministers, and Committee of Provincial Governors.

"The former organ of state security (SECO) is to be transformed into the Committee on National Peace (CNP), to be headed by Our favorite, the ever-faithful, God-fearing Christian, Leopold Zilberovich.

"All former communists are called upon to surrender their party cards at the province, county, or district offices of the CNP and to undergo confession and penitence in church.

"All Our remaining beloved subjects are called upon to maintain the peace and keep order, to expose all predatory communists and pluralists seeking to avoid registration and repentance, to display vigilance and intolerance for all signs of the false and abominable communist ideology.

"I do hereby command this Imperial Proclamation be read in the squares, the churches, and other places of public assembly, and as well in all military units and on the ships of the Imperial Navy.

"God is with us!

"Serafim the First, Emperor and Autocrat of All the Russias"

I read this ukase in the newspaper *Gazette of the Governing Senate*, which I started receiving on my first day in prison. If it hadn't been for the newspaper, I would have gone out of my mind. I was close enough to my wit's end as it was. All my life I had dreamed of witnessing some crucial historical event, the fall of an empire, a revolution, or even a counterrevolution. And what an insult that just when such an event occurs (and one I was directly involved with), I end up under lock and key for no good reason! But at least I was safe in there. Because, as I found out later, immediately after Simych (to this day I can't call him Serafim) acceded to the throne, people's courts formed spontaneously throughout the Moscowrep and tracked down former Communites with high-level needs and pluralists whom—with a simplified sense of justice—they tore limb from limb on the spot. That didn't make the papers, but the newspapers did publish long lists of those executed by sentence of the CNP's Emergency Board.

Not only that, they published endless ukases day after day, and I list them here in the order I remember them:

1. Ukase on the formation of a special commission to investigate communist crimes.
2. Ukase on the refusal to pay foreign debts.
3. Ukase on the universal obligation on the entire population

to convert to the true Russian Orthodox faith. This ukase is to be carried through the gradual baptism of all His Majesty's subjects, for which ritual purpose seas, rivers, lakes, ponds, and other such natural and artificial bodies of water are to be used.

4. On the renaming of all cities, rivers, settlements, streets, factories, shipyards producing sea- and river-going vessels, now illegally bearing the names of communist bosses.

5. All property in the form of land, all manufacturing enterprises, all means of production and transportation now pass into the hands of His Majesty and are then to be distributed free of charge by social committees to individuals capable of productive labor and who had avoided collaborating with the predatory communists.

6. Passports and other documents issued by the godless authorities are null and void and to be replaced by a single residence permit.

7. Steam, mechanical, electric, and all other forms of transportation are to be abolished and gradually replaced by draught animals, toward which end the peasant is called upon immediately to begin breeding horses, bulls, donkeys and Shetland ponies.

8. Ukase on the abolition of science and its replacement by the three obligatory subjects, which are: Scripture, *Dahl's Etymological Dictionary*, and the work by His Venerable Majesty Serafim, *The Greater Zone*.

9. Ukase on the introduction of corporal punishment.

10. Ukase making it mandatory for all men forty and over to have beards.

11. Ukase making the wearing of long clothing mandatory. Under pain of punishment, men are obliged to wear pants that do not reach above the ankles. Each pant leg must be of sufficient width to conceal the sock fully.

Women are to be God-fearing and display modesty. Their dresses and skirts should not be above their ankles.

The wearing of pants and other articles of male attire by persons of the female sex is categorically forbidden. Women are prohibited from appearing in churches, on the street, and in other public places with their heads uncovered. Women found guilty of violating these rules will have their heads shaved and be tarred and feathered.

12. Ukase forbidding women to ride bicycles.·

There were many other ukases on the tilling of the soil, the introduction of new ranks and new names for them into the army, the banning of Western dances, and a great deal else but, unfortunately, I could not remember it all.

GET YOUR
THINGS

The door opened and, accompanied by the guard, a cossack officer
entered my cell. He was wearing long billowy trousers and a cossack
jacket with tassles of some sort.

"Dzerzhin Gavrilovich, is that you?" I said, rushing to him.

Refusing to fraternize, he calmly checked a list. "Anyone here
whose name starts with K?"

After looking around, I said I was the only person there whose
name began with any letter.

"Let's go, get your things!" he growled.

I picked up my cloth cap and walked out of the cell. Leaving
the guard behind, we walked for a good while down a long winding
corridor with peeling walls and a dirty, jagged stone floor.

"Well?" he asked on the way, "are you afraid?"

"No," I said, "I'm not afraid."

"And right you are," he said. "Death is the worst that can
happen."

"And so they've let you keep your old job?" I asked. "Was it
because they found out you were a Simite?"

"No, that's not the reason," he said. "It's because they need
specialists like me. Any regime does. No matter what kind of revolution you make, you have to have something to protect it with
after. And who's going to do that? We are. Any individual can be
replaced but you can't replace all of us at the same time."

"Tell me, please," I asked artlessly, "are you still working for the CIA?"

He stopped and gazed intently at me. "I usually don't answer such questions, darling."

We continued on our way, with him in the lead. We took an elevator up a few floors to an oak-paneled corridor with a red carpet runner on the floor. At the end of the corridor, we entered a spacious reception room packed with high-ranking cossack officers.

By a door upholstered in black leatherette, a mustachioed secretary stolidly pecked at the keyboard of an Olympia typewriter with one work-calloused finger. Above him was a panel depicting Tsar Serafim entering the capital, painted by some artist who had been exceptionally quick on his feet. Amid crowds of rapturous faces, Serafim was leaning from his horse to stroke the head of a fortunate child held out to him by a fortunate mother.

"Is he in?" Dzerzhin asked the secretary curtly.

"Yes, sir!" said the secretary, jumping to attention. "He's expecting you."

Dzerzhin opened the door and allowed me to enter first. The office was as spacious and luxurious as the reception room. A man wearing the uniform of a cossack general was sitting at an enormous desk, his bald head bent over as he wrote. His hand was moving quickly. The huge painting on the wall above him portrayed Serafim on a rearing horse spearing a five-headed red dragon.

The general raised his head, set his writing aside, and came out from behind his desk. Beaming with a good-humored smile, and pulling up his trousers with their general's stripes, which were too large for him despite his pot belly, he came forward to welcome me.

It was, of course, Zilberovich, who had managed to put on a lot of weight while I was sitting in prison.

Dzerzhin stood to one side, smiling modestly—the very picture of a junior officer in the presence of a senior officer.

"You may go," said Zilberovich to him with a nod. Dzerzhin saluted smartly and left the room.

"Please, sit down," said Zilberovich, indicating a leather sofa by a coffee table on which there was a magazine I had never seen before, *The Imperial News*. Zilberovich took a seat in an armchair facing me.

"So here we are together again," he said, still smiling.

"Yes, here we are."

"You've barely changed," he said.

"But you have," I said.

"In what way?" he asked anxiously. "Do I look very old?"

"No, no," I assured him. "You don't look very old. But you look a little unusual in all those. . . ." I made a gesture encompassing his epaulettes and aiguillettes.

"Oh, you mean that." Tucking his head down in bird-like fashion, he looked himself over with a self-satisfied air. "What can I tell you, old friend. I earned all this, you know that yourself. I was loyal and true to Simych, I mean, His Majesty. I believed in him when no else did. I was at his side in his most trying hours. And now you can see how high I've risen. And, as for you, you should erect a monument to me. You should start on it as soon as you return to Stockdorf, if, of course, you do return to Stockdorf. Sim . . . I mean His Majesty was so furious at you that he wanted to deal with you the way he deals with pluralists. But I stood up for you. Do you understand?"

"No, I don't," I said. "What angered His Majesty so much? What did I do?"

"It's not what you did, it's what you didn't do," remarked Zilberovich. "You were assigned to distribute *The Greater Zone* but. . . ."

"There was nothing I could do," I said. "The floppy disk was confiscated right away at customs. And even if it hadn't been confiscated, there still wouldn't have been anything I could do. The Communites don't have computers or paper, the only thing they have in abundance is secondary matter. And they run out of that, too, because of the primary matter shortages."

"Exactly! Exactly!" said Zilberovich beaming. "That's exactly

411

what I wanted to hear from you. And so, are you critical of the communists? Do you dislike them?"

"Who could like them?" I said. "They don't even like themselves."

"Right you are!" said Zilberovich approvingly. "No one likes predators and pluralists. Everyone hates them. You and I will go to see His Majesty now. Come right out and tell him that you hate predators and pluralists and that you'll fight them to the end. And make a mental note of this—don't even think of calling him Simych or anything of the sort. Call him Your Majesty and nothing else. Don't disagree about anything. Limit your answers to Yes, Precisely, In no way—that sort of thing. Otherwise he'll become cross with you and. . . ."

Zilberovich did not finish his sentence, but jumped to his feet and clapped his hands. "My carriage to the front entrance!" he cried to his bewhiskered secretary, who had appeared in the doorway.

I thought he had used the word *carriage* for effect, but in fact there was a carriage waiting by the entrance. It was made of mahogany and fitted with leather seats; gendarmes of some sort stood on the footboards. We got in. The coachman brought the horses to a gallop at once.

The weather was beautiful, the sunlight playing on the lances of the cossack squadron escorting us. Drawing the velvet, tassled curtains, I looked avidly out the window and could see the abundant and beneficial changes that had taken place here while I was in prison. All the men were wearing long pants and all the women long dresses, and a few people even had long hair.

The new regime had evidently not fully consolidated power yet, because some streets were barricaded off by steam vehicles. For that reason we took an odd and roundabout route, though I was glad of that. First, we drove down Marx Avenue; its age-old name, Hunter's Row, had already been restored. On the other hand, First Volume Avenue was now known neither as Gorky Street nor Tversky Street, and was no longer a street or an avenue but Allee Serafim.

We did not encounter a single portrait of the Genialissimo the

412

entire way, only portraits of Simych. What I liked best was the monument on the square across from the former Palace of Love. Simych now sat tall in the saddle on the horse which had once been the mount of Yuri Dolgoruky and then of the Genialissimo. Exactly as in the picture in Leo's office, Simych was spearing a five-headed plaster dragon with brutal zeal.

Finally our carriage clattered over the cobblestones of Red Square.

The first thing I saw as we drove past the Historical Museum was two crudely constructed gallows. Horizon Timeofyevich Razin, severed hoses and all, was dangling from one, and on the other was Beria Ilich Maturin in full uniform with the exception of his pants. Nothing could have been easier than guessing where they'd gone. I looked over at Zilberovich's pants and, intercepting my gaze, he grew embarrassed and instinctively put his hands over the stripes on the sides.

I was about to make a wisecrack but, hearing a roar, I looked out the window and saw that our way was blocked by a throng of Russian Orthodox around the Place of Execution. We tarried there for a moment, long enough for me to see an executioner in a red shirt raising a huge ax. At first I couldn't make out who was about to be executed. But when the executioner brought his ax down, the crowd howled and moved back, and I could see a black, curly head rolling over the cobbles. I sighed, recognizing the head as Tom's.

"Listen," I said, turning to Zilberovich, "why was that done to him? Was it because he's a black man?"

"What are you saying!" said Zilberovich. "His Majesty is tolerant toward blacks, but you yourself wrote that Tom was a covert predator."

That disturbed me greatly. I had of course written that but, had I known my writing would bring Tom to such a horrible end, I would have crossed out every word.

While I was thinking those thoughts, our carriage had forced a path through the crowd and driven through the Kremlin's Gates of the Savior, which had been flung open wide for us.

ISKRINA

Zilberovich asked me to wait in the Tsar's reception room while he ran ahead to report. I looked around and recognized the room. Not that long ago it had been Beria Ilich's reception room, but now it looked somewhat different. The windows were curtained in drapery decorated with two-headed eagles, and while taking a closer look at them I did not notice right away that the Tsar's secretary had stopped typing and was regarding me with great curiosity. Finally I noticed her too. She was wearing a severe black dress and a white kerchief, from which her small forehead shone.

"Clasha!" said the secretary with a smile, calling me quietly by name.

"Iskra!" I cried. "Is that really you? My God! I didn't recognize you. You've changed a lot, you're prettier than ever. The dress and the kerchief look good on you. So do your bangs."

I ran over to her and was about to throw my arms around her when she put her hands out in front of her and said, "No, no, there'll be none of that."

. I was taken aback. "Why can't there be any of that? I haven't seen you for so long."

"I haven't seen you for a long time either and I've lost the habit," she said. "And it's better that way. Because you'll be leaving us soon and I have to stay here."

"Yes, that's true," I said in self-justification, "there's no way I can take you with me, because. . . ."

"Why do you think I want to go anywhere with you?" she asked in a tone of surprise.

"What?" I said startled. "You mean you don't want to leave here with me?"

"For what reason? What's for me there?"

"What do you mean what's for you there? Don't you understand? If I leave, you'll never see me again. Never ever."

"That's right," she said with a smile, spreading her hands wide. "We were going to have to say goodbye one day or another anyway."

She said that so coolly, as if the prospect of saying goodbye to me forever did not touch a single chord in her heart. This I found horribly shocking, insulting, disturbing. My male pride had been offended.

"How can you," I said, "how can you. . . . Have you really forgotten it all? But you and I even slept together."

"One among many," she said with a very cynical smile. "I couldn't leave the country with every man I ever slept with."

This frankness jolted me. I clenched my fists, I stamped my feet, I yelled at her. "How do you dare say such a thing? You should be ashamed of yourself! Does the idea of love, a woman's faithfulness and a woman's pride mean nothing to you? Is nothing sacred to you? But fool that I am, I thought about you, I suffered for you, I remembered the perfect moment when you appeared before me. Like a fleeting vision, like the genius of pure beauty."

I spoke for a long time, exalted and eloquent. And I recited Pushkin's lines without any awareness that I was stealing them. They seemed just born in my mind, or in my heart. And I sincerely believed every word I said. I had not yet concluded my oration when I noticed that Iskra had become terribly wrought up and was trembling. Suddenly, she threw herself sobbing into my arms.

"Oh my love," she murmured, swallowing her tears, "Clashenka my love, forgive me, I didn't know you loved me so much. . . . But if you. . . . Do you truly love me very much? Very, very much?"

"Of course I love you very much," I said, instantly bereft of all certainty.

"And I love you too, very very much," she said, covering me in kisses. "I'm ready to follow you anywhere. I'll go on foot, wherever you say, the past, the future, to the ends of the earth."

Human nature is so low! A second ago I had been passionately desiring to hear her say these words. And as soon as she said them, they lost all their savor for me.

Her kerchief had slipped off. I ruffled her short hair, said a few words, all the while thinking, My God, what have I gone and done now! Why did I talk her into it, what am I going to do with her?

"It would bring me such happiness, my dear," I said, "if you could come with me, but. . . ."

She closed my lips with the palm of her hand. "No buts. I'm going with you wherever you want."

"Yes, yes," I said, "of course, but you do understand I have a wife there. . . ."

"That doesn't matter," she objected hotly. "I know you have a wife. But I'm sure she's a good woman and will understand everything and she and I will be friends."

I have to say that I found this idea very amusing, and though I didn't explode with laughter, I did chuckle. I said that of course my wife was a good woman, even a very good woman, but, as to her being understanding about everything, I had a few doubts on that score.

"You see," I said choosing my words carefully, "my wife lives back in the past, in the old capitalist world, and she has all those outdated prejudices about her husband belonging to her and nobody else."

This statement did not cool Iskra's ardor in the least. "Fine," she said, "if your wife is that backward we won't traumatize her. You and I will just see each other every once in a while. And if even that's impossible, I'll be happy just to catch a glimpse of you, even if only from afar."

These women! They never know what they want. First they

416

just want to see you even if only from afar, even if it's through a telescope, and then later they realize this isn't enough and start demanding more.

"The Tsar will summon you in a minute. Tell him that you can't leave without me. He's strict, but just. He'll understand everything. Just tell him."

"Fine, fine," I said, looking over at Zilberovich, who was beckoning me with a finger from the half-opened door.

TSAR
SERAFIM

"I have four and a half minutes for you," said Tsar Serafim, setting the timer on his Seiko wristwatch.

He was seated before me in a gilded throne, with an iron staff clenched between his knees. The Tsar was wearing the Cap of Monamakh, which must have been taken from the armory. It was a hot day and sweat streamed out from under his cap; from time to time, the Tsar wiped it away on his brocade sleeve.

"I am deeply grateful, Your Majesty," I said bowing deeply.

"I was about to have you executed but then I changed my mind."

"I am deeply grateful," I said again, and, falling to my knees, I kissed his left boot.

"There's no reason for that," he muttered. "Rise! You wrote a lot of rubbish, and you allowed yourself smutty remarks in regard to me. But," and here his voice became perceptibly warmer, "I have learned that you have suffered a great deal and refused to delete me despite everything the predators did to intimidate you. Good man!"

"I was glad to do my part, Your Majesty!" I said, springing to my feet. "But I have to admit I can't take any credit for that. How could you ever be deleted! You could not be chopped out with an ax, as the saying goes, Your Majesty. Those predators think they can write anyone they want into history and anyone they want out. But I know that's not possible."

"So!" said the Tsar, pleased. "You may be a birdbrain, but

you've understood something. And that must be why I'm letting you go back home. I have banned the flights of all iron birds, but I have detained the Lufthansa plane especially for you. This will be the last flight over our empire. But I'll let you go on one . . . actually, two absolute conditions."

"You have my full attention, Your Majesty," I said humbly.

"First, as soon as you get back to 1982, immediately write a detailed account of everything you've seen here and send it by express mail to me at the Solace estate."

"Yes, Your Majesty!" I said.

"And you must write about that bitch Stepanida and her Tom, too, so then I'll know right away what to do about them. Second, I want you to tell all pluralists what tomorrow has in store for them."

"You can count on me," I promised, completely sincere.

Just then the timer on his watch buzzed, but he turned it off and asked me if I had any requests.

I said that I did have one request. Was it possible for me to leave through a back door or a window?

"Why would you do that?" asked the Emperor, knitting his brows.

"Please don't be angry, Your Majesty," I asked. "But your secretary . . . I had a little affair with her here and now she's head over heels in love with me."

"So that's the story!" said the Tsar frowning all the more. "What a lowlife you are!" he cried and struck his staff against the parquet floor. "That's what you've been up to here! That's why you weren't distributing copies of *The Greater Zone*!"

Taking fright, I collapsed to my knees. I explained that the predatory communists had assigned Iskrina to me without my even asking, as a way to honor their guest. I hadn't lived with her for the pleasure of it, but only to distract their attention, lull their vigilance, and hasten His Majesty's coming.

"And why did she live with you?" he asked, narrowing his eyes in contempt and mockery.

Of course I could have told him that the woman who wouldn't

want to live with me has yet to be born, but I was afraid of incurring his wrath and said that she lived with me as a part of her Party workload.

"What depravity!" cried the Emperor. "So that's what my secretary had been doing. Leo!" he shouted into space even though Leo was standing right beside him. "I command you to arrest that . . . what is her name, I command that she be flogged publicly, that her hair be shaved down the middle, and that she be tarred and feathered."

"Your Majesty!" I cried without rising from my knees. "Simych," I said, sensing I could call him that. "It's not her fault at all. The predators forced her to cohabit with foreigners. But she was always very God-fearing and always a faithful Simite. She always wore your portrait around her neck."

This seemed to mollify him, and he finally said that, alright, he wouldn't have her flogged, but sent to a monastery. I felt somewhat sorry for her but, being the jealous type, I was also pleased that she would be unable to cheat on me.

"Alright then," said the Tsar, removing the Cap of Monamakh and wiping his face with it. "You may go, but remember what you are to do for me. Leo, take him out through that door."

I sprang to my feet, dusted off my knees, and, bowing low, began backing toward the door.

"Vitya!" Sim Simych called out suddenly, calling me by name for the first time in his life.

Astonished, I stopped, my eyes wide open. "Yes, Your Majesty!"

"Have a good trip, Vitya!" said the Tsar, wiping away a tear with his cap.

"And you have a good stay here, Simych," I said, my voice faltering, my rear end banging up against the door.

EPILOGUE

I returned to Munich on September 24, 1982. My wife did not know I'd arrived, so I had to take a cab.

On my way through Munich, I was stunned and even overwhelmed by the profusion of lights and advertisements, the automobiles of every color, and the festively dressed people on Marienplatz. It was hard to imagine that I'd arrived in the past from the future and not the other way around.

That evening, I had no sooner walked in the door, embraced my wife, and unpacked my bag when the telephone rang.

"Hello, Vitya," said a familiar voice. "This is Bukashev."

"Bukashev?" I said in surprise. "The Genialissimo?"

"The what?" he said bewildered. "What did you call me?"

I was not quick to answer that question. I thought it might not be the Genialissimo—he didn't seem to have much chance of staying alive when I spoke with him last. But then I realized that now time was playing new tricks on me and I knew things about Lyoshka Bukashev he didn't know about himself yet. For all my adventures, I still wasn't used to all time's whims and vagaries.

"I'm sorry," I said, "I'm a little tired from my trip and my brain's not working too well."

"I can understand that," he said. "It's a long way from Honolulu. Alright, I'll call you back after you've rested up."

I had barely hung up when the phone rang again.

"Hello, old friend, this is Zilberovich."

"I wish you good health, Your Excellency," I said.

Of course he didn't understand why I called him that, but he wasn't surprised either. "Are you busy?" he said.

"What's up?" I asked.

"Run to the airport, buy a ticket, and fly to Toronto."

"Right this minute?"

"That's right," he said. "Why not?"

"It doesn't matter," I said. "You may see me yet."

I slammed down the receiver and began thinking. Clearly, Bukashev and Sim Simych were dying for information from me so that they could adjust their plans accordingly. At first I even wanted to be of help to them, but then I thought — what do I need all that for? And do I have the right to interfere in history?

Now, there's a responsibility I don't think I'd want to take upon myself. That was my decision, and so I followed up with appropriate actions. Or, to be more precise, inactions. I stopped answering the phone and told my wife to get rid of anyone who wanted me for anything. And she did, but in an extremely polite way. She told everyone who called that I had either just stepped out or had not yet returned.

To Bukashev's credit, it must be said that he quit calling rather quickly. Zilberovich proved more persistent and called me nearly every day at first. Then he stopped, too, but, as I was to see, not for very long.

As for the Arabs who had given me the advance, I didn't hear a word from them and I know why. There had been a military coup in their country, and the prince who had wanted me to learn the secret of the hydrogen bomb was assassinated by a palace guard. The new leaders may not have known about our agreement.

While I'd been away, the *New Times* magazine had gone bankrupt; they made no demands on me, and I didn't press them either. And, while living a quiet, country, family life in Stockdorf, I wrote this novel. The work went easily and quickly, because I had lived everything described here, and the novel itself came to me as if I'd read it before I'd written it. The whole story seemed to take shape all by itself, and I can no longer say which parts are primary matter and which parts are secondary.

While I was pondering all these questions, word of my modest artistic success spread quite far. Then, out of the blue, Zilberovich arrived in Stockdorf in person to present me with categorical instructions: Simych was to be deleted immediately from the novel. Upon hearing this, I threw up my hands, thinking, here we go again! Wasn't it enough that I risked my life for my fiction in the future, do I really have to fight for it again here in the present too?

"Why are you always badgering me about Simych?" I said angrily. "Why should I delete him and not someone else, for example, the Genialissimo?"

"The Genialissimo can stay in," said Leo magnanimously. "And you can even paint him in the blackest colors, but leave Simych out of it."

During the stormy exchange of views that followed, Leo tried to intimidate me by saying that my novel would only play into the hands of the predators, who would certainly seize upon it and might even publish it in a mass edition. I listened to Zilberovich with a bitter grin and sadly shook my head as I recalled Beria Ilich's iron safe.

"No, Leo," I said, "you underestimate the predators. They didn't like my novel either, and if I don't maim it like they did Supey—if I don't throw out everything except the upbeat dreams—they'll keep it in their safes for at least sixty years."

That, more or less, is what I said to Zilberovich. Meanwhile I was thinking, But what if the predators read what I've written here, meet in secret session, discuss my novel thoroughly, and admit that in some ways the author might be right? Maybe they'll decide that if they don't turn from this predatory path, don't correct the existing situation, they'll inevitably reach a pass where the difference between primary and secondary matter ceases to exist. And, reaching that sad conclusion, they will set about making corrections, not in the author or his work, but in life itself. And then my novel will be taken from the safe and published in a mass edition as the product of an idle, inoffensive imagination.

Well, personally speaking, I could not object to that turn of events. May the reality of the future not resemble the one I describe here. Of course, in that event, my reputation for exceptional honesty will suffer some damage, but that I'm willing to accept. To hell with my reputation. As long as life's a little easier on people.

And that, ladies and gentlemen, is the whole point.